SUSAN A JENNINGS

# In the Wake of Sophie's War

*Book 3 of The Sophie's War Novels*

*Best Wishs*

*[signature]*

SaRaKa InPrint

Cover Design and author photo: SAJ Designs

Stock images:

Shutterstock ID 1483136078/https://www.shutterstock.com/g/ysbrand

Shutterstock ID 1693136374 https://www.shutterstock.com/Darya Komarova

Shutterstock ID 127854155/https://www.shutterstock.com/g/tkemot

This book is written in Canadian English Style with Canadian spelling.

First edition

ISBN: 978-1-989553-29-9

Editing by Meghan Negrijn

This book was professionally typeset on Reedsy.
Find out more at reedsy.com

*I dedicate this book*
*with sympathy, gratitude and understanding.*
*To*
*Doctors and nurses, soldiers, mothers and all those loved ones who*
*fought the brutal battles on or off the battlefields*
*and suffered the silence of The Great War*

# Contents

# Prologue

Sophie's story begins in the early 1900s in Italy, a young girl growing up on her family's silk farm. Her father moves his family to Derby, England, to manage the silk mill, leaving his brother to look after the farm in Italy.

However, tragedy befalls the family and Sophie is forced to take a maid's position at the prestigious Sackville Hotel in Bexhill-on-Sea, Sussex, England.

Seeking more purpose in her life, she leaves the hotel to train as a nurse. When The Great War ravages London, Sophie vows to serve her country as a nurse in war-torn Europe.

It is now 1919 and the war is over, leaving tragedy in its wake, and Sophie is back at the Bartley Hospital, resuming her nursing career in London, after serving in Passchendaele.

# Pause

Hushed is the silence and then we pause ...

# Epigraph

*"Yesterday I visited the battlefields of last year. The place was scarcely recognisable. Instead of a wilderness of ground torn up by shell, the ground was a garden of wild flowers and tall grasses. Most remarkable of all was the appearance of many thousands of white butterflies which fluttered around. It was as if the souls of the dead soldiers had come to haunt the spot where so many fell. It was eerie to see them. And, the silence! It was so still that I could almost hear the beat of the butterflies (y's) wings."*

*Unnamed British officer, 1919*

# Sophie's Escape

## May 1919 - Lucca, Italy

'Escape.' That was the only word Sophie could think of that explained why she was sitting at the kitchen table in her villa in Lucca, Italy. Her family home, the place where she grew up, fell in love, but had not set foot in or, for that matter even thought about, for seven whole years.

The end of the war was supposed to bring a sense of relief, peace and hope, along with opportunities for new beginnings. Sophie felt none of these things. It was the overwhelming feelings of guilt, anxiety and silence that consumed her emotions, gripping her insides so tight she could barely breathe. The silence. This by far, was the worst. The guns and bombs were silent and that had brought relief. But now, the other quietness, the silence beneath the grief, fear and helplessness. She saw it daily in the eyes of her patients and it was more than she could bare.

It had been over a year since the doctors had declared her fit enough to return to nursing, not to the front as a war nurse but to the Bartley Hospital. Her injuries from the bomb blast, although healed, meant she would not pass the medical to return to Passchendaele. She had always intended to resume her career at the Bartley, so she accepted it had just happened sooner than expected. And then, the war ended only a few months after Sophie took up her position on the Women's Ward.

At first, she enjoyed being in solid buildings and not under canvas. Living at River House with young probationary nurses was refreshing; reminding her of those early days as a probationer and the friendships that had bonded with Hillary and Trixie long before they served in the war. And, now they were back at River House, no longer probationers but fully qualified and experienced nurses and Hillary a medical student.

She relished walking to the hospital every morning with Hillary, who had continued to live at River House as a paying boarder when she entered university to study medicine. Sophie felt a great deal of pride in her friend as she bravely, and against all odds, studied medicine to become a doctor. Trixie's circumstances had forced her back to the Bartley and River House before the war ended, after her secret marriage to pilot Christopher Belingham was revealed.

As time went by, Sophie began to feel more discontent. She tried to talk to Hillary, but she had spent the war in medical school and, despite witnessing some horrible scenes in the London air raids, had not seen the battle fields, nor the despair Sophie witnessed in her patients at the Bartley. Others just brushed off her concerns and worries, making her conclude that she was losing her mind.

Sophie's life had been full of tragedy and trauma, none of it her own doing, and yet she always managed to find a way to stay confident and move on, until now. She was frightened. One more demand was going to tip her over the edge. Perhaps she had not healed as well as she had thought. Andrew, her fiancé and a psychiatrist, had assured her that her reactions were normal. He at least recognized she had been through more than most. Healing the mind took longer than the body, but she felt unheard and, coincidentally, it was the great silence that haunted her the most.

She couldn't or didn't want to make decisions, even important ones she was expected to make about her career, treating patients and her personal life, including Andrew's increasing urgency to set the wedding date. Not only was she not sure about Andrew, but she questioned her desire to marry at all. She felt a deep and passionate friendship with Andrew, but was that enough?

What made Sophie snap should have been a good thing and ultimately was, but in that moment, she could take no more. Matron called her to the office and told her she had a promising career and had recommended her for a teaching assistant position, working with the incoming probationary nurses. Her ambitions had turned towards furthering her nursing career and this was an opportunity, a stepping stone towards becoming a staff nurse or even a sister. Sophie heard Matron's words and stared at her, overcome with self-doubt. Unbidden tears filled her eyes and her mind went blank. A sudden yearning for comfort flashed an image from her distant past; her late mother and the villa in Italy appeared. She frowned, stilling the flutter in her heart as the shadow of a young man reflected in the kitchen window. It was brief, no more than a second or two, but quite clear. It was a message,

3

a warning that if she didn't escape, she would never recover.

Creases of concern knitted Matron's forehead as she spoke. "Nurse Romano, are you quite well? Do you have a fever or symptoms of influenza?"

Sophie shook her head. Her throat hurt from holding back tears, but she didn't feel feverish. Matron leaned towards her, placing the back of her hand against her forehead. Relief flooding her face that Sophie was not suffering from influenza, but Matron saw the truth in her tear-filled eyes.

"I understand what ails you and it is not physical." Matron gave her a reassuring pat. The same shadow of contradiction showed in Matron's expression. They both wanted to trust and believe in the new world, but knowing the reality, the depth of the scars of war, curbed any willingness to celebrate either the end of the war or looking to the future.

Sophie took a raggedy breath. "I'm broken. I can't do this anymore, Matron." Hearing her own words, she realized she had just ended her nursing career.

Irregular breaths were the only sound in the room. Matron's expression softened and her cheeks plumped into a half smile. Her voice just a whisper, she said, "Believe me, I empathize and this will pass. You need rest so I'm putting you on leave for two weeks."

Sophie croaked, "Thank you Matron." She accepted, wondering if Matron was being kind but believing she had lost her mind. Afraid to ask what might happen at the end of two weeks, she decided she would deal with that later. For now, she had to leave London.

River House, the nurse's residence and the place she called home, was quiet. Even the housekeeper was out. Sophie quickly packed a bag and wrote a note to Cook with a little grin as she wondered why no one ever called her by her name. She certainly was the cook and a good one too, but she had taken over as housekeeper and housemother after Mrs. Wilderby's untimely death. A freak accident from the force of a bomb blast that threw the cellar door off its hinges, landing on and killing, poor Mrs. Wilderby. Sophie was a young probationer at the time and took it very hard. Having lost her own mother when she was a child, it brought back painful memories. She sighed. Going to Italy would bring her comfort and closer to her mother.

Sophie pinned a second letter to Hillary's door, telling her she had been called away and would write soon. Undecided what she should say to Andrew, she slipped her pen and note paper into her bag and telephoned a taxi. The cheerful cabbie asked where she was going and she answered with 'the fastest way to cross the English Channel.' He informed her there was a train leaving for Dover in half an hour from Victoria Station. Having made no plans, Sophie couldn't believe her luck and thanked the driver, asking if he could get her there in time for the train. The urgency of rushing to catch the train filled her with excitement. She needed that to cover her doubt at such irrational behaviour, especially her decision to return to Italy. Travel was not recommended, a second wave of Spanish flu was thought to be imminent. With that in mind, she took the muslin face mask from her pocket, and tied it around her face. She needed to be careful.

The port of Dover was bustling, mostly with ships full of troops returning home with many more to come. The first available crossing to Calais was early the next morning. She paid for a third class ticket and wandered around the port. She needed to find a cheap hotel. Grateful she had had the sense to bring all her money with her, she found a scruffy looking place and pulled the muslin tighter round her nose and mouth. She ventured in, hoping it looked better inside. The landlady gave her a big smile, "How can I help you, miss?" the woman asked. Peering around Sophie, she frowned. Sophie wasn't sure if it was the face covering or that she was alone.

"Do you have a single room for the night?"

"On your own, are you?"

"Yes." Sophie hesitated, not sure what to say next. "I'm booked to cross the Channel in the morning."

The landlady gave her a sympathetic look. "Looking for your man, are you?"

Sophie realized the landlady had interpreted her hesitation for grief and worry about her beau or husband. She went along with the assumption, easier than explaining.

"Yes, they said he might be in Italy."

"That's a long way, lass. You must love him a lot. Here's the key to Room 2, top of the stairs. That'll be ten shillings. Lavatory is down the hall."

Sophie climbed the stairs, turned the key in the lock and opened the door slowly, letting out a breath of pleasure at the smell of disinfectant. The room looked tired and worn but spotlessly clean. The bed only creaked a little when she sat on it. A jug and washbasin sat on the washstand. The room reminded her of her first job as a maid at The Sackville Hotel in Bexhill, long before she started nursing. Memories tumbled into her head, making her ask why was being pulled to her roots in Italy and why now? A knock on the door jolted her from her thoughts.

Mrs. Jones stood, holding a cup of tea. "Here, lass, you look as though you could do with a cuppa."

"Thank you, that is very kind of you."

Mrs. Jones gave a nod and left.

Sophie placed the cup on the dresser, noticing two biscuits in the saucer. She sat on a very wobbly chair, and sipped the tea, nibbling the biscuit. She was hungry and, reluctant to spend money on dinner, very grateful for the tea and biscuit, especially as such things were scarce. Fumbling in her bag for her handkerchief, her pen and note paper caught her attention. She must write to Andrew and post it before she sailed in the morning.

*Dear Andrew,*

*I hope this reaches you before you worry and wonder where I am. I had to get away. I took the train to Dover and will cross the English Channel tomorrow morning. I have decided to go to Italy.*

*I cannot explain why, but I need to connect with my roots. I told you about the villa my father left me in Lucca and that's where I'll be.*

*Matron must have seen my distress and has put me on two weeks leave. I might have destroyed my nursing career, but I just could not continue in such turmoil.*

*Please don't worry. I'm sure rest and solitude is all I need.*

*Affectionately,*
  *Sophie*

She addressed and sealed the envelop before tucking it away in her bag. The next morning she woke early having slept soundly. She crept down the stairs and headed to the port. Across the street from the port, she spotted a busy café, mostly full of sailors and young men in uniform. She squeezed her way through to get a cup of tea and bun, pulling the mask to her nose. Avoiding the crowd and cat calls, she took her tea outside and sat on a wall to eat. At last, the ship's horn blasted noise and steam, telling passengers to board. Deciding it was safer to stay on deck, Sophie waved to no one in particular as the ship pulled out of Dover Harbour.

It had taken several days to get to Lucca. Few trains were running and angry demonstrations made it difficult to get from the port to the train station. Dawn was breaking the morning sky when the train finally pulled into Lucca Station. She hailed the only taxi to take her to the villa. The drive was much longer than expected. She had forgotten the farm was several miles outside of the city. They finally passed through a small hamlet she recognized. The driver stopped abruptly.

"This is as far as I going, Signorina," he said, his eyes on the rusty, ornate iron gate twisted off its hinges and leaning towards the overgrown driveway. "Those craters will damage my motorcar."

Sophie looked at the road or what was once a road. "I understand."

He frowned as she placed money in his palm. At first, she thought he was questioning the payment, but his expression was that of concern.

"Signorina, are you sure this is the right address? I don't

think anyone lives here."

"I live here, at least for a while. Grazie, Signore. I will be fine." She smiled, as the driver opened the motorcar's door and handed her bag.

Sophie watched the taxi pull away and stood at the gate, feeling like an abandoned orphan from a tragic novel. She pushed her cloche hat tighter as the morning stillness broke into a strong breeze. At the same time she loosened her woollen coat, too warm for the Italian sun.

In front of her, the red tilted roof of the villa rose above the tree tops. She turned to look behind her, toward the small row of houses, as though she needed to know there was a way out.

*What was she doing here?* Suddenly it didn't seem real. *Was she dreaming?* The aroma of baking bread filled her with warmth and hunger. She felt her mother's hand in hers, a little girl walking to the bakery. A bell tinkled and she glanced up to see the bell perched on the door. The door that she had opened. *What is happening? How did I get to the bakery?* Panic rose in her throat. *Am I having hallucinations or am I going mad?* "No!" She said aloud.

A voice from the back called, "Who's there? We're not open."

Attempting to bring herself back to the present, Sophie realized she had not slept or eaten in twenty-four hours, which would explain her behaviour.

"Hello!"

A weary looking man appeared, pulling back a grubby looking curtain. "Si Signorina, we are closed," he said wiping his hands on a once white apron. Sophie explained in Italian that she had just arrived from England. The baker shrugged his shoulders and turned to go back to his baking.

"Please, sir!" Sophie recognized him and wondered if he would remember her mother. "My name is Sophie Romano.

"Romano!" He looked suspiciously at her. "Alberto's daughter!?"

"Si, Signore!"

"Bella, bella!" Suddenly he threw his arms in the air, kissing Sophie on each cheek and then, just as suddenly, his face turned to sadness. Shaking his head, he added, "Such tragedy." He frowned, taking her hand. "Why are you here? The silk farm is gone."

"I know, but the villa is mine. Papa put the title in my name before he died. So much has happened, not to mention the war. This is the first time I've been back."

"Si a longo!" A long time.

Sophie smiled, trying to think of the Italian expression for the bread smells good, "Le pane profumo!" She laughed, knowing that her Italian grammar was sadly lacking and then asked if she could buy supplies.

He shook his head with a frown, gesturing to the empty shelves and then suddenly smiled. "Uno momento." He disappeared into the back and returned with a small bag of coffee, a loaf of bread, still hot from the oven, and two thin slices of ham.

"Grazie!" Sophie said. The smell of the food making her mouth water, she waved goodbye, knowing it would be all around the hamlet that the Romano girl had returned.

Clutching her treats from the bakery, Sophie enjoyed the fresh air and sense of freedom, picking her way through over grown bushes and deep holes in the once gravel driveway. It was quiet, except for the chirping insects, birds and the occasional rustle of leaves from scurrying animals.

The red tiles of the villa peering through the tall cypress trees made her breath shorten and freedom turned to fear of what she might find. Long ago memories of fun summers with her aunt and uncle arose. Then there was falling in love with Carlos, unrequited love, even though their paths had crossed many times since. She felt the hurt of his letter, not only informing her of the ruined silk farm, but breaking their engagement. Even now, it made her eyes prickle with sadness.

Her steps slowed in anticipation of what might confront her as she turned the corner. She tried to brush away irrational visions of destruction; dead silkworms and the bodies of her murdered aunt and uncle. To her relief and surprise, there was no evidence of either, just over grown Mulberry trees. The villa looked strangely as she had left it, but her aunt's house, hidden by the massive pomegranate bush, was falling apart, windows broken and the door bashed in.

Climbing the steps to her villa, she hesitated, sensing she was being watched from inside. She glanced expectantly at the empty window, and turned the key in the rusty lock until it released. The door opened, stiff at first, the hinges creaking either welcoming or objecting. She didn't know which until it was fully open.

A musty smell greeted her and dust motes lingered in the air but everything looked the same. Nothing had been disturbed. It was as though they had never left or visited, and yet she remembered it as though it was yesterday.

She walked, leaving footprints in the thick dust as she entered the bright sunny kitchen, the red and white cloth, dusty but undisturbed, covered the kitchen table. There was wood in the box by the stove, ready for the fire, and clear water ran freely from the taps. The kettle, once rinsed, was ready.

She wandered into the lounge, dark and cool, and opened the shutters, usually closed to keep out the heat of the summer. The May sun made it a pleasant space. Excitement filled her and she ran upstairs to her old bedroom with pictures and dolls and teddy bears. The family had moved to England when she was twelve, although she had visited many times after the move, but had always stayed at her aunt's house. Her parents' room seemed even quieter than the rest of the house, filled with a big bed and heavy furniture.

She ran downstairs, made coffee and tore a chunk of bread from the warm loaf and ate hungrily. It had been too long since she'd eaten.

A familiar voice, husky but warm and audible said, "Benvenuto, Sophie, bellisoma." There was her mother, leaning against the cupboard, welcoming her home and looking as young and pretty as she remembered.

# Andrew's Dilemma

## May 1919 - London, England

A ndrew had a bad feeling about Sophie. She hadn't been herself for some weeks now. He had tried to reassure her, but she had withdrawn and wasn't talking. He stamped his foot, annoyed with himself. He was a psychiatrist, a doctor of troubled minds and yet he had not seen how *troubled* she was, or if he had, he'd conveniently ignored it. Now she'd disappeared.

He called at River House to speak with her best friend Hillary who was not at home. Cook said Sophie had left a note to say she was away but it contained no details. She invited him to wait in the common room. Overly anxious and restless, Andrew declined, choosing to pace outside River House while waiting for Hillary.

Trying to stay calm, he replayed his time with Sophie during the last couple of weeks. He'd ignored the signs. She was always so strong. Guilt seized him for not seeing the symptoms of battle fatigue, even shell-shock. *No*, he thought, *Sophie was too strong for that. What am I missing? Is it our relationship? I don't understand why she won't set the wedding date.* He gave a long sigh and rubbed his forehead, as if it would stop the questions without answers.

"Hello, Andrew. What are you doing here?" Hillary said, surprised to see Andrew pacing and obviously upset. He was normally so calm.

"Oh gosh. I didn't see you coming. I'm waiting for you! Have you heard from Sophie?"

Hillary put her hand in her pocket and pulled out an envelope. "Yes. She left me a note to say Matron had put her on two weeks leave and she was going away. Why do you ask? You look worried."

"I am worried. She didn't say anything to me. I know she hasn't been herself," Andrew said.

"I am surprised she didn't tell you and I agree it is sudden, but I think a break is what she needs." Hillary's expression changed as the concern in Andrew's voice matched his agitation.

"Did she say where she was going? Perhaps I can join her."

"No, actually she didn't, and that is odd too, but she did say she'd write when she was settled. Now you have me worried. But if there is one thing I know about Sophie, she can take care of herself."

"Normally I would agree, but…" Andrew hesitated. "She's been different lately. I should have known something was wrong." Andrew pulled his watch from his waistcoat. "I have to go. Maybe she sent a letter to my digs. I'll check the afternoon post. Thank you, Hillary."

"Try not to worry. I'm sure she's all right," Hillary called after him. She re-read her own note and frowned. She too had the feeling things were not quite right.

Andrew ran the four blocks to the house where he rented a room. Pushing the door open, he let out a long sigh of relief seeing a letter address to him on the hall stand, post marked Dover.

"Dover!" he said aloud. "What is she doing in Dover?"

Normally calm and rational, the panic in his own voice startled him and all kinds of medical diagnoses about Sophie's state of mind crossed his thoughts. He had known she was troubled and, deep down, he'd known it was more than the after-war melancholy so many were feeling. He saw it every day with his patients. Why hadn't she come to him? It was irrational, but he felt hurt that she had not confided in him. Then he chastised himself because he should have seen the signs. He was the professional. He considered following her, the thought of her travelling alone frightened him, but he sensed she would not thank him for appearing unannounced. He didn't even have an address but perhaps there would be one in the letter. His stare fixed on the postmark. Reluctant to open it, he continued to stare.

"It won't read itself," the landlady's voice called from the kitchen, making Andrew's heart jump into his throat.

"No, no, of course not. Good afternoon, Mrs. Humphries," Andrew blurted, his voice cracking. "I'll be back for dinner but I have to go somewhere." He shoved the letter in his inside jacket pocket and ran to his car. Cranking the engine seemed to bring him back to reality. He drove to his office at the Spring Gardens Convalescent Hospital where he was treating shell shocked officers. Staring at Sophie's photo on his desk, he took the letter from his pocket and opened it.

"Italy!" he said, reading the letter. Glancing at the date on the post mark, he added, "two days ago." He turned the letter

15

around, looking for an address, but there was nothing. He couldn't even write to her. He re-read the letter and consoled himself that she sounded quite rational. She was right, rest was good, but the solitude might not be. He remembered her talking about Lucca and a terrible tragedy, long before he met her. The physician in him didn't think going to the scene of a tragedy was a good place for Sophie to be in her current state of mind. He wished he'd paid more attention to her history. He racked his brain for more information and the only name that came to mind was Carlos Wainwright. That's where she'd met him, on the family silk farm. Did Carlos have something to do with her departure? He shook his head, more to shake off the feeling of jealousy. Carlos was an honourable man and had walked away, but Andrew was no fool. Carlos was in love with Sophie. Could he be sure of *her* feelings? Of course, she had accepted his proposal. She wore his ring. Andrew turned his thoughts back to Sophie's state of mind and her travels. He assumed she would be in Lucca by now. All he could hope for was a letter with an address.

Having slept little and unable to contain his worried thoughts, the next morning Andrew drove to the Bartley to see Matron Hartford before starting his rounds at Spring Gardens.

"Come in!" she called as he knocked on her door. She smiled as he entered, pointing to the chair across from her desk. "Take a seat. I was expecting you. You are worried about Nurse Romano?"

He nodded. "She's gone to Italy. I'm not sure it is safe to travel. Italy is reporting more cases of Spanish flu and she is troubled."

"If anyone can take care of herself, it is that girl." Matron grinned knowingly. "I didn't know she was heading to Italy. I just granted her leave. But she does speak fluent Italian and maybe she has relatives to go to."

Andrew shook his head. "No, her mother died when she was a child and her father passed away in a tragic fire when she was only sixteen. But she does own a villa in Italy that her father willed to her." Andrew took a breath. Frowning he asked, "Why did you feel it necessary to grant her leave?"

"Nurse Romano is one of the best nurses I have ever come across in my career. I had asked to see her to discuss her future here at Bartley. I'm not a psychiatrist, Dr. Cuthbert, but I know my nurses, especially the sensitive ones. Nurse Romano has been showing signs of stress, even battle fatigue, for some time. The ordeal she suffered in Passchendaele left scars, compounded by her work here. She needs time and that's what I've given her. I'm afraid I can only help with the nursing responsibilities. It is up to you to help your fiancée deal with the personal ones." Matron's eyes seemed to pierce into Andrew's, making him uncomfortable and unsure how to reply.

He coughed and cleared his throat. "Yes, Matron." He hesitated for a moment. "Should I find out where she is and join her?"

"My advice is to write to her and only visit if invited. Nurse Romano is strong willed and if she needs time alone, bursting in on her will not end well."

"You're right. I don't even have an address to write to."

"Then wait until she writes again. I only gave her two weeks. That's not long to wait. Be patient, Dr. Cuthbert."

"Thank you. I will." Andrew gave a nod, adding "if you hear

from her, would you let me know?"

"Of course."

"Italy. Lucca," Andrew muttered under his breath. Matron's words reassured him. Sophie could take care of herself. He'd witnessed her strength in Passchendaele and he pushed away the thought that everyone had their breaking point. He should know. He'd seen many of his patients, strong seasoned military men, crack like eggshells. And yet, if he was honest, he believed Sophie to be stronger than ten men. What was it *he* was not dealing with? Most of all he couldn't shake off the sense that things were not right. He could not grasp or understand why she'd left without telling him and *Italy* of all places. He glanced at the big clock in the hospital lobby and hurried to his motorcar. He was late for rounds at Spring Gardens. He gave a chuckle. Matron Mills was quite the opposite to Matron Hartford, as tough as nails and obsessed with punctuality. Andrew's stepmother had been the same, but she was cruel. He didn't think Matron Mills was like that. She could be tender when needed, but her strictness often evoked unpleasant memories, annoying him.

Matron believed that strict routines and schedules helped the patients to recover quickly. Andrew thought there might be some truth in it, but compromise with disturbed, battle fatigue and shell shocked men was necessary in some instances. This was an ongoing battle between Andrew and Matron and he braced himself for the reprimand as he pushed open the double doors. Matron Mills was standing in front of him, arms folded, with a look that would terrorize the bravest of soldiers.

"Matron! Is something wrong?" Andrew squeaked out, clearing his throat.

"It's a disaster! Come into my office." It was a command, rather than a request. "And why are you late?" The latter was said with pursed lips. In spite of his concern, Andrew had to keep a smile in check.

The door slammed behind him all thoughts of Sophie banished. Matron moved to her desk, sat down, and with her finger pointing to the chair said, "Sit!"

Andrew blinked, but did as he was told, feeling like a pet dog who had left a puddle on the carpet.

"My apologies for being late for rounds. I was detained by Matron Hartford at the Bartley but I am here now. How can I help?" Andrew attempted to sound conciliatory and helpful.

"Dr. Cuthbert, we have a situation. Influenza."

Andrew felt panic and understood Matron's distress. "How many?"

"Just one so far. Major Lambeth, admitted two days ago."

"I met with him yesterday. A severe case of battle fatigue with episodes of aggression. Has he been in contact with other patients?"

"No. In fact he refused to come out of his room. Normally, I would have insisted," Matron Mills pursed her lips so tight Andrew was surprised she could speak. "I was not informed until the ward sister expressed her concern about the fever last night. I immediately limited access to one nurse and ordered face coverings at all times."

"Thank you, Matron. How is he today?" Andrew didn't wait for a reply. "It's possible he has an infection and it's not influenza," he said hopefully. He was only too aware of the complications 'flu' would be to staff and patients, not to

19

mention the effect the illness would have on the malnourished and sickly patients.

"Will you accompany me on rounds this morning?" Andrew said, hoping Matron had other duties to attend to.

"Of course. It is imperative infectious protocol is followed at all times with staff and patients." As irritating as Matron could be, Andrew had to admit that her obsession for stringent order, rigorous compliance with rules of hygiene and a draconian view to non-compliance, were perhaps their only hope of keeping the Spanish 'flu' out of Spring Gardens, or at least containing it.

The morning rounds went well. No fevers or flu-like symptoms were detected. There were only two outbursts from Matron. The first fell on poor unsuspecting staff, not wearing face coverings. The second was the result of objections from two patients being forced to wear masks, citing their rights to freedom. Matron quickly quashed that with reference to the war they had fought and won. Andrew was glad of the muslin tickling his nose as it hid his smile when big strong men, brave soldiers, and many high ranking, buckled under Matron Mill's glaring posture.

Spring Gardens was a big Victorian house, the London residence of a wealthy duke, that had been commandeered by the War Department towards the end of the war. The big reception rooms and dining room on the ground floor were perfect for wards and housed twenty officers; although, during the war, there were three or four times that many crowded into the rooms. The garden was large for a London townhouse and offered peace and tranquility to shell shocked patients. Having completed rounds, Andrew took the stairs to visit the severely ill patients who occupied the more private bedrooms. Today the Major was the only occupant on the first floor, which alleviated some concern regarding the spread of flu.

"Good morning, Dr. Cuthbert," a nurse said, peering through a muslin mask and wearing an extra grown. Her voice sounded young, but it was hard to tell.

"How is the Major?" Andrew asked, tying a second mask around his face.

The nurse shook her head. "His fever is high and he's having difficulty breathing."

Andrew opened the door to find the Major propped up on pillows, wheezing and glassy-eyed. There was no doubt that he had Spanish flu. He no longer had the energy to be aggressive and Andrew doubted he would last the day.

"Has the family been informed?"

"He only had his mother. His brothers were both lost." The nurse's eyes were wet with tears. "His mother just died of 'flu' and I don't think he knows."

"Thank you, nurse. Keep him comfortable and let me know if there is any change." Andrew stripped off his mask and replaced it with a clean one, washing his hands before returning to Matron's office.

Major Lambeth died that night and Spring Gardens was spared a 'flu' outbreak, mostly because of Matron's diligence. Andrew never made it to his digs for dinner. Mrs. Humphries would keep a plate warm for him. She meant well but usually, if he was late, the meal was dry and inedible. It was gone 10 o'clock by the time he finished, uneasy, worried and hungry. Needing fresh air, he walked towards the Thames, looking for a pub. He found himself dodging around the nighthawks searching for a good time. The women glittered and giggled, the men laughed raucously and the pubs were lit up with flashing neon lights promising fun. Andrew only wanted a quiet corner, a pint and a beef pie. He couldn't remember the last time he'd laughed or had fun and realized how much he missed it. However, tonight was not the night to start so he walked to the Embarkment. He leaned on the wall and watched the Thames as the barges drifted on the night tide, wishing he could board a ship to Italy. Sophie filled him with concern, probably because he felt helpless, knowing something was wrong, but he couldn't decide on what.

A loud giggle and a woman's voice said, "Oh darling, that sounds so utterly boring. Fabulous jazz is what I need. Please…" Her partner muttered an inaudible reply. Andrew turned to see the women burying her head in her beau's shoulder, her voice now muffled, but they were both laughing, a little worse for wear perhaps.

Listening to the couple jolted Andrew from his morose thoughts and he began to recall how he and Sophie had met. The first time had been a disaster. She had misread the conversation and thought he was suggesting she was unbalanced and needed treatment. Much of the relationship was based on their mutual interest in the study of the mind. Perhaps the problem was the lack of fun. Now he thought about it, they were always so serious. "That," he said aloud, "has to stop right now." And, with a determined gait, he marched into the nearest pub, where he thought the couple had just come from and to his surprise the place was almost empty.

"I walked by here half an hour ago and it was full," Andrew

said to the barman. "What happened?"

"The club!" The barman shrugged, flipping his finger against his nose. "Posh-like members only, serve fancy cocktails drinks and there's an American jazz band playing all this week. Country's gone mad. What's wrong with a pint and a chorus or two of 'Pack up your trouble?'"

"What indeed!" Andrew replied thoughtfully. "I'll have a pint of ale and a meat pie please?" He pointed to a massive jar of pickled onions. "And a couple of those."

Andrew moved from the bar to a table. He suspected the barman was looking for company and he wanted to be alone. He thought about The Club. One of the doctors had mentioned The Kingfisher Club and he wondered if it was the same one. He'd heard references to jazz music but didn't realize it was popular. A smile broke the seriousness of his face as he decided to take Sophie for a night out and listen to American jazz. Fun, that's what they needed. He leaned back with satisfaction as though he'd solved their problems. He did his best to ignore the niggling question in the pit of his stomach: Was Sophie really in love with him?

# Villa di Seta

May 1919 - Villa di Seta, Lucca

The sun poured in through the cracks in the shutters, waking Sophie from a deep sleep. She blinked and stretched, feeling rested and peaceful, something she had not felt for years. Smiling at her favourite teddy bear, who seemed to be staring at her from his chair, she surmised he had a look of 'why did you leave me?' At twelve years old she had concluded teddy bears were for babies and decided not to take him to England. She jumped out of bed and picked him up, brushing off the dust. "Sorry, Teddy. I missed you terribly. I wished I had taken you with me, especially when Mama died." She smiled. "But Mama's spirit came back to the place she loved and kept you company."

Sophie flung the shutters open and took a massive breath of Tuscan air, gazing at the quiet countryside and the sun shimmering on the river. A cloud of dust caught her attention as it moved along the driveway. Someone was coming to the house. Suddenly she noticed the sun high in the sky; she had slept through the morning.

After running her fingers through her long thick hair, she quickly tied a ribbon around it and smoothed the creased dress she had grabbed from her suitcase. Who would be visiting? No one knew she was here.

Sophie opened her front door and stood at the top of the steps as a small van with faded lettering on the side gave her no clue as to who the visitor might be.

"Buongiorno!" Sophie called as a slim young woman stepped out of the van and carried a large wicker basket up the steps towards Sophie.

"Buongiorno! Signorina Romano, my father sent me with some supplies."

Sophie ushered her inside, taking the basket and placing it on the kitchen table.

"Grazie!" Somewhat perplexed, Sophie lifted the linen cloth that covered the contents, "I think there has been a mistake. I didn't order anything."

The woman smiled. "My name is Paola Bianchi. I help my father at the bakery."

"Oh yes. I stopped yesterday to buy bread and coffee, but I didn't order anything."

"This is a gift from our family. Papa was so excited to see you yesterday. He remembers your family and is sad. Mama remembers your mother. Such a nice lady. And she insisted I bring you some food."

"Oh! That was a long time ago." Sophie gestured to pay but stopped.

"A gift," Paola said, shaking her head.

"This is very kind and generous of you. Are you sure? I know how difficult it is to get food these days." She watched Paola's face full of kindness. "Please thank your mother.

Would you like a coffee? I was about to make some for myself."

"Grazie. I have to finish the deliveries. Papa is so proud that we have petrol today and can make the deliveries. Tomorrow, maybe not. I will come by for coffee another day. That is if I may?" Paola said, remembering her manners and adding an excited, almost romantic tone in her voice. "I would love to hear about England."

"Please come by, anytime. I would enjoy the company. I will be here for another 10 days."

"Oh, you are not staying?" Paola said with disappointment.

"I have not been well …" Sophie cleared her throat, not wanting to say more. "I am a nurse at the Bartley Hospital in London and must return to work." Sophie was surprised at her own sense of disappointment at the thought of returning to London so soon.

"I understand. Papa thought you had come back to live." Paola looked through the kitchen window with a frown. "I was only a little girl when you left for England. Papa told me about your aunt and uncle. He felt sorry for your father who had worked so hard, only to have your uncle destroy it all. I don't blame you not wanting to stay."

Sophie caught a massive lump in her throat at the memory of happy summers with her aunt and uncle. Unbidden, her thoughts added, 'and Carlos.'

She audibly caught her breath at the thought of his name and admonished her reaction, twisting Andrew's ring on her finger.

"Ciao!" Paola called, waving as she ran down the steps.

Sophie forced a smile as Paola turned the van around in a cloud of dust.

Quite suddenly, as if someone was calling to her, her eyes

were drawn to her aunt's house, opposite the villa. The pomegranate bush was twisted and overgrown, stretched across the weed covered path leading to the once red door. Its redness was now a pale pink as it hung at an angle, half closed.

Sophie slowly descended the villa steps and walked up the path into the house. A squawking bird fluttered past her, making her jump. The place had a stale and rotten earthy smell, dark shadows hiding in the corners. The only light came from the kitchen window above the sink. Dishes sat on the draining board, waiting to be put away, the only sign of normalcy. The kitchen cupboards had been emptied, contents scattered and broken. Empty drawers and furniture were smashed. She stepped carefully around holes in the floor where even the floorboards had been pulled up. Sophie shuddered when her foot rolled over a shell casing. The stained floorboards made her stomach turn. Could that be blood? She swallowed hard, feeling the violence of desperate people.

Sophie ran out of the house, gulping the fresh spring air and found herself under the mulberry trees, staring across the land towards the neighbour's neat rows of grape vines, such a contrast to the chaos she was facing. The outbuildings, where the silkworms had lived, were nothing but piles of rotting wood with the occasional wisp of raw silk caught on a rough board. There was no evidence of the caring sericulture farm her ancestors had handed down from one generation to another. She stared across at the storage hut, lying in ruins, the roof completely caved in and sheltered only by overgrown mulberry trees. She wrapped her arms around herself, remembering her first kiss and the many trysts behind the shed. The thought of Carlos once again made her heart beat faster. Or maybe she was afraid there might be evidence of murder inside the shed.

The solicitor had said, 'Their mutilated bodies were found in the shed,' or words to that effect. She gave a weak laugh at her morbid curiosity as she scanned the contents, but saw nothing more than old, rusty farm equipment. That didn't stop an involuntary shudder prickle down her spine. The barbarity of the events clung to her, contaminating her clothes and her skin. She felt dirty and marched towards the villa, wishing she was not alone. Why hadn't she asked Andrew to come and join her? But it wasn't Andrew's touch she craved.

After bathing and changing, Sophie felt better and returned to the kitchen for coffee. She removed the linen towel from the wicker basket and peered inside. It only took seconds for her appetite to return at the sight of crusty fresh bread. *Only Italians could bake bread like that,* she thought. She tore a piece off and chewed as she unloaded butter, cheese, pasta, a jar of home preserved tomatoes, more coffee, a bottle of red wine from the local winery and, tucked at the bottom, homemade biscotti. Grateful for the food, she realized just how selfish she had been, wrapped up in her own problems. It had not occurred to her that postwar life in Italy was no better than England. The least she could have done was brought her own supplies.

Had she become so self-indulgent? It wasn't like her to escape from hardship. Had the war changed her so much that she had no empathy, no thought for her friends, her patients? At the casualty clearing hospital in Passchendaele, there was

28

no time to indulge in ones needs. Injured soldiers needed her and, even at the Bartley, patients needed her. It all became too much, the burdens of others too heavy to carry. She had almost lost her own life. *She cupped her hands over her ears, hearing the bomb explode, her legs running, escaping the Hun's bombs blasting the hospital and then silence.* She hadn't been able to save them. Their faces were etched on her memory, dying, screaming for their mothers. Had her aunt and uncle screamed for mercy? And what about her father? His image of agony as flames licked his body almost always brought her to her knees. Was violence and carnage to follow her all her life? Thick hot tears welled up from deep inside and flooded down her face. No longer able to hold back, she gasped and sobbed, retching at times as the anguish, terror and innermost sorrow erupted and poured out of her. Eventually, the sobs subsided. She cradled her head in her arms on the tear-soaked table. She closed her eyes, grieving and mourning the countless losses of family, friends, soldiers and lives. Too exhausted to stay awake, she slipped into a fitful sleep.

Barely able to open her swollen eyes, she rubbed her stiff neck and tried to sit up, glancing towards the window and wondering how long she had been sleeping. Her throat hurt and her face felt like a balloon. She stretched out her arms and stood up shakily, but felt lighter, brighter. Much of the heavy sadness and grief had gone. She leaned her swollen face towards the afternoon sun streaming through the window, relishing its warmth coaxing her puffy eyes to open wide.

Sitting down again, she leaned back in the chair, ravenously hungry. Tearing off another piece of bread, she added the last of the ham. The coffee was strong and she felt her heritage as she sipped the dark brown liquid, not weak and milky like the English coffee. Perhaps that was why she drank tea. There was nothing more British than drinking tea. She chuckled with amused bewilderment. Did it come down to tea or coffee?

She always considered herself British but she had easily slipped into Italian ways, the language quickly coming back to her, the coffee tasting strong and bold. She felt strong and bold herself, even connected, certainly to her mother here at the villa, but not her father. He, or his spirit, had not returned to Italy. Although Italian and born on this very farm, he had expeditiously adopted the English way of life. She struggled to remember her father here at the villa. Typically, she saw him in his study at Oak House in Derby, elbow on the mantlepiece, cigar in one hand and brandy in the other, the perfect English gentleman.

Where did she belong?

She had convinced herself that the desire to come back to her roots was nothing more than fatigue, but now she was questioning if Italy meant more. But what? There was nothing here for her other than tragedy, hurt and a love lost. In England she had nursing, a fiancé, friends. She felt confused and in limbo, floating between two different worlds, each seducing her with their lure of love and protection, better things to come, happiness perhaps. She wasn't sure either could provide what she was looking for. Was she really seeking happiness?

Memories of her happy childhood with her mother's love and father's protection made her feel safe, but the unrequited love from Carlos and the tragedy of her aunt and uncle's murder wiped all that away. The love of nursing and friends like Hillary and Trixie, and Andrew's love with constant attention and protection made her feel wanted and somewhat safe.

"Andrew," she said. "A wonderful man and I have treated him badly." Sophie knew how worried and hurt he would be by her disappearing with only a brief letter of explanation. She must write to him, immediately. Aware that she was distracting herself from making any kind of decision, she took her note paper and pen from her bag.

*My dearest Andrew,*

*What you must think of me, I dare not surmise. I ask for your forgiveness for disappearing so suddenly and for such a brief letter with no explanation as I boarded the boat to France and on to the train to Italy.*

*I arrived at Villa di Seta safely yesterday after a gruelling journey. I wish I could be more precise in my explanation, but I cannot. I find myself very confused and...*

Sophie hesitated, staring out of the window and picking her words carefully. Should she write *I wish you were here*? But that was not being honest. She only wished to talk to him. Andrew was the only person who truly understood her. He was always understanding, just as he was with his patients. Did he treat her like one of his patients or like the woman he loved?

*...wishing I could talk to you. My muddled thoughts and anxiety prompted uncontrollable weeping and how I wished you could comfort me. I can hear your words 'have patience, dear Sophie. You will soon feel better' and today, I do feel a little better, as though the weeping drained away the heavy burdens.*

*I understand you are worried but please, my dear, do not. I am safe here. Even the local baker remembers me and my family and kindly brought a basket of food, including some amazing crusty Italian bread. One day, when you come to Italy, you will understand what I mean about Italian bread. I am sure I have made you smile talking about such a small thing, but it is the small things that seem important to me.*

*I will be home soon. My leave is only two weeks and, including travel, five days have passed. I long for your comforting and reassuring words and the feel of your strong arms.*

*Affectionately,*
*Sophie*

She read the letter before sealing the envelope and then wondered how she could post it. She tried to remember if there was a post office, or if she would have to go to Lucca. Paola or her father at the bakery would know. The clock struck five o'clock. The bakery would be opening after the afternoon siesta. She smiled, loving the Italian habit of the afternoon siesta to escape the heat of the day and staying open during the cool evenings.

Brushing her hair and throwing cold water on her tear-stained face, she dared to look in the mirror. Shocked to see the puffiness in her eyes, she soaked the facecloth in cold water and held it to her face for several minutes. She brushed her hair again, leaving it loose around her face, deciding she didn't look too bad, and slipped on her shoes.

She was surprised at how light she felt walking down the driveway and swinging the empty wicker basket. Reaching the bakery, the doorbell jangled as she went in.

"Ciao, Signorina!" Paola greeted her.

"I am returning your basket. Grazie. It is a long time since I ate such wonderful bread."

Paola frowned. "You want more?"

"No, no. I have lots of bread, thanks to your generosity." Sophie held up the letter. "I need stamps. Is there a Post Office near here?"

Paola shook her head. "No, it is closed. Signore was killed in the war. But I am going to Lucca tomorrow. I can post it for you there." Paola hesitated. "Would you like to come with me? I have to pick up flour for Papa."

"Si, bella, I'd love to," Sophie said, beaming.

"Good. I shall enjoy the company and you can tell me all about England." Paola's voice was full of excitement. "Meet me here at eight in the morning."

"Si, grazie!" Sophie said.

"Ciao, Signore Bianchi." Sophie handed him the empty basket. "Grazie!"

After a few pleasantries, Sophie walked back to the villa, trying her best not to look at her aunt's house or the devastated farm. She wondered how the villa had escaped damage when the thugs attacked. A frown wrinkled her forehead. Her father had made sure her name was on the deed and title to the villa, but what about the farm? Originally, the villa, house, farm buildings and land had all belonged to her grandfather, passed to his sons, her father and uncle. At what point had the buildings been split up, if at all? After the raid on the farm and house, she had assumed her uncle had lost it to debtors. Who were these debtors? She glanced at the buildings. It was obvious nobody had been near the place since the raid and murders. She recalled Carlos saying the police had done little at the time, perhaps afraid of the gangsters. That had been years ago. Curious, she searched her father's office but found no papers relating to the property. Remembering he had kept most at his solicitor's in Derby, she decided to contact Mr. Fotheringham when she returned to England. The house had been ransacked. Was that what the thieves were looking for?

Finishing off a plate of pasta, Sophie gave a sigh of satisfaction. *I can't believe I ate the whole plate and those tomatoes are like nothing I've tasted,* she thought with some surprise. Her appetite had returned and she had cooked something edible. *I must tell Hillary of my new cooking skills,* she laughed. *I will write to Hillary as I could post it with Andrew's letter tomorrow.*

*Dearest Hillary,*

*I hope this letter finds you in good health and your studies are progressing without difficulty.*
*I do miss you, wishing I could share my thoughts and adventures with you. I arrived safely, but it was a long*

*journey. I am at the villa in Italy. I know that will surprise you but I needed to come here, although, I have yet to determine the reason. But I have had time to think and put my life in some kind of order. We can talk about that when I get home.*

*I actually cooked myself pasta with tomato sauce tonight. I know you will have trouble believing that and the thought of telling you made me laugh. The local baker remembers my family and kindly brought some supplies.*

*I am quite comfortable here at the villa, but I'm not sure about my melancholy thoughts, which brought me to a bout of uncontrollable weeping. I do not understand what is wrong with me, but after a good sleep I feel much better. My dear friend, please keep this confession to yourself. I would be mortified if Matron was to find out.*

*I have written to Andrew, poor boy. I have not treated him well, but intend to make that up to him on my return.*

*I have made a new friend, Paola, the bakers daughter. She is young but very pleasant. She invited me to accompany her to Lucca tomorrow.*

*As you can tell, I am well and safe. Matron only gave me two weeks so I will be home soon. I would love to hear from you, but I suspect the post is slow and I will probably be home before you can reply.*

*Affectionately, your dearest friend,*
  *Sophie*

# A Day in Lucca

S preading her arms wide, Sophie twirled and skipped along the driveway, the morning sun warm and the breeze cool. It was hard to believe that in such a short time she had shaken off years of burdens. She felt light, happy, almost carefree. At the latter, she shook her head slightly. *Not too carefree,* she thought. *I do have responsibilities.* A sudden tightening in the pit of her stomach told her there might be some lingering burdens. *But for now, I will enjoy the sunshine, a day in Lucca and Paola's company.*

She pressed her fingers against the letters in her pocket, especially the one addressed to Andrew, feeling a little guilty and hoping the letter would ease his anxiety. If nothing else, Andrew had always been there for her and she had treated him badly. It was time to make amends.

Paola waved from the bakery, already loading the van with orders to be delivered on the way to Lucca.

"Ciao!" Paola called.

"Good morning!" Sophie said, climbing into the van, "Ah… the aroma of fresh bread is making me hungry."

Paola cranked the engine and jumped into the driver's seat, handing Sophie a small package. "From Mama." Paola laughed. "And, there is a basket of food in the back. Mama will not hear of anyone being hungry."

Sophie laughed, unwrapping two pieces of biscotti. Her stomach gave an audible rumble, making them both giggle. They crunched the biscuits as Paola steered the van onto the main road.

Heavy traffic greeted them as they drove past the ancient city wall and into Lucca. The van jostled between other automobiles, horse drawn carriages and bicycles. Sophie held her breath as Paola maneuvered through the narrow-cobbled streets, barely wide enough for one car, let alone one in each direction, plus pedestrians sauntering alongside, some raising their fist at the traffic, others unperturbed. Large buildings towered over the quaint row houses, with pretty flower boxes among the lines of washing high above them.

Sophie recalled her schoolteacher telling the class about the ancient buildings of Lucca and even as a child she had been in awe of the deep sense of time and history. Something she had not thought about for a long time. The knowledge that these buildings had stood the test of time for thousands of years gave her comfort, a sense of proportion. The Great War and her immediate woes were a small blip in time and would, one day, be history.

Paola had completed the deliveries and they were now at the wholesaler, loading bags of flour into the van. Sophie sat waiting, watching the people mill about. She noticed a group of young men in black shirts, harassing passers-by. She sensed an undercurrent, the same one she'd felt at the train station. Two black shirts moved closer, making her nervous. She was glad when Paola returned to the van and they drove away.

"Now we have lunch, si?" Paola said. "I will take you to the Piazza, famous for the wine and…" she pinched her fingers to her lips, "pasta magnifico." Sophie laughed at the typical Italian gesture.

The Piazza was full of people strolling and enjoying the sunshine; a large decorative fountain spouted water from marble ghouls and angels. The café was as she expected, white-clothed tables outside in the shade, waiters with long white aprons and the aroma of food cooking, exactly what, she couldn't tell, except it made her mouth water.

The waiter placed a carafe of rich red wine on the table and Paola ordered food for both of them and raised her glass. "Saluti!"

"Cheers!" Sophie repeated, taking a sip of wine. She nodded, appreciating the taste. "This is lovely, Paola."

Sophie scanned her surroundings, feeling on edge and wondering if there were any black shirts in the Piazza. She was relieved to see only people gathering to talk or eat.

"You noticed?" Paola asked. "The black shirts?"

Sophie nodded, surprised her nervousness had shown.

"I saw them too. That's why I drove away quickly. They are young idealists, who think it is manly to taunt young women. Italy is an unhappy country, looking for justice and a new way of life, especially the youth. There is a lot of unrest, I'm afraid."

"Yet another result of war." Sophie felt tears in her eyes. "In England too, in the form of strikes and riots."

Paola touched Sophie's hand. Taking a deep breath, she said, "Let's speak of nicer things. I see you have a ring. Tell me all about him?"

"Not much to say. He's a doctor. His name is Andrew and I worked with him in Passchendaele. We both have an interest in illness of the mind, soldiers with battle fatigue and shell shock." Sophie twisted the ring around her finger. "He's anxious to get married and I'm in no hurry."

Paola raised an eyebrow and asked, "Why? Is he not in love with you?"

"He is." Sophie really didn't want to discuss Andrew.

"A handsome Englishman. Very romantic. And, you love him?" Paola fixed a gaze on Sophie that made her uncomfortable. Her cheeks were hot and she did not know how to answer the question.

"Of course. He is very handsome, kind and so gentle with his patients. He is my friend, the only person I can talk to and share my thoughts."

Paola seemed to push her eyebrows even higher, eyes questioning Sophie's answer. "Friendship is not love."

"For me, it is." Sophie said, cutting her off. Realizing her bluntness had offended Paola, she added, "you said you wanted to know about England."

Paola gave a long thoughtful sigh. "Green countryside, rolling hills, heroes on horseback rescuing ladies in big villas—estates, I think you call them."

Sophie smothered a laugh and smiled gently, afraid she might offend Paola again. "I'm not sure that is typical England. Have you been reading Jane Austen?"

"Si!" She giggled. "Amore! Signore Darcy."

Now it was Sophie's turn to raise eyebrows. "The England you speak of is in books. *Pride and Prejudice* is romantic and I love the story too, but that is not what England is like now. The countryside is very green and pretty but the cities are full of devastation from the German bombs and the heroes are war heroes. Before the war I worked in a big posh hotel. Lords and ladies, dukes and duchesses came to stay and there were handsome young men. But if you are looking for romance, you would be better with an Italian." Paola's face showed disappointment. Sophie wanted to comfort her and pointed towards the centre of the Piazza. "A handsome man like the one over there in uniform." Sophie frowned at first then laughed. "Perhaps I am wrong. I believe that is a British officer's uniform." Seeing the funny side of Sophie's lecture about Englishmen, they both laughed loudly, making the soldier turn and stare at them, his eyes fixed on Sophie.

She froze, afraid to breath. Her heart thumped out of her chest and she thought she might faint.

"What is wrong?" Paola's face paled with fear, staring at Sophie and rising from her seat. "Is it the wine? You are so pale."

The officer slowly walked towards them, his eyes never moving from Sophie's. His lips moved with soft words. "Sophie, is that really you?"

"What are you doing here?" Sophie squeaked out.

Paola sat back in her seat, her gaze switching for one to the other. "You know each other?" Once again she was ignored.

The officer, eyes on Sophie, was now standing next to the table. "I might ask you the same question."

Paola cleared her throat. "Scusi!"

"Oh, where are my manners? Paola, Signorina Bianchi, Captain Wainwright."

"My pleasure," Carlos gave a bowed to Paola. "Forgive the correction, Major Wainwright."

Sophie blushed. "I had forgotten. My apologies."

"Are you well and fully recovered from your injuries?" Carlos asked, concern in his voice.

"Yes, thank you. I am quite recovered. Are you working at a hospital near here?"

Paola jumped up from her seat again. "You must be Andrew! I am so happy to meet you. Sophie has told me all about your work with shell shocked..." She stopped talking, realizing something was wrong.

There was an awkward silence. Sophie had no idea how to break it and detected a flash of hurt in his eyes at the mention of Andrew. The waiter suddenly appeared, placed two plates of food on the table and broke the silence by asking Carlos if he was joining the ladies.

"No, grazie. I must return to the hospital." He bowed to Paola a second time. "Major *Carlos* Wainwright, Signorina," he said with deliberate emphasis on his Christian name.

"Pardon, Major," Paola said, her cheeks pink with embarrassment.

Carlos shifted his attention to Sophie and lingered so close she could feel his warm breath on her cheeks. Was he going to kiss her? She leaned towards him and just for a second her desire clouded her judgement, before quickly pulling back, her hand covering her mouth, and pretending a cough.

"Are you staying at the villa?" A tone of surprise in his voice.

"Yes." Her voice trembled and she coughed again. "A break from the Bartley. I'm nursing again." She cleared her throat again. "They wouldn't let me go back to the front."

"I'm sorry to hear that." He gave her a cheeky grin, teasing. "Perhaps, that cough needs attention."

Sophie blushed, wafting her hand to dismiss his comment.

"Ciao, ladies! We will meet another time."

Carlos marched across the Piazza, looking as handsome as ever. She followed his every step until he disappeared down one of the cobbled streets. Sophie didn't dare look at Paola. Her heart was pounding and she was mortified by her reaction. Attempting to calm herself, she gulped down almost a full glass of wine.

"He's an old friend. He worked for my father and we spent a summer at the villa many years ago, before the war. I was very surprised to see him," Sophie blurted out, needing to give Paola an explanation. Or did she need to rationalize her reaction?

"You have many men friends. Your fiancé is a friend you love, but not a lover. And this Carlos is more than a friend. The look in his eyes tells me he's a lover. I do not understand you English." Paola smiled with an expression of curiosity.

"I don't understand either. Let's eat before it goes cold." Sophie desperately wanted to talk about something else, anything but Carlos. She was in shock, trembling inside. Her memory of the last time she saw him was hazy and vague. Badly injured from a bomb blast, she had been lying in a hospital bed in France, recovering from surgery. Carlos was the surgeon. She vaguely remembered he and Andrew were together at her bedside.

Andrew told her later that Carlos had been promoted to major with orders to take up his command at Base Hospital in France, tending to soldiers' limbs for the remainder of the war. She had not inquired what happened to him after. She assumed he would, by now, be married to Rosamond. She had never expected to see him again.

Paola was quite right. The food and wine were delicious, although the wine had made her feel quite woozy since she'd downed several glasses, hoping it would make her feel better. By the time they reached the parked van for the return journey, Sophie was out of explanations and excuses for Paola's many questions and perhaps, as an escape or the result of too much wine, she slept most of the way home.

Sophie left Paola and her father to unload the van and walked to the villa, mostly to clear her head, pinching herself to make sure she hadn't dreamt seeing Carlos in Lucca. With an involuntary sigh, she thought, *he looked handsome in his officer's uniform. Other than a few more pips for major, he hasn't changed.* She couldn't stem the flood of memories, first of fondness, and then a fury of anger boiled up from deep inside. How did he do that? He always came barging into her life at times when she thought everything was settled. He would disrupt her life, her emotions, confusing her and then he would disappear again. Was this some kind of game to him? And yet, seeing him in the Piazza was a coincidence. He was as surprised as she was. And why was he in Italy? Obviously, working at a hospital in Lucca. The war was over. Why would he still be in uniform? There must be a military hospital here.

She had noted the surprise in his voice when he had asked her if she was staying at the villa. He could not have known she was there. But, she wondered, being so close to the villa would he have taken a trip to check it out? She shook her head. *Why would he? The time when the villa meant anything to Carlos was long gone.*

She hated feeling so restless, feelings see-sawing between sadness and anger, all because of Carlos Wainwright. Again!

# Belonging and Ownership

F ollowing the trip to Lucca, Sophie spent two days of moping around the villa. She could not mollify her feelings towards Carlos. She liked the man, of course she did, even though she often found him a source of annoyance. She had loved him a long time ago; but it was young puppy love, a fling, as his mother had told her. And, years later, chance meetings at the both the Bartley and Passchendaele had been a surprise. Ultimately, she'd been shocked when he announced he was engaged to be married. Even that hadn't stopped him flirting, though. She wanted him out of her life and, more to the point, out of her thoughts. She had made her choice. Andrew was her betrothed and she was happy about her decision. *Damn, Carlos!*

Mostly to distract herself, she kept busy cleaning the villa. She had cleaned every cupboard and now she was bored. She glanced across at her aunt's house, in such a mess, she wanted to start cleaning it up. But who owned it? Mr. Fotheringham, the solicitor in Derby, had told her the property had been seized for her uncle's debts and yet, it was obvious no one had set foot on the farm since his death. She had searched the property for documents but her aunt's office had been ransacked, only a few unreadable papers lay on the floor scorched, possibly burnt. She searched for a For Sale sign, but found nothing old or new, except an old bicycle in the woodshed. What had happened?

Sophie's head now full of questions about the farm, she wheeled the bicycle out of the shed. It was in good condition all things considered, although dusty and dirty, and the tyres needed air. But with a clean, it would be as good as new and perfect for getting around. Checking out the woodshed a second time, she found a can of oil and a bicycle pump, a bit rusty but it worked.

Sophie stepped back and admired her handy work, feeling a little nervous. It had been a long time since she had ridden a bike and her leg injury from the bomb blast sometimes troubled her. She bravely hopped on and, to her surprise, she stayed upright, pedalling down the driveway. The wind in her hair felt liberating. She pedalled faster, cursing her skirt, and admitting trousers would be perfect for bicycling. She reached the Bianchi's bakery and parked her bike.

"Ciao!" Sophie called, opening the bakery door.

"Bella biciclatte! Where did you find it?" Paola asked, peering through the shop window.

"I needed a distraction and started cleaning." Sophie felt her cheeks warm and hoped Paola wouldn't ask why she needed a distraction, although she probably already knew the reason. "When I finished the villa, I looked around my aunt's place and found the bike in the woo 'shed. Perfect for running errands and coming here for supplies."

"Scusate, Sophie," Paola said, apologizing, "but we have no bread this late in the day."

"Oh, I didn't come for bread. I wanted to show you, my find. However, I do have a question. Do you know who bought my uncle's house and the silk farm?"

Paola frowned, shrugging her shoulders. "No, but Papa might know." Paola turned and called towards the back of the shop. "Papa pronto?"

"Si," Signore Bianchi pulled back the curtain that divided the shop from the bakery. "Ah, Signora Romano, what can I do for you?"

"Do you know who owns the farm?"

"Voi, you! Did you not inherit from your father and uncle? Roberto and Maria had no children."

"The villa, yes. Papa had put the title and deed in my name. The farm was owned by the family and I was told it was lost to my uncle's debtors."

"No!" Signore Bianchi shook his head. "Your uncle's debtors were gangsters. They were convicted of the murder and jailed. Have you check the records?"

"No. Where do I go for that?"

"Le municipalità, the town hall, will have the records."

"Is it far? Can I bicycle?" Sophie asked.

Signore Bianchi frowned. "Biciclatte?"

Paola laughed, nodding towards the window and the parked bike. "Si, Sophie found an old bike."

He shook his head. "No, le municipalita is in Lucca. Paola will drive you tomorrow."

Sophie and Paola left for Lucca next morning. Sophie stopped at the town hall, while Paola picked up supplies. The town hall had records of all the properties in the district. Villa di Seta, farmhouse, and ten acres of land, clearly listed the original owners as her great-grandfather and grandfather until the current owners were listed as Alberto and Roberto Romano with an amendment showing Sophie's name on Villa di Seta. She questioned the clerk to make sure nothing was missing, explaining her situation. He assured her as the only relative she was the owner of the property but she needed to consult a solicitor to formalize everything.

"Grazie Signore. Do you know a solicitor near here?"

"Si," He pointed across the hall to the writing on the glass panel of the door, Signore Cavaliere Notiao e Avvocato. He is a nice man and will help you."

Sophie thanked him again and knocked on the door. A young female voice called "Si accomodi!"

Sophie explained to the receptionist why she was there and asked for an appointment. To her surprise the young women said there had been a cancelation and Signore Cavaliere could see her in ten minutes, if she'd like to take a seat. No sooner had she sat down than Paola knocked on the door, the clerk having told her where to find Sophie.

"I can't believe it, Paola. Everything is mine. There are no debtors. I am the only next of kin, just as your father said."

The office door opened and Signore Cavaliere smiled at Sophie and then frowned when he saw Paola.

"Paola, is something wrong? Your papa, he is all right?"

"Si, I am here with my friend, Sophie Romano. Papa is quite well." Paola turned to Sophie. "Signore Cavaliere is an old friend of my father's. I would have said something but I did not realize this was his office."

"Sophie Romano! You must be Alberto's daughter." Signore's face grimaced with sympathy. "I am so sorry for your loss and tragedy. I knew your father and uncle well. Your father was a good man, a great friend. Your uncle, he had problems. Please, come into my office. How can I help you?"

Shifting in her chair, Sophie explained her discovery, that she was the rightful heir to what was left of the farm and land and asked if he could help her.

Signore explained the legalities and what had to be done. He needed documents from Sophie, which fortunately she had brought with her to Italy, in case there were any issues with the villa. He agreed to visit the villa the next day and reassured her it was a simple process and he could have it completed before she returned to London.

When they arrived back at the bakery, Paola insisted she come inside and meet her mother and tell her father the good news. Sophie wasn't sure whether it was good news. What was she going to do with a rundown farm and ten acres of land? She had been wondering what to do with the villa, aware that years of neglect was going to cost money. The remaining property, the house and outbuildings, were in much worse condition. She was overwhelmed by the whole thing.

Signora Bianchi gave Sophie a gentle, understanding smile. "Bella, come sit down. A glass of vino, si?"

Sophie thought of refusing, but the warmth of the welcome, including the wine, was what she needed. "Grazie, Signora!"

It took but a few minutes for Sophie to relax and forget about land and property. Her Italian came back quickly as she laughed and chatted with this kind Italian family. She felt loved, appreciated and secure in a way that only family can make you feel. It had been a very long time since she had felt this way. Since her father's death, there had been no family. Happiness filled her heart to be with these wonderful people, but with a touch of sadness for the family she missed and mourned.

Signore Bianchi must have sensed her sadness and poured more wine, making them all laugh with stories of Sophie's mother scolding her when she asked for cake. Sophie laughed. "And you always found a treat for me," Sophie added. "And Pietro teased …" The room fell silent and Sophie realized that Pietro, the Bianchi's son, the same age as Sophie, had not been mentioned once, either by his parents or Paola.

Signora Bianchi spoke first. "Alpine troops. He insisted on going. He loved the mountains." Her eyes glistened with tears.

"1916, the Battle of Isonzo, the first one. The men were exhausted from climbing the Alps, the cold in March froze fingers and toes. Brave men were slaughtered, including Pietro. Many battles followed but Pietro did not see the victory." Signore stared into space. "It was not worth the death of our son."

Sophie brushed tears away. "I am so very sorry for your loss." *And sorry I mentioned his name,* she thought.

"You understand, but many don't," Signora said.

"I do. I nursed soldiers in Passchendaele, in different terrain but terrible conditions. I held their hands and stroked their brow. I wrote letters of condolence to their wives and parents if the commanding officer wasn't available. I do understand and I feel your pain."

The mood changed. Signore Bianchi got up and said, "I must lock up the shop."

"Si," Signora said. Taking a deep breath, she added, "Dinner will not cook itself."

"Oh, I must be going," Sophie said, realizing it was dusk and getting late.

"No, you have dinner with us tonight." Signora waved her arm, telling Sophie to sit, and pointing to Paola to pour more wine.

"Don't argue with Mama," Paola said, with a laugh.

"Grazie, Signora," Sophie replied, looking forward to a home cooked meal.

Turning to Paola, Sophie said, "I am so sorry, Paola. I didn't mean to upset your parents. I had forgotten about Pietro until your father mentioned me in the store. He used to tell me the cake would make me fat."

"That sounds like Pietro. Can you imagine how he teased me, his little sister? I miss him so much. What I would give to hear him tease me again. Papa gets mad sometimes that Italy joined the war and Mama has bouts of sad tears. As time goes by, the pain lessens and sometimes Mama and Papa can talk about the memories."

Signore Bianchi returned from locking up the shop and joined Sophie and Paola as a large steaming bowl of pasta was placed in the middle of the table.


The sun had disappeared behind the horizon, leaving an orange glow as the stars began to twinkle in the darkening sky. Sophie walked backed to the villa, full to overflowing with food, wine and love from a wonderful family. She thought about Pietro and the Bianchis' terrible loss. *The war might be over, but we are all still paying the price and how long will it go on?* She sat on the villa steps, gazing at the stars, as they brightened and the night darkened. A slight breeze brushed her cheeks and the night insects chirped noisily.

"What am I going to do with all this?" she said, sweeping her gaze along the farmhouse, the outbuildings and land beyond the mulberry trees. Her eyes heavy, she yawned, pulling herself up the remaining steps and closing the front door. Sleep would come easily tonight.

The noise of the engine made Sophie peer through the kitchen window. A red Fiat bounced down the driveway and stopped outside the villa. Signore Cavaliere jumped out of the automobile and, carrying a leather bag, he mounted the steps to the villa. Sophie had already opened the front door.

"Buongiorno!" Sophie said, stretching her arm to shake his hand.

"Buongiorno, Signorina Romano."

Sophie led the way into the kitchen. She had thought about using her father's study but decided she was more comfortable in the kitchen. She handed Signore a folder with her papers.

"Grazie," he said, leafing through the documents, reading and nodding. "Everything is in order. It is good that you had the foresight to bring them with you."

"I wanted to make sure the title to the villa was in my name. At the time, I had no idea the farm and land were still in my father and uncle's names."

Signore Cavaliere read and explained all the documents and, with her signature, Sophie was now the sole owner of the dilapidated silkworm farm. Taking the documents from him, she stared at them before looking at him. Shrugging her shoulders, she said, "What do I do now?"

"Signorina, it is yours to do as you wish. You are not happy?" He frowned, seeing the confusion, when he expected her to be pleased with such an inheritance. "If you do not want it, then sell it. Would you like me to help you?"

"Signore, I am a nurse. I live in London. I neither have time, nor money, to repair the house and the farm is in ruins. Even my beloved villa needs repairs I cannot afford." Sophie felt near to tears. Yet more problems to resolve.

"Do not be upset. I will help you. You want to keep the villa, si?"

"Si, but it has been neglected for too long. How will I do the repairs?"

"It is simple. You sell the farm and land and use the money to repair the villa. I will help you with the sale and hire workmen for the repairs."

At first, Sophie was stunned. Could she really do that? She broke into a big smile. Of course she could. "So simple. I never thought about that. But who would buy a run down farm?"

"The house and outbuildings are worthless but the land is fertile soil and probably perfect for a vineyard. Signorina, will you trust me to find a buyer for your land?" Sophie gave a hesitant nod. She needed to talk to someone. This was happening too fast. Seeing her hesitation, he added, "I will first make enquiries and then we can discuss what can be done. Now I must return to my office."

Sophie couldn't help but admire the red Fiat with its polished brass fittings as it drove away. She liked the gentleman, as well as his automobile. She giggled, surprised at how excited she felt at the prospect of selling the land. Jumping on her bicycle, she pedalled to the bakery to ask Signore Bianchi what he thought of the idea and if she could trust Signore Cavaliere.

When she arrived, Signore was outside the shop. "Sophie, I am just closing up for siesta. What can I get you?"

"Signore, what can you tell me about Signore Cavaliere? He has suggested I sell the land. He said the soil is good for a vineyard. Is that true? He said he would sell it for me. You know him well. Can I trust him?"

"Si, Sophie. I would trust him with my life. He is a good man and only wants to help you. He was a friend of your father's. The vineyard is a good idea. Franco Bianchi, your neighbour, has been talking about extending his crops."

"Franco. Neighbour?" She frowned and then remember the neat rows of grape vines past the mulberry trees at the end of her land. "Is he a nice man? Should I talk to him?"

"Leave it to me. Franco is my cousin. Now I need to get out of the heat and rest. You do the same."

"Grazie!" Sophie got on her bicycle and pedalled to the villa.

# Expect the Unexpected

Three days passed and Sophie was anxious with no word about the vineyard or from the solicitor. Italians have a reputation of moving slowly, but she was due back in London and did not have the luxury of time. She knew that her nursing career was at stake, and that Matron had, with good reason, doubted her abilities. *I have to prove to Matron that I am well, in mind and body, and both worthy and capable of the promotion.* She pondered for a moment, then nodded with the realization that, thankfully, she was not losing her mind. She really did feel well and strong, just like her old self. She was looking forward to going back to London, the Bartley and Andrew.

A loud knock on the front door made her jump. "Ah, speak of the devil, that must be Signore Cavaliere." She peered through the window but there was no red Fiat outside.

A stranger stood on her doorstep; a tall wiry man in his fifties, although she thought his tanned weather beaten face made him older than his years. He lifted his straw hat and beamed a kindly smile. "Good morning, Signorina. My name is Franco Bianchi. I am your neighbour," the man said in perfect English.

"Good morning! You speak English," Sophie said with

surprise.

"Si. I spent several years in England in my youth and I served with you English during the war. My, how you say, cousin, the baker, said to me that you were selling the Romano land."

"Yes. My solicitor is looking into it for me. Are you interested?" Sophie answered cautiously. She really wanted the solicitor to deal with this and she had no idea how much the land was worth. "Your cousin did mention you were planning to extend the vineyard."

"I have been waiting a long time, since before the war. I did not know who owned the land after the death of Roberto. I consulted Signore Cavaliere, who tried to contact the brother, your father," he said hesitantly. "Only to discover he too had died and he could not find you."

"Signore Cavaliere is your solicitor?" *This man seems to know everyone,* she thought. *Is this a good thing or should I be looking for someone impartial?*

Signore must have guessed her thoughts. "Do not worry. He is a good, honest man. In a small place like ours, he knows everyone and treats everyone fairly."

She wasn't sure. It seemed so different from the English way and Mr. Fotheringham's formality. Another knock on the door and this time the red Fiat was parked outside.

"Signore, please come in. I have company."

"Si. I have spoken with Franco. He is interested in buying your land."

Glancing from one man to the other Sophie felt uneasy. Was there a conspiracy going on?

"Signore Cavaliere, as yet, we have not discussed any details and I think it inappropriate to discuss this in the presence of a potential buyer."

A pacifying smile formed on his face. "This is business and best discussed between gentlemen. I'm sure you understand, Sophie. May I call you Sophie?"

"No, you may not!" Sophie retorted, annoyed at his placating tone. "I have taken care of my own affairs since I was sixteen. I do not appreciate being treated as though I were a child." Her stare pierced right through him, making him shuffle his feet and clear his throat.

"My apologies, Signorina Romano. You are quite right. We have not discussed the terms of the sale. In my capacity as your solicitor, I thought it be beneficial that Franco join us …"

Interrupting him, Sophie said, "Beneficial to whom? It certainly is not beneficial to me." Sophie took a breath, turning to Signore Bianchi, whose eyes had a twinkle and his lips a grin, obviously enjoying the drama.

He raised his hand, to prevent Sophie from speaking. "I apologize for the intrusion." Speaking directly to Sophie and in English, he added, "I will leave you to discuss business. You are an amazing lady, Signorina. I shall look forward to hearing from you."

He picked up his straw hat, raised it slightly above his head, acknowledging Signore Cavaliere, and, with a broad grin, said in Italian, "Signore, I wish you luck."

Sophie gave him a conciliatory smile. She liked Franco and would indeed sell the land to him but first she needed to deal with Signore Cavaliere. A nice enough gentleman, but from his purplish complexion and controlled breathing, she doubted any women had ever challenged him before. Somewhat perplexed but a professional, his colour returned to normal. Choosing his words carefully, he discussed the sale process and what he considered a fair price for the property and suggested Franco Bianchi be approached. Sophie agreed. It would be preferable for the solicitor to negotiate the terms of the sale and she stepped back, confident things would come together before she returned to London.

Sophie waited on the steps for Paola. The sun was already slipping behind the mountains and she felt excited and nervous. Paola had talked her into going dancing at a club in Lucca. It seemed American jazz had arrived at the sleepy town of Lucca, courtesy of some American service men. Although she had never been to the clubs in London, she was aware of the modern music and even more modern, dancing. Flappers, they called them in London: young women in provocative, short, fringed and sequined skirts, with long cigarette holders and bright red lipstick who danced outrageously. Certain members of the population frowned on the new age, but Sophie found it exciting and she could do with some fun. She wasn't sure her blue dress was appropriate. It was rather plain but she had shortened it and, anyway, that was all she had to wear. She styled her long hair with finger waves to look like a bob and tied a blue band around her forehead, to tame her often unruly hair and give her a modern look.

She ran down the steps to the van. "You look smashing, darling!" Paola said in broken English, mimicking what she perceived to be a flapper.

Sophie laughed, jumping in the van. "Why do you have a coat on?"

Paola looked sheepish. "I didn't want Mama to see me in

my new dress. I doubt she would approve and Papa would have a fit. I told them we were going out for a special dinner to celebrate the sale of the land."

"Oh!" Sophie said, seeing a twinkling of sequins where Paola's coat had parted. "But the land isn't sold yet."

"It will be. I heard Cousin Franco talking to Papa."

Paola parked the van several streets from the club, tied a sequined band around her forehead and removed her coat.

Sophie gasped, as Paola spun around in a pink drop waisted dress, trimmed with fringe and decorated with pearl sequins, highlighted by a long string of faux pearls.

"Paola, you look amazing. I feel so underdressed."

"You are fine. There are all sorts at the club."

"Have you been here before?" Sophie asked, realizing this was not Paola's first visit.

She shrugged. "Si, maybe?"

The club was dark and noisy, a trumpet blared above the chatter, but Sophie had no idea of the tune being played and her eyes stung from the haze of cigarette smoke. Paola led her to a table and sat down with a group of American servicemen, who she had obviously met before.

"This is my friend, Sophie Romano," Paola yelled over the music and introductions were made.

Sophie smiled and nodded, catching only one name. Harry, a young, good-looking officer, offered her a seat next to him. In broken Italian, he asked if she would like a cocktail. When she answered in English, he was delighted.

"You are English," he shouted, waving to the waiter and sending a signal for drinks. With a puzzled expression, he asked, "but Romano is Italian?"

"Both," she answered simply, not wanting to get into details.

"I have a villa about five miles from here. I live in London," she shouted back as a tray of cocktails appeared on the table. She picked up a glass of what looked like champagne with all kinds of fruit floating on top. She took a sip. It was quite nice, if rather sweet.

"I didn't realize there were American troops still here. I thought you'd been shipped home."

"Oh! Good heavens no. I am not American. English like you. Those guys," he nodded towards the dance floor, "Americans." Sophie followed his gaze. The dance floor was packed and Paola was dancing, her feet moving very fast and the fringe on her dress shaking provocatively. *You are a dark horse, innocent looking Paola. No wonder you don't want your mother to see your dress.*

"Want to have a go?" Harry asked.

"Oh, I couldn't do that," Sophie said, feeling panic rise in her chest.

"Ah, come on." He grabbed her hand and dragged her to the dance floor. Paola gave her a thumbs up.

She felt the rhythm of the music and it was hard not to tap and move and suddenly she was dancing. Hands in the air, palms out, and kicking her legs, it felt wonderful. Her partner bounced to the same rhythm and they started laughing. She could not remember the last time she'd had so much fun.

By the end of the evening, they were happy, giggly and exhausted. Paola drove Sophie to the villa and, as they passed the bakery, she groaned.

"The lights are on. That means Papa is up waiting for me. Do you mind if I come in and change? It is late and I will have some explaining to do, without explaining this." She pointed to her dress.

"Of course not. Do you have clothes with you?"

Paola stopped the van and reached in the back for a small bag. They ran up the steps giggling and Paola quickly changed into an ordinary dress.

Sophie pointed at her face. "The lipstick is very bright. I doubt your father would approve."

"Grazie!" Paola rubbed her handkerchief across her lips. "Remember, we went to the Café Supreme and came back here afterwards."

"Si, I understand," Sophie said with a smile. "Now, off you go. It is nearly midnight. Ciao!"

The van chugged off along the driveway, sounding loud in the quiet of the night. Sophie felt light-headed from the champagne as she locked up and went to her bedroom. The first thing she saw, hanging on the wardrobe door was Paola's dress. She held it against her and swung around in front of the mirror. The temptation was too much and she quickly undressed and slipped the silky gown over her head.

Humming, she began to dance, watching the sequins sparkle and the fringe swing with her hips. Laughing at herself and feeling extremely happy, Sophie flopped on the bed and stared at the ceiling, thinking about dancing with Harry and having fun. She felt just a little guilty and wished Andrew enjoyed dancing but, now she thought about it, they had never had the opportunity. But with the war over there were clubs in London.

"Andrew, you must take me dancing. We need to have fun," she said with a resolute tone. Giving a whimsical sigh, she added, "Why do men in uniform look so handsome?" She bounced into a sitting position, a sudden thought flashing in her head. *The uniform! Harry was wearing the exact same uniform as Carlos the day we met in the Piazza.* It had been too noisy for conversation on the dance floor, so other than names, they had not revealed anything about themselves. *Is it possible that Harry is a doctor at the military hospital?*

Sophie took off the dress and crawled into bed, a hollow feeling in the pit of her stomach. It had been a wonderful evening but having fun, enjoying herself, made her feel guilty. She gave a big sigh. *Guilty about what? Why shouldn't I enjoy dancing with Harry? Andrew isn't here and I wish Carlos would stop intruding, playing with my feelings.* Pouting like a petulant child, she pulled the covers over her head and fell asleep.

Having slept off the childish feelings, Sophie woke excited and happy, thinking about the dancing and fun of the previous night. When the issue of the officer's uniform had popped into her head, she brushed it away with annoyance. She had too much to do today and silly random thoughts were not going to change her good mood.

The red Fiat pulled up in front of the villa, not unexpectedly, based on Paola's celebration comment from the night before.

"Come in," Sophie called in Italian, as she placed coffee cups and biscotti on the table.

Signore Cavaliere entered, immediately opening his well-worn leather satchel. "Buongiorno! Signorina, I have good news. Franco has agreed to buy your land and wants to close the deal quickly so he can work on preparing the soil for planting vines this autumn."

"That is good news," Sophie said, taking the documents from his hands.

"I have taken the liberty of asking Franco to join us." Signore gave Sophie a tentative glance, "I hope that is all right by you. We will have finished our business before he arrives."

Sophie smothered a grin. Obviously, Signore had taken her words seriously. "Grazie, Signore. That is an excellent idea. Please enjoy your coffee while I read the documents."

Concentrating hard, Sophie read through the legal jargon. She asked a few questions but understood most of it. When she got to the last page with the amount of lira, she gasped. It would be enough to repair the villa plus more for a deposit on a house in London. She and Andrew could have their own place.

Signore cleared his throat, looking at her with a smile. "What do you think of the price?"

"It is very generous. Is it a fair price?"

"It most certainly is. The land is good soil and if we were not recovering from the war, it would be worth much more. Franco needs the land and has the money. He knows the value. Are you in agreement?"

"Si," Sophie nodded her head, her smile stretched from cheek to cheek.

Signore pointed to the document. "Sign, here and here. As soon as Franco signs, I will finish the transaction at my office.

No sooner had she signed, than Franco appeared at the door, holding two bottles of his best wine. Franco signed the papers and opened the wine.

"Saluti!"

The gentlemen drank their wine and departed. Sophie sipped hers, not used to drinking so early. Although it was close to lunchtime. What happened next made her take a large gulp.

A small green sporty motorcar screeched to a stop in front

of the villa and first Harry, the driver, got out and then Carlos. He stood quite still, a pained expression on his face as he looked around at the ruined house and farm. Sophie could have sworn his eyes lingered on the old shed.

"Come on, old chap. We don't have much time," Harry called, his gaze checking out the villa. "I hope I got her name right and this is the right place."

Sophie stepped back from the window, her heart firmly lodged in her throat, making it difficult to breath. She gulped down the remainder of the wine, which released her throat and allowed her to take a deep breath.

The knock on the door, although a normal one, sounded like a booming hammer. "Hello," a voice called, "anyone home. It's Harry. Remember me from last night at the club?"

Sophie spun around from the kitchen. "Harry, how did you find me?" Peering around his shoulder, she saw Carlos come through the door.

"Carlos!" she said, her voice barely a squeak.

"Hello, Sophie."

Ignoring Carlos, she switched her gaze to Harry. "I realized last night when I got home that you were wearing the same uniform as Carlos and wondered if you knew him. What a small world we live in. Carlos and I go back a long way." The words tumbled out of her mouth. She wasn't even sure what she was saying, but suddenly came to her senses adding, "Oh, my goodness, where are my manners? Please come in, take a seat…" She hesitated. "What brings you two gentlemen here?"

Carlos stared at the wine bottle, a slight grin on his face, "It's a bit early for drinking."

"Franco, my neighbour who owns the vineyard, brought it to celebrate. He has just bought my property. The solicitor was here and we signed the papers this morning."

A deep audible gasp came from Carlos, as he blurted out with an accusatory tone, "You didn't sell the villa, did you?"

Sophie gave him a curious look. His reaction was inappropriate. "Why is it any concern of yours? As a matter of fact, no, my father had put the villa in my name before he died. But then you wouldn't know about that, would you?" Sophie was annoyed. It still hurt the way he had abandoned her when she needed him the most. Her sarcastic comment was deliberate.

"Harry, when did you realize that I was a," she cleared her throat, "friend of Carlos'. You are a doctor too?"

"Yes, orthopaedic, same as Carlos, except this chap runs the hospital. We normally come to the club together but an emergency kept him at the hospital last night. When I got back to base, I told Carlos about this beautiful woman I met and one thing led to another and he realized who you are."

Sophie felt her cheeks blush. "Yes, Carlos and I have a habit of bumping into each other in unexpected places. Would you not agree?" Sophie directed the last comment to Carlos.

"It does seem that way, but you will be the one leaving this time." His sarcastic tone surprised her as much as his admittance to leaving her on past occasions.

"True. I will be returning to London the day after tomorrow." Sophie felt smug and lifted her eyebrows. "Perhaps the tables have turned, Major." She felt a certain satisfaction at her barbed words and then regretted them. He stared at her, hurt in his eyes. He was subdued, not the confident man she used to know. *What happened?* she wondered.

Carlos perked up, laughing as though someone had cracked a joke and motioned towards the almost empty wine bottle, "May I?"

"I'll get some glasses. Why don't you open the new bottle, Carlos?"

Harry glanced at his pocket watch. "Just one, then we have to get back to the hospital."

Carlos circled this left hand around the bottle, while his right hand turned the corkscrew. Sophie stared at the unadorned hand splayed around the wine. He was not wearing a wedding ring.

# Boat, Train and Motorcar

Sophie's last night in the villa had been restless. Conflicting dreams had woken her several times, especially the dream of a man and woman throwing wedding rings in a fire and then burning themselves trying to retrieve them. Confusing and muddled as dreams often are she wondered if there was a message but discarded them as only dreams.

She squinted at the sunlight flicking through the shutters, stretched and jumped out of bed. It was going to be a long day. She dressed and flung the shutters open, taking one last look at the Tuscany countryside.

It was with a heavy heart, she had gathered the household things, organized them in cupboards, thrown dust sheets over the furniture and packed her suitcase. It was a much larger one that she had found in the attic, than the bag she had arrived with. She was returning to London with some family treasures and memories of her childhood.

Signore Cavaliere and Franco Bianchi were to oversee the renovation work on the villa until her next visit. When that would be, she had no idea.

A loud honk-honk from the bakery van told her Paola was waiting outside to take her to the train station. She lingered in the doorway, waiting for her mother to appear as she had done when she arrived. It occurred to her that she had not seen her since then. "Mama, I will be back soon." Perhaps she imagined her mother leaning on the kitchen counter, blowing her a kiss, but she heard her words quite clearly. "Follow your heart and be safe, my darling Sophie." And then she was gone.

Paola drove slowly and they hardly spoke, both close to tears. Upon arrival at the train station, Sophie took her bag from the van and hugged Paola.

"I'll be back and maybe you can come to England one day."

Brushing her sleeve across her face, Paola nodded. "I will miss you. Ciao!"

Sophie waved until the van was out of sight and walked into the station. First, she went to the telegraph office and sent a telegram to Andrew. She checked the time and schedule of the train. As expected, it was late, so she settled in the Ladies Waiting Room. Plenty of time to think. *Why was it that whenever,* she thought, *she had things straight in her mind, something happened to disrupt it? Carlos. He is always at the bottom of it and the ringless finger had shaken her.*

Miss Harvey knocked on Dr. Cuthbert's door and handed him a telegram. "Just arrived, sir, but no reply is expected."

Andrew took a breath. Telegrams brought bad news. "Thank you." He sliced the brown envelope open.

*LEAVING ITALY TODAY STOP IN DOVER SATUR-*
*DAY STOP EARLIEST TRAIN TO LONDON STOP*
*NOTIFY RIVER HOUSE STOP SOPHIE*

Andrew's face lit up like a beacon, a broad smile stretching from ear to ear.

"She's coming home. Thank heavens for that," he said aloud. He wondered how she was. She had sounded pretty upset in her letter. It wasn't like Sophie to weep. What she described was a breakdown, or close to it. She was strong, too strong. He'd seen the signs so many times in his patients and it was so much harder to see it in someone you loved. He did love her with all his heart and couldn't wait to feel her in his arms. He missed her company, not being able to ask her opinion about patients and treatment. Most of all, he missed the soft lavender scent of her skin and the silkiness of her beautiful hair. He smiled at the memory of its usual unruliness and her frustration as wisps sprang from the pins.

His happiness was marked with caution. Her letter said she felt a little better. Had she reconciled some of her demons about the war, her work and, dare he think, their wedding? Oh, how he hoped she would come home and set the wedding date, make plans to start their life together. If he was honest, he was tired of the delays and of Sophie's excuses. He only tolerated it because he was afraid if he pushed her, she would say no. As hard as he tried, the niggling feeling that she was not committed, small as it was, would not go away. He brushed it off as his own insecurities, and not Sophie's indecision.

Picking up the telephone, he called Cook at River House to tell her to expect Sophie home late Saturday. He thought about calling the Bartley but decided against it. Sophie would be back at work soon enough.

Taking a look at his own schedule, he decided that with a few changes he could take a couple of days leave and drive to Dover and meet her at the ferry. They could have a nice leisurely drive back to London. Maybe they could stay overnight at an inn, make a little holiday of it. The thought of having her all to himself was very appealing.

"Dr. Cuthbert." His secretary's head leaned round the door. "You are due at the meeting in five minutes." She frowned. "Is everything all right, Doctor? I don't want to be nosy, but telegrams are not always good."

"All is well Miss Harvey. My fiancée, Miss Romano, is on her way home, so it is good news. I've decided to take a couple of days off. Would you be kind enough to find a doctor to take my calls and reorganize my schedule for tomorrow and Saturday?"

"Of course. The meeting, Doctor? Matron Mills is waiting." Miss Harvey gave him a sympathetic glance.

"On my way," Andrew replied, picking up his notebook and almost skipping out of the office, until he was confronted by a scowling Matron Mills.

"A very good afternoon to you, Matron. Do we have a busy meeting today?"

Matron frowned and stuck her nose in the air, as was her habit when displeased. It didn't bother Andrew today. He was too happy at the prospect of seeing Sophie.


Andrew loaded the picnic basket Mrs. Humphries had packed for him into his T Ford. By the weight of the basket, there was enough food for an army. He wondered how she did it when there were such food shortages. She was a good housekeeper and felt it her duty to keep her boarders well fed and healthy and she succeeded. Andrew noted that no one in the house had contracted the Spanish flu. Good food contributed to good health. He hoped Sophie was looking after herself and taking precautions. The flu was, once more, rampant in Italy and France and travelling by train and boat with who knows who was not recommended. At least he could spare her the train from Dover to London and she was a nurse, wearing a face covering was second nature, and she would keep her distance from others. *Wouldn't she? Of course she would. I am being ridiculous.*

The engine started with a healthy splutter on the first turn of the crank handle. The gears ground into place and Andrew proceeded to maneuver the motorcar through London's morning traffic. The horse drawn carts slowed things down and annoyed him. He was anxious to get out of London. It was drizzling, making the drains smell nasty and the horse droppings worse. Even though the war was over, rubble from bombings still littered the streets. The gaping holes where homes once stood made him shudder.

It seemed the sun wanted out of London too, because it wasn't until he drove onto the country road that the clouds parted and the spring sun shone through. Andrew pulled the leather window straps, letting the window down and the fresh air in. Drawing in a deep breath, the light fragrance of spring blew away the street odours of London. The wind in his hair was refreshing, making him wish he had a sportier model, but this little motorcar served him well.

London to Dover was the longest trip he had ever attempted. He was mildly anxious about finding petrol and if the T Ford was up to it. The condition of the road was another issue, although he was told the Dover Road was a well-used one and not too bad. He just hoped they were right. Seventy-five miles was an extremely long journey. Doubts were slipping into his head. *What if I break down, or I'm too late and miss Sophie?* His heart rate went up at the thought, but which thought? The thought of Sophie or breaking down. He sat straighter in his seat and said into the wind, "I am well prepared with a spare wheel and two cans of petrol in the boot and a basket of food on the seat beside me." He smiled, adding, "When am I not prepared? And, I have plenty of time. The ferry doesn't arrive until the morning."

The rain pounding on the window woke Andrew with a start. He blinked, trying to make out where he was and why he was fully dressed. The room was dark, except for a street light shining through big raindrops sliding down the window pane. He could hear music and muffled voices. *Where am I?* He rolled over, his back sore from a lump in the mattress. Then he remembered booking into a lodging house, a recommendation from a seaman on the dock, 'clean, comfortable and the best breakfast this side of the Channel,' he had said.

Of course, he was in Dover.

He reached for his pocket watch 1:30 am. He had slept since dinner time, exhausted after the drive from London. He recalled how bad the roads were and how relieved he had been when he found a petrol pump. The T Ford had done well. He rubbed his sleepy eyes and remembered parking at the dockside to make enquiries about the ferry. He had wanted to get a message to Sophie but the ticket office was closed and the telegraph office couldn't send a telegram without an address.

Andrew had stood outside the Telegraph Office wondering what to do. He must have looked awful. He certainly felt tired and disappointed. He had begun to think his idea of meeting Sophie was rather rash. A passing seamen, assuming he was lost, offered help. Andrew asked him about the ferry from Calais and where he could find lodgings. The seamen obliged. The ferry was due at mid-day and directed him to Mrs. Beaton's Boarding House where he met a round, cross looking woman. She led him up the stairs, while reciting a list of rules and pushed open the bedroom door, handing him a key. And here he was, lying on the bed where he had flopped after kicking the door closed.

He hauled himself out of bed and undressed, brushing his jacket and folding his trousers, sighing at the mud on the cuffs and the rumpled creases. He stepped over to the window to see where the music was coming from. Other than beams of light, he could see nothing through the rain. Yawning, he crawled back to bed and this time he pulled the covers up, falling into a deep sleep and not waking until daylight.

The seaman had been correct. Mrs. Beaton's breakfast was more than worth the lumpy bed and he ate heartily before venturing back to the dockside to wait for the ferry.

The dock was a busy place with ships coming and going, cargo being loaded and unloaded, soldiers, sailors and dock workers milling around. Andrew walked around, locating the ferry dock and where the passengers disembarked. He grinned, pleased he had made the decision to come. He tried to imagine Sophie's face when she saw him, her touch when she kissed him. His grin turned to a smile. *I can't wait to see her and I'll have her all to myself on the journey back to London.*

A loud horn blasted. A ship was cruising into the harbour,

smoke billowing from the funnel. Andrew moved to the entrance, wishing he'd found a place sooner. He was surprised there were so many people. He glanced up at the people on deck, mostly men in uniform, coming home. Mothers, wives, children and girlfriends were all jostling to greet their loved ones. He scanned the deck for Sophie, but it was impossible to make out individuals, especially as most people were wearing some kind of mask. A tightness gripped his inside. How was he going to find her? She would get lost in the crowd. If she had luggage, she'd be looking for a porter. He walked over to where the porters stood waiting for business. At first, he could see everyone as they disembarked but then there was a crowd and the porters had moved on. He watched, his eyes intent on the crowd, but panicked he couldn't remember what she looked like. The crowd had thinned to stragglers, many searching for lost luggage and she was not there. How could he possibly have missed her? He sat heavily on a bench, his head in his hands. He wanted to weep.

"Andrew? What on earth are you doing here?"

He lifted his head slowly, staring into a crowd and heard it again. "Andrew!?"

He whipped his head around, blinked and rubbed his eyes. "Am I dreaming?" Sophie moved from behind the bench and stood in front of him. "Sophie, darling." Emotion gripped his throat, making him stutter. "I, I thought I'd missed you. I am so glad to see you." Andrew threw his arms around her in a bear hug and kissed her, rather awkwardly as they were both wearing muslin face coverings.

Gently pushing him away, she said, "Why are you here?"

"To meet you." He hesitated, sensing some edginess, unease. "I drove down from London yesterday. I thought you'd be pleased."

She smiled. Removing her mask, she pecked him on the cheek and gave him a hug, enjoying his warmth. "Of course, I'm pleased. Just very surprised." She heard him sigh, realizing that she had perhaps not given him the welcome he was expecting.

Andrew, put his arm around her waist. "How are you feeling? I am so happy to see you."

"I am feeling much better, practically my old self again. You drove your motorcar from London to Dover to meet me, just to drive all the way back? Andrew, you are such a wonderful, thoughtful man. Is it any wonder I am to marry you?"

He smiled, relieved she had mentioned marriage and delighted by her praise. Pointing to the suitcase and the carpet bag, he said, "Is this all your luggage?"

She nodded, laughing. "I went with my mother's carpet bag and returned with this large suitcase. I brought a few treasures from the villa."

Andrew picked up the case in one hand and the carpet bag in the other and led the way to his parked motorcar. He strapped the case on the back and placed the bag on the back seat.

"You are looking a bit pale. Are you feeling alright?" he asked with a frown. "How about a cup of tea? There's a café over there."

"A cup of tea sounds wonderful. I'm thirsty and hungry. The sea was choppy, I didn't like to eat anything …." She added, "just in case."

Sophie recognized the café as the one she had stopped at on her way to Italy, but it wasn't so busy and they sat at a table. Andrew ordered two teas and one bun. He was still full from breakfast.

"I can't believe you are home or that I am here in Dover." Andrew took her hand, squeezing it. "It took me a long time to get here. The rain slowed me down and I did get stuck in the mud a couple of times. I left London in the morning and it was getting dark when I arrived. It might be wise to consider finding accommodation, a place to stay overnight."

"Oh. Is that proper?" Sophie said.

"Don't misunderstand me. It will be a respectable establishment." A bright red colour emerged from his collar. "Two rooms, of course … and if we make good time, we might make it back to London." He tried to hide both his disappointment and concern. He doubted they would reach London before dark. Sophie's frown told him she did not approve of staying overnight, respectable or not.

"I am anxious to get home, you understand," Sophie said appealingly, not sure he did understand. His eyes, his face, his touch were expectant although she wasn't sure what he wanted; her company, affection or was it more? No, Andrew was a gentleman. *Dear Andrew, you are a kind man* she thought staring directly into his eyes, *such love and devotion. What a gallant effort but quite unnecessary.* She sighed, not looking forward to hours in a motorcar. What will we talk about? It occurred to her that their conversations were always about patients, treatments and illnesses of the mind. Outside of the hospital, what was there to talk about? Suddenly it struck her that they'd perhaps talk about their plans, which up until now she had avoided, setting the wedding date, finding somewhere to live. Was that what he was expecting?

"Penny for your thoughts?" Andrew finished his tea. "We had better prepare to leave. I would like to get to London before dark."

"I am ready." She placed her cup in the saucer, took Andrew's hand in hers and they walked to the motorcar.

# The Road to London

ophie was enjoying the drive. The Kent countryside was green and pretty, the last of the spring flowers adorned gardens in the little villages they passed. So far conversation had been light, discussing the hospital, Andrew's brush with the Spanish flu, and the dragon Matron at Spring Gardens Convalescent Hospital. She talked about Italy, selling the property, her night out with Paola dancing dances with strange names, although she omitted to mention meeting Harry or having seen Carlos without a wedding ring in Lucca or at the villa. In fact, she was careful not to mention the villa at all. It seemed Andrew didn't belong there.

Andrew eased the motorcar onto the grass at the side of the road. "I need a break. My legs are tired and I'm hungry."

Frowning, Sophie repeated, "Hungry?"

"Mrs. Humphries packed me a picnic basket." He leaned over the seat and pulled up a wicker basket. "I ate much of it yesterday, but there is still some food left." He pointed to a wooden style in the hedgerow. "A public pathway leading to the river."

"That looks charming. It is a beautiful day and warm. I don't need these," Sophie said, taking off her brown jacket and matching hat and placing them on the back seat.

Andrew stared as her hair, loosened from the hat, catching the sun with little jewels of gold in her dark tresses. He admired her white silk blouse that seemed to flow over her body and the slim brown skirt showed off her curves and ankles.

"Will you join me?" he said with a deep bow. Throwing the blanket over his shoulder, he took Sophie's hand and carried the basket in the other.

After eating what was left of Mrs. Humphries' picnic and drinking homemade elderflower wine, they stretched out on the blanket. Sophie rested her head on Andrew's chest, watching the white clouds move gently across the unusually blue sky. The water lapping on the river bank and the occasional quack of a duck and a distant cuckoo call made for a peaceful afternoon. She always felt relaxed with Andrew. There was no conflict or pressure and she never doubted his passionate love for her. She could not reciprocate the same kind of love, but she did love him in her own way.

A little pang of guilt struck her, aware of her feelings for Carlos. Was her passion for Carlos like Andrew's passion for her? She admitted it had been easy to dismiss Carlos when she thought he was married to Rosamond, but seeing his ringless finger had suggested he was a free man. Theirs was a volatile affair, it always had been. He had hurt her many times, played with her emotions, walked out on her, even disappeared more than once and yet she saw love in his eyes. What kind of life would they have? Passionate perhaps, but always in conflict. How well did she know him? So many things had interfered, first his mother's lies, her father's death and her change of circumstance, not to mention the war, his betrothal to Rosamond, and finally, Andrew, *her* fiancé.

Perhaps it was for the best that events had intruded in their lives, keeping them apart and now it was too late. She had lost all trust in Carlos. On the other hand, she would trust Andrew with her life.

She reached for Andrew's hand, pressed it against her cheek and kissed it. He was the man she was going to marry.

"What was that for?" Andrew said, entwining his fingers in hers. "Do you know how much I love you and want to marry you?"

"I do and I want to marry you."

Andrew bent over kissing her head. "Does this mean you are ready to set the date?"

"What about June 21st. That was my mother's birthday."

"So soon!" Andrew could not believe his ears.

"I have made you wait long enough. Neither of us have families to worry about. A simple wedding with friends will be easy to arrange."

Andrew kissed her with more passion than she had ever felt and she returned it. "You, my darling Sophie, have made me so happy. And, absolutely, the sooner the better." He gave a laugh. "I will need to find you a home. I doubt we'd be comfortable at Mrs. Humphries' and Cook would not appreciate a married couple at River House.

"We can buy a little house in London. I was going to surprise you. I have enough money from the proceeds of the property sale in Italy to buy, or at least put a deposit on, a house."

"I cannot believe it. Our own house with a garden." Andrew pulled her up from the blanket and they embraced, holding each other tightly.

Sophie felt his passion hard against her and a warmth stirred inside her, making her kiss him lustfully. She gave a shudder of pleasure and wanted more. Breaking away, a pink hue rose in her cheeks. "Oh, I don't know what came over me," she said breathlessly, her hands covering her face.

Andrew gave her a wry grin, wrapped his arms around her and, equally as breathless, whispered, "I think it would be prudent to pack up and retreat to the motorcar. We have many miles before reaching London."

Andrew cranked the engine and jumped in the driver's seat, giving Sophie a loving pat on her lap. They exchanged smiles as he put the motorcar in gear. The next hour or so of the journey was spent in a comfortable silence, both having drifted into their own thoughts.

Andrew had a permanent grin on his face, pleased he had taken the risk of driving to Dover. He had been quite nervous about Sophie's reaction, but that had turned out even better than he expected. The road conditions were another story but so far the roads were dry and no rain clouds appeared in the sky. He decided that stopping over night at an inn was not a good idea. If he was honest, he couldn't trust himself, knowing his desire to make love to her was intense and had been heightened by Sophie's response to his embrace. He shifted uncomfortably in his seat just thinking about how easy it would have been to lay beside her, kiss her and make love to her right there under the sun. It had been hard to pull away but he had. Next time, he might not be so strong. *Staying in an inn tonight is out of the question. I hope the road stays clear and dry, and we make it to London before dark.* He glanced over to the passenger seat. Sophie was fast asleep. *My lovely Sophie, you look beautiful as you sleep. Two days travelling and no sleep. At least I had a night's rest. I wonder what you are dreaming about.* A massive bump in the road drew his attention back to driving. The rain yesterday had left big ruts and holes in the road. He tested the steering wheel and listen to the motorcar, but all seemed well and he drove on.

The bump had jarred Sophie from sleep but she kept her eyes closed, feeling embarrassed about her reaction to Andrew's embrace. It felt sensual and she liked the sensation and was ashamed that she had wanted Andrew to keep caressing her, kissing, even touching. She was a nurse and touching the male patient's testicles and penis were body parts to be washed and treated, nothing to be embarrassed about. This was different. Her general impression of copulation was a man's pleasure, so what was wrong with her to be feeling this way. One would normally talk to one's mother about such things but who did you go to when there was no mother? Hillary? Would she know more? Would this be taught in her doctor training? The only married friend she had was Trixie. Perhaps she would be the right person to talk to and then she remembered Trixie telling her about the pleasures of her wedding night. Sophie felt better. Maybe these feelings were normal. Normal or not, she felt her cheeks getting pink with warmth and kept her eyes closed, hoping Andrew had not noticed. Would she ever get used to it?

Clouds had rolled over the sun, but so far, there had been no rain. Andrew was anxious as they were still several miles from London. So far, they had made good time but if it rained, it would slow them down and he estimated there was only about an hour's daylight left. If the clouds darkened with rain, there would be even less. On top of that, he needed petrol. He'd used both cans of petrol earlier. The road was deserted and he couldn't even see a farmhouse. This late in the evening, even if they found a petrol pump, it would be closed.

Sensing his anxiety, Sophie glanced at him. "Is everything all right? You look worried."

"Everything is fine." He hesitated. "Actually, no. I am worried. We are in need of petrol and I don't see anywhere to buy it."

"Keep driving and if we run out, I'll push," she said, laughing.

"It might be a long way."

"Over there," Sophie shouted, pointing ahead of them. "There's a house and is that a petrol pump in front?"

"I believe it is." Andrew drove faster to the house and there was a petrol pump, but it was closed. He let out a long sigh.

Sophie jumped out of the car. "I'll knock on the door and see if anyone is home."

Andrew watched as a young boy of about ten answered the door and a woman stood behind him. The conversation seemed long and Andrew couldn't make out what they were saying so he got out of the car and joined them.

Sophie turned to him. "Mr. Target, who mans the pump, is not here, and his wife doesn't know how to operate the pumps."

"Mrs. Target, is there anyway of contacting your husband? If I don't get some petrol, we will be stranded."

Before Mrs. Target could answer, the boy said, "I can operate the pump, Ma. Pa showed me how to do it and I know where the key is."

"Oh, son, I would be so grateful." Andrew glanced at the mother. "Is that all right with you, Mrs. Target?"

She nodded towards the boy, who ran in the house and came out with the key in hand and unlocked the pump and filled the motorcar's tank. Being very grateful and relieved, Andrew paid them handsomely. Even Mrs. Target's face had a bright smile on it as she thanked them.

It was dusk when they reached the outskirts of London and the light was fading rapidly. The street lamps were already lit, making the last of their journey easy. Andrew pulled up in front of River House and knocked on the door, placing Sophie's luggage on the doorstep and waited. It was a long time past curfew and he wanted to make sure Cook answered the door. Muttering could be heard as the bolts slid back. Her hair wrapped in a scarf, and a thick dressing gown pulled tight around her, Cook opened the door. Her irritation soon passed when she saw Sophie and Andrew on the doorstep. Picking up the suitcase, she chased Andrew away. It wasn't proper to have young gentlemen hanging around this late in the evening.

Sophie peered into the common room, hoping Hillary might still be up.

"Everyone's in their bed this late," Cook said returning to the kitchen. "You look as though you could do with a cuppa. Put them things down and join me in the kitchen. I have a message for you from Matron."

Her own bed was what Sophie really wanted but she nodded, following Cook to the kitchen. The tea was already made, *Cook's nightcap,* she thought except there were two cups and a plate of shortbread biscuits and an envelope on the table. Sophie opened the envelope and read the brief instruction to report to Matron's office at eight the next morning.

"Dr. Cuthbert told me you was coming home tonight. Mind you, I almost gave up on ya'. Sure you're all right? Treated you well, did he?"

Sophie felt a blush coming, wondering what Cook meant by 'treated her well'. Did she know about the tryst by the river? "Of course. Andrew, Dr. Cuthbert, is a perfect gentleman." She rubbed her eyes and yawned. "I'm fairly wilting with fatigue. I have never been on such a long journey by motorcar."

Cook scoffed, almost spilling her tea. "Motorcars. Modern fan-dangle things. I don't trust 'um. I'm glad you're home safe. Are you feeling better? You were not at all well when you left for your holiday. Where did you go near Dover?"

"I went to Italy, to a place called Lucca, where my family comes from. I took the ferry from Calais to Dover. That was after the train from Lucca."

"Italy! That's a foreign country." Cook shook her head. "Italy, you said."

Sophie grinned. "Yes, Italy." Not wanting to get into any explanations, she finished her tea and added, "Thank you for waiting up and for the tea. I'll get to my room now." She was amused by Cook's reaction to Italy, obviously the end of the earth to her, but Sophie saw genuine concern in her expression and comment. The previous housekeeper had been very caring, but Cook was more pragmatic and rarely, if ever, showed emotion for her charges. Yet, there was no doubt in Sophie's mind that she cared very much.

Sophie dropped her bags inside her bedroom door and stepped across the hall. Tapping lightly on Hillary's door she whispered, "Are you awake? It's me, Sophie." She heard the rustle of bedding and Hillary's door opened, the young woman ushering Sophie to enter.

"I am so glad to see you," Sophie said as they hugged.

"I've missed you. How are you? You look well. A bit tired but a lot better than when you left."

"I am much better. I really loved it in Italy and made a new friend Paola and her family. I rested, had fun, and did much thinking."

Sophie and Hillary sat on the bed talking. Sophie did most of the talking, bringing Hillary up to date on the situation in Lucca. This time talking to Hillary she did not leave out the two encounters with Carlos, but she did make light of it.

Hillary was aware that Andrew had driven his motorcar to Dover. As Sophie's best friend, he had asked her opinion she had encouraged him, saying it was a gesture to show Sophie how much he cared.

"How was the motorcar ride from Dover? It must have taken hours," Hillary asked innocently and then raised an eyebrow when Sophie blushed. "Did something happen on the journey?"

"Not exactly." Sophie put her hands to her hot cheeks and told Hillary about the picnic and the unbidden sensations and wanting more, even the lustful kiss. "I am so ashamed, but I could not stop the feelings. I wondered if your studies mention these sensations."

"Unfortunately not. The lady students are asked to leave when the lectures are about sensitive subjects. But one of my fellow students, Maggie, is a real woman of the world and is quite blunt about these things. She said that women can get as much pleasure from," her voice dropped to a whisper, "sex, as men. She goes to the jazz clubs and flirts and maybe more, with different men."

"This was not flirting, Hillary. I really wanted him to touch me and we are not married."

"You worry too much. When you are married," Hillary giggled, "you can tell me what it's like."

"That's not very helpful. I almost forgot. Andrew and I

have set the wedding date, June 21st, and I want you to be my maid of honour." Still somewhat confused, and blushing with embarrassment, Sophie thought changing the subject to the wedding would put an end to the conversation and it did. However, she was not expecting it to open up another conversation that she definitely did not want to have.

"I am happy for you, truly I am." Hillary gave her a quizzical look "Does this mean Carlos is out of the picture altogether, even though he might be a free man? I told you I could find no announcements and you just told me that he was not wearing a ring. Did you speak to him? Ask him what happened to Rosamond?"

"No! I'm finished with Carlos." Sophie's harsh tone reflected her determined expression. "Andrew is everything that Carlos is not, reliable, kind, considerate, attentive and he is in love with me." Her tone softened and she smiled. "And, I want him to be my husband. So that is the end of the matter. I do not wish to speak of Carlos again."

Hillary nodded, her expression not convincing, but she smiled. "Of course, I will be your maid of honour. June 21st does not give us much time."

Sophie smothered a yawn. "We can talk about this another time. I need to get some sleep. Tomorrow I have to face Matron and whether or not I still have a career."

# Back at the Bartley

ophie and Hillary walked in silence, both tired from having stayed up talking half the night. Running down the steps to the underground, Hillary waved goodbye and Sophie continued on to the Bartley. She was early for the meeting with Matron and headed to the Women's Ward, not sure if she had a shift today.

Needing a familiar face, she was grateful to see Trixie at the nurses' desk. "Good morning, Trixie!" Sophie said. "Am I working today?"

"Sophie, how lovely to see you," she said, embracing her. "I'm glad you are back. How are you?" Trixie sounded odd and she looked very pale.

"I'm better thank you. How are you?"

"All right. A bit tired and not feeling myself these days. We've been so busy while you were away. I'm glad you're back." Trixie frowned, looking at the schedule. "I don't see your name here. Sister Kay makes it up a week ahead. Maybe she didn't know when you were back."

Sophie felt uneasy. Why wasn't she on the schedule? "I have to see Matron at eight this morning. I was not feeling well when I went on leave. Perhaps I don't have a job anymore." She felt her eyes prickle with tears, remembering almost turning down or at least postponing an opportunity. "I had the feeling at the time that I was jeopardizing my career."

"Oh, that is unlikely. Sister Kay was talking about you only yesterday. I think Matron has plans for you. Perhaps they are moving you to a different ward."

"Perhaps. I will find out soon enough. I had better go. I'll see you later."

Sophie rushed along the corridor towards Matron's office. Not being on the schedule of the Women's Ward confirmed her worst fears. She was to be fired or demoted. *Taking the time to sort myself out obviously was not the right move. I should have stayed.* She shook her head, knowing she could not have continued and, had she stayed, things would be worse. *At least I feel better and I am able to cope. I will just have to make the best of it.* Her throat tightened at the thought of having to find new work.

Beth Filly, Matron's secretary, gave her a big smile. "Nurse Romano, how lovely to see you. Are you feeling better after your holiday?"

"Yes, thank you. Is Matron in? She asked to see me."

"She's expecting you. Take a seat and I'll let her know you are here."

Sophie sat down, taking deep breaths to calm herself and prepare for the worst. Beth returned to her desk, giving her a smile, but said nothing and it seemed like hours before Matron opened her door.

"Come in and take a seat, Nurse Romano. How are you feeling?"

"Quite well, thank you. Fully recovered. My visit to Lucca was very relaxing and I was able to sort out some family issues."

Matron frowned, glancing at Sophie's opened file on her desk. "I didn't think you had family."

"I don't but I was born in Lucca. My late father had property there, our family home. It is very beautiful and quiet in the Tuscany region of Italy, a perfect holiday setting. I have not been there since a tragedy befell the family. I took the opportunity to sell the property as London is my home now."

"Forgive me, I did not intend to pry into your private affairs." Matron looked genuinely apologetic. Although she was always supportive and took a great interest in her nurses, she rarely intruded in their private lives.

"Few people know of my Italian past, except for my very Italian name." Sophie smiled. "I had a wonderful childhood with my parents in Lucca, but it ended in tragedy." Sophie felt awkward and, not wanting to say more on the subject, she added brightly, "But as a result, I eventually became a nurse and, for that, I am grateful."

"As are we at the Bartley, which brings me to my reason for this meeting. Before you went on leave, I had mentioned an assistant teaching position and, if you are interested, that offer is still there. But I need to know right away as we have a new group of nurse probationers starting next week."

Sophie could not believe what she was hearing, having convinced herself she no longer had a nursing position. This explained why she was not on the Women's Ward schedule. She looked up to see Matron staring at her, waiting for an answer. "Yes, Matron, I accept the position. I am honoured."

"Good! There are some stipulations and this would be a trial for three months. Your health is of concern and I understand you are to be married."

"I am quite well, Matron, I assure you." *Marriage? What*

*does that have to do with my job?* Taken by surprise with this, Sophie was not sure how to respond.

"I am sure you are well, but your service during the war and the severity of your injuries must be taken into account. Dr. Cuthbert has assured me that you are recovered. However, I note that he is the man you are to marry."

Sophie hesitated, giving some thought to Matron's words. Could she be implying that Andrew was not being accurate with his assessment of her health?

"Dr. Cuthbert is an honourable gentleman and physician. If he did not consider me fit to nurse, he would not hesitate to tell both of us." Sophie's voice was harsher than she intended. The woman's insinuations had angered and surprised her. This was not like Matron. "And, you are correct, we are to be married, but I have no intention of giving up my nursing career, married or not." Matron did not respond so Sophie continued. "I am happy to take on this position in a probationary capacity in order to prove to you neither of your concerns are valid." Sophie sat back in her chair, feeling proud for speaking out until she glanced at Matron's dark and silent expression. *Oh dear, I might have said too much.* Reflecting on her remarks, she realized they were bordering on insubordination. Her brow creased in thought. There was something different about Matron. She was usually open minded.

Taking a deep breath, Matron said, "Be that as it may, Nurse Romano, but what are your plans when babies come along?"

"Babies!" The word flew out of her mouth with an almost disgusted look on her face. "I have, we have, never talked about a family. It was always the two of us. I have no desire to have children," the words sputtered out at the same time as her thoughts raced on in her head. *Is that what I really want? It is something we have never discussed and I have never given it any consideration. No, I do not want children. What if Andrew wants a family? What then?* At this final thought, her stomach tightened into a knot and she felt sick because she knew the answer.

Sophie swallowed hard. Taking an audible breath, she sat up straight. "Matron, I want a nursing career and it is not beyond the bounds of possibility that I will aspire to be Matron or, at the very least, a senior nursing position. I will expect any suitor, including Dr. Cuthbert, to support me. If this is not to be, then I will remain a spinster, committed to nursing."

Matron broke her silence, first with a beaming smile and then she spoke. "I have known from the first day I met you that you had the making of a special nurse." She gave a hearty chuckle. "But I wonder, are you implying there is someone else other than Andrew?" She put her head to one side with a puzzled look. "Your beau, Andrew or not, has a challenge ahead of him."

She was surprised that Matron referred to him by his Christian name although she had known they were friendly. She liked the familiarity, but Matron's question regarding beaus caught her attention. Why had she even said that? There was no one else. Andrew would support her. She acknowledged that children were serious business and yet the subject had never come up.

"I am committed to Andrew. I wear his ring." She hesitated, wondering if she should tell her they had set the date. Under the circumstances, she thought it better not to say anything just yet.

Matron handed her a thick book, with many pages hanging

loose. "I want you to read this and report to Sister Kay tomorrow morning at eight sharp. She will appraise you of your schedule on the ward and your studies. Sister Kay is in charge of probationers for the first three months. Find yourself a quiet place, the nurses' lounge perhaps, and read this cover to cover."

The large book tucked under her arm, Sophie immediately went to the nurses' lounge, made a cup of tea and put her feet up on the couch. She couldn't remember having a book to study when she was in training. Sister Singleton, an unpleasant woman who spent more time belittling than teaching, had been in charge of the probationary nurses.

Sister Kay had put the manual together, a very different person who cared about her work, the patients and the nurses. Sophie was looking forward to working with her again. Deeply immersed in Florence Nightingale's teachings of hygiene, the principals adopted and enforced by the Bartley Hospital, she had not noticed she had company.

"It must be nice to play the wounded soldier."

"I beg your pardon!" Sophie said with a look of puzzlement at the comment. Then she saw Nurse Hogan, a miserable older nurse, making tea and buttering bread. "What a strange thing to say. I am fully recovered from my injuries and have been for some time."

"I heard you had been forced to take time off or join the soldiers, you know …" spinning her finger towards her head she continued, "the crazy ones."

Fury stirred inside Sophie. Describing shell shocked soldiers as crazy always made her angry. She and Nurse Hogan had crossed paths before when Sophie was a probationary nurse. Normally, she tolerated most people but not Nurse

Hogan. Her total detachment from empathy or sympathy or any kind of emotion rendered her nefarious in Sophie's eyes. The woman was a jealous, lying, trouble maker. She had almost cost Sophie her job when she expected to be assigned to the Casualty Clearing Station in Passchendaele, albeit Nurse Hogan's lies were caught and she was almost fired. The shortage of nurses at the Bartley meant she had a second chance and was transferred to the operating room, where her skills of precision and accuracy would be heralded with no chance of upsetting conscious patients.

"My time off was holiday time. I had business to attend to in Italy. What are you doing here in the middle of your shift?" Sophie said, attempting to curb her anger.

"You really do reach above your station. Why on earth would you be in Italy? Why am I here? Because we are between surgeries and it is a convenient time to take my lunch. At least I am not loafing around, reading."

Sophie's blood was on the boil. She felt her face flush, but knew it was important to stay calm and not give Nurse Hogan any reason to continue the conversation. She was obviously fishing for information that she would no doubt turn into rumours. Recalling her opening comments, she wondered if she had already set rumours in motion. "I am not reading for pleasure. I am studying nurses' training, as instructed by Matron."

"What!?" Nurse Hogan yelled, and stood in front of the couch, pointing a knife covered in jam at Sophie. "Are you the new training nurse working with Sister Kay?" Sophie nodded but before she could answer the woman continued, "I asked Matron for that position. Sister Singleton told me, before she went to the convent, that I was perfect for the job."

Completely mystified, Sophie stared at Nurse Hogan. Sister Singleton had left the Bartley in disgrace years earlier. She had to admit that the two were birds of a feather. Nurse Hogan was quite unsuitable to train young nurses.

"I can see you don't believe me. I had a long discussion with Matron while you were away. I'm surprised not to hear from her."

"Is that so!" Sophie said, with sarcasm. "Matron appointed me this morning. That's why I am studying this book." *I wonder. Was it Nurse Hogan that fed Matron rumours about my well-being? She was rather odd at first during the meeting. Would Nurse Hogan mention marriage and babies.* Sophie looked down at her hand, where the ring would be. *But I never wear my ring on duty. How would she know I was to be married?* Sophie decided to ignore the woman and concentrated on the book, although she was no longer absorbing much. Finally, Nurse Hogan gave a frustrated huff and went back to the operating theatre and Sophie let out a long sigh of relief and a giggle at the thought of her dealing with young nurses in training.

Lying on the couch to study was, perhaps, not a good idea. Sophie was tired from her travels and talking with Hillary half the night. As hard as she tried to stay alert, her eyes closed and she drifted off into dreams.

*Andrew held her tigh; wedding things came and went, people came and went. Matron, patients and Nurse Hogan all mingled with anger and happiness. It was all such a mess and she had worked so hard in Italy to be assertive and decisive and her dreams were telling her to be careful.*

Something warm on her forehead disturbed her and she opened her eyes to see Andrew leaning over, kissing her forehead.

"Andrew!" She looked around the room, pleased to see they were alone.

"I know I'm not allowed in the nurses' lounge. Will you join me in the canteen? I went to find you on the Women's Ward. Trixie told me you weren't on the schedule. What are you doing in here? Reading?" Andrew frowned, concern in his eyes.

"I am to assist Sister Kay with probationary nurses starting tomorrow and I have to read this," she said, closing the manual. "We need to get out of here, before someone like Nurse Hogan sees us. What are you doing at the Bartley?"

"A consultation for Dr. Wilcox, not your favourite doctor. I don't think he will ever forgive you for telling him off for being insensitive. He certainly deserved it and he may even have changed his ways. He actually called me for my opinion regarding a patient with shell-shock. That's why I am here."

"Two adversaries in one day, my first day back. I hope that isn't a reflection of things to come," Sophie said, finding a table in the canteen.

"Nurse Hogan. Wasn't she the one who made false accusations about us?" Andrew said, placing a tray of tea and scones on the table.

Sophie nodded affirmative. "She definitely has not changed her ways, still loves spreading rumours. She appeared in the nurses' lounge this morning, questioning me about what I was reading. I can imagine what she might say if she had seen you kissing me." Sophie laughed.

"There will be no need for rumours when we are married. No second thoughts, the date is still June 21st? He reached across the table and stoked her hand.

"I already asked Hillary to be my maid of honour. I didn't

95

mention it to Matron. Andrew, Matron was a bit odd with me this morning. She's still concerned about my health and also expressed concern about us getting married. The hospital has archaic opinions on married nurses, although that has recently changed. I assured Matron I had every intention of pursuing advancement in nursing." Sophie stared at Andrew, trying to detect his reaction, even analyze his frown and puzzled expression. "We have never really talked about how things would work after we married." She stopped talking, her thoughts on another delicate subject. *Dare I mention babies. What kind of a woman doesn't want a family? Am I that kind of woman?* Staying silent on the subject, she waited for Andrew to speak.

"It never occurred to me that you would not continue nursing at the Bartley after we were married. I know how important nursing is to you. I guess we will be a very modern couple. That is what you want, or have I misunderstood? You seem hesitant about something."

"Oh, no misunderstanding. You are correct I want to continue nursing. It's just that we had not discussed..." She paused. *Was this the right time to mention children, family?*

"Sophie, please tell me. What is it? Something else is worrying you."

"We have never talked about babies, children, a family. Andrew, I know this is perhaps a terrible thing to say, but I don't want children, at least not now, if ever." She sat back heavily in her chair, holding her breath and waiting for his answer.

He stared at her. His eyes, full of love and so gentle they lifted his lips into a smile, or a kiss. She so wanted the kiss. "I had always thought it was just the two of us." He looked over his shoulder where the canteen was getting busy. "We need some privacy. Walk with me to my motorcar. I have to return to Spring Gardens."

They walked out of the hospital in silence. Andrew slipped his hand in hers as they approached the motorcar. He put his finger under her chin, looked into her eyes and said, "My sweet Sophie, it is the two of us working together. I have no desire to be a father. My father was a cruel man and I would never inflict that on a child of mine." He leaned in and kissed her and she kissed him, those same sensual feelings filled her with desire, but this time there was no shame.

"I'm sorry about the way your father treated you and yet you are a gentle, loving man."

"Most of it came from my mother when I was young. She died when I was nine. My father turned to drink and beatings. I think he realized and sent me to boarding school for safety. Finally, the drink killed him when I was fifteen. I stayed at boarding school until I was old enough to go to university. The school physician took an interest in me. He treated the bruises from my father's beatings when I returned to school after holidays. I remember him suggesting I stay at school for the next holiday but it didn't matter as Father died. Doc and his wife were kind to me and from then on, I spent school holidays with them. Doc inspired me to study medicine. He was the one who taught me people weren't crazy, that illness of the mind was a medical condition to be treated."

Sophie wondered why she had never asked him about his family. She was aware that his parents had died when he was young, as had hers. She found the similarities in their young lives part of the attraction.

"Andrew, being with someone who understands what it's

like to be orphaned is a great comfort to me. It seems every time I turn around, there is something else we have in common. I've known for some time that our interest in healing shell-shocked patients bonded us in an unexpected understanding. We are both committed to a life in medicine, opposed to raising a family." She stood on tiptoe and reached up to kiss him. "Let's plan a wedding."

# All Things New

Beyond asking Hillary to be her maid of honour, Sophie had done little to plan the wedding. Andrew suggested, and Sophie agreed, on a civil ceremony, followed by luncheon with friends. She recognized the simple wedding was her idea, but it seemed anticlimactic. The simplicity suited Andrew, who was a no-fuss kind of person. Sophie felt an urge to have fun. After all, a wedding was a once in a lifetime occasion. Thinking back to their time in Passchendaele, she couldn't recall having fun, except maybe at the Christmas concert. It was a serious time and they were mostly grateful to get a few hours off duty. *When was the last time I had fun?* She asked herself. *Italy, the jazz club with Paola, dancing with Harry. That had been fun.* She stopped her thoughts from going any further, knowing Harry would lead to Carlos and quickly switched back to having fun. *I will talk to Andrew about going to a club after the wedding ceremony. Goodness knows when I'll have time.* She exhaled a big sigh.

In spite of her new position, Sister Kay still expected her to work most of her shifts on the ward. Fortunately, Sister Kay was in charge of both and Sophie did not mind the extra work. She always enjoyed nursing on the ward and the prospect of introducing pupil nurses to her passion filled her with excitement. One thing she had not expected was the title of Sister-Tutor, albeit she was only assisting, but she took pride in having a title, even if no one used it. She made a mental note of the sister part, allowing Sister Romano to roll off her tongue, giving her something to aspire towards.

The split duties took up all of her time. It occurred to her that she might be using the lack of time as an excuse to stall things. Dismissing that thought, she acknowledged she was truly run off her feet and enjoying every minute. However, it left her little time to plan the wedding. There was no alternative. She would have to forgo the planning and delegate or postpone—the latter was not an option. As much as she wanted to make the arrangements, her work came first. *I will ask Hillary to take over. She is my maid of honour and perhaps Andrew can do more.* Satisfied she had found a solution, she asked both of them to meet her that evening.

Glancing at her timepiece, Sophie realized she needed to hurry to the hospital lobby to greet the new girls starting the program. This was the first time Sister Kay had allowed her to do the preliminary introduction. The bulk of the new group of probationers had arrived the previous week, but two had dropped out. These late arrivals were the replacements.

Both girls had arrived at River House, the nurses' residence, yesterday. Cook introduced them at dinner. Miss Clarice Harrington, a society girl, tall and plain looking with a high and mighty attitude had bright green eyes that reminded Sophie of a cat waiting to pounce. Miss Dotty Fox, on the other hand, was quite the opposite. She was petite with thick, golden brown, curly hair and green eyes that shone with enthusiasm. She had seemed shy. Sophie liked her and wondered if the shyness was due to her appearance. Her dress hung on her at least one size too big and her stocking had been mended but her boots were new. Sophie sensed a mystery, surmising that this poor young woman had a benefactor.

The girls were standing awkwardly by the reception desk. Miss Fox looked nervous and Miss Harrington was catching her breath, with quite the flush on her cheeks. *Arrived just in time,* Sophie thought, but made no comment.

"Hello and welcome to the Bartley. I hope you had no trouble getting here," Sophie said with a bright smile.

"No, Miss …I mean Nurse Romano." Miss Fox blushed at her almost mistake.

Sophie gave her an assuring smile. "It takes a while to get used to the titles. You will notice that now you are in uniform, I will address you as Nurse or Probationer. And you, Nurse Harrington?"

"I took a wrong turn. I'm not used walking. The chauffeur usually drives me to places." Nurse Harington's lips pursed, ready to complain and then relaxing as she realized how inappropriate she was being.

*Ah,* Sophie thought *that's why she's flushed and out of breath. A bit of a rush. Chauffeur indeed. I'm assuming it was beneath her to accompany Miss Fox. I have my work cut out with this one and yet there is a deep sadness in her eyes.*

"Oh, you didn't come together?" Sophie looked from one to the other, lingering a few seconds longer on Nurse Harrington, hoping she would get the message. But the flash of deep sadness in her eyes took Sophie by surprise. It was brief, but unmistakable. "In future I would advise you to walk together. It is safer, especially if you are on night duty. It gives you an opportunity to get to know one another. There are no chauffeurs here, Nurse Harrington."

"I realize that, Nurse Romano. I was explaining the reason," she replied defensively. "I am trying my best. This is all new to me."

"So it is and I do understand. It is new to all of us. I'll do whatever I can to help you. Quite often you will find the best support comes from your fellow nurses as you become friends. Another reason to walk together."

Nurse Harrington gave a weak but positive smile and Nurse Fox nodded with enthusiasm. Although the girls came from different backgrounds, in their identical probationer's uniforms, they looked much the same and Sophie sensed, perhaps for different reasons, they were both committed to nursing.

"Today you start your training with a tour of the hospital and an explanation of what is expected of you during the training. The first three months are filled with lectures and hygiene, practical and theory. The practical will be cleaning the wards and scrubbing floors. Menial tasks, I'm afraid, but when you are on the wards, you will get a sense of how the wards are run. Sister Kay is a good teacher and will make the training as interesting as possible. The practical nursing will come later."

Sophie glanced at both girls, remembering how she had scrubbed floors and listened to Sister Singleton's disgusting descriptions of bedpans prompting her to defend the more gentile probationers turning green. Nurse Fox's acceptance came with an enthusiastic nod of her head, no stranger to scrubbing floors. Nurse Harrington's blank look might or might not have been acceptance. In truth, Sophie doubted she had ever cleaned anything, beyond her personal care, and even then she probably had a maid. She suddenly felt sympathy, or was it pity, for Nurse Harrington. Her upper-class attitude would do her no favours in this environment. And yet, there was a strange mixture of defiance with extreme sadness. Something had happened to her, maybe she'd even been mistreated. Sophie couldn't quite put her finger on it. Perhaps the family had come on hard times. The memory of her own father's death came flooding back to her, followed by the indignity of being thrown out of her comfortable upper-class home to scrub floors in a hotel. *Is that why I feel empathy towards her, or is it something else?*

Sophie led the way through the wards and all the patient care areas including a brief glance at, what Sophie thought was, an empty operating theatre. Nurse Hogan suddenly appeared from nowhere.

"Good morning, Nurse Hogan. May I introduce two new probationers …" The sour look of hatred on Nurse Hogan's face stopped Sophie from finishing her sentence.

"Get out! I will not have you in my operating room. You, Nurse Romano, should know better!" She yelled at the top of her voice, her face red with fury as she glared at Sophie. As though realizing her outburst was both unnecessary and unprofessional, she turned her attention to the probationers. She smiled, adding in a controlled softer voice, "This is a sterile area. I'm preparing for surgical procedures. I will have to ask you to leave."

"Of course! I understand." Sophie guided the two into the hallway, closing the door behind them. Embarrassed at the unwarranted reprimand by a colleague and shaken by the hatred, Sophie took a deep breath to compose herself.

"What was that all about?" Nurse Harrington asked, visibly shaken by Nurse Hogan's violent outburst.

Sophie didn't answer, not sure what to say.

"Sum'at got up her nose, al'right," Nurse Fox added, making Sophie smile.

"Ladies, I think it is time for a break. I'll show you the nurses' lounge. This is where we can relax, before or after shifts and for break time. If you want a full meal, it is best to go to the canteen, but for tea it's a comfortable place to put your feet up."

Sophie made tea and sat the nurses at a small round table. Taking a sip of tea, she savoured the warmth before speaking. "The tour is almost complete. Do you have any questions?"

Nurse Harrington asked, "Are all the other nurses as contentious as the operating room nurse? I found her most unpleasant."

"No, most nurses are kind and helpful. I'm afraid what you witnessed was personal. Nurse Hogan and I, had … shall we say … a disagreement about the care of shell-shocked patients. That was a long time ago, before I went to Passchendaele. It seems she holds a grudge." Sophie smiled, realizing she was saying too much. "However, the operating rooms are, as she says, sterile areas. It is of the utmost importance to prevent infections. In retrospect, I should have asked before entering."

"Mi brother were in Passchendaele." Nurse Fox took a ragged breath, tears filling her eyes. "He didn't come home. It broke mi mam's heart."

Sophie leaned forward. "I am so sorry. I treated many young boys like your brother and they were all very brave and always cheerful, despite their injuries." Sophie glanced at Nurse Harrington. "What about your family?"

"My brother was in France." Her face warmed. "He was in the medical corps and spoke highly of the nurses. It's because of Edwin that I decided to be a nurse. He's been very encouraging, not like ..." Suddenly her demeanour changed she clenched her jaw. "... my father. He was a colonel and fought in Egypt. He came home unscathed, physically that is. He's always had a nasty temper, but the war made his anger boil into rage and now he treats the family and servants as though they are the enemy on the battlefield. Sometimes I wish he hadn't come home." Sophie glanced towards Nurse Harrington and witnessed her green eyes flash with animosity. She turned to Nurse Fox and noticed she had the same, albeit warmer green eyes, an usual colour.

"The war did terrible things to all of us and our families and I am sorry for both of you. Nursing is one way to help both patients and yourselves. You will see much of the fall-out in your patients. Surprisingly, your personal experiences will help you manage and treat patients who come into your care."

Using Sister Kay's manual, Sophie spent the next hour going through various tasks and procedures that had been taught to the probationers in the lecture hall the previous week.

"Now, ladies, follow me into the basement. There are no patients on this level. It is mostly for the operation of the hospital, the boiler for heating and hot water, storage and supply rooms. There is a large laundry, which you will be expected to work in from time to time, plus storage rooms for hospital supplies and a broom cupboard for cleaning tools. Across the hall is where the bedpans are cleaned." Sophie was trying to be cheerful. Her memories and experience of the basement were not pleasant.

As they descended, Sophie continued. "I will give you fair

warning, it is hot and steamy. These room are functional and none are pleasant and some smell really bad. A trick I use when the odour is more than I can bear is to think of spring lilacs and their sweet scent or any strong flower fragrance works just as well."

Nurse Harrington hesitated halfway down the stairs, her green eyes staring into the darkness below. "I cannot see any value in cleaning. Goodness, I have never cleaned in my life. That is maid's work. And I refuse to have anything to do with bedpans. Surely there are orderlies that do that kind of thing. I came here to train as a nurse," she said. Turning on her heels, she flounced to the top of the stairs.

Sophie touched Nurse Fox's arm and grinned. "Wait for me at the bottom of the stairs while I deal with this," she sighed, returning her attention to Nurse Harrington and repressing the urge to roll her eyes.

Considering the situation, Sophie was not surprised, but she was perplexed as the nurse had been quite compliant up until now. "I know scrubbing floors is not what you expected to do in nurses' training. But this is the way it is. It lasts for three months and if you do well, you move on to the wards."

"It is an outrage to expect me to do this kind of work," Nurse Harrington retorted with her hands on her hips.

"Be that as it may, if you want to nurse, you have to start here. However, there is one other option. You can pay a substantial fee and be excused. Perhaps you could speak to your father."

The colour slowly drained from her face and tears trickled down her cheeks. "I know my father refuses to pay for anything to do with nursing. He's been quite unreasonable. He hopes I'll find it too hard and give up. I don't know why he hates me nursing."

Gently putting her arm on Nurse Harrington's shoulder, Sophie felt for the girl, as snobby and privileged as she was. Her father sounded cruel. "Believe me, I do understand what it's like. I once lived in a big house with maids and suddenly, through no fault of my own, I found myself scrubbing floors."

"How did you manage?"

"I worked hard and did what was expected of me, eventually reaping the reward and I became a nurse. Will you just come downstairs and join Nurse Fox? You don't have to do anything today."

Nurse Fox put out her hand and Nurse Harrington, to Sophie's surprise, took it and smiled. Sophie did a quick tour and sent them off to River House to study.

# Best Made Plans

Andrew sat in the pub, waiting for Sophie and Hillary. He was tired. It had been an exceptionally busy day, although he had managed to get to his digs and enjoy Mrs. Humphries' excellent cooking. Now, he would prefer to be in his room reading a book, rather than sitting in a noisy pub. He had missed Sophie's phone call. The message read 'Meet me at the *Rose & Crown* at seven o'clock. I've asked Hillary to join us so we may discuss the wedding.' Andrew sighed. He loved Sophie and couldn't wait to be married but these wedding plans, simple as they were, were taking up much of his time and he suspected Sophie had new ideas. He couldn't imagine what. He had booked the justice of the peace to conduct the ceremony, but had not yet found a groomsman. He wasn't the outgoing type and chose his friends carefully. Sadly, his small pool of friends had diminished during the war. He thought about asking Christopher Belingham, but wondered if that would require inviting his family. Since his brother's death Chris was now heir to both his father's title and estate.

"Andrew! Andrew!" Sophie called, standing next to the table.

Andrew looked up and laughed. "Darling, I am sorry I

was miles away, thinking about the wedding." He stood up, bending forward, and kissed Sophie, realizing she wasn't alone. "Hillary, hello. Lovely to see you. What can I get you ladies to drink?"

"Um… champagne cocktail with fruit," Sophie said.

"Pardon. Did you say champagne cocktail with fruit?" An amused grin creased Andrew's face. "I doubt they have cocktails of any kind in this pub. When did you learn to drink cocktails?"

"In Italy, Paola took me to a jazz club one night and the drinks were divine." Seeing Andrew's quizzical look and not wanting to make any further explanation of that evening, Sophie laughed. "I'm teasing you. We did go to a club that was featuring an American jazz band. I can assure you Lucca is not exactly the hub of modern music and dance but they did offer American cocktails. I'll have my usual half pint, please, darling."

"I'll have the same," Hillary said. Leaning towards Sophie, she whispered, "Tell me more."

"Later."

Andrew put the drinks on the table. Stifling a yawn, he opened the conversation. "So, what news do you have about the wedding? You have some new ideas?"

Clearing her throat, Sophie gathered her thoughts, a little concerned by Andrew's appearance; tired and pale, even distracted.

"I am concerned about our wedding plans. I am run off my feet with ward work and training and can't find enough time to make the arrangements. I would like to delegate some things to you, Hillary."

"Of course. It's my job to attend to the bride. However,

remember I have examinations coming up in two weeks. I'm not sure how much I can do before then."

"I thought about that and wondered if you and Andrew could work together." Sophie glanced at Andrew, who had not reacted to her request. "Is that too much for you, Andrew?"

"Not at all. I'll do what I can, but I too, am busy. What else needs to be done?"

"We need to decide who we're inviting. Neither of us have family, so my thoughts are just our immediate friends. Trixie and Chris for sure, and I thought I'd try and find Emily and Captain Evans. I believe they settled in Wales. I assume they married, but I'm surprised we didn't get an invite." She realized, as had Andrew, that some friends had not survived the war and others were scattered around the country.

"I was thinking of asking Chris to be my groomsman," Andrew said, "but I wondered if we would be expected to invite his family?"

"Oh, Andrew, that is a great idea and no we are not expected to invite the family. We will be a small group. Perhaps we could make it up for the size by doing something different. A plain wedding breakfast is a bit boring, don't you think?"

"What do you have in mind?" Andrew asked with a great deal of caution in his tone.

"We were just talking about jazz clubs and I know there are a few in London." Sophie paused for reaction from Andrew and, when none came, continued. "We could have the ceremony as planned, followed by the wedding breakfast, following that later in the evening with a night at a club, where we can dance and drink fancy cocktails and have fun."

"Absolutely. That is a fabulous idea, Sophie." Hillary wafted her arms and shuffled her feet, humming *Tiger Rag*. "What do you think, Andrew?"

"Um, well, I am not familiar with this new jazz music and I've never been to a club. One of the doctors at Spring Gardens mentioned one called the Kingfisher Club. It features famous jazz bands from America." He gave a laugh. "I'm sure they would have fancy cocktails. I intended to take Sophie there one night, just to have a look." He gave Sophie a wink. "I'm afraid I can't even dance the waltz."

Laughing, Sophie felt exhilarated. Andrew seemed keen on her idea and she wanted to keep the momentum going. "You don't need to know anything to dance these new dances. I couldn't believe how easy they were. You kind of bounce to the music, it's just a lot of fun."

"Something else you learned in Italy?" Andrew smiled but his voice sounded stern.

"Paola taught me. That's another thing. You don't need a partner. Most people do partner up, but it can be a man or woman. I danced with Paola and it was a hoot." In her excitement, Sophie had said more than she intended and hoped she had averted any questions about who she was dancing with in Italy. Although dancing with Harry had been innocent, she wasn't sure Andrew would see it that way.

"Perhaps we need to focus on wedding plans," Hillary said. "What else needs doing? What about flowers? Shall I order a bouquet?"

"I had not thought about flowers. In fact, I haven't even thought about what I will wear. Maybe I should decide on that first." Sophie leaned over and kissed Andrew. "I doubt you are interested in what I wear, darling. Hillary can help me with that and all you need is your best suit."

Andrew nodded. "I am concerned about living accommodation. Mrs. Humphries is excited that we are to be married and, much to my surprise, kindly offered us two rooms on the top floor. I declined, and told her we were purchasing property, a house of our own." Andrew's face lit up with a smile as he squeezed Sophie's shoulders and kissed her cheek adding, "If I am to carry my beautiful bride over the threshold, it is imperative we have a front door. Wouldn't you agree, darling?"

Sophie felt an unexpected sense of panic. It certainly had been her suggestion to purchase a property. In her mind, the house was hers. There was no 'we.' Ridiculous as it seemed, it had not occurred to her that as a married couple, of course they would share the house. Slowly, it dawned on her what the implications of 'we and sharing' really meant once they were married. Although married women were allowed to own property, thanks to the Married Women's Property Act past some fifty years ago, men were still head of the household. Most women in her situation did not have the privilege of owning anything. It was only due to her father's forethought that she owned the villa and it was little more than chance circumstances that had put money in her pocket. At the thought of her beautiful villa, her throat tightened, Andrew did not belong at the villa. This, she could never share. *Thank heavens I never told him about Villa di Seta. Am I being selfish? Doesn't Andrew deserve to share in my good fortune?*

Andrew stared at her, waiting for an answer. "Darling?"

Sophie could not give him the answer he was expecting. Her mind franticly searched for an appropriate reply. Finally, she spoke. "That is very kind of Mrs. Humphries. Perhaps we might consider two private rooms." Seeing Andrew's heartfelt disappointment and a childlike hurt in his eyes,

Sophie quickly added, "I believe with our busy lives and only four weeks to the wedding, renting rooms would give us time to settle before making big decisions." Cleverly avoiding the mention of a house, Sophie felt deceitful and guilty for misleading Andrew. The implications of purchasing property, especially for Sophie, warranted much more thought and consideration.

"I am being thoughtless. Sorry, my dear. I agree choosing a house is a big decision. I am just so excited about having a real home." Andrew yawned and rubbed his eyes. Taking several deep breaths, he added, "Forgive me! May we continue this another time? I am overwrought with fatigue. If we are finished, would you excuse me, darling?"

Sophie frowned, wondering if there was more to his tiredness. "Are you feeling unwell?"

"No, it has been a long day." Andrew took her in his arms and kissed her. "Good night. I'll call so we can discuss this further and we'll set a date for the jazz club. Good night, Hillary."

Sophie watched him leave and waved as he closed the pub door. "I hope Andrew's not coming down with something. He's always quiet, but he wasn't himself today."

"I am surmising he is tired and completely overwhelmed. He certainly looked it. I'm not sure he's keen on celebrating at the club, but wants to please you and he definitely does not want to rent Mrs. Humphries' rooms."

"Wise as always, Hillary. You are right. I will have a talk with him."

"Now, tell me more about Italy?" Hillary said, her eyes bright with excitement. "You were at a jazz club and dancing with Paola. She sounds like a nice friend but I don't believe your partner was Paola."

"She was, most of the time. Paola is a wonderful person. I must write to her and tell her the news. She might come to the wedding. She's dying to come to England."

"I thought it better not to mention it in front of Andrew," said Hillary, "but I've been to the Kingfisher Club. It was exciting, dark, smoky and a lot of fun with amazing music and fabulous champagne cocktails. The dancing is lively and sensual at the same time. Unless Italian clubs are different, I think you were, shall we say, cautious in your story."

Sophie beamed a mischievous smile. "I was being careful. He is a wonderful man but his idea of fun is a stroll around the garden. I was fine with that when we were in Passchendaele. Although there were no gardens, we walked in the woods." Closing her eyes, she paused, not seeing the pleasant stroll in the woods but the horror of bombs and death.

"Sophie! Are you quite well? You are as white as a ghost."

"I'm… fine," she stuttered. "The last time I was near those woods was when I was injured."

"It must have been awful. Sometimes I feel guilty having stayed here."

"Hillary, please don't. You are serving your country by paving the way for women physicians."

"I am and there are times when it is a struggle."

Sophie's impish smile returned. "Let us move on and count our blessings. The war is over, I am fully recovered from my injuries. Matron is happy with my work and I'm ready to advance my nursing career. It's time to have fun. I don't deny that the jazz club in Italy made me realize how dull I'd become. Like most of us, I had forgotten how to have a good time." Sophie relayed an animated description of her night out with

Paola, dancing with Harry, and the unexpected connection to Carlos, followed by the surprise visit to the villa.

Hillary listened intently and they giggled, describing the strange dance steps and fancy cocktails. She slipped her head questioningly to one side at the mention of Carlos.

"It is uncanny how that man keeps popping into your life. Didn't you say you would never speak of him again?" Hillary paused with an expectant look, waiting for Sophie to respond but she said nothing. "Are you sure there is nothing there? How many times do I have to tell you I found no wedding announcement regarding Lady Rosamond, or anyone else."

"Maybe not, but if he is a free man, why didn't he tell me? He's made no attempt to court me. Anyway, I have made my decision. While I was in Italy I had a lot of time to think and you are right again, it is uncanny how Carlos appears and disappears. I cannot deny my feelings for him. At times it's passionate and the scary thing is I see it in his eyes too. It's too volatile, lust not love, and he's let me down too many times. I do not trust him. A marriage to Carlos would be a complete disaster. It might have worked all those years ago, before his mother interfered, but not anymore. I need someone I can trust and I can trust Andrew."

"I understand. And you and Andrew make a happy couple. He really adores you." Hillary laughed. "I'm not the right person to advise on matters of the heart. I don't remember the last time I courted anyone."

"You need to do something about that. Who will you bring to my wedding?"

"I don't have much time for courting, but there is someone I study with. Reginald Davies, Reggie. He's open minded about women physicians and has helped me tremendously. I'd like to invite him. He'd fit in well."

"Oh...?"

"No, it is not romantic, a good friendship, that's all. He would be an ideal escort."

"I'm happy you have a friend. I'll look forward to meeting Reggie." Sophie looked up at the clock behind the bar. "We have been here a long time. If we don't get moving, Cook will lock us out."


Sophie had slept fitfully. Either she stared at the ceiling, worried about sharing her property with Andrew, or slipped into sleep, only to wake covered in perspiration. The nightmares left her in suspense because she was not able to remember why she was so frightened. She washed and dressed quickly as it was already past seven and she was due to assist Sister Kay with a lecture on Spanish Flu and the importance of hygiene at eight o'clock. On top of that, she had promised to escort Nurses Fox and Harington to their first lecture. Entering the dining room, her stomach churned from lack of sleep. Cook put a plate of bacon and eggs in front of her. Just the sight of it made her want to retch, but she had a big day ahead of her and needed the nourishment. Hillary had left early to study at the library. Sophie smiled, wondering if today's studying included Reggie.

"Good morning! How are you?" Sophie smiled across the table at Trixie who was a temporary residence at River House, while husband Chris was finishing his military service although the temporary part had stretched to a year.

"I am well, and you?" Trixie replied.

"Me too, I have been busy with the new probationers and

planning the wedding."

"Chris called me this morning. Andrew has asked him to be groomsman."

"That was fast. We only talked about it last night. I suppose he wanted to make sure Chris could get leave."

"He already asked when you announced your wedding date and he's taken three days, so we can have time together. I have to find somewhere for us to stay."

"Cook still won't let you stay here?"

Trixie shook her head again. "Have you decided where you'll live after you're married?"

"Mrs. Humphries has offered us two rooms until we can purchase a house. I think we should take her up on her offer. Andrew's not so keen. Sorry, Trixie, I have to rush. Will I see you on the ward later?"

Trixie nodded. "We are working together today. I'll see you later." She scrunched her eyebrow together, something she did when she had concerns about something. "Sophie, I should warn you. Nurse Hogan has been talking to Matron about you. Be careful. I don't know about what, but she can be nasty."

"Oh not again!" Sophie sighed. "Thank you for telling me. Bye!" *As if I don't have enough on my mind.* She placed her hand on her stomach, anxiety causing nausea, and wished she had not eaten breakfast.

# Innuendos or Lies?

The day was moving along smoothly, better than she had expected. Sophie escorted Nurses Harrington and Fox to the lecture where they were formerly introduced to the latest group of probationers.

Nurse Harrington seemed contrite, in contrast to her attitude the day before and she appeared to have befriended Nurse Fox. Quite the odd couple, Sophie thought and decided they could learn much from each other, hoping the friendship would continue. Now the two were in the group Sophie's work was done unless Sister Kay needed her. She elected to stay and listen to the lecture. Most of the information she had learned from her own orientation plus two years of experience. However, she found the current references to Spanish flu of great interest. Particularly its ease of spreading, which was quite frightening. The hospital and staff took precautions, of course, wearing face coverings and hand washing. Diligent hygiene was essential in the hospital, but keeping one's distance was difficult when treating patients. Sister Kay encouraged maintaining these precautions even off hospital property, especially when in public places, with great emphasis on keeping one's distance.

Sophie questioned how careful she was outside the hospital

and thought about their visit to the pub to discuss the wedding. After listening to Sister Kay, perhaps it was not the wisest place to meet in a pandemic and this wave of Spanish flu appeared to be more lethal than previous ones.

The lecture over, she searched for her charges and smiled encouragingly as they were led away to begin the cleaning regime. Nurse Fox showed confidence, no stranger to scrubbing floors and it pleased Sophie to see her lead Nurse Harrington, obviously preparing her for the chores in a gentle and kindly manner. She doubted Nurse Harrington's congenial attitude would last once a scrubbing brush was placed in her hand.

The Women's Ward looked overcrowded, reminding her of the wards in Passchendaele after a brutal battle, except the metallic smell of blood was missing, replaced with the smell of fever and sweat. She gave an involuntary shudder, frowning. The ward was quiet, too quiet.

"Sophie, how was the lecture? I'm glad you're here. I'm behind with the morning beds. The orderlies brought in extra beds last night. Several cases of pneumonia," Trixie said, tucking in clean sheets and helping a patient back to bed. "Can you go to the pharmacy? Dr. Wilcox has ordered aspirin for the new patients."

"On my way. Were there any messages for me?" Sophie said glancing at the nurses' desk.

"No, I haven't checked. I've been too busy settling patients." Suddenly Trixie realizing why Sophie was asking, she added, "Oh! Nothing from Matron. Maybe I misheard."

"Or Matron ignored it," Sophie replied, heading to the

pharmacy. Aware of Nurse Hogan's propensity to twist the truth, sometimes to the point of downright lies, it was possible that Matron had dismissed any accusations. A pleasant thought, but Sophie knew Matron would have to deal with it. *What made somebody behave like that?* Sophie mused. *Always needing to 'report people,' often for minor infractions, embellished until there was only the smallest nugget of truth. Did she believe her own lies? Was it an unhealthy need for attention or perhaps for whatever reason an obsession with precision and perfection?*

Nurse Hogan's dislike of Sophie bordered on hatred and the feeling was mutual. Perhaps not to the point of hatred, but Sophie did not like the woman. Jealousy was an ugly trait, especially when coupled with revenge. Sophie had exposed her lies, which almost caused her to lose her job, but that was two years ago. Nurse Hogan took pleasure in holding a grudge, no matter how much time had passed, and Sophie's recent promotion only added to the woman's angst.

Sophie returned with the prescribed aspirin and quinine. She glanced towards Trixie. Something was wrong and Trixie looked stressed. "Is something wrong?"

"I need your help," Trixie said, throwing the covers off the patients. "Cold water. We need to sponge her down. Her fever is dangerously high.

Sophie hurried to the bedside and placed two bowls of cold water on each side of the bed and they began sponging her. Sophie couldn't believe how young she was. Twenty-two or three, her cheeks were bright pink from the fever and her breathing laboured.

"Miss Summer, I'm going to lift you up on the pillows to help you breath." Trixie lifted her and Sophie pushed the pillows behind her."

"We're losing her," Sophie said feeling the heat from her body rising like steam from a kettle.

Trixie yelled to a young probationary nurse, "Nurse, fetch Dr. Wilcox now!"

Dr. Wilcox walked on to the ward, a look of disdain on his face. "Nurse Belingham, what is so urgent that you see fit to interrupt my morning rounds?"

"Miss Summer is in distress. Her fever is 104.5 …" A loud cry from the patient stopped Trixie mid-sentence and they watched in horror as her body shook violently and then she began convulsing. Even Dr. Wilcox moved fast, his expression changed to concern and possibly surprise.

"Remove those dam pillows and hold her down," he shouted at Sophie, his eyes squinting with recognition. "Nurse Belingham, I need a syringe and phenobarbital."

After the injection Miss Summer stopped fitting. Dr Wilcox stared at Sophie, "I know you, Nurse…"

"Romano, Sir. Nurse Romano and you treated me last year. I was a patient after I was injured in Passchendaele during the war."

"Ah, you lost your sight and hearing. I never forget patients especially ones so rude," He gave her a stern look and then to Sophie's surprise a smile brightened his face and she saw a much different man. "You put me in my place. Still rude, but perhaps I deserved it. I did not realize you were a nurse. You recovered fully?"

"Yes, sir. My hearing is not perfect but everything has healed."

"Good, good. Well done."

Now it was Sophie's turn to smile. His remark sounded as though she had won a race, not recently recovered from injuries.   But he was trying.   Perhaps her words about respecting women had had an effect.

"Leave Miss Summer to rest and I'll return after rounds." Dr. Wilcox patted the patient's hand and walked out of the ward.

"He's a strange one," Trixie said. "Some days he's congenial and others rude and disrespectful. What did you say to him?"

"I hardly remember but I was angry at the way he talked over me and I told him so. I believe I was rather rude. He remembered. I think he tries, but he's old and his generation have an Edwardian perspective towards women.   I was surprised he would admit to deserving my comment."

It was only an hour later that Dr. Wilcox returned with Sister Kay for morning rounds, later than usual as a result of the Miss Summer's emergency. Rounds were fast, and Sister Kay complimented the nurses on their organization of the overcrowded ward, making it abundantly clear that hygiene and ward cleanliness was even more important than usual.

All nurses accepted cleanliness as a priority, dating back to Florence Nightingale's revolutionary teachings, so why the emphasis today? Sophie could not shake off a sense of foreboding, nor could she explain her feelings.

"Sister, I noticed you expanded your talk regarding the Spanish flu at the lecture today.  I thought it had subsided somewhat."

"I want to make sure all my nurses protect themselves. There is an increase in the number of cases. The doctors are concerned with the rising cases of pneumonia, as you are experiencing right here on the ward."

Trixie gave a knowing nod, resigned to a busy day on the already full ward and an episode with Miss Summer. There would be more before the shift was over.

"Nurse Romano, I need to speak with you."

Sophie swung round to face Sister Kay. "Is something wrong? Is everything all right with Nurses Fox and Harrington?"

"Of course. You did a fine job, particularly as they are so different. Matron asked me to have a word on another matter."

Sister Kay led her to a screened off portion of the ward, offering a little more privacy. Sophie felt her heart drop into her stomach. *Nurse Hogan!*

"First of all, I am pleased with your first introduction. You did well up to a point. However, it has come to Matron's attention that you did not follow protocol when showing the probationers the operating room."

"I am sorry, Sister. I know I should have asked before entering. It won't happen again." Sophie's apology didn't seem to be enough.

"It was a little more than entering without permission, was it not?"

"No. The room was empty until Nurse Hogan entered and reminded me that I should have approached her first. I apologized and immediately escorted the probationers out."

"I am surprised at your response. I always considered you to be someone with high integrity. Covering up such an indiscretion is worse than the infraction itself." Sister Kay scowled, her normal pleasant demeanour replaced with what appeared to be anger. "I am very disappointed in you. I expected you to be following in my footsteps, as did Matron."

Sophie shook her head, her throat tightened, not believing what she was hearing. She felt paralyzed and lost for words.

"Your silence is puzzling. I expected you to explain yourself. This is a very serious violation." Sister's words were clipped with anger.

"I, I ... don't know what to say. I'm not sure what you are talking about. I just told you what happened and there was nothing more. Please tell me what you heard?"

"You are telling me you did not walk into a sterile operating room fully prepared, including a patient, and proceed to give a lengthy lecture on operating procedure."

"Good heavens, absolutely not. The operating room was empty when we entered. Ask Nurse Fox or Nurse Harrington?"

"I'm afraid I did. Nurse Harrington corroborated the incident as I described to you, although she did deny the lecture part. Nurse Hogan must have misled Matron on that point."

Sophie could feel her cheeks flushing with anger. How had she twisted the event and coaxed Nurse Harrington into lying?

"Sister, this whole incident is a lie, beyond me not asking before I entered an empty operating room. And Nurse Fox, what did she say?"

"I have nothing more to say. This incident is grounds for dismissal. You are relieved of duties until you report to Matron at eight tomorrow morning."

Stunned, Sophie sat staring into space for how long she did not know. She went into the ward to find Trixie but she had left and the evening shift had taken over. It was past six o'clock. Seething with anger, she marched towards the operating rooms and saw Nurse Hogan running down the stairs. Seeing Sophie, she stopped for a brief second, raised an eyebrow, smirked and muttered something Sophie could not hear. Sophie ran after her but she disappeared through a back door.

Collecting her cape and handbag, Sophie exited the hospital through a back door, not wanting to speak with anyone. It had begun to rain and she pulled her cape tight around her. The dampness felt cold, or was it the despair? *How could this happen? I trust Sister Kay and Matron and yet this woman has managed to convince them both of these lies.* She walked aimlessly for hours and found herself by the common and sat on a bench. The rain had stopped and there was an earthy smell from the wet grass, mixed with a wet wool odour coming from her cape; quite heavy from the rain. She cursed, realizing it would take days to dry out and she'd have to make excuses to Cook for being late for dinner. That was better than facing Nurse Harrington. Had she deliberately lied or had she been bribed? It didn't really matter. Sophie was at a loss as to how she could counter Nurse Hogan's story and ask Matron to believe what really happened.

Sophie left River House early the next morning, telling Cook she had an early start with probationers, knowing that she would tell Hillary. Normally she would have discussed this with Hillary. Yet, for some reason, she didn't want to talk to anyone. It all seemed bizarre, as though she was in a dream or nightmare and couldn't wake up.

She sat outside Matron's office, too early even for Beth Filly to be at her desk. She swallowed a few times, feeling thirsty and wanting a cup of tea, but dared not go into the Nurses' Lounge or the canteen, for fear she might meet someone.

"Good morning!" Beth's cheerful voice startled her for a second. "You are early. I think Matron said eight o'clock."

"I know, but I'd rather wait here," Sophie said, trying hard to smile.

Beth shrugged her shoulders and unlocked the office door. "I'm making a cuppa. Would you like one?"

"Please. I would appreciate some tea."

Beth disappeared and reappeared ten minutes later with a two cups and saucers and sat next to Sophie. "I heard what happened and I don't believe it. That woman, you know who, has caused so much trouble."

"Thanks Beth, but I don't think Matron has seen though her this time. There's a credible witness."

Before Sophie could answer, Matron's heels could be heard on the hard floor and Beth ran into her office.

"Nurse Romano, you are early."

"Yes, Matron. I'd rather wait here. Beth kindly gave me tea. I can wait."

"I have a few things to attend to first but when I'm finished, I'll send Beth to get you."

"Thank you," Sophie said, almost in a whisper. She'd expected Matron's tone to be angry, but it wasn't. It was worse, disappointment. The same as Sister Kay. Sophie felt tears pooling under her eyelids and willed herself not to cry. She hated disappointing people and worked hard to please those she loved or respected.

Five minutes later, Beth ushered her in to Matron's office. Sophie sat down, staring at her feet and waiting for Matron to speak.

"I am, at least, happy to see that you are remorseful."

Sophie looked up and frowned. "Matron, I have little to be

remorseful about. I am upset because I do not know how to convince you that what you were told is complete fabrication, almost. I did go into the operating room without first asking, but as I told Sister Kay, it was empty until Nurse Hogan came in."

Matron let out a long, frustrated sigh. "I am so disappointed that you are clinging to this story. We have not one but two reliable witnesses. Nurse Harrington and the patient who was waiting for an operation."

"I can assure you there was no patient in the operating room when we entered and I do not know why Nurse Harrington said whatever she said, because we were together. Has anyone spoken to Nurse Fox?"

"That will not be necessary. I have no choice but to terminate …."A loud bang came from Beth's office. Someone had slammed the door and Beth was arguing with them. Matron rose from her seat and opened the office door. "Miss Filly, what on earth is going on?"

"Nurse, um, she wants to talk to you."

"Matron, I must speak with ya'. It's about Nurse Romano. It in't right. She did nau't, I mean nothing, wrong."

Matron moved into Beth's office and closed her door, leaving Sophie to wonder who the mysterious nurse was that demanded to see Matron. Sophie had tried to eavesdrop, and recognized the voice, it was Nurse Fox. They talked in whispers. It seemed like hours before Matron returned, only to ask Sophie to wait there. She would be back shortly. Hearing the outside door close, Sophie crept to the office door, wanting to talk to Beth, but her desk was empty.

What had happened? Nurse Fox seemed to be defending her, but she had learned long ago that things weren't always what they seemed and she was afraid. Why had they left the office?

Half an hour later, Beth returned and sat behind her desk. Sophie stood up, ready to speak to Beth when Matron returned with Sister Kay.

"Take a seat, both of you." A smile radiated from Matron and Sophie had no idea why. Her stomach and chest felt like steel, they were so tight and she dared not relax as tears lingered, waiting to release.

"Nurse Romano, we both owe you an apology and we are guilty of a grave misunderstanding. It has come to our attention that you entered an empty operating room. Your only misdemeanor was not asking permission, which might have been a courtesy, but no rules were broken."

Sophie glanced from one to the other. "I don't understand. What has happened?"

"You are absolved of any wrongdoing. I am not at liberty to say more at this time. Return to your duties and Sister Kay will speak with you later."

Sophie wanted to argue. She felt annoyed at how she had been treated and it looked as though she was getting the brush off, but at least they believed her. It was Sophie's turn to be disappointed. Perhaps I need to be cautious who I trust. Maybe I've misjudged Matron and Sister Kay. Lesson learned, she thought.


At River House that evening, Nurse Fox and a very guilty Nurse Harrington knocked on her bedroom door. Nurse Harrington apologized for her part in the incident. Being new, she had not realized the magnitude of the consequences of her actions. Nurse Hogan had bribed her by promising to excuse her from all cleaning duties, a promise she could not keep. Nurse Fox would not be bribed and had come forward, which prompted Matron to check up on the elusive patient who was supposed to be in the operating room. The poor guy, having been prepared for surgery, had no memory as to whether he was in the operating room at that time, but he assumed if Nurse Hogan said so, he must have been there. The ward nurse, however, confirmed the patient was still in the ward and not in the operating room.

# All Work and No Play

B ack on course, learning more about training every day, and being run off her feet on the ward, Sophie counted her blessings. Part of her was sad that Nurse Hogan had left under a dark cloud, but the other part was relieved she no longer had to look over her shoulder. Matron had cleared her of any wrongdoing and, thankfully, her career was still intact.

She and Trixie were used to crowded wards from the war, but this was different. The women were dying of a mysterious chest ailment, often after suffering and surviving the Spanish flu. Miss Summer had died during the night and her bed was already occupied by another young woman. It was hard to keep up with so many women with high fevers. Sister Kay allowed nurse probationers to help on the wards. Nurse Harrington and Nurse Fox were delighted to be assigned to Sophie's ward, although Sophie thought their delight had more to do with being excused from scrubbing floors. They were both fast learners and a great help cooling down patients.

Dr. Wilcox arrived on the ward pale and tired. Sophie noted his exhaustion had overcome his arrogance. She didn't immediately notice that his entourage of doctors included Hillary until a voice whispered at her back. "Hello. I'm with

Dr. Wilcox."

"Hillary," Sophie whispered, eyeing the group and Dr. Wilcox as they moved from bed to bed. Making sure she wasn't heard, she whispered again, "See you later in the lobby."

Their shift over, Sophie and Trixie met Hillary and walked to River House. Hillary explained that the current situation on the Women's Ward was the same across the hospital and medical students had been asked to assist the doctors.

"It is exciting. I wasn't sure when I was assigned to Dr. Wilcox but so far it's been good. I could not believe how many beds you have on the ward. How do you manage?" Hillary said.

"We have to manage. They sent us probationers for the same reason they sent you to the doctors. It's a help." Sophie pointed to Trixie. "Remember, we worked in worse conditions during the war, but I did not expect it in peacetime."

"I don't think any of us expected this." Trixie shrugged her shoulders. "I haven't seen Chris in ages. He's not allowed out of the barracks until it's clear of 'flu.' Neither of us are enjoying being apart so much. When you mentioned taking rooms at Mrs. Humphries, we decided it would work for us too. I know his parents are expecting us to move into Beech Hall, but Chris wants to stay in the RAF for as long as he can."

"River House won't be the same without you two." Hillary pulled a sad face. "I might look at moving too."

"If I buy a house, I will rent you a room," Sophie said, quickly adding, "I doubt that will be for some time."

"Newlywed love birds? I doubt you will want me hanging around." Hillary giggled. "If you know what I mean?"

"Love birds indeed." Sophie giggled.

Hillary exhaled a long sigh. "I'm bored, in spite of how busy we are at the hospital. Anyone else feel bored?"

"I'm not bored but I am tired of living from one crisis to another. I want to get out and have some fun. Dance, listen to music and use words like 'fabulous and absolutely,' while calling everyone 'darling' and carrying a long cigarette holder."

"Sophie, I can't imagine you smoking and aren't you tired? I doubt I could dance. My feet are killing me, or what is it they say, 'my dogs are barking.'" At this last remark, everyone burst into hysterical laughter, causing passers-by to stare and even step around them.

"Darling, dancing sounds absolutely fabulous!" Hillary said drawing out the syllables with a true county accent and tears of laughter. Finally catching her breath, she added, "Let's go to the Kingfisher Club. What do you think, Sophie? We said we'd check it out for the wedding."

"Andrew said he'd check it out but I doubt he has yet. I can call him and tell him to meet us there."

Sophie squeezed Hillary's arm as they approached the flashing light that read, Kingfisher Club. It was just the two of them. Trixie had begged off, feeling too tired, and Andrew was on call, but said he might come later.

"I'm glad we decided to come. You look great by the way," Sophie said, admiring Hillary's loose fitting dress. Her tall, thin frame suited the fashion and the peacock blue complimented her blue eyes.

"So do you. Green is your colour and the fringe is rather risqué, even for you. The glitter on the head band is a perfect contrast to your dark hair. Great finger waves. I don't remember seeing that dress before?"

"It's new. After going to the club in Italy in a very plain cotton dress I decided I needed something more appropriate. This is the first time I've worn it and I do feel a bit risqué." They both burst into giggles.

"Good evening, ladies!" The doorman smiled, opening the door for them.

Noise and thick cigarette smoke greeted them, making both of them cough. Neither had picked up the trendy habit. The hostess showed them to a small table. Hearing the jazz music, loud over the chatter, Hillary began to sway to the rhythm and yelled, "I think that's *Tiger Rag,* one of my favourites." Turning to the waitress, "Two champagne cocktails, please!"

Sophie's eyes darted around the club. She had an amazing sense of excitement. The worry of accusations, dying patients and overcrowded wards just disappeared. She felt alive and happy. People were laughing, the dance floor was full and the jazz had changed to a slow romantic waltz. She would have liked to dance and she glanced towards the door, wondering if Andrew would make the effort to join them. The drinks arrived and they clinked glass just as the trumpeter blasted a lively jazz tune of unknown origin, American, no doubt. The drinks went down very smoothly. Sophie nodded to the waitress for two more.

Hillary stood up and extended her hand. "Come on. Let's dance."

Sophie took a look at the dancers and they all seemed to be couples. She wasn't sure she was brave enough to dance with Hillary, until she spotted several women without male partners. "Okay, why not."

It didn't take long for them to get into the dance rhythm. Sophie couldn't stop laughing. She quickly got the hang of rolling her hips to make the fringe flip out with her moves. Her shoes, with the little heels, were perfect for twisting and kicking on the wooden floor. The music stopped with the band announcing they were taking a ten minute break. Out of breath and laughing, Sophie and Hillary went back to their table, two full glasses sat next to their half empty ones.

"Where did these come from? Did you order more drinks?" Sophie asked.

"No! A mistake perhaps?" Hillary beckoned the waitress.

Obviously used to such acts of kindness, the waitress grinned. "The tall gentleman at the bar ordered them for you."

Hillary turned to witness a tall handsome gentleman waving as he slid off the bar stool and, with long strides, walked to their table.

"Reggie!" Hillary said with surprise. "What are you doing here?"

"I could ask you the same question." His eyes sparkled with laughter.

"Touche! We wanted a night out to have fun. Oh, Reggie, this is my friend, Sophie Romano,"

"Ah, you are the famous Sophie. I am pleased to meet you, Miss Romano." He brushed a kiss on her hand, "Hillary talks about you all the time."

"She does? Forgive me, where are my manners. It is a pleasure to meet you, Reggie." Sophie's words were drowned as the jazz band began to play a fox-trot.

Reggie bowed, took Hillary's hand and guided her to the dance floor. Sophie watched wide eyed as Reggie swept Hillary around the dance floor, amazed at how well Hillary danced. Sensing someone behind her, Sophie turned to see a dark and very handsome gentleman stretch out his hand. "May I have the pleasure of this dance?" She smiled and was just about to accept when she saw Andrew being directed to their table.

"Thank you for your kind offer, sir, but I am spoken for." Sophie let out a breath. *That was close and he was handsome.* She glanced up and realized the stranger must be been with Reggie's party and felt a flicker of disappointment.

"There you are, darling," Andrew said. "Who were you talking to?"

"Oh, I don't know. He asked me to dance. A friend of Reggie's perhaps."

"Reggie?" He deliberately stretched the name.

Sophie frowned, detecting jealousy in Andrew's tone. "Reggie is a fellow medical student and friend of Hillary's. They are on the dance floor. It's good to see you, Andrew." She leaned over to kiss him. "Shall we dance? I love the fox-trot."

"Aren't I supposed to ask you to dance? I need to catch my breath. I only just arrived."

"Of course. Why don't you order a cocktail? We can dance later."

"I'd like a beer. They do serve beer, right?" Catching Sophie shaking her head, he added, "Alright, I'll try one of your fancy cocktails."

Andrew took an empty chair from the next table and sat beside Sophie, putting his arm around her shoulders. The waitress placed a colourful drink in front of him. He frowned, lifting the glass to his lips. "The is a fruit bowl, not a drink." Giving Sophie a cheeky grin, he added, "do I drink it or chew it?

Sophie playfully punched his shoulder. "Drink it, of course.

So what do you think?"

"Um … it's quite nice. A little sweet for my taste, but it's alright."

"What's quite nice?" Hillary said. "Hello Andrew, pleased you could come. I see you are trying a cocktail."

"Come join us, Reggie. I'd like you to meet my fiancé, Andrew. He's in charge of Spring Gardens Hospital."

"Pleased to meet you, Andrew. Spring Gardens. Is that the mental hospital for officers suffering shell-shock? An interesting field to be in, illness of the mind."

"You are a doctor?" Andrew asked.

"Almost. I'm in medical school. That's how I know Hillary."

"It is unusual to find someone interested in mental illness."

"My father came out of the war suffering nightmares, so it's an area of medicine that is close to home. He insists there is nothing wrong and refuses to seek treatment. Do you have any advice?"

"It is very difficult for men like your father to understand this is not a weakness and, with treatment, it can get better. Can you persuade him of the benefits for him and his family? I'd be happy to talk to him."

"Thank you. I'll see what I can do. Excuse me, I had better return to my friends. Hillary, I'll see you at school tomorrow." Reggie gave a little bow and went back to the bar.

The music suddenly returned louder than ever with a trumpet solo, making everyone shout to the point that no one could have a conversation. Sophie stood up, pulling on Andrew who was shaking his head and yelling, "No I can't dance!"

Hillary stood up and grabbed Sophie's hand and headed for the dance floor. Andrew stared in surprise, feeling uncomfortable as his fiancée danced with a woman. He waited for a break in the music and tried to wave Sophie off the dance floor, but Reggie turned up and began dancing with Hillary leaving Andrew no choice but to dance with Sophie—if you could call it dancing. Try as he might, Andrew's stiff wooden legs would not bend to the rhythm, causing Sophie to stifle the giggles. Finally, she led him back to the table and they both laughed.

"You did tell me you couldn't dance. I'm sorry, Andrew. I embarrassed you."

"I'm sorry too. I wish I could dance. I always make a mess of it and, to be honest, when I was growing up, there was no one to teach me."

"I could teach you, at least just one dance for the wedding. Speaking of the wedding, why don't we find someone to ask about our plan to come here after the wedding breakfast."

Andrew beckoned the waitress, ordered more drinks and ask who he should speak to about a wedding party reservation. The waitress immediately sent the hostess to their table. The reservation was made for two large tables for the early evening of June 21$^{st}$.

Hillary returned from the dance floor, delighted the arrangements had been confirmed.


Trixie knocked on Sophie's door early the next morning. It was Sophie's day off, but she was dying to know how the evening had gone. She heard a groan, followed by a sleepy, "Come in."

"So, it wasn't such a good night at the club?" Trixie concluded from Sophie's paleness and serious expression.

"No. I mean yes, we had a great time. I think I drank too many cocktails." Sophie sat up in bed and ran her fingers through her long, tangled hair. Rubbing the sleep from her eyes, her face brightened as she told Trixie about the evening.

"I was so pleased Andrew joined us. I was afraid he wouldn't come and I'm happy he made the reservation for the after-wedding party. It eased my mind."

"Eased your mind? Why?" Trixie said with a deep frown. "Is everything all right between you and Andrew?"

"Of course. Sometimes Andrew doesn't seem to enjoy the things I do."

"Like going to jazz clubs."

Sophie nodded. "I know he's a serious kind of person. Everything was so serious in Passchendaele, but it doesn't have to be here, now. I love that he's kind, steady and reliable but judging by last night, he is uncomfortable having fun. I know that doesn't make sense."

"It does make sense. Chris and I have been married a year now and agreed our set up is different to most, but we don't like all the same things. We support and perhaps tolerate on occasions each other's likes. Andrew has already shown he supports you by going to the club and booking it for after wedding. And, you are right, there is nobody more reliable than Andrew. I have no doubt he'll be the perfect husband. You worry too much."

"Ha-ha! Wise words from an old married woman," Sophie teased.

"I must run." Trixie glanced at her timepiece. "I'm late. I won't see you tonight or tomorrow. I'm meeting Chris and tomorrow is my day off. We are going to look for accommodation."

# Memories of Silk

Sophie lay in bed, snoozing, waiting for the quiet that came over River House after everyone left for the hospital. Usually, she planned her day off and often spent the day with Hillary, but Hillary was working at the hospital today, so she had the whole day to herself. The aftermath of too many champagne cocktails was making her feel groggy, but staying in bed made it worse. A long soak in a hot bath was the answer and she decided to wash her hair, which was always a chore as it was long and thick, and took ages to dry. She wondered if she should be brave and have it bobbed. No, she liked her long hair and was quite proficient at finger waves. Twisting the length into the nape of her neck gave it the appearance of a bob.

Cook gave her a scowl when she entered the kitchen, a thick towel across her shoulders to catch the wetness of her hair loose down her back. "It's too late for breakfast," Cook growled. "I made myself tea. Would you like a cup?"

"Thank you. That would be lovely." Sophie looked around to see if there was any food.

"I shouldn't spoil you, but there's some bacon left over from breakfast and I can make you some toast."

"Thank you, Cook. I would like that." Sophie smiled

because in spite of Cook's tone of annoyance, she had kindly saved the bacon for her.

Cook was a strange woman. Sophie thought she was what you might call 'a diamond in the rough.' On the outside, she was tough and not afraid to speak her mind and rarely showed any kind of emotion. On the inside, Sophie suspected she was quite different. She showed her affection by doing little things, like saving bacon for Sophie, or comforting the homesick girls with a chat and cup of cocoa. Cook, unlike Mrs. Wilderby her predecessor, was not motherly, but she did her best, caring for the young nurses.

"What's upsetting you today, missy?" Cook said bluntly, placing a plate of bacon and toast on the kitchen table. "You've been moping ever since you got back from that foreign place. I don't trust them foreigners. Drink ya tea."

Sophie took a sip of the hot tea, putting her hand to her mouth to prevent her from spitting it out as the tea burnt her tongue and Cook's question had taken her by surprise. *Have I been moping? And what does it have to do with Italy?*

"Cook, we are so busy on the wards. I'm tired. I don't think that's moping."

"I know you girls work hard, but did some'at happen in Italy? I notice things, you know." Cook pointed towards her eyes.

"Nothing's going on. I am marrying Andrew on June 21st, and you are invited to the ceremony and the wedding breakfast afterwards. We are going to the Kingfisher Jazz Club later that evening and you are welcome to join us."

Cook blushed. "You want me at your wedding?"

"Of course, and afterwards."

"I'll come to the wedding. So, who's doing the wedding

breakfast?" Cook looked hurt, even annoyed.

"I don't know. We haven't made any arrangements yet. Why do you ask?"

"If it's a small do like you say, I could do that here. You'd have to pay for it, mind. All the girls, except the wedding people will be at the hospital."

"Cook, that is amazing. I would love that and I'll pay for all the food and Andrew can arrange the wine. We'll have champagne of course, then we can go to the club and dance the night away." Sophie stood up and hugged Cook. "Thank you."

"Now, now, we'll have none of that love stuff," she said, pulling away. "I'm not going to any fancy club. I don't hold with them fancy drinks and dancing. It's not natural to dance, kicking ya' legs, showing your unmentionable."

Sophie had trouble hiding a laugh, assuming unmentionables were knickers or even old fashioned bloomers, and no one under the age of forty or fifty wore such garments these days.

Pushing her chair back, she removed the towel from her shoulders. Flipping her hair over the back of the chair, she leaned towards the hot stove to dry her hair.

"You're blessed with beautiful hair. Mine's got thin over the years, but I won't have it cut. It's not natural. I've had long hair all mi life." Cook put her hand up to the brown and grey bun at the back of her head. "Enough chatter. What do you have planned for the day?"

"I'm taking a trip to Selfridges to buy a dress for the wedding."

"That sounds better than butcher and green grocer. I'll leave you to it," she said, taking off her apron and pinning her hat on. You'll need a Mac or umbrella. It looks like rain," she added, buttoning up her well-worn grey Mac and picking up her wicker shopping basket.

Enjoying the peace and quiet, Sophie ate the rest of her toast and let her hair dry by the stove. She giggled aloud at Cook's, 'it's not natural' and 'unmentionables.' *I must remember to tell Andrew.*

It rained heavily during the journey to Oxford Street. Sophie cursed for taking the autobus, instead of the Underground, but thankfully it was only spitting when she got off, not even enough to put up the umbrella. She always felt excited going into a big department store and Selfridges was special. The scent of exotic perfumes greeted her as she walked through the door. Perfume reminded her of her mother, giving her a warm but sad feeling. As a little girl, she'd sat with her mother, dreaming of princess brides in long flowing gowns. Suddenly she felt alone in the world and wished she'd waited to come with Hillary. But time was short and, as it was her idea to have the wedding so soon, she really couldn't complain.

"May I help you, madam?" The polite voice startled Sophie from her thoughts.

"Thank you. I'm looking for a wedding dress." She gulped at the words and quickly added, "just something very simple."

"Of course." The shop assistant raised her hand in a motion for Sophie to follow. They stopped at the lift. As the door opened, the assistant spoke to the lift attendant. "Madam is looking for the bridal department."

As the lift approached the second floor, the attendant called, "Second floor, ladies and bridal wear and ladies' shoes! Bridal wear to the right, madam."

Sophie had never seen so many dresses in one place, with veils, hats and gloves of all sizes and styles. Completely overwhelmed, she stood and stared, not knowing where to start when a stiff older woman approached her.

"Good afternoon!" she said with a smile that did not reach her eyes, "How may I help you?"

"I'm looking for a wedding dress," Sophie stammered. "But these look too fancy. It's a simple wedding."

The woman looked her up and down. "Perhaps madam would prefer a more economical dress?"

Sophie frowned thinking, *economical? Is the woman implying the bargain basement? The cheek of it, although that is not a bad idea.*

Straightening her shoulders and pinning the woman directly in the eye, Sophie hissed, "I said simple and that does not imply cheap." She waited for the woman's reaction. When none came, she said, "My fiancé and I have decided on a small civic ceremony. I'm sure with your expertise you would agree, a long flowing gown would not be appropriate." Sophie grinned as the assistant's mouth twitched and a slight blush coloured each cheek.

The woman said nothing but guided Sophie to a rack of white and rather ornate wedding dresses. Sophie shook her head, a little irritated, wondering why the woman didn't understand simple.

Biting her tongue, trying to be polite, Sophie touched the dresses and commented, "The dresses are beautiful but too formal for me." Sophie took a deep breath. She wanted this experience to be pleasant. Deciding she had a choice; she could either walk away and come back another time or try to get the sales assistant to understand. She decided on the latter.

"My parents passed away before the war and my fiancé has no family. We both served in the medical corps during the war and lost many friends. Perhaps you can understand why we want a nice, small and unpretentious wedding?"

"I am sorry. The war was hard on us all and I do understand. My name is Mrs. Dover and I think I have an idea." Her face brightened into a genuine smile.

*Well, that worked.* Sophie thought. *She is a different person. I wonder if she lost someone in the war?*

"If you would be kind enough to follow me, I have some beautiful designs over here. I think you will like them."

Mrs. Dover's heels clipped on the wooden floor as she led Sophie to a discrete corner of the department, which was set out with chairs and vases of flowers. "Please take a seat." Glancing at Sophie and then studying the dresses, she smiled and nodded. Selecting several dresses from the rack, she passed them to an assistant.

Sophie sat a little awkwardly. After having felt insulted in the beginning, she now felt a little intimidated by Mrs. Dover's attention and wasn't quite sure what came next. Taking one dress at a time, Mrs. Dover presented the dress for her approval, and to her surprise, she liked them all. Leaning forward, she touched the fabric of one that caught her eye. Memories of her father and the silk trade came flooding back. The dress felt like Romano silk, so soft and rich it brought tears to her eyes. How she wished she could marry in Romano silk.

"Are you quite well? You look a little pale Miss… ?" Mrs. Dover realized she had not asked her name. "Forgive me, I

144

didn't ask your name."

"Romano. Sophie Romano, and I am quite well, a little overwhelmed perhaps. My father was in the silk business. We had a silk farm in Italy and a factory in Derby. My apologies, the feel of this silk felt just like Romano silk. A bit of a shock, that's all."

"You are the daughter of Alberto Romano. My father was a bespoke tailor and I was his secretary before I married. Your father used to meet my father to discuss the silk orders. There was a high demand for Romano silk."

"What a coincidence. I hadn't thought about the silk trade in so long, but when I touched this dress, it all came back to me. I used to help my father at the silk mill in Derby." Sophie brushed away tears. "I'd like to try this dress, if I may?"

Mrs. Dover pulled back the curtain on the change room and handed Sophie the silk dress. She slipped the dress on and gave a gasp of pleasure. The butter blond colour and fit were perfect. The soft silk shimmered and the light scalloped lace over the top gave it a richness. Sophie closed her eyes, wishing her mother was by her side. She knew she would approve the dress. If only her father could feel the silk. He was always so proud of exquisite Romano silk. She slid her hand between the silk and lace.

*Mama, Papa, this may not be Romano silk, but it feels like it. You have been gone so long and yet, on days like this, it feels like only yesterday. I feel your presence every day. How I wish you were here.*

Blushing and keeping her tears at bay, Sophie stepped out of the change room and Mrs. Dover beamed a smile.

"You look beautiful, Miss Romano. How does it feel?"

"I could be wearing Romano silk." Sophie held back tears as

a matching beaded headband was secure around her forehead.

"The colour is perfect for your dark hair, Miss Romano. Beautiful, truly beautiful."

"Thank you. I'll take the dress and headband."

The pavement glittered from the wetness of yet another downpour as Selfridges' doorman held the exit open. Sophie hesitated at the curb, awkwardly clutching the large box containing her Romano dress. Uncertain whether to make a run for it to the Underground across the street or, at the risk of dropping her cherished box, opening her umbrella. She peered down Oxford Street, preparing to cross the road when a red autobus appeared. She decided not to open her umbrella; a few minutes in the rain wouldn't hurt while she waited.

She climbed up the step and found an unoccupied window seat and rested the box across her lap. Watching the rain trickle down the window, she thought not of her impending wedding, but of the silk mill, the clatter of the looms filled her head, the feel of the luxurious fabric. Her hands caressed the box as though she could feel the silk inside. She had bought a cherished memory, not a dress for her wedding. An unrecognizable sensation slipped through her. *What is happening to me? Why do I feel this way?* Afraid she was slipping into the abyss she'd experienced before the trip to Italy, she sat up straight in her seat and focused on the road ahead. Surprised to see the sun had broken through the rain clouds, she realized she was only two stops away from hers.

Wrapping her arms around the box, Sophie walked to River House, hoping Cook would offer her a cup of tea. She realized she hadn't eaten since breakfast. She had intended to treat herself to afternoon tea at Selfridges' Tea Room but, in the delight of buying the dress, she had completely forgotten.

Sophie ran upstairs, placed her box on her bed and knocked on Hillary's door. There was no answer. Disappointed and wanting to share her purchase with her best friend, Sophie went back downstairs.

"Hello! Cook are you there?" Sophie called as she opened the kitchen door.

"Come in! I just made tea. How was your shopping trip?" Cook stood at the stove, stirring something that smelt delicious. "Pour the tea, then. I'm almost done here."

"Tea sounds lovely. I had a good day at Selfridges." Sophie chose to be vague because she wanted to share her purchase with Hillary before anyone else. "Have you seen Hillary?"

"No, I haven't seen her all day. Said she was working at the hospital." Cook took a sip of tea. "Did you get ya' shopping? I don't hold with them fancy department stores. Too busy. I don't know how you can decide on what to buy."

Sophie smiled, amused by Cooks reference to things being too fancy. It seemed to be her staple answer to anything she didn't understand. "It's a great experience. You should try it one day."

"Na', not for me. Now run along. I've got work to do. Oh, nearly forgot. There's a letter for you on the hall stand."

Sophie picked up the letter, reading the Italian post mark as she ran upstairs to her room.

# News from Italy

Excited to hear from Paola, with news from Lucca, Sophie ripped open the envelope and began reading, slowly at first, as she geared her brain into Italian. Despite her mother tongue being Italian, for the most part she spoke better English than Italian, meaning she found herself translating Paola's letter in her head.

*Ciao Sophie*

*I hope you are well. We are all well, although Mama and Papa are struggling, trying to keep the bakery going. The Blackshirts are making it hard to get around and Papa gets into arguments with them when he goes to town for supplies. I'm afraid one day they'll throw him in prison. So far, they just taunt him.*

*Thank you for inviting us to your wedding. Papa says he can't leave the shop and Mama won't travel any farther than Lucca. As you know, my dream has been to come to England, but I'm not sure I can make the journey on my own. The Blackshirts are everywhere and they frighten me. I am constantly harassed by them when I go to Lucca and Mussolini encourages them. It makes me sad that I won't be at your wedding, but when things settle down, I will make the journey and meet your husband.*

*I am happy to hear you set the date for your wedding but surprised it seemed quite sudden. You didn't talk about Andrew much when you were here. I always thought there was something between you and Carlos. However, Andrew must be a perfect gentleman and care for you very much to drive all the way from London to Dover. I bet you were surprised to see him when you got off the ferry. It all sounds so romantic. Are you sure you didn't read that in a novel?*

Sophie laughed at this remark. Paola was mature for a nineteen-year-old, but still young in the romance department.

*I went to the jazz club last night and danced with Harry. He really is nice and I would like to get to know him better, but Papa would not like it if I fell for an Englishman. Carlos was there too, but he looked sad and didn't speak to me except to say hello. I checked the villa today, to make sure the repairs were being done. Giuseppe is doing a great job. The roof repairs are finished, but the rest of it is slow as it is difficult to get supplies.*

*This is going to sound strange, but as I drove the van along your driveway, concentrating on missing the holes, the spring rain has made them worse, I was sure I saw*

*Carlos driving away. Why would he be at the villa?*

Looking up from the letter, Sophie frowned. Why would Carlos be at the villa? Her heart skipped a beat or two at the thought of Carlos there. She shook herself, annoyed he was intruding on her life again, and pulled her focus back to Paola's letter.

*Cousin Franco has already started to clear the land, ready for planting the grape vines. You wouldn't recognize the place. He's taken down the old shed, but restored the outbuilding for storing wine.*

*I must close now, as it is late and I must be up early tomorrow to help Papa.*

*Ciao*
  *Paola*

Folding the letter back into the envelope, Sophie stared at the dress box on the bed, her eyes tracing the bold letters that spelled Selfridges across the top. A soft tap on the door drew her attention from the box.

"Come in!"

"Sorry. Am I interrupting?" Hillary said, glancing at the letter.

"No, not all. The letter is from Paola in Italy. Keeping me up to date on the villa. It arrived in this afternoon's post, while I was at Selfridges."

"I am dying to know if you bought a dress." Hillary's eyes scanned Sophie and then the box. "You did. Oh, let me see. Is it gorgeous? Of course it is."

"You sound more excited than me." Sophie laughed at her friend's enthusiasm. "And yes, it is beautiful, but not a typical wedding dress. It could be worn at a fancy club." She laughed. "As if I ever go to fancy clubs. I never thought I would wear such fabric. It feels and looks like Romano silk. It is perfect. I was waiting for you before I opened the box."

The tissue paper rustled as Sophie gently lifted the lid. She couldn't help but gasp again, as she unfolded the dress.

"Oh, Sophie, it is beautiful. Try it on for me."

Sophie pulled off her cotton dress and let the silky dress slide over her head and body. She turned to look in the mirror and handed the hairband to Hillary, allowing her to tie it around her hair.

"I am overwhelmed. I don't know what to say. It is very beautiful, Sophie. How much did it cost?"

"£8, a month's wages. I can't believe I spent that much on a dress, even if it is for my wedding. I couldn't resist. I tried it on and said 'I'll take it' and didn't even look at the price. It could have been £20, and I would have taken it."

"I can see why. What shall I wear? I can't afford a new dress."

"I'll buy you a dress. After all, it is my wedding."

"No, I couldn't let you do that. What about my blue dress, the one I wore to the club?" Hillary looked tentative, waiting for Sophie's reply.

"I think the blue will compliment this pale yellow, or butter blond as they call it. Go and fetch it and let's see."

Hillary returned, dressed in her peacock blue dress. They

stood side by side, looking in the long mirror. In unison, they nodded and said, "Absolutely divine, darling!" and then collapsed on the bed in fits of laughter. Hearing Cook call that dinner was ready, they quickly slipped out of their dresses and back into day clothes.

The dinner table seemed somber, even Nurse Harrington looked tired and Sophie felt guilty feeling so elated, although she did have to get back to work tomorrow.

"How are things on the wards?" Sophie ventured to ask.

"Busy with fevers," Nurse Harrington said. "I've sponged dozens of patients. It's sad they are so ill. A lady died today while I was sponging her forehead." Her voice quivered and tears filled her eyes.

"I'm sorry, Nurse. It is hard to lose patients and I'm afraid it doesn't get any easier. She was not alone and feeling your soothing hands would be a comfort to her. You did well." Sophie remembered how hard it was seeing her first patient die. "If you want to talk about it, I'm happy to listen."

Hillary took a breath and smiled to lift everyone's spirits. "Are you getting used to working on the wards?"

All the probationers nodded with enthusiasm. Sophie understood that cleanliness was important and the nurses needed to know how to clean, but she couldn't help wondering if scrubbing floors was good for their morale, or even the best use of their time. They were all doing well on the wards and, even in a crisis, they had shown how willing they were to work hard. *I think I'll have a word with Sister Kay, maybe Matron too.*

"The nurses are doing better than the doctors," Hillary said. "Two consultants have gone down with 'flu' and the rest are trying to fill in the best they can. Dr. Wilcox was relieved to see the pneumonia cases have stabilized, and he thinks it will improve. I can relate to you, ladies. Like you, I prefer working on the wards. I don't have to clean but classroom work can get boring. Working with puffed up doctors also has its challenges."

A soft tittering of laughter went around the table. The probationers and young nurses were in awe of Hillary, first because she had been a senior nurse and a good one at that, and now she was training to be a physician. Most of them thought they were being brave nursing, either to get out of poverty or to escape undesirable suitors.

Cook blustered into the dining room, carrying a steaming bowl of pudding. "Did you enjoy the stew? The butcher is proud of you girls and insists you have the best beef to keep your strength up. I made ya a rice pudding today," she added, returning to the kitchen. Cook only ate with the girls on special occasions, which Sophie thought was odd. The chair at the head of the table was vacant at most meals.

As soon as the meal was over, Sophie excused herself and returned to her room, wanting to reply to Paola's letter. Hilary followed to study, burying herself in a mound of text books.

Admiring the dress one more time, Sophie touched the exquisite silk, its softness and warmth reminding her of her father's smile and of happy times at the silk mill. Was this a good omen for a happy marriage? Her sudden sense of uncertainty alarmed her. *Why would I be uncertain? Wedding nerves, that's all,* she thought. She slid the dress on to a satin padded coat hanger, before draping a cotton shirt over the top and carefully placing it at the back of her wardrobe.

Paola's letter lay on her desk and she re-read it before picking up her pen and smoothing out the writing paper.

*Ciao Paola,*

*I was delighted to hear from you and to know you and your family are well. I am quite well, thank you, although very busy at the hospital.*

*I am sad that you are not able to come to the wedding, but I do understand. I bought my dress today and I am very pleased.*

*Giuseppe is a good man. I trust his work. Don't worry about time, as it will be many months before I will be back in Italy.*

*My friendship with Carlos is a long story and it started at the villa. Perhaps that is why he was visiting. He has let me down several times and I have accepted that a permeant relationship with Carlos just would not work. Andrew is quite the opposite, kind, generous, attentive—at least as attentive as his work allows, but I have a great interest in mental disorders. I saw so many soldiers suffer during the war. I admire Andrew for his gift for treating such patients, so even his work doesn't keep us apart. Goodness, I am writing too much about me.*

*I am pleased you returned to the American Jazz Club. Did your father forgive you or are you still sneaking out without his permission?*

*Harry is a good dancer. I enjoyed his company too. I found him to be a nice and considerate gentleman. I am sure your father would see that if they met, although he probably sees all Englishmen as untrustworthy after your brother was killed, which is understandable. It was a terrible war with horrendous repercussions.*

154

*I can see your father arguing with the Blackshirts and that is so dangerous, but he's an outspoken man. I don't see Blackshirts here, but there is an undercurrent of dissatisfaction and the unions are active and aggressive. I'm told there are underground groups. Many of them shout their philosophies in Hyde Park, but I don't see them as dangerous.*

*It is past my bedtime. I had a day off today, but it's back to work tomorrow, so I will close now.*

*Ciao with love,*
  *Sophie*

Writing about Andrew reminded Sophie she had not heard from him for a few days, which was not like him. It was too late to telephone. She needed to remember to call him in the morning.

Sophie and Hillary were alone in the dining room, eating breakfast the next morning when, much to Cook's annoyance, the River House telephone rang. "Who's calling at this hour in the morning?" she huffed, muttering, "I don't know why we need such a contraption. Six-thirty, indeed."

Sophie jumped up, calling, "I'll answer it. It might be Andrew."

"A gentleman he might be, but tell him it's too early for telephone calls. Don't be long. Ya eggs 'ul get cold. There's a fresh pot of tea on the table."

"I'll tell him, and thank you," Sophie said as she picked up the receiver.

"Andrew, good morning. Cook says the call is too early." She laughed and listened carefully before returning to her cold eggs.

"Andrew says hello, Hillary." She giggled. "I won't repeat his comment regarding Cook. I suggested we go to the Kingfisher tomorrow night, but he's busy at the hospital. They are having a similar problem at the Bartley, several cases of pneumonia, and he's exhausted. He sounds it too. Oh well, I was looking forward to a night out. Maybe next week."

"Why don't we go on our own? I need a night out and so do you, Sophie."

"A night out where?" Trixie said, walking into to the dining room, yawning.

"Good morning, Trixie. You're up early," Sophie and Hillary said in unison.

Rubbing her eyes, Trixie poured herself a cup of tea. "Chris is picking me up later. He has a couple days leave and I'm off today. Chris found us rooms, not far from here. He's taking me to view them and meet the landlady. If I like the place, we can move in straight away. I can hardly believe we'll have our own place."

"That is good news. Have you told Cook?"

"She's happy, as she has two new nurses coming at the end of the month." Trixie sighed. "Chris plans to tell his parents about the rooms. They are expecting us for luncheon at the estate. I'm not looking forward to Lady Belingham's reaction. She will blame me for leading her precious son astray."

"She'll always blame you," Sophie sympathized. "Wait until Chris is Lord Belingham and you live on the estate. You'll be Lady Belingham. I can't imagine how his mother will handle that."

"At least that is not going to happen for a long time, so we can enjoy our marriage for a few years. We have to make sure his father stays healthy. Sophie, have you and Andrew decided to stay at Mrs. Humphries?"

"I have but I'm not sure about Andrew. He has his heart set on a house. Time for us to go. See you later."

# The Kingfisher Club

Hillary, Sophie and Trixie were at the Kingfisher Club for the third time in the last two weeks. The hostess, her welcoming smile barely visible in the darkened, smoke filled room, carefully guided the group through a maze of small round tables that surrounded the dance floor. Sophie blinked her stinging eyes, as cigarette smoke swirled into her face from a particularly long cigarette holder. Arriving at what was becoming their regular spot, close to the band, a loud trumpet seemed to hail them to their seats and they ordered a round of drinks. Five of them squeezed around the little table. There was Trixie with Chris, who was on leave to settle into their new accommodation and Hillary had invited Reggie to join them once again. Andrew had declined, his excuses becoming more tiresome.

The music prompted everyone, except Sophie, to get on the dance floor. She watched Chris and Trixie dancing like a couple of pros, laughing and having a good time. They seemed really happy since moving into their own rooms. Reggie and Hillary were more the slow waltz type, but Sophie noticed they were getting closer each evening, presenting as a handsome couple. Hillary insisted they were friends and study partners, but Sophie saw much more going on. She hated to admit that she was jealous of both couples and really missed Andrew. Here she was, a dud, a wallflower, of her own doing. Never short of offers from dance partners, she refused, feeling disloyal both to Andrew for dancing with other men and to her unknown partners. It seemed unfair, knowing she was not free to encourage the flirting, although she did enjoy it.

Sophie loved to dance, the music and dance steps making her feel alive. She didn't mind who she danced with. She just wanted to dance. If the girls came alone, they would dance together but tonight they both had partners, so here she was sitting alone, staring at a damask tablecloth of undetermined colour, sipping cocktails of unquestionable origin.

"May I have this dance," a sultry male voice asked, breathing into her neck. Sophie turned cautiously, wondering who was causing this amazing tingling sensation down her spine. She gasped, "Andrew!"

He shook his head. "I can't believe the most beautiful woman in the room is sitting alone. So, will you dance with me?"

"Of course." Andrew led her to the dance floor. Sophie felt the rhythm bounce into her legs, kicking and laughing she swung her hips, her hands on Andrew's shoulders, his on her waist. He tried his best to keep up with her. Sophie ignored his awkward, non-rhythmic moves. She was dancing and Andrew was with her. Nothing else mattered. The band played and the trumpets wailed until the dancers were exhausted and all three couples retreated to the table. Reggie ordered drinks all round, which resulted in animated conversation, probably as a result of several such drinks earlier in the evening. Andrew seemed reserved, sipping on his first drink and watching the group. He put his arm around Sophie and she snuggled into his shoulder.

The table next to them burst into raucous laughter, drowning out any conversation. Suddenly a blond woman in a short red flapper dress stood up and focused on Andrew, yelling, "Dr. Cuthbert!" Amidst peals of laughter and undoubtedly too many cocktails, the woman added, "Surprise, surprise!" with an American accent. "The great doctor is partying." With a look of disdain, she continued. "Rather stay at home like an Airedale, not used to night life. Oh, do I see a handcuff? Should I congratulation you, darling?" Her last words slurred.

Andrew stared at the woman and Sophie leaned in to him and whispered, "Who is she?" He shook his head without answering.

"Who am I?" the woman shouted, alarming her table companions. One gentleman pulled on her arm, suggesting she sit down, and gave Andrew an embarrassed smile, mouthing, *too much to drink.*

Andrew stood up to face the woman. "Madam, you have the advantage of knowing me. My apologies but I cannot recall meeting you. Perhaps you would be so kind as to introduce yourself and your friends?"

Visibly swaying, her retort shocked everyone. "The crazy doctor works in a looney bin and he doesn't remember me! Try remembering my lunatic husband. He went to war a great man and came back a lunatic, chasing German killers in his twisted head. You said you would make him better." The woman burst into heavy sobs, finally falling into the arms of her friend who gently eased her away from the table. Another man joined them and helped her walk to the door.

Andrew was stunned. Tears glistened, and struggling not to

spill them, he looked to Sophie for support. "She's the husband of one my patients, one of Major General Macdonald's men. I treated him in France at the end of the war and transferred him to Spring Gardens. Originally, he showed signs of recovering. I hoped to get him home but something happened on a home visit and he's deteriorated ever since. We've tried everything and there is nothing more I can do for him. He's in a locked ward, a danger to himself and others, even his wife."

"That's why she is so upset and has to blame someone, which unfortunately is you. I'm sorry, Andrew. The poor woman is distraught and excessive drinking brought out the worst." Sophie used her calming nurse's voice. "Let's call it a night and go home. Perhaps Mrs. Humphries would allow us to sit in her sitting-room for a while."

"Thank you. I would like to sit with you. I'm quite shaken." Andrew took Sophie's hand and addressed the group. "Not quite the excitement I was expecting. Would you excuse us? I'm not feeling my best. Lovely to see you all." Andrew nodded a goodbye as he and Sophie left the club.

Mrs. Humphries was surprisingly accommodating. Without giving her details, Andrew explained they had had a bit of a shock and needed to talk for a while. She offered them her sitting-room, making it clear she would not be far away in the kitchen, should they need her.

Sophie smiled. "I think we are being chaperoned and I expect a tray of tea to arrive shortly to make sure we are behaving."

"No doubt in my mind that you are correct. She is a lovely person and a pleasant landlady." Andrew winked. "But I have an undying need to kiss you."

"An undying need? My goodness, Dr. Cuthbert. You had better kiss me before the tea arrives." Sophie's giggle went unheard as Andrew pulled her towards him and kissed her with such passion she almost swooned. Returning the kiss with eagerness, she felt the tension of the evening melt away.

Snuggled together on the sofa Sophie said, "The war still lingers in so many lives. That poor woman is a casualty of war, as much as the fighting men. She sounded American and possibly resents the British for encouraging the Americans to join forces. Her life is ruined and there are many more woman like her, trying to make sense of what happened to their husbands." Her forehead creased above her nose. "Do you know why she called you an Airedale?"

Andrew laughed. "No idea, and a handcuffed one at that. Some kind of American slang, perhaps. Sophie, you do believe me that I do my best. Some men can't be helped, others struggle to make a partial recovery and a few make a full recovery. I can only take comfort in that I am able to help some, who would not otherwise recover."

"Of course, I believe you. One of the things that attracted me to you was your unselfish caring for your patients in an area of medicine that is so little understood and often maligned. You are a wonderful man and doctor. Never ever doubt your motives or abilities. Now, I think for all that flattery, I need another kiss." She giggled. "Perhaps not."

As expected, a gentle knock on the living room door announced Mrs. Humphries' arrival with a tray of cocoa and sweet biscuits. "I thought you might like a cuppa to help you sleep." Setting the tray on the coffee table, Mrs. Humphries sat down and passed the cups around.

"Thank you. This looks lovely," Sophie said, amused by her protectiveness, and, she suspected, Mrs. Humphries might have another motive for joining them.

"I am happy that Dr. Cuthbert has found a lovely bride and I wanted to tell you how pleased I am. I have become very fond of our doctor. He's been kind to me and life hasn't been easy since my husband was killed in the war. We were young and had not had time to have children. Dr. Cuthbert is like a son to me." She stopped to take a drink of cocoa. "Miss Romano, I would like it if you and the doctor would come and live here after you're married." Hesitating briefly, she added, "I'd make the rent reasonable."

Sophie felt like hugging the woman. Already having decided she didn't want to buy a house just yet, Mrs. Humphries rooms would be ideal. Would her emotional plea convince Andrew?

"Mrs. Humphries, that is very generous of you. Andrew, how do you feel about staying here for a few months, even a year? We can buy a house when we are more settled." Sophie smiled, making a mental note that one of Andrew's tasks was to ask Mrs. Humphries about the rooms and he obviously had not spoken to her. She waited for his answer, feeling a slight irritation.

"I was looking forward to a house and garden, but you are right Sophie, renting rooms for now and saving for a house is the best thing for us." Andrew yawned and looked very pale. "I am tired. I had better walk you home."

"It's not far. I'll walk home. You are tired and need your rest."

"Independent Sophie. No, I can't let you walk home in the dark this late." Andrew's tone was quite clipped.

Mrs. Humphries cleared her throat. "I have an idea. I wanted to show you the rooms upstairs. I'll show you the rooms and you could stay the night. The bed is all made up, towels and everything. Try it out so to speak." She sat back, looking very satisfied.

"That is very kind, but Cook will be worried if I don't return to River house."

"Don't you worry about that. I'll call Hilda and tell her you are trying out my spare rooms."

"You know Cook? I never knew her name was Hilda."

"We go back a long way and helped each other, with being war widows. Hilda was cook to a big posh family after her husband was killed. That was before she went to River House."

"We always call her Cook, and never thought to ask her name. And thank you, I'd like to see the rooms." Sophie gave Andrew a side glance. She had a feeling Mrs. Humphries had already spoken to Cook.

The three climbed to the third floor. There were two rooms, a bedroom and a sitting room and, to Sophie's surprise, a small bathroom under the eaves, making it cramped for anyone over 5' 4" to stand except for over the sink, but having their own bathroom was definitely a bonus.

"I'll leave you two to check things out, make yourselves comfortable. Miss Romano and Doctor, don't dally too long." Her look was that of a stern house mother, confirming the meaning of the word dally. "I'll see you both in the morning, breakfast at 6:30, early. You'll have plenty of time to get to River House to change for your shift."

"What do you think about living here, Andrew? The bedroom is small but room enough for two of us and the living room is spacious and bright. And look, there's a little hob and kettle. We can make our own tea. I think we'd be comfortable here, just for a little while."

"I agree this is very comfortable. I'll tell her we'll take it and move in right after the wedding. Mrs. Humphries is an excellent cook, unless you would prefer rooms with a kitchen to do your own cooking?"

Sophie laughed. "Believe me darling, you would suffer if I cooked. We will hire a cook when we have a house."

Andrew kissed her and went to his own room on the second floor. Sophie picked up the towel and a white nightdress dropped on the floor. "You thought of everything, Mrs. Humphries." She sighed with pleasure. "A whole bathroom all to myself is like living in a palace."

Sophie lay on her back, staring at the ceiling. "Will these rooms really be my home in two weeks' time?" A sense of uncertainty crept over her. She liked the place. Mrs. Humphries was a good landlady and excellent cook. The rooms couldn't be more perfect, two armchairs by the fireplace where they could sit reading in the evening. Snuggling into the comfortable double bed, she blushed slightly as she imagined Andrew at her side. The place was warm and cosy. It felt like a home.

# Illness Strikes Close to Home

Andrew and Sophie were the only two in the dining room at six in the morning. Although the bed was comfortable, Sophie had slept badly and wasn't in the mood to meet those who might become her fellow residents. Mrs. Humphries buzzed around, serving an excellent breakfast of eggs, bacon and crispy fried bread, toast and homemade marmalade, with a choice of tea or coffee. Sophie preferred to stick with tea but she noticed Andrew drank coffee. She didn't know he liked coffee. She smiled to herself, thinking of the small things they knew so little about each other. Music hung in the air. Mrs. Humphries hummed, occasionally singing the words, slightly off key, but well enough for Sophie to recognize the popular song *Roses of Picardy.* She was undeniably happy that her favourite boarder was not leaving and delighted at the prospect of having a married couple settle in her third-floor rooms. The move-in date had been set for two days after the wedding, assuming the bride and groom would plan a short honeymoon. Something else they had yet to discuss, but she consoled herself that most of the arrangement had been made and the honeymoon, if there was one, was up to the groom.

The motorcar ride to River House was short and Sophie

frowned as she stared at Andrew quiet, pensive and very pale. "Is something wrong? I thought you would be pleased that we have settled our living arrangement."

"I am pleased." He gave her a weak smile. "I am feeling fatigued and not quite myself. Too much excitement," he laughed. "You, my darling, are wearing me out. I'm not used to nightclubs and some of the, less than polite, patrons."

"That awful woman upset you, didn't she?"

"A little. I wish I could give her back the respected army officer husband who went to war, and not the man who returned. So much more needs to done. You know that."

Sophie nodded, understanding what Andrew was saying and wishing she could be of more help. "Do you think studying Freud would help? I've read quite a lot and would like to understand more."

"Perhaps, but I'm not sure these war injuries are curable." Andrew sighed. It wasn't like him to be pessimistic. He rubbed his stomach. "I don't think cocktails suit me. Can we, just the two of us, go to the *Rose & Crown* tomorrow for a beer and a steak pie?"

"I'd like that. I'm on nights all next week and you're on call so a simple night out would be lovely."

The motorcar stopped at the curb and Sophie waved as Andrew drove off to Spring Gardens Hospital. She ran in to change into her uniform. Hillary had already left and she was running late, not for the ward, but to Sister Kay's office to discuss the trainees' progress and she wasn't prepared. Clubbing was interfering in her work. Andrew was right, a quiet beer was a lot less taxing and cocktails made her head fuzzy the next day. She resolved to only go the Kingfisher club on her days off.

Clutching the nurse's training manual to her chest, Sophie immediately headed downstairs to Sister Kay's office, which was more of a broom cupboard than an office. Judging by the distinct odour of carbolic emanating from the walls, it was exactly that, a broom cupboard. It gave Sophie the heebie-jeebies, reminding her of her own training and a cruel sister attacking her in a similar cleaning room only a few yards away.

Sister made the best of the space, pushing the desk against the wall and adding a desk lamp that struggled to brighten the place. A pretty china inkwell and pen stand sat above a blotter with a photograph of an old couple, possibly her parents.

"Good morning, Nurse Romano. Take a seat."

Sophie sat down on the only other chair, pulled close to the side of the desk. She sat very still as her knees almost touched Sister Kay's. However, it did make it easy to follow the reports spread on the desk.

"You have a new schedule?"

"I thought your idea of reducing the cleaning time and adding more practical time for the probationers was solid. We need help on the wards and charwomen can take over the cleaning. It's far more practical. I have yet to get the hospital governors to approve, but I am taking advantage of the current crisis to try it out—give the board proof of its value to the hospital.

It seems the peak of these infections has passed. Admissions are down so we need to be quick."

Sister Kay went on to describe how the time was to be broken up and Sophie was expected to monitor the probationers, especially making sure the hospital was clean. The ward nurses would monitor them on the wards. She wasn't sure where she would find the time. She'd have to use her breaks checking the cleaning, knowing the nurses would prefer to be on the wards.

"I realize I'm asking for a lot of your time. Do I have your commitment?"

"Of course, Sister."

"It is none of my business what you do in your spare time but a word of advice. It might be prudent to spend less time at jazz clubs. You will need all your strength for your new duties."

"A conclusion I had come to just this morning, Sister. I won't let you down."

"Good. I have some concerns regarding Nurses Harrington and Fox. They have become very friendly and that in itself is good. They are from such different backgrounds, and ..."

"Why are you concerned?"

"Nurse Harrington is a troubled young woman. Her brother, not her father, registered her in the nurses' program. Aristocratic families hide behind their privileged lives and have secrets. In my experience, probationers with Nurse Harrington's background flaunt their privilege and can be mean and hurtful, even destructive. A perfect example was her involvement with Nurse Hogan." Sister looked at Sophie with regret. "I apologize for misjudging you. I am truly sorry."

Sophie nodded, accepting the apology. The incident had hurt her deeply. Afraid of what she might say, she felt it better to remain quiet. She also noted that it was unusual for Sister to single out probationers, making her wonder why the interest and need to defend Nurse Harrington. "Nurse Harrington apologized to both me and Nurse Fox over that incident. She was quite genuine and remorseful. I agree she is troubled and it may have to do with her father, possibly a result of the war. However, I suspect there is more. She did mention her fondness for her brother, at least she has an ally in him. I will try and spend some time with her and Nurse Fox. It is a strange friendship, but I believe it to be beneficial to both nurses."

"Indeed, it could be, particularly for Nurse Harrington. It is a difficult transition from being pampered to your every whim, with a busy day being little more than polite social calls. I remember it well." Sister stared into the grey walls and then, at Sophie's puzzled expression, replied. "I was a mean and privileged girl when I started nursing at St. Thomas'. It was Esther Hartford, Matron, who was my friend. We trained together. My father disowned me for wanting to be a nurse and my mother wept because of the disgrace. It was my brother who helped me. I see the puzzlement in your face, but now you can understand my concern. I also know that without a friend or understanding superior, it is easy to take the wrong path. Matron is the only person, to my knowledge, that is privy to my background and now you. I would appreciate your discretion."

"Of course, Sister. I had no idea. I understand. I will do my best for both nurses."

Sister Kay put her head to one side and smiled. It was a smile of endearment, as much as approval.

"I have so much faith in you. One day you will be sitting in my place in this office. Hopefully, by then, they'll have found the sister-tutor something larger than a broom closet." They both laughed at the humble surroundings. "Matron has promised she will find me something more suited to the position." Her eyes were bright with amusement. "I understand there is a storage cupboard on the main floor, larger than this, with a window looking onto the courtyard, which I'm told has my name on it."

"Broom closet to storage cupboard, with a window. Definitely a step up," Sophie said with a humorous and sarcastic tone.

Sister laughed. "Indeed!"

The new schedule complete, Sophie and Sister met with the probationers and gave them their new instructions. As expected, Nurses Harrington and Fox were assigned to the Women's Ward and duties commenced immediately.

Sister McPherson, who was covering for Sister Kay, was in the process of checking the patients ready for doctor's round. Upon seeing Sister Kay, she instructed Trixie to continue. The two sisters conferred and agreed to put the probationers to work. The ward actually had spare beds for the first time in weeks, confirming Sister's Kay's thought that they needed to hurry in order to present their case with evidence to the board of governors. However, several patients with pneumonia had high fevers, needing constant care, care that the regular nurses did not have time for. Nurse Harrington was assigned to an older woman who had recovered from Spanish flu two weeks earlier, but now had a high fever and difficulty breathing, possibly pneumonia. Nurse Fox's patient was a young woman who had injured her leg in a motorcar accident and was showing signs of infection.

The timing appeared perfect as Dr. Wilcox and his entourage entered the ward minutes after everyone was settled. Sophie gave the nurses an encouraging smile and slipped away, leaving Sister McPherson to do the rounds. She sensed someone was watching her and realized Hillary and

Reggie were among the doctors as student observers. They exchanged knowing nods and smiles.

Dr. Wilcox, always full of his own importance, must have notice as he bellowed, "Miss West, perhaps you could give us your full attention." He muttered under his breath, "women don't belong here."

Sophie raised an eyebrow, stared right at him and smiled. He quickly moved on. When he reached the patient Nurse Harrington was assisting, he examined the chart and listened to the woman's breathing and turned to the young doctors. "This woman is showing signs of respiratory distress, perhaps pneumonia. What other diseases would be possible?"

Silence ensued. The young doctors seemed afraid to speak up. Not sure if she was allowed to answer, Hillary decided to anyway. "Sir, it could be a bronchial condition or asthma, a chronic condition that has recently been associated with reactions to a foreign substance, causing the patient to wheeze. However, the fever indicates classic symptoms of pneumonia. It appears she has recently recovered from Spanish flu, often a sign that the pneumonia is somehow caused by the 'flu.'" Hillary cleared her throat. "Sir."

Dr. Wilcox tensed. He knew Hillary was correct, but hated that she had more than adequately answered his question. Ignoring Hillary, he directed his next question to the group. "Gentlemen, would you concur with Miss West's rationale?"

It was Reggie who spoke this time. "Yes, sir. In recent weeks, more and more patients have developed a chest infection, like pneumonia, associated with the Spanish flu."

"Excellent deduction, Mr. Davies. This patient is suffering from advanced pneumonia and careful nursing will determine whether or not the patient recovers." He glanced at Nurse

Harrington. Sophie had moved forward, expecting rebuke or comment, as he realized she was a trainee nurse. "Sister, I take it this nurse has the skills to treat the patient?"

"Yes, sir. Nurse Harrington has been assigned to stay with the patient to bring her temperature down." Sister McPherson hesitated. Sophie thought she might be deciding whether to bring the doctor's attention to the overworked nurses and the use of trainees to help on the wards. She was pretty sure if it was Sister Kay, she would have said something. Dr. Wilcox was old fashioned in his views, so few nurses stood up to him, including Sister McPherson. Nothing more was said.

The group moved to another patient and Sophie went to Nurse Harrington, whose eyes were flashing brilliant green. Sophie wasn't sure if it was fear or indignation.

"Don't be alarmed. You are doing a great job," Sophie leaned in and whispered. "My opinion of this doctor is the same as yours. Full of his own importance."

"But I didn't say anything."

"You didn't have to. I saw it in your eyes."

"What if I …I lose the patient."

"It happens, but you are doing your best, making the patient comfortable, keeping her fever down and comforting her worries. You cannot do anything more and, if the patient does not recover, it is God's will."

Sophie continued her work on the ward. Although the number of patients had lessened and fewer were being admitted, most patients were very ill. It reminded her of the Casualty Clearing Hospital. The men were nearly always cheerful, even those who were dying, and there was a certain expectation of death but here, in a civilian hospital, recovery was expected, not death. Yet she knew a few of these patients would not make it through the night. The empty beds were not due to patients being discharged.

Two days later, Sophie was pleased to see patients recovering and fewer deaths. Nurse Harrington's patient had survived as had many others. Sister Kay had enough evidence to write a report for the board of governors, proposing better use be made of probationers' time and skills, which would result in faster recovery and fewer deaths.

Having finished the report Sophie and Sister Kay left the crummy basement office. Sister Kay headed to the admin office with the report and Sophie met Hillary in the lobby. She enjoyed walking with Hillary, hearing about her studies and blatant opposition from both her fellow students and lecturers or doctors, although Dr Wilcox had finally complimented her on her knowledge. It made Sophie wonder if the man appreciated a challenge and perhaps respected women more than he was admitting. Hillary did not agree.

Cook had already been informed that Sophie was eating out with Andrew and she waited for him in the sitting room until she heard the motorcar pull up.

Andrew kissed her and opened the motorcar door. "Beer and steak pie awaits at the *Rose & Crown.*"

"I'm hungry. Cook made a stew tonight and the aroma has been teasing me for the past half hour," Sophie said, settling in her seat.

Andrew ordered two pies with chips and carried two half pints to the table. "Only half?" Sophie said.

"I'm not overly thirsty tonight."

Sophie took a sip of beer and looked at Andrew, whose

colour had not returned to normal. When they last met, he'd implied he wasn't sleeping well. She thought it had been the unpleasantness at the club, but there seemed to be no explanation today.

"Are you having trouble sleeping?" Sophie asked with concern.

He began to cough and took in a deep jagged breath. "This cough kept me awake last night, and it was a busy day. They are closing some of the military hospitals in Europe, so we've had an influx of new patients. I've been doing assessments all day." He took Sophie's hand and squeezed it. "Don't worry. I'm fine. Just a bit of a cold. How was your day?"

"Interesting. Sister Kay was very complimentary and I'm really enjoying working with the new nurses. We are establishing a new program, pending the governors' approval. It has been busy with pneumonia cases, but seems a little better, and the probationers have been helping us on the ward."

"You know your eyes light up when you talk about nursing and the new nurses. You are passionate about your work. Not many are, you know."

"I have an excellent teacher in Sister Kay and even stuffy old Dr. Wilcox keeps me on my toes." Sophie laughed.

"Wilcox is so old fashioned. He actually suggested my patient wouldn't understand our conversation." Andrew laughed. "An intelligent experienced colonel…" Andrew stopped talking as a bout of coughing took over.

"Andrew, that is not a cold." She went to put her hand on his forehead but was interrupted by two plates of pie and chips.

"Stop fussing. I just got something caught in my throat. Now eat up while it's hot."

Sophie watched him eat his pie, which was good that he had an appetite, but she was by no means convinced he was alright. He had stopped coughing, but there were beads of sweat on his forehead

"I'm pleased Sister is happy with your work. What else did she say?"

Sophie laughed. "She suggested I spend less time at the club. Implying it might interfere with my work. I told her I'd already decided on that subject. I didn't say it was your suggestion."

"Why? Does she think marrying me will distract you from your work?"

"That's an odd question. She's never mentioned our marriage since the day I told her I intended to keep nursing. You do understand, I will not give up nursing." Sophie's words came out with more emphasis than she intended.

"Absolutely. I would never ask you to give up nursing. Remember, I said we would be a very modern couple." He leaned over to kiss her but started coughing again. He was close enough for Sophie to feel his forehead.

"Andrew, you have a fever. I'd say around 102. Don't tell me you're fine." She couldn't keep the irritation out of her voice. She wanted to be sympathetic, but his denial was annoying. "I'm taking you home right now."

"All right. I don't feel well but I didn't want to miss our night out. A good night's sleep and I'll be fine."

Andrew drove home and Sophie insisted on coming in with him. She wished him goodnight and sent him off to his room and knocked on Mrs. Humphries' private sitting room door.

"I'm sorry to disturb you, but I wanted to let you know that Andrew, Dr. Cuthbert, is not well."

"Not well? Whatever is the matter?" Mrs. Humphries' face creased with worry.

"He has a cough and a fever. I sent him to bed. Would you mind taking him some water? He needs to drink, and give him an aspirin if you have any. And, Mrs. Humphries, if he isn't any better in the morning, I think he should see a doctor. I'm quite worried about him."

"Don't you worry, Miss Romano. I will take care of him. I have some aspirin and I'll make him some hot lemon and honey to ease the cough."

"I doubt he will, but he should take a few days off work too," Sophie said.

"He'll not get past me to that door, unless he makes a miraculous recovery. Don't worry, lass. You get off to bed. I'll look after him."

Sophie walked to River House, worried that Andrew's symptoms were much more than a cold, but she had every confidence that he was being well looked after.

# Not Always as it Seems

The bed shook violently. Sophie panicked and opened her eyes. "Oh Hillary, I must have been dreaming. I thought there was an earthquake.

"You were dead to the world. Me shaking you was the earthquake. It is late."

Sophie sat up on her elbows. "What time is it? Did I sleep through my alarm clock?"

"It's a quarter to seven. What happened? It's not like you to oversleep."

"I was awake most of the night, worried about Andrew. I took him home last night with a terrible cough. I must call Mrs. Humphries and find out how he is today."

"You don't have time. You have fifteen minutes to get dressed and have breakfast. I'm sure Mrs. Humphries is taking care of him. Call from the hospital." Hillary took her uniform from the wardrobe. "Here. Get dressed. I'll go grab a tea and some toast. You can eat on the way. Cook won't be pleased, but at least you won't be late."

Sophie gulped down a couple of mouthfuls of tea and put a slice of toast in her mouth as they walked out of River House. She could hear Cook tut-tutting as the door closed behind them.

Hillary waved, running down the underground steps and Sophie ran to the Bartley, flinging her cape in the nurse lounge. She'd put it away later. Brushing her uniform and taking a calming breath, she arrived on the ward. A tired looking night nurse was pleased to see her.

"I'm sorry I'm late. I overslept. Has Sister arrived yet?"

"No. Sister McPherson is off today and Sister Kay has a meeting with Matron. She'll be late. Nothing to report. Mrs. Lamb had a bad night, but she's sleeping now. The charts are all done."

"Where's Nurse Belingham?" Sophie checked around the ward. An orderly was delivering the breakfast tray, but she was the only nurse.

"I don't know. She's late too." The nurse yawned. "I was beginning to think I had to work a double shift. If that's all, I need to get some sleep."

"Of course. Sorry. I didn't intend to keep you. Have a good rest."

She watched the nurse leave, hoping to see Trixie running to the ward, but the corridor was empty. Taking a large gulp of air, she gave a long, slow sigh, her eyes going from one bed to the next. *Okay, where to start,* Sophie thought to herself. *I'll start with temperatures. Trixie, where are you?*

Sophie wheeled her trolley around the ward and was relieved that most patients were getting better. Mrs. Lamb's pneumonia was getting worse as was the pain in her leg injury. But Sophie had to wait for doctor's rounds to increase the dose of morphine. *Oh gosh, doctor's rounds. I can imagine Dr. Wilcox's sarcastic remarks with no nurses on the ward and Mrs. Lamb in distress.*

"Nurse Romano, are you alone?" Sister Kay asked, as she

entered the ward. "Where is Nurse Belingham?"

"I am alone. I don't understand why Nurse Belingham isn't here. I was hoping you would know. I've done the temperatures and they are all good, except Mrs. Lamb. She needs attention. Her fever is high."

Sister shook her head. "Carry on. Treat Mrs. Lamb and I'll find some help."

Sophie sat beside Mrs. Lamb, gently cooling her brow. Her deathly white face relaxed as she felt the soothing cloth. It was never easy to watch the life leech out of a patient. Some patients with the will to live could rally and recover. Sophie knew it would not be long for Mrs. Lamb. A widow of many years, with her only son killed in the war, she had no fight left.

Her lips moved and Sophie bent to listen. "Don't fret, Nurse. I see in ya' eyes how much you care. I'm ready to meet my Ernie and my boy. We'll be a family again. Thank you, and that young lady yesterday. You are kind. I just want to rest awhile before I go."

"Shush. Save your strength." Sophie lifted her up on the pillow to ease her breathing and gently wiped her shoulders and arms to cool her skin. She had a smile on her face as she slept and looked peaceful for the first time in days. The coughing had stopped and her laboured breaths eased, making Sophie wonder if she might recover.

"Sister Kay sent me to help. What would you like me to do?" Nurse Fox breezed into the ward. Sophie smiled. The girl was like a ping-pong ball, incapable of walking at a normal pace, bouncing from one thing to another, and frequently being reprimanded for running. But, she got things done, and in record time.

"Sit with Mrs. Lamb. Let her sleep and sponge her, if necessary, while I get the medicine trolly."

"Isn't she Nurse 'arrington's patient?"

Sophie gave her a puzzled look. "Nurse Harrington did nurse her yesterday, but patients do not belong to any nurse in particular. We treat all patients. Generally, you give as much time as the patients need. Mrs. Lamb is very ill and needs extra time. Actually, she just needs someone to be with her. Can you do that?"

"Yes, Nurse. I don't wanna get on the wrong side of her, that's all."

"Just do as I ask. Please." Sophie's response was short but she really did not have the energy to deal with squabbling nurses.

Sister Kay returned with a nurse from the orthopaedic ward and Nurse Harrington, who was, to Sophie's surprise, indignant that Nurse Fox was with Mrs. Lamb. Sister Kay ordered the morning routine to be completed, checking her timepiece. Doctor's rounds were due to start in half an hour.

"Any word from Trixie, I mean Nurse Belingham?" Sophie asked.

"She has food poisoning and will be off for the rest of the day. Matron suggested she take tomorrow too."

"Poor Trixie. I hope she is not alone. She no longer lives at River House. They have their own rooms and her husband is often on the base."

"I believe it was her husband who notified the hospital. Now, beds have to be changed and patients washed. We have work to do. Get a move on!"

Sophie finished writing up the charts and handed them to the next shift when she noticed Nurse Harrington was at Mrs. Lamb's bedside. "Where's Nurse Fox?"

"I asked to take over. I can't leave her." Nurse Harrington's eyes filled with tears.

Sophie took the patient's pulse, so faint she could hardly feel it. She sat beside them and waited. Mrs. Lamb passed away, still smiling. "She's gone." Sophie put her arm on Nurse Harrington's shoulders, giving her a sympathetic smile. "Now, record the time and update the chart. The evening shift will take over."

"I'm sorry for crying. I expect you are used to it."

Sophie helped her put on her cape and took her hand, "You did well today. A good nurse mourns her patients. It is nothing to feel ashamed about, but we have to be professional and not distress the other patients. That means keeping our emotions in check until you are off the ward."

"Oh, I didn't think about that."

"You are not expected to know everything. Come, walk with me to River House and we can talk on the way." Sophie led the way to the lobby. "It is something you never quite get used to, but death is as much a part of nursing, as treating the sick and life itself. It's important that we are stoic, but respectful."

"I felt it my responsibility to nurse Mrs. Lamb until she got better. It feels as though I failed, like I always do." Tears trickled down her cheeks and her shoulders slumped and curved more than usual, in an attempt to make her look small. Sophie had the sense she was not just talking about Mrs. Lamb.

"Clarice, one thing you learn early is to be impartial. Being overprotective or becoming attached to patients never ends well. Nurse Fox seemed to be concerned that she would upset you if she nursed Mrs. Lamb. Why was that?"

"I didn't want to get the blame if she made a mistake. I wanted to do a good job, but I guess I failed, like always."

"You are not failing. You are new, young, and have a lot to learn. So far, you are doing well. Have you had a bad experience at the hospital?" Sophie was thinking of the terrible treatment the old sister-tutor gave the probationers.

She shook her head. "No, but they all expect me to fail, except my brother. My mother ignored me. Said I was too plain and had my head into too many books. My older sisters are both beautiful and found suitable husbands. I'm the ugly sister and not good for anything. My mother wanted to marry me off to an old man." She scowled with disgust. "I refused and told her I wanted to be a nurse. She laughed and my father lost his temper and threatened to throw me out. Edwin was furious and threatened to walk out if he spoke to me like that again. Then he helped me apply for the nurses' program here." Clarice took a sudden breath and concern creased her face. "I've said too much. Please, don't tell the other girls, especially Dotty. Please!"

"My lips are sealed. Thank you for confiding in me. I hope you find some friends and encouragement here. You and Nurse Fox get along well. Perhaps she will be your first friend and supporter. You can support each other."

"I like her, but she's lower class from London's east end. My parents would not approve. It's as though I've known her all my life. She's alone, since her mother died. I don't feel sorry for her. She was lucky her mother cared about her." Sophie caught a flash of jealousy in her green eyes.

"Um …sometimes you need to compromise." *This will certainly be a strange friendship,* Sophie thought. *I'm not sure Clarice can overcome her privileged background, even though she is at odds with it. Poor girl has so much growing up to do.* "Why nursing? Are you passionate about it, or was it a way to get away from home, or a little of both?"

"Edwin. He served in the medical corps in the war. He told me how wonderful the nurses were and he thought I would make a good one. Edwin has always seen things in me that no one else sees. I'm not sure about being passionate. Dotty is passionate about nursing. She's a good example."

"She is and you need to give it some thought. Here we are. Cook's looking for us through the window. We had better hurry. Before we go in, please know you can come to me anytime, Clarice."

Clarice gave Sophie a smile with more warmth than she'd seen before and yet there was still a hint of mistrust.

Cook was indeed waiting for them. Dinner was seven sharp and the delay at the hospital and sauntering home meant that they were a few minutes late. Sophie gave Cook a brief explanation for their tardiness, which was accepted among a considerable amount of tut-tutting. Everyone seated at the table, Cook carried a large casserole of macaroni and cheese to the table. Everyone sucked in the amazing cheesy aroma. This was one of Cook's specialties and, judging by the quietness of the dinner table, very much appreciated.

Sophie pulled herself up the stairs, so tired she could barely walk and flopped on her bed. "What a day!"

"Knock, knock," Hillary closed the door. "A bad day? You look exhausted."

"Just very busy. Trixie was off with food poisoning and the

ward is busy. Nurse Harington needed some extra care after a patient died. Just one of those days."

"How's Andrew?"

Sophie gasped. "I can't believe it. I forgot to call him. I never stopped all day. Fine bride I am, forgetting my sick fiancé. Wait here. I'll call now."

She ran down stairs and called Mrs. Humphries but she didn't like what she heard. Rubbing her forehead, she returned to her room.

"So, what did she say?"

"Andrew tried to go to work this morning, but she made him go back to bed. He still has a fever and a cough. She sounded worried."

"Did you speak to Andrew? Mrs. Humphries is a bit of a mother hen and you mentioned Andrew was her favourite. Maybe she is overreacting."

"No, he was sleeping so I said not to disturb him. I'll call in the morning. She promised to call if there was any change. If he's no better tomorrow, I'll call the doctor."

Six o'clock the next morning, Sophie knocked on Hillary's door to say she was leaving early, intending to call at Andrew's digs on the way to the hospital. Cook was not pleased when she refused breakfast. She couldn't explain the bad feeling she had and telephone calls were not enough. She had to see him and make sure he was all right.

She walked with determination, as she practised what she would say to convince Andrew he needed a doctor. That was going to be difficult. Mrs. Humphries answered the door, her irritation obvious at an early morning caller. Seeing Sophie, she lightened up. "Good morning, Miss Romano. You'll be wanting to know how Dr. Cuthbert is doing. Come in and have a cup of tea." She leaned in and whispered, "He says he's better but I think he should stay in bed one more day at least. He's in the dining room."

"I'll talk to him, see what I can do," Sophie whispered back.

"Good morning, darling. How are you feeling? Are you sure you should be out of bed?"

"Good morning, Sophie. So many questions so early in the morning and why are you here?" He sounded flat, in spite of his obvious effort to be cheerful.

Sophie studied his face and did not like his pallor. Although he was not flushed with fever, his raspy voice and jerky breaths sounded terrible.

"Andrew, you do not look well. You need to stay in bed for another day or two. How's the cough?"

"My dear Sophie, I have a cold. The cough has almost gone and see …" He put his hand to his forehead, "no fever." The effort of talking made him breathless and he started coughing. "See … now you …made me cough." He tried to laugh, either to cover up the cough, or maybe the laughing had prompted the coughing.

"Andrew!" Sophie said with exasperation. "You are a doctor. You know you are ill."

"Exactly. I am a doctor with a cold and I am fine. Now, sit down with me and have a cup of tea and a slice of toast with Mrs. H's marmalade."

"Mrs. H's marmalade wins." She rested her head on Andrew's shoulder, deliberately to hear his chest. Andrew took her head in his hands and kissed her, but not before she heard what she was sure was a rattling chest. "Will you not consider staying home just one more day?"

"I have patients to see, but what I will promise is that I will come home early." He kissed her again. "Eat up your toast and I'll drive you to the Bartley.

Sophie reluctantly agreed. Waving goodbye, as he drove off, she had a terrible sinking feeling in her stomach. Andrew behaved as though he was getting better, but she knew he was covering something up. He had no fever. His chest rattled, but that could be the cold. He seemed alright, but he wasn't. She hoped the doctors or Matron at Spring Gardens would see it too and send him home. *Should I call Matron with my concerns? No, he'd never forgive me. I'll have to wait and call at his digs on my way home.* Resigned there was nothing more she could do, Sophie started her shift on the Women's Ward, expecting another busy day as Trixie was still not back.

# Dark Nights

The orderly placed a cup of hot tea on the nurses' desk. "Thank you," Sophie said, yawning. The first couple of nights on the night shift were always a challenge. Sophie found it difficult to get into the routine of sleeping during the day, every little sound waking her up. It didn't help that she was worried about Andrew.

Matron Mills had insisted he see one of the doctors at the Spring Gardens Hospital. The diagnosis was a chest infection and the treatment bed rest. She had spoken to Mrs. Humphries. He was in good hands but it didn't stop her worrying, for two reasons: his health and the wedding, which was less than two weeks away. In spite of his insistence, he would be better by then, Sophie was not convinced. Everyone kept telling her he'd be alright and not to worry, the wedding would go ahead as planned. An unease grew inside her, and she no longer had a vision of her wedding day. It had completely disappeared as though there had been no wedding planned in the first place.

Hillary wrote it off as wedding nerves. Trixie reported she had felt the same way and it would be fine in the end. And, there was another thing. Trixie was not well. She had not fully recovered from food poisoning. The thought of food made her bilious and the lack of nourishment made her weak and pale. What was happening to everyone?

Trixie was due to relieve her in half an hour. Sophie completed the charts and closed her eyes, hoping that the tiredness she felt now would still be there when she arrived home to sleep. Most mornings the walk woke her up and Cook's breakfast filled her with energy. She decided she would visit Andrew after breakfast and sleep later.

"Good morning!" Trixie called cheerfully. "How was the night?"

"Trixie, good to see you. A quiet night. The charts are all done." Sophie looked up to see Trixie pale and very anxious. "Whatever is wrong? Are you unwell?"

She shook her head. "I'm feeling better. It's not me. I bumped into Dr. Wilcox on my way here. It's Andrew. He was admitted to the Men's Ward during the night and he's not doing well. Dr. Wilcox asked that you meet him on the ward as soon as possible."

"Andrew's here in the Bartley and Dr. Wilcox wants to see me?" Sophie repeated parrot-like. "I'll be back for my things."

She ran down the corridor, and up a flight of stairs to the Men's Ward. Seeing Dr. Wilcox at the nurses' desk, she stopped to compose herself, expecting the worst.

"Ah! Nurse Romano, a word please." He guided her back out into the corridor and lowered his voice. "I believe Dr. Cuthbert is your fiancé. He has been asking for you. As a professional courtesy, I wanted to explain my findings."

"What happened? The doctor at Spring Gardens said it was a chest infection and he needed rest."

"I'm afraid it is more than a chest infection. You are a nurse and I need to be honest with you. The infection has gone beyond his chest and I suspect sepsis."

Sophie leaned against the wall, her knees feeling weak. Few people survived sepsis. Suddenly she was angry with Andrew, for not taking care of himself. Had he taken care of the infection early, this may never have happened.

"Your prognosis, Doctor?"

"The same as yours, Nurse." He gave her a sympathetic, knowing glance. "As you are aware, there is no treatment. It is up to the patient to fight and some patients do survive. Dr. Cuthbert is a fighter." He smiled, but there was no reassurance. "I have ordered round the clock nursing and fluids. As far as I can see, his organs are still working and, if we can stop it spreading, he has a chance. I have given you permission to stay as long as you wish. Encourage him to fight this terrible disease. I wish I could offer more."

Blinking back tears, Sophie managed to squeak out, "Thank you. I'll go to him now."

"I will return after rounds. I have left instructions to be called if there is any change. Nurse Romano, you are a brave lady with more courage than I've seen in a woman. Use every ounce of it and pray." His words were genuine and surprised Sophie.

Andrew lay very still. Sophie stared at his chest to make sure he was breathing. The nurse in attendance stopped mopping his brow when she saw Sophie. "Please continue. I'm Dr. Cuthbert's fiancée. I'm not here as a nurse. I'm in uniform because I just finished my shift on the Women's Ward."

"He's very poorly." She hesitated.

"I know. I spoke with Dr. Wilcox. Has he lost consciousness?"

She shook her head. "Sleeping."

Sophie took his hand. "Andrew, I'm here darling." She stroked his arm, wet with perspiration.

"Sophie, I'm sorry …" Andrew whispered.

She squeezed his hand. "I will get mad with you later, but right now you need to fight for your life. How are you feeling?"

"I'm… so … so tired, Sophie I love you … if I …" Andrew's voice faded and Sophie bent forward to hear.

"Shush." She eased him up and placed the water glass to his lips. "You need to drink. Doc said lots of fluids." Andrew coughed, spilling the water. Sophie pushed another pillow behind him, persuading him to take more water. He shook his head, coughing. She gently eased him back on the pillow, his eyes closed. She felt his arm again and called an orderly to bring her water and a cloth.

Sophie glanced at the nurse. "My name is Sophie, Nurse Romano. What is your name?"

"Jill Clark. My last year in training. I'm pleased to meet you. I've heard a lot about you. I'm a friend of Clarice Harrington. We went to boarding school together. She talks about you all the time. She really likes you. I am terribly sorry for Dr. Cuthbert, he's very poorly."

"I know. All we can do is keep him cool and bring that temperature down. He's a fighter, so he has a good chance." Sophie's voice sounded firm and far more confident than she felt. Talking to Jill as a nurse, she was able to distance herself, and treat Andrew as a patient, making it easier to cope.

The orderly handed Sophie a bowl of water and several cloths. "Thank you. We need ice in the water to keep it cold. See if they have some in the kitchen." The orderly gave her a strange look, but did as he was asked.

Sister McPherson accompanied Dr. Wilcox on morning rounds. He was pleased to see Andrew's temperature, although high, had not increased since his morning visit. He nodded a smile to Sophie and spoke to Sister, before moving down the ward. Sister lingered.

"Nurse Romano, Dr. Wilcox wants you to get some rest." She put her hand up as Sophie attempted to speak. "I understand you don't want to go home, so I suggest you go to the canteen and get a cup of tea and something to eat. Can you do that for me?"

Sophie hesitated, but tea sounded good and Andrew seemed stable. "I'll go first and then Nurse Clark can take a break too."

Sister nodded and joined Dr. Wilcox's entourage.

The sound of her footsteps in the corridor seemed to bounce in her ears as she headed to the nurses' lounge. She felt lightheaded and decided tea and a rest was all she needed. Beth Filly was in the lounge, making tea, and offered her a cup.

"You look exhausted. I heard about Dr. Cuthbert. How is he?" Beth asked, passing her a cup and saucer.

"He's stable for now." Sophie sat on the sofa, afraid if she lay down, she would fall asleep. She could only rest for a few minutes.

Beth produced an egg sandwich and gave Sophie half, plus two ginger biscuits. Sophie welcomed the sandwich and biscuits. She found even Beth's idle chatter a pleasure. Nodding occasionally as she ate and sipped her tea, she was surprised how much better she felt. The light-headedness had gone and she didn't even feel tired. Thanking Beth, she went back to see Andrew.

Sophie stayed with Andrew until the afternoon. His condition had not changed, which was a good sign, and she went back to River House to get some sleep. She returned to the Bartley early for her shift to check on Andrew. The night nurse promised to let her know if there was any change.

It seemed the crisis of pneumonia cases had peaked and the Women's Ward was back to normal and particularly quiet. A situation most nurses relished, but not that night. She sat at the nurses' desk, reading the charts. Andrew kept flashing in her mind. He was seriously ill and, although he hadn't gotten any worse, he had not improved either.

What would she do if Andrew died? She had faced death many times before. Her mother's passing, although she remembered little about that. Her father's death had broken her heart, as did losing her friends in the Passchendaele bombing. But life went on. The wedding would be off and she would miss him, but her life wouldn't change very much. Was that normal, she wondered. *I am not thinking straight, I would be devastated if Andrew died. He's a bright light of friendship. I trust him and we get along so well together. There's nothing not to like about Andrew. 'A good solid gentleman,' as my father would say.* She smiled at the memory of her father, always there for her. Andrew had the same qualities. She felt safe with him, as she did with her father. What she couldn't figure out, was if this was a good thing to base a marriage on.

Checking the time, Sophie did her rounds. Everyone was sleeping. She checked the supply cupboard and busied herself with anything to pass the time, glad to see the first signs of dawn. There was no news from the Men's Ward, so she hoped Andrew had had a good night.

Finally, she was relieved from duty by the day nurse; not

Trixie, as it was her day off.

Andrew's fever had broken during the night and she was both surprised and delighted to see him open his eyes. His pale face smiled as she walked to his bedside.

"Andrew, you are awake. How do you feel?"

"A little better. Tired and weak. Dr. Wilcox says I'm over the worst. He implied I was some sort of miracle, which he attributes to you."

"Me! I just wanted you to fight and you did." Sophie gave him a stern look. "You are not out of the woods yet. It will take a long time to get your strength back." She hesitated, not sure whether to say what was on her mind. "Andrew, you are not going to be well enough…"

"I know. This has given me a scare and I agree to be sensible. That means we have to postpone the wedding. I'm sorry."

"We can rebook it for next month. You'll be better by then." Sophie was trying to sound cheerful, but felt apprehensive.

"Let's not rebook until we've talked to Dr. Wilcox. Maybe we'll take our time and see how I'm doing," Andrew said with something like hesitation in his voice.

Puzzled, Sophie said, "Whatever you feel is best."

"I need to rest. Come back and see me later, please!"

"Of course. I'm going to get some sleep and I'll come back this afternoon before my shift." Sophie bent down and kissed him. "Do as you are told and rest." Andrew smiled, giving her a salute, followed by blowing a kiss.

Grateful to be able to get some sleep and feeling relief that Andrew would get better, Sophie walked to River House. She had lots of questions in her head and she couldn't make sense of any of them.

By the time she arrived at River House, her anxiety was

almost overwhelming. She had been relieved of one kind of tension, only to feel herself tighten with even more, and she had no idea where it came from.

She knocked on Hillary's door, delighted when she opened it.

"Do you have time to talk?" Sophie said, not sure if Hillary was leaving for university or studying.

"Of course, I do. No classes today. I'm studying for exams, but I could do with a break."

Sophie laughed. "At eight in the morning, I think you have just started. I appreciate the falsehood."

"How is Andrew?" Hillary said, her voice sorrowful. "Is that what you want to talk about?"

Tears filled Sophie eyes, precipitated by the kindness in Hillary's voice. The emotions of the last twenty-four hours were on the brink of bursting into a cascading waterfall. She didn't know where to start. Hillary gave her a hug.

"My dear friend Sophie, did something terrible happen?" Releasing the hug, she waited for Sophie's answer.

Sophie shook her head, rubbing the tears from her face, futile as it was. More tears continued to flow. She took a deep breath, at least able to calm the sobbing.

"Oh no! His fever broke this morning, even Dr. Wilcox called it a miracle, quite expecting something terrible to happen." She sat on the side of the bed. The tears released the tension. Sophie had not realized how frightened and anxious she had been and now she felt confusion.

"He was awake and well enough to talk to me. We both agreed to postpone the wedding."

"You must be disappointed, but it is for the best. Don't worry, I'll deal with all that. When is the new date?"

"Hillary, that is the odd thing. I suggested we make it at the end of next month, giving him plenty of time to recover. Andrew wouldn't set a new date. He wants to wait until he's better."

"Dear Sophie, that isn't odd at all. He needs time to recover. Andrew has always been overwhelmed with wedding plans. It is too much for him right now."

"Overwhelmed? I have been so consumed by everything in my life that I didn't see it. I made it so much worse, asking him to take on more. He never said a word to me. How could I have been so insensitive?"

"Sometimes the closer we are, the less we see. You and Andrew are so alike, you both work too hard and care too much about your patients." Hillary paused. "And not enough about each other."

"We care very much about each other," Sophie replied, indignant at Hillary's remark. "Sometimes, in Passchendaele, we worked together with patients. I liked working with him, being with him, talking to him, solving the puzzles of the mind. I think I miss that comradeship. And you are right, we are alike." Sophie found her thoughts drifting into what might be a hidden corner of her mind. "Hillary, is that enough to base a marriage on? Am I doing the right thing?"

"You and Andrew are a perfect couple. You are tired. You have been through an ordeal. What you need is rest and I need to get back to my studies."

Sophie nodded her agreement, only too aware that sleep would not be forthcoming.

# Recovery

It took Andrew two long weeks to recover well enough to be discharged from the hospital into Mrs. Humphries' care. His pallor, weight loss and what seemed like melancholia, distressed Sophie. Medically, he had recovered from the disease, but she worried. The effects of the illness either lingered inside him or perhaps, had taken something away.

Very much aware of how much Andrew hated being in hospital, doctors rarely made good patients, she worried about his overall apathetic demeanour, something she had never seen in him before. She hoped that once home, Mrs. Humphries' attentive care, home cooking and cheerfulness would bring him back to his old self.

Andrew's convalescence added yet another task to her already busy life. Every evening, after her shift, she took a detour to see Andrew and often stayed for dinner. He was gaining weight and his colour was almost normal. He tried hard to be cheerful, but he could not hide the underlying apathy.

Sophie had the strangest sense of dread, almost a bad omen feeling and yet, as much as she searched for a cause, nothing seemed to fit. Certainly, the wedding was cause for concern.

A new date had not been set, but it was easily explained by Andrew's slow recovery, which hopefully, also explained his lack of desire to return to his patients. She sensed he was pulling away from her, although it may have had more to do with the fact that they had so little time alone. Mrs. Humphries protected Andrew as one of her own and rarely left them alone, making intimate conversation impossible. Grateful as she was for Mrs. Humphries dedication to Andrew, she wondered if he was enjoying the care and attention a bit too much.

Sophie's feet hurt from a long day on the ward. Happy to be back on day shift, she was still adjusting her sleep pattern. Some kind of union riot near Hyde Park had filled the Casualty Department to overflowing with knife wounds, head injuries and broken knuckles. Two women, caught in the riot or maybe taking part in the riot, were admitted to Sophie's ward. Angry hate filled the women, both with foul mouths and knife wounds. They'd screamed and yelled incoherent chants about injustice, until the doctor was called to sedate them both.

The chaos meant a delay in leaving the hospital, but now she could breathe easier and was on the way to Mrs. Humphries. *My dogs are barking.* She chuckled at the modern description. She had notice strange flapper expressions slipping into her vocabulary, picked up mostly from the club. It had been a long time since she had had fun at the club. Hillary's time was spent studying and Trixie's health kept her at home most evenings. Sophie's time off was spent with Andrew, who was in no fit state to do anything. Perhaps that's what he needs, a night out to cheer him up.

Andrew and the other boarders were all at the dining room

table when Sophie walked in, an empty chair set especially for her. Mrs. Humphries already considered her one of the boarders. Had she and Andrew married as planned, she would indeed be living here.

"Sit yourself down," Mrs. Humphries said, placing a steaming steak and kidney pie in the middle of the table. "You look peaky, Nurse Romano."

"A busy day. We had some injured patients from the riot at Hyde Park." Sophie glanced at Andrew, sitting next to her. He gave her a weak smile. Sophie searched for his hand under the table and gave it a squeeze.

"I don't hold with those riots. People get hurt," Mrs. Humphries said, as she cut and served the pie. "If they paid them fair wages, there would be no need for riots. Help yourselves to spuds and beans, fresh from the garden next door. Now eat up while it's hot." She served herself a plate and marched back into the kitchen.

Sophie cleared away the pudding plates and everyone but Andrew, left the table. She took his hand, leading him to the lounge for a few minutes of alone time while Mrs. Humphries did the dishes and tidied the kitchen.

"How are you feeling today?" Sophie leaned forward and kissed his forehead.

"Much better, but still tired. It seems I can't get enough sleep."

"I think you need cheering up," she said, forcing extra cheerfulness into her voice.

"What do you have in mind? Just sitting next to you cheers me up."

"Let's go out. We haven't been to the Kingfisher since before you became ill."

Andrew stared at her in horror but did not reply.

"All right, maybe the Kingfisher is too much to start. How about a walk to the *Rose & Crown* for a pint?" Glancing towards the kitchen, Sophie added, "We could get some privacy and talk about the wedding, you going back to work or the crazy day I had on the ward."

"We can talk here. We can go to my room."

"You know Mrs. Humphries won't allow us alone in your bedroom."

"She'll have to when we're married."

"But we are not married. I'd like to talk to my fiancé without someone else's opinions interrupting us." Irritation clipped Sophie's words, said louder than she intended. She lowered her voice to a whisper. "Andrew, I want to be alone with you."

"We won't be alone in a public place and I don't feel up to it."

"When will you be *up to it*?" All of a sudden something snapped. She was tired of treading carefully, choosing her words so as not to upset Andrew. Unedited words tumbled out of her. "What has happened to you? Dr. Wilcox says you are fully recovered and yet you show no interest in going back to Spring Gardens and I'm sure they need you. You sit around here being coddled by Mrs. Humphries. You won't take me out, not even to the pub. I had a terrible day and you ignored me. I don't understand. Please explain to me what is wrong? Is it me? Have I upset you?"

Andrew looked at her with moist eyes and ran his fingers through his hair. "I'm not myself. I can't explain and I'm sorry. I need more time. Time to think and work things out."

"Fine. I'll leave you to think, if that is what you want." She cleared her throat to hide her own tears. "It's my day off tomorrow. If you want to see me and maybe go somewhere, telephone River House." She kissed him on the cheek, turned and walked out of the front door, tears dripping gently onto her cheeks. She avoided Mrs. Humphries, who would want an explanation and there wasn't one.

She couldn't be certain what had prompted the tears. Was it the sense of something ending, Andrew's malaise or something lost? Walking beside the River Thames, relishing the cool night air on her hot, tear strained cheeks, she stopped and leaned on the Embankment wall. She watched the barges and envied their journey to a known destination. Dusk coloured the western sky pink as the sun disappeared and the lights glistened in the grey waters of the Thames.

The peaceful scene was in contrast to the anger and frustration that churned inside her and filled her with guilt. Something was wrong. Andrew was ill, not physically but, dare she admit what had been lingering in her thoughts, suffering from a disturbance in his mind. She had seen this during the war; a soldier whose injuries healed, but they cared for nothing, lost interest in everything, despondent and afraid of the future. These were the soldiers Andrew treated and made better. Was this happening to Andrew?

Sophie opened the door of River House, delighted to see Hillary sitting alone at the dining room table finishing a cup of tea. Hillary took one look at Sophie and, like the true friend she was, quietly poured her a cup of tea

"Do you want to talk about it?"

"Hillary, something is wrong with Andrew. He needs the best doctor in the house. Except he is the best doctor for what ails him."

"Are you saying he needs a psychiatrist?"

Sophie nodded and explained Andrew's behaviour and their exchange of words.

"It could just be the after effects of the illness. Why don't we ask Chris to go visit him? Maybe he needs a friend. We could visit Trixie and see what she thinks."

"If you saw him, you would know it is more than effects of the illness. He needs a doctor, not a friend. But, Chris is sensible and might convince him he needs help. Okay! Let's go now."

"Slow down. May we telephone first?"

Sophie immediately went to the hall telephone and had a long conversation. Even Cook appeared from the kitchen, shaking her finger. Although the telephone was essential for the nurses, long personal calls were frowned upon because of the expense.

"I'll pay for the call," Sophie called to Cook, as she hung up the phone.

Sophie nodded towards the stairs and Hillary followed her to her room. Hillary jumped on the bed and sat cross-legged. Sophie sat in the chair, her feet up on the bed, feeling calmer and more relaxed after talking to both Trixie and Chris.

"So, what did she say?" Hillary asked.

"We timed it right. Chris is home until tomorrow afternoon. He has offered to visit Andrew in the morning. Trixie has invited us for lunch and when Chris gets back, he can tell us how it went. I'll go visit him later. I explained my concerns. I didn't know Chris had visited Andrew several times. Funny Andrew didn't mention it. Chris said he'd seen the same lethargic person I described and, like all of us thought it would pass as he recovered."

"I'll come with you. I can catch up on my studies in the

202

evening." Hillary stood up. "I really have to go and get some reading done tonight. You look as though an early night would do you the world of good."

"I agree, and thanks, Hillary. I'll see you tomorrow."


The next morning, Andrew called Sophie and explained that Chris was paying him a visit, suggesting she visit later and, if he was well enough, they could go to the Rose & Crown. Delighted with Andrew's change of heart, she began to relax.

Her thoughts wandered to Italy as they often did when she was worried. She sighed, wishing the villa was closer and she could sit at the kitchen table and ask her mother for advice. Things made sense in the Tuscan countryside. It would be a perfect place for Andrew to convalesce, but instead of Andrew sitting next to her, the image was Carlos. Why was it that Carlos belonged there, but Andrew didn't? Her whole body stiffened. Quickly, almost violently, she pushed Carlos' image from her mind and forced herself to think of practical things about the villa.

It had been some time since she had had news of the repairs on the villa. She was concerned about the roof repairs. A leaky roof could do a lot of damage. Although Paola had not seemed concerned in her last letter, it was time to write again; writing would keep her mind occupied for the morning.

Hillary stalled her studies at noon and they shared a taxi to Trixie's new digs. Trixie, always an excitable person, seemed overly excited. She had made a wonderful lunch of Scotch eggs, ham and salad, with custard tart for pudding.

"Trixie, this is a feast. What are we celebrating?" Sophie said and received an impish shrug from Trixie, just as Chris walked in the door.

"Well, how did it go?" Sophie scanned Chris' expression for clues.

"Mostly, it went well. He was glad to see me and wanted to talk. At first it was about you, Sophie. He knows he upset you are and is sorry. We talked about getting back to work, and to my surprise there was no opposition. He said he'd thought about it and just this morning, he had called Matron Mills to discuss his return. Whatever happened between you two yesterday has had a profound effect on Andrew."

"I'm glad to hear that. I was worried. I left in bit of a huff. Actually, I was angry and Andrew didn't deserve to be spoken to like that. I wish he had told me he was contemplating going back to work, but I'm glad he told you. Did he mention the wedding or anything else?"

"No, now I think about it, he didn't mention the new date. After that, we talked about the war and my situation as a pilot and heir to the estate. My father is losing patience, plus we have new developments." He winked at Trixie. "Father wants me on the estate and I want to stay in the RAF."

"Chris, I can't thank you enough. I plan to see him later and I'll see if we can get a date for the wedding."

"Take it easy, Sophie. My advice would be to wait until another time. Men don't like to be rushed, you know," Chris said with a raised eyebrow. "One thing at a time."

"Alright. enough progress for one day. Um! This looks yummy." Sophie joined everyone at the table.

Chris opened a bottle of wine and poured everyone a glass. He took Trixie's hand and they stood together at the end of the table.

"Trixie and I have something to celebrate." Chris smiled

like the Cheshire Cat and his cheeks reddened. "We are going to have a baby."

"Oh, congratulations! This is wonderful news," Sophie said, chorused by Hillary.

"What I thought was food poisoning was morning sickness. We are very happy, but it is a little sooner than we planned. We'd appreciate it if you would keep it quiet. I'd like to keep working for a few months, at least until I show. Then Matron will probably kick me out anyway."

"How will it affect you, Chris? Probably not much as you already have permission to live off base?" Hillary asked.

"I'm afraid it will affect me tremendously, change my life actually. This will be the catalyst that Papa has been waiting for, to lure me back to the estate. We will be expected to give up our London flat and move to the estate. Ultimately, it will be the best place for Trixie and the baby but, for now, we have decided to stay here until Trixie has to resign. It means not telling either of our parents. We have to keep the baby a secret."

"What about obstetric care?" Sophie frowned. "Trixie, have you seen a midwife or doctor?"

"Don't worry, Sophie. Dr. Leamington-Smythe is my obstetrician. I saw him yesterday and he confirmed I was pregnant. He is a highly reputable Harley Street doctor and a very nice man." She giggled. "In spite of his long double-barrelled name. He understands the situation and has agreed to our secret, somewhat reluctantly. He's old-fashioned and believes women, especially pregnant ones, belong in the home. When he realized, I would continue working with or without his consent, he agreed with conditions. I have to attend regular appointments, more than usual, and to stop working if any complications arise. He gave a few other instructions about getting enough sleep and not lifting patients. I may need your help with that, Sophie. I am healthy, a bit sickly in the mornings, but that will pass." Trixie leaned into Chris and he kissed her cheek. "We are so happy."

"Well, you will have to excuse me. Duty calls. I must get back to flying." Chris shrugged his shoulders. "More secrets, I'm afraid. These flights are classified." Chris took Trixie in his arms, beaming with love and pride and kissed his wife. "See you tomorrow, darling."

# Difficult Times

Grunts and sighs came from the wardrobe, Sophie's head inside, as she flipped hangers from one side to the other. Her clothes were mostly old and worn out except for two dresses; one blue cotton dress and her green flapper style dress, which was perfect for the club, although she'd worn it so many times it was time for a new one. There was a wool skirt and two silk blouses that had seen better days. Spending most of her time in uniform, she had not realized how few clothes she owned. Her hand touched the soft smooth fabric of the Romano silk dress as she called it. She sighed again. *I'm afraid you'll have to wait a little longer for the wedding.*

That night, she wanted to look nice for Andrew, to make the evening special for his first night out. The green dress was too fancy for the pub, but the blue cotton with a white cardigan, was perfect. She brushed her hair until it shone, waved it in the front and carefully wrapped it into her neck. Every time she did this, she questioned if she should cut her hair, but always came to the same conclusion. She liked her long hair. She added a little rouge to her cheeks and, feeling quite daring, took a bright red lipstick to her lips. Checking herself in the mirror, she was pleased with the overall effect. Grabbing her umbrella and handbag, she set out to Mrs. Humphries', later than usual, having declined dinner.

Several of the boarders were still in the dining room when she arrived and they greeted her with whistles. She blushed, looking for Andrew.

"My, my, aren't we dressed up tonight," Mrs. Humphries said, with a scowl. "Mind how you go. It's not natural. Painted lips, indeed." She gave a long sigh.

"What's not natural, Mrs. H?" Andrew jumped off the last stair, looking handsome in a charcoal grey suit and white shirt. "You look lovely, Sophie." He took her arm and they walked to the *Rose & Crown.*

The pub was quiet and Sophie sat at a small round table tucked in the corner. It was an old fashioned pub, with a Nook as a separate room for unaccompanied ladies, the bar for men only and the lounge, for mixed company, where they were sitting. The wood panelling and heavy oak beams made the place feel dark, but not depressing. The whole place felt welcoming, warm and cosy. Andrew carried the drinks from the bar, smiling as he placed them on the table.

Sophie raised her glass. "Here's to our first night out. How do you feel?"

"I'm much better." He put his arm around her shoulder. "Really. You worry too much."

"I do worry about you." Her comment hung in the air and a quietness, even awkwardness, passed between them. It felt like a first date, as though they didn't know each other, not a couple about to get married.

Andrew broke the silence. "It was good to see Chris today. He told me the good news that he's going to be a father. I'm pleased for them."

"Me too, and Trixie is excited. Did Chris mention they would eventually move to the estate?"

"He did and he's resigned to it, but not happy about giving up his career. I feel for him. Being a pilot and a military career was his lifelong dream. He never expected to step into his brother's role but he's very stoic about it. I'm not sure I would be."

Sophie stared off into space. "The German attack that last day in Passchendaele changed a lot of lives. Colonel Belingham's death turned Chris from a pilot to an earl-in-waiting." Sophie sighed, glancing at Andrew whose demeanour had become sombre. "Let's change the subject. This is supposed to be a fun night."

"Death changes many things. A glimpse of death makes you wonder if life is worth it. I found myself envying those that died. What do you think?" Andrew gave a harsh humourless laugh.

"I think we are being morbid and I'd rather talk about pleasant things, like our wedding. Now you are feeling better, are you ready to make a date?" Sophie leaned in and kissed his cheek. "I have a beautiful silk dress in my wardrobe waiting for our special day."

"As always, you are right, my lovely Sophie, and you shall wear that dress very soon." He squeezed her hand, attempting a smile.

Waiting for him to name a date, she studied his face. His smile had not reached his eyes. They were still full of pain, so much so that she stifled a gasp.

"Andrew, you would tell me if something was wrong?" She paused. "You haven't changed your mind, have you?"

Andrew cleared his throat and Sophie detected a slight

hesitation, "Of course not. First, I need to get back to my patients. Give me a little time. Maybe September."

"An autumn wedding. Yes, that sounds nice. When you've settled back at the hospital, we can set a date. Are you worried about seeing patients again?"

"A little." Andrew rubbed his forehead and brushed his fingers through his hair. "Sophie, I am worried. I don't have much strength and I'm having trouble concentrating. I need to be able to listen to my patients. I'm not sure I can do that at the moment."

"You will be fine. Take it easy at first, one patient at a time. Tell the board and Matron you can only consult with less complicated cases to start with. I'm sure they'll understand. They have managed without you for the last month." Sophie held his chin and gently moved his face so she could see into his eyes. "Andrew, you are one of the best psychiatrists in London, if not the country. Most of your colleagues see less than half the patients you treat. Slowing down won't even be noticed."

"What would I do without you? It will be hard, but I have to get back." He gave a laugh. "Get back on the horse, so to speak."

"Absolutely. And the longer you leave it, the harder it will get. Mrs. Humphries is making you too comfortable."

"Ha, she is indeed. At times, she reminded me of my mother. I felt as I did when I was six years old, especially when she scolded me for not eating my vegetables. It's a nice feeling to be loved in a motherly way."

"Yes, it is. I miss my mother's advice and reassurance. What do you think your mother would say to you today?"

"I'm not sure, but I know what Doc would say. 'Enough

210

moping around, lad. Just get on with it.'" Andrew deepened his voice, making them both laugh.

"And?" Sophie said, her head to one side. "Would you take his advice?"

"Yes, I would and he'd be right. Doc was always right. I will phone Spring Gardens and have them schedule patients next week."

"You were lucky to have Doc and his wife, to support you during your father's drinking and after his death. It was the butler who took care of me when Papa died, and then Mrs. Banks, the head housekeeper at the hotel where I worked."

"Count our blessings," Andrew said giving her a hug. "It's time I counted mine, instead of feeling sorry for myself. I promise you, I will make the effort." He yawned. "I'm tired. Shall we call it a night?"

They walked back to the digs in companionable silence. Sophie was pleased with most of the evening. It had been awkward in the beginning, but turned out well. She was surprised how much Andrew had talked. At last, she could see some of the old Andrew returning.

Spring Gardens welcomed Andrew's return but the slow start only lasted for the first week. An influx of patients from overseas hospitals filled their beds. Most of the overseas military hospitals had closed. As the troops were sent home and patient numbers declined, the remaining soldiers still requiring treatment were admitted to British hospitals.

Andrew never turned anyone away, so his case load with both in and outpatients was about twice as many as the other doctors. Anxious about his health, Sophie called at Mrs.

Humphries two or three times a week. Andrew was often not there, but Mrs. Humphries assured her he was doing well; tired but otherwise fine. There was nothing she could do, except leave a message for him and hope he would call. An evening out was what she wanted. She hadn't been to the Kingfisher Club for ages. Hillary and Reggie were close to exams with no time for fun and Trixie's delicate condition prevented her from going out like they used to. Andrew wasn't keen, but she was convinced one evening would not hurt and she dragged him to the club.

The club was a mistake. Andrew was beyond tired and didn't have the energy to dance. When Sophie danced with strangers, he was jealous. Conversation was impossible, because of the loud music and finally she gave up and they got a taxi to Mrs. Humphries and walked from there to River House, so they could talk.

"Not a very fun evening," Sophie stated.

"No. I don't like the club much. I only wanted to please you," Andrew replied, brushing his fingers through his hair. "You have no idea how tired I am."

"The fact that you wouldn't dance indicated that." Sophie was annoyed. They had seen little of each other since the night in the *Rose & Crown* and that had been such a good night.

"I'm sorry I am so busy. It was impossible to take things slowly with so many new patients. There is some good news. Many of these men are ready to go home. In a few weeks the hospital will be back to treating those patients who are too ill to go home and I can get back to my research on shell-shock."

"That is good news. Do you think we can name a wedding date, now?"

"Um, yes, soon. When I get an idea of how many will be discharged and the hospital is back to normal. Mrs. Humphries is anxious too. I suggested I move into the rooms and pay her the extra rent. She can at least rent my room out then."

"That is kind of you. I'm sure Mrs. Humphries will appreciate your concern." Sophie could not help her sarcastic tone. It was as if Andrew was more concerned about his landlady than his fiancée.

"Here we are." Andrew stopped at the bottom of the steps. "It will get better. I'm on call tomorrow, but I'll telephone sometime."

"Goodnight, Andrew!" Sophie jumped up the steps before he could kiss her. His 'I'll telephone sometime' made her very angry.

Andrew waved and blew a kiss, seemingly oblivious of Sophie's dismissal and anger.

The evening did not improve, Sophie stomped up the stairs and slammed her bedroom door. Hillary came rushing into her room.

"What on earth is the matter? I have never seen you so angry."

"I'm sorry, Hillary. Andrew is, is… impossible." Sophie went on to repeat the events of the evening.

"He does sound over worked and not quite himself but that's no excuse to ignore you. Still no date for the wedding?"

Sophie shook her head. "He wants to wait until things settle down at Spring Gardens. Do you think he's changed his mind?"

"No, he's just not coping well."

"You're right. He's not coping. Hillary, I'm not sure I want to go through with this."

"Sure you do. Things are a bit difficult now, but it will straighten out." Hillary took a deep breath, as though to speak, but decided not to.

"Where are my manners? I'm so wrapped up in my affairs, I didn't ask you how the exams were going."

"Not good. I had some bad news today. I failed one of the biology exams. I don't understand." Hillary wiped tears from her cheeks. "I know I answered the questions correctly. I talked to Reggie and he passed with flying colours and I gave the same answers as he did."

"There must be some mistake," Sophie said with a comforting arm on Hillary's shoulder.

"Reggie wants me to go to the Dean and ask for the exam to be remarked."

"You can do that?"

"Yes, but this professor already hates me. If I challenge him, he will refuse to allow me to retake the exam."

"Why does he hate you?" Sophie scowled.

"Quite simply, he doesn't think women belong in the medical profession beyond nursing. I unfortunately have argued several points with him in class. I have been correct on all occasions and his ego does not like that. I made an enemy. The other female students got a pass with a low mark, which means they can qualify, but with a fail I may not." Hillary shrugged her shoulders.

"If it was me, I would go to the Dean. What do you have to lose? The prof failed you anyway. If the Dean agrees with him, he might at least give you a chance to retake the exam and if he doesn't agree, you will pass. I doubt he'll deliberately fail you if the Dean is involved."

"When you put it like that, it makes sense. Reggie said something similar."

"As a matter of interest, what is the Dean's opinion on female doctors?" Sophie asked.

"It's hard to tell, but he's always been respectful towards us. He hasn't implied any concerns and seems like a fair gentleman. It's worth a try. I'll see if Reggie will help me."

"How are you and Reggie getting along?"

"Just friends, no more," Hillary said in a warning tone.

Sophie didn't agree. She had watched them together and they were perfect for each other. It would take some time for them to realize this, but she was convinced it would happen.

# Reality and Truth

Trixie was already at the nurses' desk, looking a little sickly and annoyed, when Sophie arrived.

"Not feeling well this morning?" Sophie whispered.

"I'm all right. It's those Nurse Probationers that are irritating me, giggling and not paying attention. I think we should split them up. I'll see what Sister has to say."

"No need for that. I will talk to them. It is my job to help the probationers settle. If Sister gets involved, they will go on report and that's not necessary."

"Am I being overly sensitive? Sorry, it's ... you know." Trixie placed her hand on her stomach.

Sophie nodded. "Shush! Here comes Sister."

"Good morning, ladies! What do we have today?" Sister Kay said, glancing at the charts, while the nurses waited for morning instructions.

"Mrs. Webb s to be taken for X-Rays and I see we have one discharge today and no new patients overnight. I also need to speak to you about hygiene. There has been an increase in pneumonia and some Spanish flu cases have been reported. The infections need to be stopped now. I want you to be extra vigilant in cleaning bed frames and anything

216

the patient touches. Carbolic for general cleaning and Lysol for any instruments. Probationers, use your training and be thorough." Sister glanced at her timepiece. "And report back to Nurse Romano in one hour for inspection. Nurses, morning rounds as usual. That will be all. Carry on."

The day passed quickly, for which Sophie was grateful since she was still tired and irritated by Andrew's behaviour. The extra cleaning filled the ward with a stronger than usual smell of disinfectant, making Trixie feel queasy. Sister had given her a couple of puzzled glances. Trixie wafted her hand. "It smells awful, that stuff," implying it was just the smell she didn't like. It was imperative Sister did not guess she was with child.

At the end of the day, Sophie noticed that Nurses Fox and Harrington were constantly in deep conversation and, by the end of the shift, they were giggling. Sophie joined them and suggested they walk to River House together. She considered it important to get to know them better. Both these probationers had the makings of good nurses and Sophie wanted to do a good job of mentoring, which would impress Sister Kay. If she was honest, she thought she had found her calling as she really enjoyed teaching. There was something about them that intrigued Sophie, as though there was a secret between them and yet they were strangers from extremely different backgrounds. Dotty Fox had had a tough life of poverty, a drunk father who had abandoned her, a loving mother and a kind benefactor who supported her nurse's training. Clarice had money and privilege, but had been abandoned by emotionally absent parents. Her benefactor, her brother, cared deeply for her and supported her nurse's training. So perhaps they weren't so different.

"It is good to see you two making such good friends. Were you acquainted before nursing?" Sophie asked, knowing the answer, but not quite convinced that they had not met before. It was also a way to open a conversation.

"Not likely," Dotty said with a giggle. "There's no one posh from where I come from. Mi Mam, I mean, Mother, might know some posh people. She were in service in a big house, but that were, was, a long time ago. Never saw her until we met here. In't that right, Clarice?"

"Isn't that right," Clarice muttered almost under her breath and then smiled.

"Sorry." Dotty looked at Sophie. "She's teaching me to speak posh. I want to be like the other nurses."

"That is commendable, both of you. It's always good to improve oneself and, Clarice, you are kind to help. It does my heart good to see such friendship, but it is important you are professional when you are on the ward, or even in the hospital. There have been comments about the giggling on duty, which can be perceived as not paying attention to your work."

"Are you saying we don't work?" Dotty retorted with pursed lips.

"No, I am not saying that. You both work hard. There is a certain, shall we say, sombre decorum expected on the ward." Sophie eyed Clarice. "I think you know what I'm trying to say, don't you, Clarice?"

"Yes, I do but Dotty is awfully funny at times." Clarice's eyes sparkled.

"I understand and sometimes, when things get tough, a little humour is a pleasant relief but save the giggles for when you are out of the hospital or at least in the nurses' lounge. Hold yourself tall." She noticed Clarice hunch her shoulders. "I know you are considered tall for a lady, Clarice. Ignore it and be proud of your height. Carry yourselves with confidence. Now, practice walking around as though you are Matron or Queen Mary." Sophie laughed and the girls giggled. "Now, you understand. All right, lecture over for today."

"I'm curious, Sophie... May I call you Sophie?" Clarice paused, continuing when Sophie nodded her approval. "Why are you so interested in us?"

"I like you. I am reminded of my own days as a probationer. I was a bit different, like you two. My mother died when I was young. I was raised in a wealthy family but when my father died, I was penniless and alone. I worked as a maid scrubbing floors in a hotel to get by. When the war came, I decided to train as a nurse, so I could help the soldiers, which I did. Now I'm back at the Bartley and one day I hope to be a nursing sister."

"What happened to your father?" Clarice asked

"Oh, a long story for another day. I loved him and miss him every day. He was a loving, wise father."

"More an' I can say about mine, nor yours, ay?" Dotty nudged Clarice.

"My father is a busy man with responsibilities. He leaves the children and household to Mother." There was fiery anger, or was it deep sadness, in those expressive eyes.

Having arrived home, Sophie frowned and said, "Ladies, please mind what I said about the wards."

"Yes, we will," they replied in unison.

"Nurse Romano, Sophie, I am inspired by your words and understanding. I will do my best." Clarice straightened and stood tall. "Thank you."

"I'm pleased to help."

The smell of Cook's famous beef stew mixed with baking wafted from the kitchen as the girls entered.

"I was hungry before I got home. Now I'm starving," Dotty said running upstairs, Clarice following.

Sophie went into the kitchen. "Hello, Cook, it smells wonderful. Oh, what's the occasion?"

"It's Nurse Dotty's birthday," Cook said, as she wrapped a pink ribbon around a cake covered in white icing. "Almost finished. How should I write her name? Nurse Dotty or Fox?"

"Just Dotty. That's what we call her off duty. You have quite the talent, Cook. The cake is beautiful. How did you know it was her birthday?"

"Nurse Clarice told me yesterday. She said poor lass had never had a birthday cake. I planned to bake today so I added a Victoria sponge and some icing. There!" Cook finished piping Dotty's cake, swooshed the tail of the letter y and placed candles on the top. "I found these in the cupboard. Probably not enough for each year, but I'm not sure how old she is, 21 perhaps. Plenty to blow out." Cook looked up. "Don't say anything. This is a surprise."

Sophie tapped her lips and went to her room. She decided to change out of her uniform for the occasion and put on a skirt and blouse. There was something sad about not celebrating birthdays. Even at The Sackville Hotel, they had remembered birthdays and the chef always made a cake. Sometimes there was a little present from a friend. *A present. What do I have?* She took a package from her dressing table drawer, carefully opening the tissue paper. "Perfect!" she said, picking up a delicate lace handkerchief. She had brought several back from Italy. They were always plentiful in Lucca market and she'd thought they would be nice Christmas presents. Just as nice for birthdays too. The handkerchief neatly tied with a pink ribbon, she put it in her pocket and went down for dinner.

Clarice and Dotty had changed and Sophie suspected Cook had told Hillary because she had a fresh blouse on. There was a festive mood around the table, but most of the diners did not know what was coming. The mood was perhaps for Cook's beef stew with dumplings, a favourite at River House. She didn't disappoint. Everyone came back for seconds.

Cook gave Clarice a nod and she disappeared into the kitchen, returning with the cake lit with candles. Sophie started singing, "Happy Birthday to you," indicating that everyone should joined in. They quickly realized the cake was heading for Dotty. "Happy Birthday, dear Dotty, Happy birthday to you."

Dotty stared at the cake, unable to speak for the tears streaming down her face. Brushing her wet cheeks, she tried to smile. "I …dunno what to say."

Cook spoke up. "First, blow out the candles."

Cheers went round the table as the candles were snuffed out. "Thank you," she mumbled in the midst of more tears. "I've never had a cake … mi mam didn't bake." Suddenly frowning and wiping her cheeks she said, "How did ya know? Clarice, did you do this?"

"I certainly did and Cook agreed to make you a cake. We kept it a secret but it looks as though a few found out." Clarice handed her a box "Happy birthday!"

Dotty opened the box and held up a long strand of glass beads in different shades of green. She put them round her neck, her sparkling eyes catching their reflection. She jumped up and hugged Clarice.

Sophie put her hand in her pocket and handed Dotty the handkerchief. "A little present from Italy."

Dotty untied the ribbon, admired the lace and dabbed her cheeks. "Thank you. This is beautiful. How can I thank you all?"

Cook handed her a knife. "I'd start by cutting the cake. A nice big piece for everyone. I'll make a pot of tea."

The remainder of the evening was spent chatting and laughing. The celebration had bonded the group of mostly new probationers. The evening had focused on Dotty and Clarice and once again, Sophie wondered if there was a secret. They were so a like, she sensed something was missing but had no idea what. In fact, they were an odd couple with an odd friendship.

Sophie and Hillary, a few years older and perhaps wiser, retired to Sophie's room, leaving the youngsters to celebrate.

"I'm glad we are alone. I have some news regarding the exams," Hillary said, sitting in her usual crossed legged position on Sophie's bed.

"Did you see the Dean?"

"I was so impulsive. I bumped into him in the corridor and suddenly I blurted out that I was upset by my exam results. Not very professional, and I thought I had blown my chances."

"So, what did he say?"

"At first, he looked shocked and I wasn't sure if it was being accosted in the corridor or my outburst. He went quiet, frowned and said, 'Miss West, why would you think you had failed? I've seen your work and it is excellent.' My mouth fell open. I couldn't believe what he was saying." Hillary laughed. "I'm sure I looked stupid. I thanked him for the compliment and told him I was given 48% on my last biology exam. He asked me to make an appointment with his secretary to discuss it further. I see him the day after tomorrow at 4 p.m."

"Hillary, that is wonderful news. What did Reggie say?"

"I had to apologize because I was quite rude to him, saying the Dean wouldn't listen to me. He forgave me and suggested we get him to look at all the ladies' papers. I know Margaret wants her exam looked at. She did get a pass, but the mark was 52%, not a fair one."

"Reggie is such a gentleman and really supports you. We should make a foursome and go to the club one night. Andrew is getting better and he doesn't mind the club if he has a friend there."

"Actually, Reggie asked me if I'd like to go to the Kingfisher on Friday after I've talked to the Dean. He's convinced we will be celebrating."

"I'm not sure. It might be too soon for Andrew. We had a bit of a tiff the other day but I'll ask. If not this week, maybe next."

"I'll talk to you tomorrow." Hillary opened the door. "Good night."

Lying on her back and staring at the ceiling, Sophie thought about Andrew. He did seem better since he'd gone back to work, but she wasn't convinced he was coping. Things were not right between them. When she suggested going out, there was always an excuse, as though he was distancing himself from her. And yet, when they were together, he leaned on her. She fell asleep whispering, "Time. Give him time."

Early morning, just before or after breakfast, was a good

time to catch Andrew. In fact, it was a good time for them both. Sophie picked up the telephone on her way from the dining room. Mrs. Humphries answered and immediately invited her for dinner that night. It was impossible to refuse, so Sophie accepted, thinking it would be a good opportunity to ask Andrew about joining Hillary and Reggie at the club. Andrew came on the line, sounding cheerful, but he was brief. Once again, she felt the distance. He always had a valid excuse about patient care or hospital meetings and she always accepted the reasons. Today, she asked him how he was feeling and his reply that he was fine, was not only short, but curt. He rushed off the telephone, saying he'd see her tonight, having overheard Mrs. Humphries' invitation. He didn't sound too pleased about that either.

Sophie let out a very long sad sigh. It was obvious a night out at the Kingfisher Club was out of the question and she was disappointed. She whispered, "He just needs more time." It was becoming a mantra.

"Pardon?" Clarice said, walking in the hall. "Did you say something?"

"Oh, nothing. I was talking to myself. Are you leaving? Mind if I walk with you?"

"I'd like that. Dotty is off today. I'll enjoy the company and you look as though you could do with some." Clarice gave her a knowing smile.

"A few personal issues. Nothing to worry about." As much as she liked Clarice, she wasn't about to share her concerns over Andrew. "You are observant and that is a good trait to have in nursing. Patients often don't tell you when they are in pain or need something."

"I learned to assess people's moods and behaviour a long

time ago. Nobody in my family, except my brother, says what they really mean. My sisters constantly made fun of me, and my father shouted his displeasure. I learned when to stay out of people's way, especially Papa's and to comfort Mama when she needed me."

"I'm sorry. It must be hard to live with such a family. I'm pleased your brother is a comfort, but I'm assuming he's away."

"He writes to me. At least I receive his letters, living here. My sisters, when they lived at home, use to tease me and hide his letters. Do you have sisters?"

"No. I'm an only child. I have no family, so my nursing colleagues have become my family and my best friend is like a sister."

"I would like that. Dotty is my best friend. I want to make a career of nursing and support myself. It's a bit more difficult than I thought."

"You will do well. Work hard, study and pay attention. One other thing. Be patient. You have almost three years ahead of you. Learn everything you can." Sophie paused. "Can I ask you a personal question?"

"Of course," Clarice replied.

"I think your friendship with Dotty is good, you will help each other a lot. I know you said you have never crossed paths before nursing but you are so comfortable together."

"It is strange you should mention that, because I feel I have known her forever. She's a real friend, not like most of the girls in boarding school. I want Edwin to meet her. One day, I'll take her to Beech Hall."

"Good friends are very important. Nurse Belingham and I were probationers together and this kind of friendship never dies. Treasure yours with Dotty."

Sophie smiled as they parted company. She felt rather motherly, as a mentor, and she liked the role. She liked listening and advising probationers. Her association with Dotty and Clarice confirmed her ambition to become a ward sister and maybe more. She felt excited by the prospect and keen to learn all she could.

# Hearts Change

Tired and hungry, Sophie knocked on Mrs. Humphries front door, expecting Andrew to answer, but one of the boarders let her in. Andrew had not arrived. He'd called to say he was delayed and had left a message for Sophie to wait for him.

Sophie ate dinner and chatted with Mrs. Humphries and the other boarders. They sat at the table for a long time, drinking tea. It was getting dark when Andrew finally appeared. He looked strained and pale, hardly touching his dinner and causing Mrs. Humphries to fuss.

"Doctor, you need to keep your strength up." She turned to Sophie. "Talk some sense into him, will you?"

"She's right, Andrew. You look exhausted. You'll feel better after a meal."

"Stop it! Stop fussing, both of you," Andrew snapped, obviously irritated. "I've had a long day and didn't get chance to eat lunch until late, so I'm not hungry." He grabbed Sophie's arm tight enough to make her flinch. "Let's go for a walk. I need some fresh air. Mrs. H, save me some pudding and I'll have it later with a cup of tea." He smiled as though to soften his harsh tone.

A fine drizzle made the pavement glisten in the street

lights. Andrew pushed the umbrella open and they walked side by side. His hand firmly gripping the umbrella's handle made it unavailable to Sophie. She slipped her arm under his, expecting to ease his irritable mood. Rather than pull her to his side, he nudged her away. Sophie felt her insides tighten and her breath stuck in her throat. They walked in an uncomfortable silence for a long time, eventually reaching the River Thames. The Embankment was busy, people rushing from place to place. Some were sombre with nowhere to go, or tired from a late session at the office. Others sparkled in evening dresses, dark suits and bowler hats; animated and cheerful, they headed for the theatre or clubs. She and Andrew didn't belong in any of those groups.

Clearing her throat and pulling in as much air as she could, Sophie broke the silence. "Andrew, are you going to tell me what this is all about or are we going to walk all night?"

"Sophie, I love you so very much. I don't know where to start." He closed the umbrella, the rain having stopped. He guided her to a sheltered bench overlooking the river. The light from the dolphin lamps lining the embankment should have been romantic, but a loud, mournful horn sounded from a river barge, making her feel uneasy. Whatever Andrew was about to say, it was not good.

"I am probably telling you something you already know, but I had to come to my own conclusion. My illness pushed me to death's door and I was so frightened. I imagined I would never recover or practice medicine again. Unfortunately, my fear set off horrible recurring nightmares of death and dying."

Sophie's hand went to her mouth, her eyes briefly closing as she felt his agony. "And you never said anything to me. You didn't have to go through this alone."

"I couldn't tell you. I'm sorry. Knowing you were there did more for me than you'll ever know. I'm not sure what I would have done without you, my darling Sophie." He leaned forward and kissed her, his tension gone. "It also caused me to withdraw and melancholia began to set in. I hoped it would improve when I returned to the hospital and my patients." He paused, rubbed his forehead and took a ragged breath before continuing. "Several things happened at the hospital. I made a few mistakes. Not big ones, but not like me and enough to make me aware that I was not coping and needed medical help. I went to see Dr. Gruber, my colleague at Spring Gardens. He came to the conclusion that there were several factors: a delayed reaction to the horrors of war in Passchendaele and the after-effect of the pneumonia, which caused the nightmares, and all that caused a form of melancholia."

"Oh Andrew, you have no idea how happy that makes me. Yes, I have known you were ill and I had a good idea what it was, but I couldn't figure out the cause, or the cure."

"I'm not sure my illness should make you happy," he teased and smiled, brushing a stray hair from her forehead. "I understand what you are saying but doctors are not supposed to have the same illnesses as their patients. It was very hard for me to admit I was unwell."

"What kind of treatment has Dr. Gruber advised?"

"Like me, Dr. Gruber has studied Sigmund Freud, and we have a treatment plan, which will also be a research assignment. He thinks the condition is situational, meaning directly related to the war, my illness, the fear of seeing death. He is recommending weekly sessions with him. He is as certain as a doctor can be that I will heal quickly and be back to normal in a month or so."

"I am happy for you and I don't doubt you will get better soon. There is something I don't understand. Why was it so hard to tell me this?"

Shaking his head, he said, "I don't know. I thought I could make it better, that it would pass." He wrapped his arm around her shoulder. "You're shivering and it's getting cold." He looked around and spotted an open café. "Let's get some cocoa and warm up. I have more to say." Andrew's expression turned sombre again.

Several tables were empty and Andrew chose a small one in the corner. He ordered cocoa, a meat pie for himself and cake for Sophie.

"Remember, you promised to have pudding with Mrs. Humphries."

"That's why I only ordered one piece of cake. I wasn't hungry earlier, but now I'm ravenous. The pie will be welcome." Andrew looked very serious. "I have more to say, Sophie."

"More about the illness?" Sophie said, with panic edging her voice. She had guessed he hadn't told her everything. Was he saving the worst for last?

"Not directly. Lying in a hospital bed, not knowing if I was going to live or die; I reflected on life and what it meant to me."

Sophie gave a small chuckle. "You mean your life flashed before your eyes."

"Something like that. Although by the time I returned to my digs and Mrs. Humphries', I was confused and not feeling myself. Many weird things went through my mind. I know you were frustrated and worried, but it took me a long time to see things clearly." Andrew dropped his eyes to the floor and when he looked up, a single tear slowly trickled down his cheek.

"Andrew, what is it? Tell me, please."

"Sophie, my darling Sophie, I love you with all my heart. I love every breath you breathe and yet I cannot marry you." His eyes full of sorrow, he wept. Taking both of Sophie's hands in his, he whispered, "I am so, so sorry."

Stunned, Sophie's own tears crept down her cheeks and fell, along with Andrew's, onto their joined hands. "Why?" she whispered.

Reaching in his pocket, he took out a crisp white handkerchief and gently wiped Sophie's tears and then his own. "I'll take you home. You stay here. I'll find a cab."

"I'd rather walk." Her voice was thick with tears. "And hear your explanation. Why, Andrew? Why?"

"This was not an easy decision but it's the right one."

"I don't understand. I've been deserted, even spurned in the past, but I never expected it from you. The stable, quiet, kind and caring man I agreed to marry. The one man who never left my side as we raced through France, until I was safely in a British hospital. The man who drove for hours to meet me in Dover so he could declare his love for me. And now you're breaking my heart. Who are you?"

She pulled her coat up to her chin. They had walked beside the river and the cool, damp breeze off the water seeped through her coat, deepening the cold feeling of loneliness. Her thoughts went back to Dover and her surprise at seeing Andrew. How she had, at first, resisted his overtures of love, even a little annoyed at his presence, wanting time to reconcile the meaning of the unexpected visitors at the villa. But, when she'd accepted Andrew's proposal, she had pushed all that securely into the past, firmly believing she wanted Andrew to be her husband. She desperately needed an explanation for his change of heart.

"Your silence is unnerving." She paused. "I need to know."

The rain had returned into a heavy shower, prompting Andrew to open the umbrella. Sophie moved closer, for shelter and a sense of privacy.

"I have to set you free, let you go, because I love you and I know you can't return my love…"

"But I do…" she interrupted.

He put his fingers to her lips. "Shush. I know you think you do, but your heart belongs to another."

Sophie shook her head vigorously, while squashing the turmoil that was churning inside her.

"You asked why I made this decision, so please listen to what I have to say." He waited for Sophie to acknowledge his words.

"I'm listening."

"I wish I could turn the clock back to the days we worked together and the hours of discussion about Freud and shell shocked patients and the deep friendship we had. I fell in love with you long before Passchendaele, here in London, in the library," he began.

"When the librarian was convinced we were German spies because we read Sigmund Freud, an Austrian." Sophie smiled.

"You remember," Andrew said returning her smile. "I regret going to Dover because that is when everything changed. You are so right when you call me stable. Although you should perhaps add boring and dull. Dancing at the Kingfisher Club was torture for me and yet I saw your eyes light up as you had

232

fun. I was jealous as you danced with strangers, your skirt swishing and your eyes sparkling. You looked so beautiful that I wanted to be that stranger. I wasn't jealous of the partner. I was jealous because I could never be that dancer."

"We don't have to go dancing."

"It would be all right in the beginning, but eventually my boring side and your fun side would cause problems. You need someone who enjoys life more than I do. My recent bout of illness and its lasting effects have made me realize that my work is my life. I can never love anyone like I love you, so I will devote my life to my second passion, psychiatry. It's over, Sophie. Perhaps one day we can ignite that friendship again." Andrew's words had a finality to them that she could not deny.

"I will miss you and our friendship very much. I promise you I will find a way to resume our friendship."

Andrew hailed a cab. He kissed her one last time, paid the cabby and provided instructions to drive her to River House.

"Goodbye, my darling Sophie. Take care of yourself and give your heart to the one you truly love."

The taxi lurched forward and she peered through the rear window and whispered, "Dear, sweet Andrew. I will miss you so very much." A hole opened up inside her. It was a loss she would never fill, but deep down in her soul, she knew he was right.

Safely back at River House, she slipped quietly to her room. Light shone from under Hillary's door, but she didn't knock. She needed to be alone.

Sophie undressed and slid into bed, wrapping an old woollen shawl around herself. It had belonged to her mother. She'd kept it all these years but forgotten about it until that night. She lay on her back, watching a little black spider walk across the ceiling and wondered what spiders thought about. How lovely to lead such a simple life, weaving a silky web, catching food and walking along the ceiling. Boring, she thought. Was Andrew so boring? He certainly didn't enjoy the clubs. She knew that. She could not deny she had had her own misgivings and, on more than one occasion, she had questioned if the strong feelings she had were friendship, not romantic love. She knew which it was and finally admitted it was a deep friendship she felt. But what did he mean, 'my heart belongs to another' and 'giving my heart to the one I truly love'. Well, there wasn't anyone else.

# Picking up the Pieces

Puffy eyes, queasy tummy and a headache greeted Sophie when she opened her eyes early the next morning. She wrapped her dressing gown around her. Hoping Hillary was awake, she tapped on her door.

Hillary, also in her dressing gown, sat at her desk. Her eyes widened when she saw Sophie. "Oh, you look terrible. A night on the town?"

"I wish it were." Sophie rubbed her aching head. "Andrew broke off our engagement. The wedding is off." She surprised herself at how easily the words came out. Not a single tear followed, perhaps because there were none left.

"Oh no! When? What happened? You look cold. Jump into bed." The two sat in bed, propped up with pillows and covered with a warm eiderdown. Sophie began to explain the events of the previous evening. At first, she sounded matter of fact, but as she relived the evening and repeated Andrew's reasons, the tears began to flow. Hillary stayed quiet, handing her handkerchiefs and nodding or shaking her head at various appropriate intervals. Otherwise, she just listened.

"I can't explain why I'm crying. Andrew is right. What we have is a deep friendship, not romantic love, although I do believe the marriage would have worked. Andrew loved me passionately and I loved him in my own way. We had a great deal of respect for each other. He doesn't think that is enough." Sophie leaned back on the pillow and closed her eyes.

"Perhaps not, but I know nothing of romance and marriage." Hillary got out of bed. "I'm going to see if I can get some tea and toast."

"Thanks. That would be nice. My stomach doesn't feel good and my head is aching. Do you have any aspirin?"

"You stay where you are. I'll be back in a minute."

True to her word, Hillary returned with a tray loaded with tea and milk and hot buttered toast and two aspirin. "I told Cook you weren't feeling well. You probably shouldn't go to work."

"I can't stay off work."

"Of course you can. Have you looked in the mirror this morning? Cook will take one look at you and put you to bed. She's cooking breakfasts at the moment. We have about half-an-hour before she comes to check on you."

"It would be nice to rest today and stop this silly crying. All I need is to burst into tears on the ward."

"I doubt that would happen, but you are grieving. Whether or not it is a broken heart is debatable but the loss of a life with Andrew, a close friend and a cancelled wedding isn't nothing," Hillary pointed out as gently as she could.

"I will miss Andrew and our long discussions. You are right. I don't have a broken heart in the romantic sense. Speaking of hearts, Andrew actually said my heart belonged to someone else. Did he think I was seeing someone else? Although he didn't say it with malice."

Hillary's eyes widened with amusement. "You are teasing.

Surely you know to whom he's referring."

"I have been at Andrew's side ever since I came back from … Italy." She hesitated. "Is he talking about Carlos?"

"Of course he is!"

"But Carlos walked away. All that is behind me. There was never a contest in my mind. I have to admit I didn't tell Andrew I met Carlos a couple of times in Italy. They were both chance encounters. Well, the last one might not have been, but that had more to do with his friend Harry. It didn't seem relevant."

"How do you feel about Carlos?"

"I made my commitment to Andrew because he was stable and I dismissed Carlos because he was, and still is, unstable. I can't live that way. There was a time I loved Carlos, but not anymore. I'm afraid Andrew had it all wrong." Sophie put her fingers to her temples. "I don't feel well. The aspirin isn't helping."

"Maybe you should go back to bed." Hillary put her hand on Sophie's forehead. "You have a fever, Sophie. You are ill. This isn't just grief. We can talk later."

Sophie had just gotten into her own bed when Cook knocked on the door, carrying a thermometer and a glass of honey lemon. She did indeed have a fever and her scratchy throat, she'd attributed to weeping, was due to a cold. She hoped it wasn't 'flu'. Cook immediately put her in isolation. No one was allowed in her room and the doctor was called.

Secretly grateful to have a day, maybe more, to sleep and sort her thoughts out, Sophie settled in bed and slept until she was rudely awakened by the doctor's visit.

"So, what do we have here?" he asked in a loud, booming voice. He ha-hummed and grunted as he took her temperature, flashed the light in her eyes, ears and throat, pressed his fingers into her neck and finally counted the seconds, taking her pulse.

"Nothing serious." He tapped Sophie's leg and turned to Cook. "I can assure you it is not influenza. She has no swollen glands. It could be the start of tonsillitis, but I think it is more likely to be a bad cold. Two days bed rest, lots of fluids and I'll pop by in a couple of days. Call me if there is any change." He packed his things in his bag and bowed. "Good day, ladies!"

Cook fluffed the pillows. "If it weren't for the fever, I'd say you had a broken heart."

"Pardon!?" *How in the world does Cook know about the break-up?*

"I hear the wedding is off."

"It is. News travels fast."

"Mrs. Humphries called me this morning. Dr. Cuthbert's in a right state and she ain't too pleased either. She'd kept them rooms for you. You need to make your mind up, girl." Cook's tone was accusatory.

"Cook, I don't know what Mrs. Humphries said to you but Andrew broke off the engagement, not me. It was an unpleasant surprise."

"Oh, did he now!" She waited for Sophie to say more, but Sophie did not want to talk about it.

"If you don't mind, I want to sleep. I feel quite unwell."

"You look poorly. Go back to sleep and I'll bring you some soup later."


Sophie's fever went back to normal after two more days and the doctor insisted she rest for three more. She took the time to adjust to life without Andrew and plan for a different future. Nursing was her future. It always had been, ever since she'd left the Sackville. More determined than ever, she would concentrate on becoming a ward sister, Sister Romano. She smiled, reflecting on the title. Excitement tickled her insides, something she hadn't experienced in a long time. She had tried hard not to show it to Andrew, but the prospect of trying to be both a wife and nurse had terrified her. The one thing that still niggled at her was Carlos and, thanks to Andrew and Hillary coming to a wrong conclusion.

She laundered and ironed her uniform, ready for an early start the next day, retired early and woke at the crack of dawn. She and Hillary walked together, both a little nervous. Sophie knew there would be lots of questions about Andrew. And, as a result of her formal meeting with the Dean, Hillary, together with her fellow female students, had been invited to meet with him again to discuss their exam marks. They wished each other luck and went their separate ways.

Sister Kay was already on the ward when she arrived, talking to the nurse probationers. Trixie arrived on her heels, looking much better. She had pink cheeks and was looking radiant.

"Good morning, ladies. Pleased to see you are early today. Welcome back, Nurse Romano. I trust you are feeling better."

"Thank you. Yes, Sister, I am quite recovered."

"Ladies, we have a busy day ahead of us. The Casualty Department is dealing with a major accident. Some buildings collapsed, as a result of a previously unexploded bomb, damaging houses, trapping women and young children. The fire department is there now with a rescue team. Make up the extra cots and prepare for trauma patients. That will be all. Carry on. Nurse Romano, a word please?"

Sophie followed Sister to the nurses' station. "I understand on top of your illness you suffered a personal…" Sister paused.

"My fiancé broke off our engagement. It was probably for the best. In fact, it is a good thing for me as I want to concentrate on advancing my nursing career."

"You need say no more. I am pleased to see your positive attitude and I will assist you as best I can. Today, I would like you to lead the probationers with the patient care. Your war service will be of great value in treating the injured, as will Nurse Belingham's."

"Thank you," Sophie said almost hesitantly, surprised that her wishes were being answered so quickly. A coincidence, perhaps.

They had just finished the morning tasks when the first patients arrived from Casualty. Sophie beckoned Nurse Harrington over. "With me, and Nurse Fox with Nurse Belingham."

A pale, distraught young woman with abrasions on her face that twisted in pain was wheeled on to the ward. Lifting the sheet, Sophie saw a leg in a splint. Glancing at the chart for the patient's name, she directed the orderly to the first bed.

"Mrs. Peat, we have to move you from the stretcher to the bed and this may hurt." She nodded to Nurse Harrington. "Hold the nurse's hand tight." Sophie and the orderly quickly moved her to the bed. She flinched without a sound. Then Sophie noticed the tears.

"Is your leg painful?"

"Only if I move it. My face is sore. Nurse, can you find out if Susie's all right and if they found Daniel? I don't know where they are," she said, new tears running down her face.

Sophie realized her face was sore because the salty tears were in the cuts.

"How old are they? I can check the children's ward."

"Susie's five. They brought her in with me, but I don't know where Daniel is. He's seven. One minute we were standing in the kitchen and the next we were covered in rubble."

Sophie dabbed her face. "I'll make enquiries. I'm sure they will be safe. You try and rest." She looked around the ward. Everyone was busy and there were more patients to attend to. She couldn't leave. An orderly walked by and she grabbed his arm. "Are you going back to Casualty?"

"Yes. Do you want something?"

"Can you find out if a little five-year-old girl, Susie Peat, and a boy about seven, Daniel Peat, are in Casualty?" The orderly hesitated. She gave him a pleading look. "Please. The mother is going frantic."

"I'll see what I can do," he said giving her a cheeky wink. "It'll cost ya.'" He laughed. "Nah, I'll take a look for ya."

Sophie shook her head, his humour welcome. They had been going non-stop all morning. He reminded her of Buster from the Casualty Clearing Station, always cheerful and willing to help. The whole scene reminded her of the war. After they settled the rest of the influx, she sent the probationers off for a break and helped Trixie to update the charts.

A soft whistle attracted her attention. The young orderly beckoned to her. "The little girl is on the children's ward. I couldn't find the boy, but the nurse told me they just had word more casualties had been found and they was on their way. He might be in that lot."

"Thank you. What's your name?"

241

"Henry. Me friends call me Flash, on account that I move fast."

"Henry will do fine. Thank you." She smiled.

"Trixie, can you manage for a few minutes? I want to check on the condition of the little girl. I hope I can give the mother some good news."

"Go ahead. I'll finish these."

The Children's Ward was as full as the women's. All they would tell her was that Susie had a bump on the head. They didn't know how serious it was, but she was talking and asking for her mother. Sophie informed them that her mother couldn't come to her, but perhaps the little one would like to know her mum was being looked after.

Mrs. Peat was grateful to hear her daughter was in the children's ward but the tears flowed when she realized her son had not been found. Sophie held her hand, not knowing what else to do when a big, burly man walked in.

"Oh John, thank goodness you're here. Susie's hurt and Daniel is nowhere to be found. Nurse, this is my husband."

"Pleased to meet you Mr. Peat. Could I have a word?" Sophie explained his wife's injuries and where to find his daughter. "Your son was not one of the injured. I understand Casualty is expecting more patients. We'll let you know as soon as we have news. Try talking to the police. Little boys can wander off. If he's lost, the police can find him."

"He is independent for his age. He's most likely searching for his mother." Mr. Peat hesitated, glancing at his wife and then Sophie.

"You go look for your son. We'll take care of your wife and daughter."

"Do as she says, John. I'll be all right. I need to sleep. The medicine makes me groggy. Go find Daniel, please."

"I'll go the police first. Don't worry, I'll find him." John waved to his wife as he left the ward.

The remainder of the day was busy, but with no new patients and by the time the evening shift arrived, Trixie and Sophie were exhausted. Trixie ran off to meet Chris and Sophie hung around the ward, hoping Mr. Peat would be back with news of Daniel. Tired and hungry, she decided there was nothing more she could do and walked through the hospital lobby and out the main entrance, not usually used by nurses. If Mr. Peat returned, this was the entrance he would use. The cool evening air felt fresh on her face and she hesitated by the big glass doors, scanning the area and checking faces as they passed her. All of a sudden, a movement behind her made her turn and look down. A scruffy looking little boy in short trousers and blue blazer stood leaning on the wall, his face dirty and wet with tears. Could it be? Was this Daniel?

Sophie crouched down. "Hello. Are you lost?"

Big brown eyes wide and frightened stared at Sophie. "I'm looking for my mother."

"Is your name Daniel?" Sophie asked, her heart thumping in her chest. Was it possible?

He nodded. "Daniel Peat. Do you know my mummy? I have a sister too."

"I do indeed, Daniel, and your mummy and sister are right here in the hospital, doing just fine. Are you hurt?"

He shook his head. "My house fell down. They took Mummy away in an ambulance. I thought she might be here."

"You are a very resourceful little boy. Come with me." Sophie took his hand and went back to the Women's Ward.

The duty nurse eyed her suspiciously, glancing at Daniel. Her expression changed when Sophie whispered who he was and where she had found him. The nurse let her through on the condition they didn't stay long. Mrs. Peat was dosing when Daniel saw her and ran to his mother, jumping on the bed before Sophie could stop him. Mrs. Peat let out a cry of pain and then wrapped her arms around him. "Daniel, I am so happy to see you. Are you hurt? Let me look."

"He seems fine, but I'll have the doctor check him over. Now, Daniel, you must be careful. Mummy has a poorly leg. Can you sit over here?"

"He's okay. I want to hug him. Where's John?"

"I don't know. I found Daniel outside the hospital, looking for you. He saw the ambulance take you away and somehow found his way here. We have to go or the nurse will get into trouble. I'll look after Daniel until your husband comes back. You get some rest. I'll see you tomorrow."

Sophie took Daniel to Casualty and had the doctor check him for injuries. After a full examination he was declared to be quite healthy. Hoping his father would return, she decided the best place to wait was the lobby.

"I see you found 'im." Henry, the orderly, walked towards them, carrying a flask and a brown bag. "On mi break. A double shift today."

The thought of food made Sophie hungry and it occurred to her that Daniel had probably not eaten all day. "Are you hungry, Daniel?" He nodded his head.

"Henry, would you go to the canteen for me? I'll give you some money. I don't think Daniel has eaten all day."

"Course I will."

"A sandwich and milk for Daniel, a tea for me and biscuits

for us all." She handed Henry some coins.

The food eaten, Henry went back to work and Daniel snuggled up to Sophie. She took the opportunity to find out what happened. Daniel was in a different room when the house collapsed. By the time he scrambled out of the rubble, the ambulance was taking his mother and sister to the hospital. Because he wasn't hurt, nobody paid any attention to him and he wandered off. He remembered walking to the hospital one time with his mother and sister when Susie had hurt her arm. He made several wrong turns and when he finally arrived at the hospital, he didn't know what to do. He tried asking passersby but they ignored him.

Sophie listened to him and was amazed at his bravery and grateful she had found him. It was getting dark and there was still no sign of Mr. Peat. Daniel had fallen asleep. Clearly, she had not thought this through. She had assumed Mr. Peat would return and she'd hand him over and return to River House and be scolded for not turning up for dinner. It was possible that, realizing visiting hours were over and not knowing she had found Daniel, Mr. Peat would not return tonight. *Oh, what was I thinking? I should have notified the police. I'll do that now.* She gently lay Daniel on the bench and asked the reception desk to call the police about a missing boy. Whatever the receptionist said brought the police within minutes, sirens blaring. Daniel woke up, clinging to Sophie and intimidated by police officers staring at him. After explaining the situation, the police calmed down and Mr. Peat, who happened to be at the station when the call came in, arrived in his own car to collect his son.

# Taking Chances

Cook slammed a plate of dried up sausage and mash in front of Sophie, quite unwilling to hear an explanation of her evening and reason for her lateness.

"You have made your point, Cook. I'm sorry for not calling but a little boy needed looking after." Sophie cut the sausage and began to eat. It didn't taste too bad. The sausage was a bit chewy, but she was hungry.

"Little boy?" Cook asked.

Sophie told Cook the story and although her scowling face said otherwise, she softened and made a fresh pot of tea, meaning Sophie was forgiven.

Hillary joined them and Cook gave her a conspirator's smile. Sophie glanced from one to the other with a frown. Cook loved to have secret information. It made her feel important if the nurses confided in her. Obviously, she knew something Sophie did not.

"I'll leave you two to chat. Miss West has some exciting news."

"You first," Hillary said. "What was all the excitement today and why are you so late?"

Once again Sophie relayed the story of the building collapse, damaged houses and the Peat family with a mostly happy ending.

"That was an eventful day. Mine was not as busy, but extremely interesting."

"Stop teasing. Is this about your examination results?"

Hillary nodded. "There are four women in our group, three of us, Margaret, Helena and myself attended the meeting. The fourth lady, Daphne, is not doing well and declined. We were shown into the Dean's office, an enormous room, a bit dark and intimidating, with oak panelled walls, heavy leather furniture and a large oak desk. There was a vase of yellow roses on the sideboard that brightened the whole room. His secretary offered us refreshments. I thought it was a good sign, and she suggested we take a seat. The Dean was held up at another meeting."

"So, what did he say?"

"First, he apologized for being late and sat down with us. His secretary handed him some papers. Then he said, 'I have reviewed all of the examination papers, not just yours. In my view, there is an inconsistency. I agree that the marks you received do not accurately reflect your work, with the exception of one student and she has decided not to continue her studies.' We assumed that was Daphne. He went on to say, 'that all the class examination papers, not just ours, were being submitted to another professor to be marked a second time. He will review the result and if he's satisfied, the final marks will be posted in the usual way in about a week's time.'"

"He sounds as though he supports women. I am surprised," Sophie said.

"He does. We found out that his wife is a doctor at St Thomas'. He said, and these are his words, 'Ladies, I am impressed with your work. You will make fine doctors. Rest assured, this inequality will never happen again as long as I am Dean. Should any of you require help in any way, do not hesitate to knock on my door. If I can't help, my wife can. Obviously, she can relate to the challenges women experience as career physicians.' He then showed us to the door and wished us a good day. Can you believe that?"

"I bet his wife had a word or two to say about the situation. I wonder what will happen to Professor what's-his-name?" Sophie asked.

"Budd. No one liked him. He hasn't been in classes all this week. Reggie thinks he's been fired. I doubt we'll ever know, and the Dean wouldn't mention it. I'm glad he's gone."

"How is Reggie?"

"Reggie doesn't change. He's fine and he's been very supportive. We are planning to go to the Kingfisher on Saturday to celebrate. Why don't you come along?"

"I'll think about it. I'm not sure."

"A night out would do you good." Hillary yawned, "It's almost ten o'clock, past my bedtime, and you look as though you might fade away."

The two climbed the stairs, both tired but feeling good after a productive day.

The ward was busy the next day but by no means as frantic as the one before. The patients were settled, some recovering from surgery and others nursing cuts and bruises. Thankfully, the pneumonia cases had been discharged. Anyone suspected of having 'flu' was transferred to isolation.

Sister Kay had asked Sophie to mentor the probationers

again. Their work was good both responded well to instructions and they were good with the patients. However, they had tendency to squabble over what Sophie could not determine. Nurses Harrington and Fox were having a heated argument, most inappropriately, in front of a patient. As she approached, they stopped and smiled.

"When you've finished the beds, please meet me in the Nurses' Lounge. And, please stop squabbling and get on with your work. Doctor's rounds in half-an-hour." Sophie felt like a school teacher, but had decided the girls needed some discipline. She also knew Sister Kay was watching how she handled things.

Mrs. Peat sat up in bed, trying to brush her long, curly hair. Her arm was stiff and bruised where a brick had landed on her. Sophie went to her. "Would you like me to do that for you?"

"Thank you. My arm is sore." She smiled. "Actually, everything is sore."

"I'm afraid that's bruising coming out from the accident. It will get better. Were your husband and little boy able to go home last night?"

"He said the authorities wouldn't let them in the house. He was taking Daniel to his parents' in Lewisham. They will take care of Daniel and he wanted to tell them what had happened and that we're all right. Do you think they'll let me visit Susie?"

"We can ask the doctor. How's the leg feeling today?"

"It's painful all the time."

Sophie lifted the sheet. There was redness on the skin. She checked the chart but her vitals were all normal, including her temperature. Something about the leg worried her. The bone had been pulled back into place and immobilized with splints but the redness indicated an open wound. She had seen similar wounds on soldiers and they almost always finished up with nasty infections.

"Mrs. Peat, I'll be back. I want Sister to check on your leg before doctor's rounds."

Sister Kay lifted the sheet draped over the cage protecting the leg and raised her eyebrows. "I'll ask the doctor to look at it this morning. Go on your break now before rounds and take the probationers with you. Nurse Belingham can finish the rest."

Sophie made tea and found some biscuits, telling Nurses Harrington and Fox to help themselves.

"I will make this brief. I am pleased to say you both work very hard, neither myself nor Sister have any complaints about you work. However, I find your squabbling annoying and inappropriate, especially when you are with patients. Why do you argue so much?"

Sophie waited for an answer, glancing from one to the other. Clarice looked as though she might pounce any minute, not too happy with criticism and Dotty, more compliant. No verbal answer was forthcoming, Clarice shrugged her shoulders and Dotty seemed thoughtful.

"That kind of behaviour I expect from two-year-olds, not from responsible nurses and it has to stop. Do you understand?"

Suitably chastised, they both nodded.

"Next time, and I hope there won't be a next time, you will go on report and Sister Kay will decide the consequences. Now, take your break and be back on the ward in ten minutes."

Sophie marched back to the ward, feeling powerful, and not sure if she liked the sensation. Was she being arrogant?

She wanted to share her knowledge and passion for nursing. Sister Kay had given her that opportunity. She had not expected discipline to be part of the process. Self-discipline was essential and she suspected this was something Dotty had learned growing up, but not Clarice.

A new doctor with no entourage of housemen or students stood at the nurses' desk, talking to Sister when Sophie returned.

"Nurse Romano, Dr. McDonald is here to see Mrs. Peat. Would you lead the way?" He looked very young and Sophie detected a nervousness about him, possibly intimidated by Sister or just new to the hospital.

"Mrs. Peat, Dr. McDonald has come to take a look at your leg." Sophie took her hand while Sister lifted the sheet and removed the cage, allowing the doctor to examine the leg. He moved the splint, making Mrs. Peat cry out. Sophie squeezed her hand. There was, as Sophie had expected, an angry, red open wound that should have been dressed with antiseptic. She tried to recall the instructions on the chart, remembering nothing about an open wound. She glanced towards Sister, who was frowning, obviously having the same thoughts.

The young doctor pulled himself tall and cleared his throat. "The bones have been positioned nicely. The wound has deteriorated since I examined it yesterday. Sister, this wound needs to be irrigated and cleaned with antiseptic as soon as possible." Sophie felt the hackles on her neck stand on end as the young whipper-snapper's tone implied the deterioration was the fault of the nurses.

"Of course, Doctor. Perhaps you would write your instructions on the chart?" Sister handed him the clipboard from the end of the bed, her finger resting on the previous instructions.

Sophie stifled a grin. Dr. McDonald's face had gone quite pink. He rubbed his hand along the back of his neck and studied the chart. Realizing his mistake, his face was now red. Sophie might have felt sorry for him except not treating the wound might have serious consequences for Mrs. Peat.

"It was of the utmost importance that the fractures be set properly first, regardless of the wound. Now, we'll treat the wound." He sounded pompous, which in someone so young was ridiculous. "Good day!"

Sister sighed. "I would like you to take care of Mrs. Peat. You have the experience with this kind of wound. How serious is it?"

"It's hard to say, but so far it's local. She has no fever. Antiseptic and frequent dressing changes should stem the infection." Sophie frowned. "Who is he?"

"I understand he's well trained, top of his class; from a hospital in Scotland but I'm not sure where. He didn't serve in the war as he was too young. He was allowed to stay in university. He will be fine. He's just a bit wet behind the ears."

Sophie smiled at Sister's rather familiar expression. She was usually formal but the words fit Dr McDonald well. "And he is head of the department?"

"A temporary measure until the hospital board finds some-one with experience to head up the department."

"I hope it doesn't take long," Sophie said as she prepared a dressing tray for Mrs. Peat.

Sophie gently cleaned the wound and was pleased the infection was mostly on the surface. "I'm afraid this will sting, but it's important we keep it clean."

"I don't mind as long as it gets better. My leg aches but he said not to move it. Nurse, have you heard anything about

Susie?"

Anticipating the patient would ask about her daughter, Sophie had enquired. "I thought you might ask. She's doing well with only a bump on the head and a cut on her forehead. If she keeps improving, your husband will be able to take her home today or tomorrow."

"Oh that is good news. John said he'd visit Susie this afternoon before he comes to see me."

Sophie replaced the cage to prevent the covers resting on her leg and pulled them up. "You look tired. I suggest you get some rest. I will clean the wound twice more today, so rest in between."

Visiting hours were from 2 - 4 pm every afternoon. Patients busy with family, the nurses often took their breaks during visiting hours. Sophie intended to speak with Mr. Peat. She sat on a bench in the hallway, not very comfortable, but at least she was off her feet.

"Nurse Romano, how lovely to see you," Mr. Peat said, seeing Sophie on the bench. "I have some good news. Susie is being discharged this evening. I promised my boss I would work tonight to make up for the time off. My parents are coming to pick her up and take her to Lewisham. Susie and Daniel love being with Nana and Grandpa. They can stay until Betty, my wife, is better and we have a home to go to. I'm staying with friends."

"Wonderful news. What do you do for a living?"

"I work in a solicitor's office, clerk to the senior partner. They have been understanding but the work still has to be done. How is Betty?"

"She's doing well. There is some local infection around the wound. I'm not concerned about it, but the treatments are

253

painful for your wife. It is too early to say how the fractures are healing. I'm afraid she may be in hospital for some time."

"It was quite a shock to see her leg. I saw the same thing on my mate during the war and he lost a leg. I never expected to see such injuries on my wife. I don't want to upset Betty, but I am scared."

"Betty will be fine. She is not going to lose her leg. It will heal but will take a long time. She is young and strong. I was in Passchendaele, nursing during the war. I have a great deal of experience treating such injuries. I will take good care of your wife and she will have the best care the hospital can provide." Sophie held her breath as she thought of the young orthopaedic doctor who didn't seem to know what he was doing. She wished Carlos was Betty's doctor. He would have the leg fixed in no time, but that was not an option. It was up to her to look after the wound and watch how the leg was setting.

"Thank you. That is a relief. I'd better go to Betty. I can't stay long today but my parents will come by when they pick up Susie."

"Try not to worry. She's doing well," Sophie said, not feeling as confident as she sounded.

Hunger grumbled in her stomach, just as Trixie, looking radiant, beckoned her to join her in the canteen. Sophie smiled. Trixie was always hungry these days. Perhaps there was some truth in the expression, eating for two.

# Bonds of Friendship

The wind howled, whipping up Sophie's skirts and she was certain she had seen flakes of snow on her way to Trixie and Chris's flat. Trixie had been secretive about the reason for the invitation. Sophie guessed she was announcing her resignation from the hospital and they were planning to move to the estate. Trixie's figure tended to be roundish and she had managed to hide the bump by suggesting she had gained weight, loosening her uniform and tying her apron loosely. She had passed her twenty-second week and it was getting increasingly difficult to hide. Trixie had commented to Sophie that by the time they met the Belinghams for Christmas, there would be no doubt as to her condition. Chris' mother was a formidable woman, entrenched in tradition and formality. They were hoping the joyous news of a grandchild and potential heir, would outweigh her displeasure of not being informed the moment Trixie was with child. Sophie was inclined to think the woman, although pleased with the news, would continue to show her displeasure.

Trixie had become an accomplished cook since her pregnancy and Sophie knocked on the front door with great expectations of a delicious meal. She wasn't disappointed by the savoury aroma that wafted into her nostrils as the door opened, but she almost fainted when she saw who opened it.

"Andrew! What are you doing here?" She hesitated, wondering whether to step inside or run for cover. She hadn't seen or spoken to Andrew since the night they'd walked along the Thames embankment.

"Hello, Sophie. How are you? Come in. Trixie is in the kitchen and Chris is pouring drinks." He gave her a quick peck on the cheek. "It's good to see you."

"And, you too, I think," she said, puzzlement written all over her face.

"I don't want this to be awkward. I know it's a bit strange, but I want us to be friends." Andrew's tone was sincere.

"Me too. Do you know why we are here? Trixie has been quite secretive."

"I heard that," Trixie called from the kitchen. "And you have to be patient a little longer."

Chris handed them each a glass of sherry. Sophie took hers into the kitchen, leaving the men to talk.

"You might have warned me Andrew was here," Sophie whispered.

"I was afraid if I told you, you'd find an excuse not to come. Besides, you two need to be friends."

"What is this all about?"

"You have probably guessed some of the reason, but not all. I'm almost finished in here. You go and enjoy your sherry. I'll call you when I need help."

Andrew was sitting on the arm of the sofa. Sophie sat at the other end and drank her sherry rather quickly before accepting a refill. She hoped it might calm her pounding heart, but it didn't. All it did was redden her cheeks. She excused herself to powder her nose. Taking large deep breaths, she looked in the mirror. "Really Sophie, what is the problem?" As she thought about it, she realized how much she still cared about Andrew and yet was fearful that Andrew would want them to get back together, which could not happen. She rubbed her cheek. "What was the peck on the cheek all about? Friends, that's all."

Sophie joined Andrew at the table and Chris laid down a large oval dish laden with a steaming roast of beef and big fluffy Yorkshire puddings. He began carving as Trixie brought dishes of vegetables. Andrew poured everyone some wine. Chris raised his glass with a cheeky twinkle in his eye. "To friends!"

*This dinner is getting more mysterious by the minute,* Sophie thought, enjoying the tender beef.

Trixie stood up. "I see your furrowed brow, Sophie, and I will make an announcement. I resigned my position at the hospital today." She patted her stomach. "Baby is getting too big and too active. A patient noticed the little monkey kicking the other day. I did not tell Matron I was pregnant. I said we were moving to the estate to help Lord Belingham. When I told Sister Kay, she gave me a warm smile. I think she had guessed."

Sophie stretched her arm out to reach Trixie's hand and gave it a squeeze. "I will miss you so much on the ward, but I wish you all the best. It will be quite a different life, lady of leisure. But the rest will do you and the baby a lot of good."

"It sure will and spending all day with Lady Belingham will be a challenge. I expect I'll be busy getting the nursery ready." Trixie gave a little shrug. "But that is not all. We have thought long and hard and have not come to this decision lightly. Chris and I had planned to ask you two to be the baby's Godparents. We did not want to make things difficult for you, but in the end, there was no one else we felt we could trust with our baby's future. You are both kind, loving, sensible people and we remember the wonderful friendship you had before you were engaged. I think that bond is still there. We are not asking you to reignite your relationship, except as friends. Would you, my dearest friend, Sophie, be our son or daughter's Godmother?"

Tears filled Sophie's eyes and she spluttered. "Yes, oh yes. I would love to be Godmother. I am truly honoured, thank you."

"And," Chris continued, "Andrew, would you do us the honour of being our baby's Godfather?

"Of course." Andrew grinned. "An honour indeed." With his gaze fixed on Sophie, he added, "Sophie and I may not be betrothed, but the bond of friendship we have will serve young Belingham well." Andrew raised his glass. "To young Belingham and friendship!"

Apple pie with custard finished off the meal and Sophie was full to bursting with too much food. She sat on the couch next to Andrew in front of the fire. Trixie sat on Chris' knee and a contented quiet descended on the room, making everyone sleepy.

Sophie's eyelids began to flutter and, afraid she might fall asleep and lean on Andrew, she pulled herself straight, clearing her throat. "When are you planning on moving?

"We are going down for the weekend to inform the family and I'd like Trixie to move into the estate shortly after that because I am away on training exercise and I don't want her to be alone."

"You're not resigning? How will that work?" Sophie asked.

"We," Trixie gave Chris a hug, "decided that I should live at Beech Hall. The place is enormous. We have our own apartment within the house. It will be fine for now. I will be well taken care of and Chris need not worry about me while he is away. Chris will stay on the base and come home when he can." Trixie hesitated. "No, he is not resigning. We have decided to stick to that part of our original plan." Trixie patted her tummy. "This little fellow decided to come a couple of years sooner than we planned. Chris wants to continue his military career for as long as he can."

"I hope you understand," Chris said. "Ever since I was in short trousers, I've wanted to be a pilot in the RAF and part of my dream came true. My brother Clive was the heir and, like my father, was passionate about the estate. Clive's death in Passchendaele changed that forever and here I am, heir to the Earl of Carberley." Chris put his arm around Trixie. "My darling wife has agreed, even encouraged me, to continue my career. There will be a time when I am needed on the estate but, for now, the estate manager and my father are managing. My parents won't be pleased, but this is our decision."

"We're hoping the news of a grandchild, and me agreeing to live at Beech Hall will soften the blow," Trixie said.

"You sound as though you have it all worked out." Sophie said, hearing hints of apprehension in Trixie's voice. "It won't be easy for either of you."

"No, it won't. But it will be worth it. I intend to split the time between Beech Hall and my parents place, while I am able to travel and then Mummy and Daddy will be my guests at Beech Hall, which will impress my mother." Trixie laughed. "You know how she loves being a society lady."

Everyone nodded, knowing Lady King only too well.

Andrew stretched and stood up. "Good food, good company, a warm fire and too much wine is making me sleepy. Sophie, can I walk you home? I could do with some fresh air."

Sophie accepted and they said their goodbyes. The wind felt cold, but the fresh air woke them up as they walked towards River House. Sophie surprised herself. She felt safe with Andrew and the old comfortable friendship from the beginning had returned, even though her heart still fluttered a little. She loved Andrew and although she welcomed the change, she wasn't sure Andrew felt the same way.

"Is everything all right?" Sophie asked, "You seem on edge. Is our breakup still bothering you?"

"Oh gosh no. I miss you terribly and it's lonely without you, but it was the right thing to do. I am delighted that the Belinghams asked us to be Godparents. I will enjoy that and, selfishly, it will keep us in touch. Who would have believed that we could have an affectionate friendship and a Godchild?"

"You do have a way with words and I agree with you. An ideal situation. But there is something you are not telling me. Andrew, what is it?"

"I'm leaving London." Sophie gasped and tried to interrupt. Andrew placed his finger gently on her lips. "Shush. Let me finish and then we can talk. Several months ago, I was approached to take over as Chief Physician of a small private mental institution in Scotland. I turned them down without much thought. You and I were to be married and I was happy at Spring Gardens."

"You never told me," Sophie said, a little hurt he had not confided in her.

"There was no point. I had no intention of taking the

position and moving to Scotland at that time. Things changed after my illness. Spring Gardens no longer has the challenges it once had and Matron Mills is really cramping my style. I want the freedom to research and treat patients so they can be well, at least as well as the atrocities of war will allow. I'm also seeing civilians with similar illnesses and I want to go beyond the military.

"Sophie, I will never fall in love again, except with my work. Two weeks ago, I contacted them to see if the opportunity was still available. They invited me to visit and even paid my train fare, it was an amazing trip. I boarded the Scotch Express from Kings Cross to Edinburgh and spent three days viewing the premises, talking to patients and staff. The Dalkeith Private Clinic is an amazing hospital that treats men and women, military and civilian. It is not afraid of new ideas or experimental treatments and they value research. It's very impressive." He paused, taking a deep breath and continued. "I accepted the position of Chief Physician at the Dalkeith Clinic. I am booked on the night train the day after tomorrow."

Sophie opened her mouth to speak but found she was lost for words. All kinds of emotions were flashing in her head.

"Sophie, say something?"

"Oh, my goodness. That is a lot to take in. First, congratulations. This is the perfect position for you. I'm a little jealous but Scotland is too far away. My career is at the Bartley and I am content with that. What did Mrs. Humphries say? You are like son to her."

"I haven't told her. I am all paid up to end of the month and I will give her a month extra, allowing her time to find new boarders. I have not told many people. The board of governors at Spring Gardens have been notified. Matron Mills has a letter on her desk." Andrew chuckled. "I'd rather not be around when she reads it. Chris has known since I made the trip to Scotland, but I swore him to secrecy."

"So that is why we had the Godparent invite before the baby was born. I am so pleased we have Baby Belingham to keep us connected. I wish you well. This is definitely your dream. Please write to me and let me know how you're doing."

"And you write to me and let me know when you get your Sister's cap. I have one more thing to say. I don't regret being engaged to you and my heart will always be yours. If you should find love and get married, it will not change us. Whoever the lucky man is, he will understand."

Sophie, playfully punched his shoulder. "Andrew Cuthbert, you are talking in riddles. I am devoting myself to nursing, friendship and Baby Belingham."

Andrew nodded with a wry grin. "If you say so." They stood at the bottom of the steps to Rive House. "It's time. I must say goodbye." He kissed her gently and they hugged for several minutes. "Keep in touch. I'll write as soon as I have an address."

"Good luck and safe journey!" Sophie watched him until he turned the corner and waved.

# A mixture of Surprises

Everyone knew the Scotch express left King's Cross Railway Station at ten in the morning. Sophie had arranged her day off to coincide with Andrew's departure but she had not told Andrew. She stood at the entrance of King's Cross station clutching a book she had bought him for the journey.

"Hello!" Andrew's voice made her swing around. "I thought about calling, but never found the time. We said our goodbyes the other night but I wondered if you might come and I'm happy you're here. Shall we go to the café? The train doesn't leave for another hour."

They sat down and Sophie spoke first. "This is awful tea." She pulled a face and Andrew did the same. "I had to come and wave you off on your new adventure. I am truly excited for you. Oh, I bought you a book to read on the journey."

"Thank you. It is a long one, eight to ten hours." He patted his leather bag. "Mrs. Humphries packed me a flask of tea and enough sandwiches and cakes for an army, so I won't go hungry."

"How is she?" Sophie asked.

"She cried when I told her, but was delighted with the extra money and I promised to write. I hope you don't mind, but I told her you would pop round and say hello. She seemed to brighten up then."

"I'd be happy to see her. It's easy to drop by on my way home from the hospital."

Andrew looked at the title, *Dream Psychology* by Sigmund Freud

"Sophie, this is marvellous. Where did you get it? It's his latest. Thank you," he said, opening the book and whispered her inscription. *"Dear Andrew, My wonderful friend. I shall miss you terribly. I wish you all the success in the world. Love always from your best friend Sophie."* Moisture gathered in the corner of Andrew's eyes. "I don't know what to say. I will treasure this always…." A train announcement drowned out his last word.

"I think that's your train," Sophie said, spreading her arms to engulf him in a massive hug.

She waved and watched the train pull out of the station, Andrew's head and arm leaning out of the window, waving until he was too small to see.

Taking advantage of her day off, Sophie took the Underground to Oxford Street to do a little early Christmas shopping and treat herself to afternoon tea in the Selfridges' Palm Court Restaurant. The stores were already festive and Selfridges never disappointed. She browsed around the windows with intricate and charming Christmas displays. She admired the children's toys, giving her an idea to buy her soon-to-be Godchild a Christmas present and making her rush into the store with purpose. Amazed at the selection of children clothes and toys, she was surprised at how excited she felt trying to make up her mind what to buy. She chose a baby rattle that sounded like bells, a white matinee coat and a soft woollen blanket in the palest blue, which she determined would be okay even if the baby was a girl. Then she spotted colourful illustrated books printed on cloth, not paper. She imagined reading Baby Belingham a story and added *The Tale of Mavis Mouse* to the pile of purchases.

"May I help, madam?" a cheery assistant asked, her eyes glancing at Sophie's stomach.

*Good grief,* Sophie thought, *does she think these are for me?* "Um, thank you. Please wrap all of these. I am to be Godmother to my friend's baby."

The woman smiled. "As you wish, madam."

She picked up her packages and decided her next stop was afternoon tea at the Palm Court.

The waiter showed her to a table. "Would madam prefer to wait for her guest?"

Sophie ignored his question. "Afternoon tea for one please. Earl Grey."

He bowed and disappeared into the kitchen, returning with a tray on his shoulder carrying a small plate of delicate sandwiches, scones, a two-plate holder full of assorted little cakes and a pot of steaming tea.

"Shall I pour for madam?"

"Thank you." His attention made her feel a little awkward until she realized she was actual enjoying the solitude. She helped herself to whatever took her fancy and ate heartily without a smidgen of guilt. Enjoying every mouthful in silence, there was no frivolous chatter requiring a meaningless response to interrupt her tea.

Sophie picked up her parcels and left the restaurant full of energy. It occurred to her that with Andrew gone, she had no need to worry about dancing. She could dance as often as she liked, but she did need a new dress. She giggled to herself as she headed to the lady's dress department. A flapper dress, not too outrageous, but fun. She didn't normally wear red as she considered it to be too flashy, but the assistant had shown her a black and red dress; short, loose fitting, with delicate sheer sleeves and sequins, perfect for the club. Her dress purchased, she continued to shop until she had too many parcels to carry comfortably and decided it was time to go home. The doorman opened the big glass door for her as one of her parcels fell. She hoped it wasn't the vase she'd bought for Trixie. The doorman rushed to rescue it for her. Glancing at her full hands, he gave her a warm smile and said, "A taxi, madam?"

"Thank you!" *Why not,* she thought, dismissing the cost. *I have had a lovely day.*

On the drive home through London to River House, she felt happy and wasn't quite sure why. After all, she had said goodbye to Andrew her ex-fiancé and part of her felt sad. But their affectionate friendly parting had eased her heart. She knew that Andrew was following his dream, making it almost joyous. It didn't take long for her to realize that a heavy burden had lifted from her shoulders. All the time she was with Andrew, she had tried to be someone she wasn't. She tried to please him or cajole him into things that made her happy. They had the same thoughts and opinions about mentally ill patients and shell-shocked soldiers, but that was all. How selfish she had been. Seeing the pleasure in his face when he boarded that train to devote his life to his work, she knew everything would be okay in the end.

Sophie's good humour continued when she started her shift the next morning, greeted by Sister Kay, Trixie and the probationers. Sister made the official announcement that Trixie would be retiring from nursing and a new nurse would be assigned by Matron. Until then, they might be shorthanded. Fortunately, the ward was not overly busy, 'flu' cases were sent to special isolation wards and trauma patients from the bomb accident had all been discharged, leaving a variety of curable illnesses.

The nurses' lounge was quiet when Sophie entered for her break. A cup of tea was all she wanted, leaving space for dinner that night. Cook had been quite put out when Sophie had not eaten dinner the evening before, having been full from her afternoon tea. She put her feet up on the coffee table and closed her eyes.

"May I join you?" Sister Kay's voice prompted her to open her eyes and quickly place her feet on the floor.

"Sister, forgive me. I thought I was alone."

"You are alone. I don't normally come in here. I like to give the nurses privacy. However, I need to speak with you." She smiled, seeing Sophie's alarm. "A compliment, I assure you."

"A compliment?" Sophie frowned.

"From Matron and from rather an unusual source. Do you remember Mrs. Peat with the badly broken leg."

"I do remember. I was worried about her treatment. That young doctor didn't know what he was doing. I'm sorry, Sister. I know I shouldn't talk about doctors like that, but I was afraid Mrs. Peat would never walk again. That's why I took over. Did I do something wrong?"

Sister smiled and shook her head. "You are so charmingly modest. You may have saved her leg, and possibly her life.

Your decision making skills are never wrong. It will serve you well as you advance."

"Thank you, Sister. You know sometimes the best teacher is opportunity. In the Casualty Clearing Hospital, I had to make decisions fast and often hope they were the right ones."

"The compliment comes from Dr. McDonald himself, through Matron. He is young and inexperienced with no head of department, although I believe that situation is soon to rectified. Heads of departments are required to send reports to the Chief Physician. Dr. McDonald sent his report and included Matron. In that report, he praised your work in the treatment of Mrs. Peat. He also mentioned you were a valuable asset to the hospital because of your experience."

"That is praise indeed and coming from a young doctor, who I thought was rather arrogant. It must have taken some courage. Thank you for telling me, Sister."

"On a personal note, I understand you are no longer betrothed. You know that single women are more likely to advance in nursing. I don't agree with it, but it is a fact. Nurse Belingham was lucky to get her position back during the war, but the pregnancy was another issue."

"You knew she was pregnant, didn't you?"

"It wasn't hard to miss." Sister chuckled, "I admired her tenacity when she arrived for her shift, green with morning sickness. I chose to ignore it. She's a good nurse. Matron doesn't know. Her resignation indicated marital commitment with her husband's family."

"Her brother-in-law was killed in the war, making her husband heir to Lord Belingham's estate and earldom. She is expected to live at Beech Hall during her pregnancy and eventually she will be lady of the house. Not quite what she expected when she married Chris."

"Life rarely turns out as we expect it to. Now, I must let you have your break." Sister had a whimsical look in her eye as she left the lounge.

Putting her feet back on the coffee table, Sophie pondered her feelings of hope and happiness. Her dream of being a ward Sister was getting closer. She felt excited and a little nervous. It seemed too good to be true.

The shift finished on time for a change and Sophie decided to visit Mrs. Humphries. She bought a bunch of flowers from the flower seller outside the hospital, hoping they would cheer her up. She was sure she would be missing Andrew.

Mrs. Humphries was at the kitchen table when Sophie arrived. Walking through the unlocked front door, she called, "It's only me, come to say hello."

"Nurse Romano, how lovely to see you." She took the flowers and sniffed the blooms. "These are lovely. Thank you. Did you see him off?"

"Yes, I did and he was well, happy and excited. He asked me to pop in and keep an eye on you. He will miss you, and I know he will miss your cooking."

"That he will," Mrs. Humphries said with pride. "Now I have to rent the rooms out. His old room and the two rooms upstairs. I thought I'd move the single beds up in the attic and get two boarders. Not sure what to do with the sitting room." A tear rested in the corner of each eye. "I wish it were you moving in."

"I know you do, but we both knew it would not have worked out. Best to know now."

"Goodness, where are my manners." She poured two cups of tea and cut a slice of Victoria sponge cake for Sophie. Refusing was not an option, but the cake was large and delicious and would definitely spoil her appetite for Cook's dinner.

"It must be a lot of work looking after boarders. How many do you have?" Sophie mumbled though a mouthful of cake.

"I have three regulars and one who comes just when he's in town on business. I don't like more than six, so it's nice if I can get a couple for the attic."

"I'll ask at the hospital. Doctors are often looking for digs. Now, I have to go. Take care of yourself Mrs. H and I'll drop by another day. Call me if you need anything."

Lying in her bed, Sophie rubbed her overfull stomach, swearing she'd never eat again. Cook had made her famous stew for dinner and treacle pudding to follow. She vowed to plan her shopping and social visits more carefully and try not to involve food.

A letter had arrived in the post from Italy. She recognized Paola's handwriting. Puffing up her pillow and making herself comfortable, she started to read the news from Lucca, which was usually written in Italian and needed concentration.

*Ciao Sophie,*

*I hope you are well. You haven't mentioned Andrew lately. Has he recovered from his illness? Perhaps you are already married.*

*First, news of the family. Mama had a winter cold and is recovered. The bakery supplies are back to normal for the regular ingredients but there are shortages of specialty items. I haven't seen Papa so happy since before the war. He sings as he bakes and serves his customers. The political situation is much the same with Blackshirts on every corner in Lucca.*

*I am afraid to go to Lucca alone. Luigi, Papa's assistant, comes with me to the suppliers. He's a big man, young and fit, and the Blackshirts walk away when they see him. I even stopped going to the Jazz Club after I was accosted one evening, parking the van. I got away, but they followed me to the club. When they saw the size of the doorman, they retreated. Harry insisted on picking me up from home, but Papa made a scene about me fraternizing with the English, so I haven't seen him or heard from him since that night. The last time I was at the club, your friend Carlos was not there. Harry said he'd had some kind of promotion. I didn't quite hear what. You know how noisy it can get. I miss Harry and I am sad, but it is for the best. Papa would never accept an Englishman.*

*Papa keeps pushing Luigi to take me out. He hired him when the bakery got busy again. He is a good baker and quite handsome, but he has not asked me out and he is not nearly as much fun as Harry.*

*The repairs on the villa are finished and Signor Cavaliere inspected it and has paid Giuseppe for his work. Papa asked if you are coming back to live or for a holiday? He is concerned about the villa being empty. There is much vandalism in the cities. He's afraid they will move further afield and suggests you rent it out. He would help you find tenants. Franco watches as best he can but with the acreage of vines between his house and*

271

*the villa, he can't see much.*

*Ciao, Paola*


Sophie leaned against the headboard. *Carlos, Grrr! Why does his name keep appearing? It seems every time I turn around, it's there. I'm being irrational. Of course, Paolo would mention him. Harry is his friend and, from what she said in the letter, I doubt she'll see them again.*

Re-reading the letter, Sophie took note of the important issues. She was pleased the repairs were finished and the solicitor had settled the account. She thought it would be safe and secure until their next visit. She hadn't thought about Blackshirts or vandals. Did she want to rent it out to strangers? She definitely did not want to sell. It was hers, her father's legacy, and her mother's spirit lived there. She chuckled. Perhaps her mother would chase off any intruders. A ghost would certainly scare them. Now she was being fanciful, as the only person who had the vision of her mother in the kitchen. Villa di Seta belonged to her, her father and mother. She could never leave them.

*However, I need to protect the property and get advice on how to go about it. Signore Cavaliere will know what to do. I will write to him.*

# Resolutions

It had been an eventful week without Trixie. The probationers had worked hard. The squabbling had stopped, which pleased Sophie, as she was forced to give them more responsibility until the new nurse started and that had worked out surprisingly well. The new nurse was due to start that day. Sister Kay was showing her around the hospital and would introduce her sometime during the morning, after rounds.

Nurses Harrington and Fox were doing a lot of whispering. Sophie suspected they were anxious about the new nurse, with good reason. They liked the extra tasks and would lose them when the new girl started.

Sister quickly made the introductions, having to rush off to a meeting with Matron, leaving Sophie to do the orientation.

As it turned out, there was no need to worry. The new arrival, Nurse Swindon, had only recently qualified and related more to the probationers than the established nurses. Nurse Fox immediately took her under her wing and harmony reigned. But for how long, Sophie was not sure. The phrase 'two's company, three's a crowd' ran through her head.

That morning, she had a surprise visitor. Hillary stood outside the ward waving to her. Knowing Sister was in a meeting, Sophie looked around to make sure everyone was busy and snuck into the corridor.

"Hillary, what are you doing here? Is something wrong," she asked, although the expression on Hillary's face was telling her the opposite.

"I am bursting to tell someone. I passed with 95%. I happened to be walking by the notice board as the secretary pinned the results up. I can hardly believe it. With those kind of marks, I get my pick of houseman jobs." She giggled excitedly. "Such a weird title for a junior doctor and I wonder if they will change it to 'house-woman.' One more set of exams in the spring and I'll be on the wards."

"Congratulations. That is wonderful news. This is so exciting, Hillary. I am so proud of you for not just becoming a doctor, but challenging that awful professor. What's happened to him?"

"I don't know, but I haven't seen him on campus. Maybe he resigned or was fired." Hillary giggled. "I don't really care. All three of us passed with over 85%. Reggie passed with 88%. I think that was the same as last time. I think we should celebrate at the Kingfisher. I'll speak with Reggie and let you know."

"I'd like that. I'm ready to dance. I bought a new dress yesterday. I'd better get back. See you later." Sophie rushed back to the ward before Sister returned. She had not been missed and everything was in order. It was almost too quiet. Days like this could be boring. The prospect of an evening of dancing made her smile. She should write to Paola and Signore Cavaliere, but that could wait one more day.

Reggie picked them up at seven, which was early for the club. Most people didn't arrive until ten. With the River House curfew for the older nurses and Hillary at ten, it cramped their style, but was better than eight, the probationers' curfew. Hillary had considered moving, mostly because she liked to study with Reggie until late, but rooms were expensive and she couldn't afford more. Sophie had never really thought about it until that night, but, as she was working the next day, she would not stay out later than ten.

Reggie kindly offered to dance with her, but there was no need as she had partners all evening. She was convinced it was the new dress. Whatever the reason, it turned out to be a fabulous evening. She didn't want it to end and from the look of Reggie and Hillary, neither did they. But they all dutifully returned to River house as Cook was about to lock up.

Far to wound up for sleep, Hillary slipped into Sophie's room and they talked about her exams and Reggie and the club. Sophie giggled over some of the less agile dancers, rubbing her toes that had been trampled on.

"You and Reggie are looking more like a couple every day. Anything new to tell me?" Sophie said.

"No, but I will admit, I think we are more than friends. He kissed me tonight on the dance floor. Just a peck but if we'd stayed longer, it might have been more."

"I am pleased for you. He's a nice man. Staying longer would be nice. It is getting tiresome having a curfew and we are not kids anymore. I've never thought about moving, but maybe we should think about getting our own rooms."

"I already thought about it. Reggie suggested I move, but I just can't afford it until I qualify. I haven't been able to work many nursing shifts because my study load is so heavy and it will get worse. The next few months are critical."

"I understand," Sophie said with a thoughtful frown. "I have an idea. Would you consider sharing with me?"

"Of course. What do you have in mind?"

"Mrs. Humphries! The rooms on the top floor Andrew and I were supposed to rent. It would be ideal. Two rooms, a sitting room and a bedroom. We'd have to share the bedroom but we'd have our own bathroom."

"You mean no more queueing for a wash in the morning?" Hillary heisted. "How do you feel about it? After all, it was to be your love nest."

"I'm fine. We worked things out and we are friends, the way it was meant to be. Now, what do you think? Our own bathroom, a sitting room where we could actually entertain friends, no curfew, and magnificent food at about the same as we are paying now." Sophie thought it might be a bit more, but she could pay the extra until Hillary qualified.

Hillary laughed. "It sounds perfect to me. If you are sure about this, I'm ready to move."

"I'll drop by tomorrow and talk to Mrs. Humphries. If she says yes, then we can tell Cook. I don't think it will be a problem. There are always probationers wanting to live here." Sophie stretched and rubbed her eyes. "Now I'm tired. See you tomorrow."

Sleep escaped Sophie once she went to bed. Her thoughts were digesting the day's events. For a quiet one, much had happened and the thought of sharing rooms with Hillary at Mrs. Humphries was exciting. The alarm buzzed while she was still thinking about the new digs; she supposed she had slept a little.

If she rushed, she had time to drop by and see Mrs. H before her shift. Now she was concerned that someone might have already taken the rooms. Sophie knocked on the back door.

Mrs. H would be cooking breakfast and she could avoid the boarders.

Refusing tea, Sophie said, "I'm on my way to the hospital so I don't have much time. I'll make this quick. Are your attic rooms still available?"

"I haven't advertised them yet. Do you know someone?"

"I sure do. I want to rent them with Hillary." Sophie smiled and then frowned when there was on reply. "Is there a problem?"

"No, no. You have made me so happy. I would like you to have them. Then Andrew might come back to visit."

Sophie continued to frown at Mrs. Humphries reply. Did she think Andrew would come back? "Andrew is not coming back, but he could visit." She decided to leave it at that. "I have to run. I'll bring Hillary around later this evening, if that's alright. One other thing. You mentioned putting two beds in the bedroom. Is that still possible?"

"Yes. I already asked my neighbour to help move the beds around. When will you move in? We'll talk about it tonight." Mrs. Humphries was beaming.

Cook was calm and matter of fact as Hillary and Sophie packed their things. It had not bothered her that they were moving out, making room for four probationers, two to a room. Sophie on the other hand was quite sad. River House had been a place of refuge when she had arrived broken-hearted and starting a new life. Mrs. Wilderby, had been kind and she had made lifelong friendships with Trixie and Hillary and others who had moved on.

Only a week had passed since they'd made the decision. The

girls hardly had time to pack suitcases and boxes and now they lined the hall, waiting for Chris to arrive. He had a big car and could move everything. He was returning from Beech Hall after delivering Trixie to his parents. In preparation for clearing out their flat, he'd invited one of his RAF buddies to help. The poor fellow finished up helping Hillary and Sophie as well. However, Mrs. Humphries rewarded them with a home cooked meal of steak and kidney pie. There were no complaints.

Hillary was twirling in the bathroom, in danger of knocking something over in her excitement. It was a small room but neither of them had had the luxury of not sharing with a bunch of other people, often strangers, and small or not, it was a novelty. Sophie dumped the last box in the bedroom and flopped onto the couch in the sitting room. She was enjoying the sitting room with a sofa and two big comfy chairs. Albeit the deep bottle green velvet had faded and worn away on the armrests, but they were comfortable. A small bureau and chair by the window was perfect for studying and letter writing and it included a fireplace. Mrs. Humphries had lit the fire and left them plenty of coal but lugging the coal scuttle up two flights of stairs might be a nuisance. Certainly, they would get used to it. It was a small price to pay for their own space.

The unpacking continued the next morning. Sophie had arranged to have two days off and Hillary put her studies to one side to sort things out, but they were finished with everything organized by noon. Hillary went to the library to pick up some textbooks and Sophie wrote letters.

Her letter to Signore Cavaliere was brief, informing him of her change of address and instructing him to look into the risk of vandalism and to suggest what might be done to increase security. Andrew's letter took a little longer, as he would be delighted she was living at Mrs. Humphries. The last letter was the reply to Paola's, explaining the details of why she and Andrew did not get married and why he was now in Scotland. She continued to say they were still friends and finally provided her new address. As she re-read the letter to herself, she couldn't help thinking her life was bizarre and the Bianchi family would quite possibly think she was crazy. Maybe she was, but she was happy crazy.

The weather had turned cold, but their little attic stayed warm with the fire and warm eiderdowns at night. Hillary and Sophie relaxed and enjoyed their day in front of the fire. They had decided to take it in turns fetching the coal and it would be unusual for them to be home all day so one scuttle of coal a day was all they needed. A sense of cosy companionship settled in their little place. Sophie usually read textbooks to please Andrew. A patient had suggested she try reading mysteries for pleasure. She was immersed in Agatha Christie's *An Affair at Styles.* Hillary mended her stockings. They made their own tea on a little hotplate and went down for dinner where Sophie introduced Hillary to the boarders.

Sophie's first walk to the hospital, although closer than River House, took her longer as it was foggy and icy under foot. When she arrived at the Bartley it was chaos. The Casualty Department was lined with ambulances, reminding her of the blitz.

"What is going on?" she asked the porter.

"Morning, miss! Road accidents. Cars sliding into each other. Some crazy drivers don't know how to drive slow. I reckon you'll be busy today."

"I agree. I'd better get to the ward."

Surprisingly, the ward was quiet. There were no new patients and everyone had arrived safely, including Sister Kay, who called everyone to pay attention.

"It is possible we could have a busy day. There have been several motor vehicle accidents, more than usual due to the icy conditions. Generally, gentlemen are victims of motorcar accidents so the Men's Ward will be busy today. I understand there are a few lady drivers and passengers injured and some unfortunate pedestrians are being treated in Casualty. Prepare for new admissions and possible trauma patients later today. Carry on, ladies!

The morning began with the usual routine, when suddenly chaos descended. Dr. Wilcox arrived early for rounds, flushed and angry. His entourage looked decidedly nervous. He immediately reprimanded Sister for not being ready. She said nothing. Experience had taught her to hold her tongue at such times. Sophie caught her eye and a wry grin escaped her lips. Blustering consultants did not intimidate Sister Kay and Sophie made a mental note to handle situations in the same manner.

A disturbance in the corridor sent Sophie to investigate and find a line of stretchers heading towards her. "Women's Ward," an orderly shouted.

"This way." Sophie stepped back to allow three gurneys to pass into the ward.

She nodded to Sister, indicating she'd take care of the new patients, while Dr. Wilcox went more colourful, his temper ready to explode. He announced loud enough for all to hear, "First the Men's Ward, now here. How am I expected to consult in such chaos?"

Sophie stared at him with disdain. He was such an odious

man, with no respect or consideration for staff or patients. She had thought he was improving. but his temper and arrogance were inexcusable.

"Nurse Harrington, transfer this patient to a bed and make her comfortable. Check the chart for injuries first. Nurse Fox, do the same with this lady, an injured pedestrian, I believe. Nurse Swindon, supervise and assist please."

Sophie glanced at the last stretcher coming towards her and her intuition told her this was not good. Judging by the woman's bobbed hairstyle and pearl necklace, still around her neck, she was no ordinary patient. Her ashen face and raspy breath made Sophie wonder if she was dying. It certainly indicated internal injuries or broken ribs from the steering wheel. She was the driver, not passenger.

"Take her to the bed in the corner. Nurse Swindon, fetch some screens, please, and I'll need your help," Sophie said, glancing at her chart. She stifled a gasp, seeing the extent of the injuries, from broken ribs and abrasions to multiple fractures of her right foot and ankle. Sophie lifted the bottom of the sheet to see a deformed foot at an impossible angle. She glanced up at the young pretty face and sighed. Only a miracle would save that foot.

Sister Kay stood at her side, Dr. Wilcox having left in a huff.

"How do we treat this patient, Sister?" Sophie's tone and body language indicated to Sister that her chances of surviving were slim. Pointing to the mutilated foot, Sophie shook her head.

Sister acknowledged with a subtle nod. "Morphine for now, as prescribed. An orthopaedic consult has been requested."

"Not Dr. McDonald?" Sophie said with horror.

"Perhaps, although I believe there is a new head of the department who started yesterday. I have not been introduced. The Board of Governors are pleased with their selection. He's experienced and served in the war. I believe he is known to them." Sister continued to study the chart. "I see the x-ray of Mrs. Thorpe's chest shows broken ribs, painful but that binding will ease the discomfort and they will heal. Keep the open wounds clean and watch her vital signs. It's about all we can do for now."

The patient groaned and opened her eyes. Sophie removed a wisp of dark hair from her forehead. "Mrs. Thorpe, you had a nasty accident and you are in hospital. My name is Nurse Romano and I will be taking care of you."

Mrs. Thorpe's eyes filled with panic. "I couldn't steer. The motorcar just slid into the wall."

"Shush. The roads were icy today. You have some serious injuries. Are you in pain?"

"It's awfully difficult to breathe, my head aches and my legs hurt." With panic, she added, "my legs, something's wrong with my legs,"

"You have injured your foot and a consultant has been called to take a look. I'll give you something for the pain. Try to relax."

Once the morphine took effect, Mrs. Thorpe calmed down and fell asleep. She looked odd lying there, badly injured, with three strands of undamaged pearls around her neck. They needed to be removed and Sophie wondered why Casualty had not done so. Deciding, she'd do it later and let her sleep for now, Sophie pulled the screens around the bed.

She heard Sister Kay greet someone at the nurses' desk and looked up and froze. *Is that ...no it couldn't be ...oh my goodness, it is.* Sophie bolted behind the screen, disturbing

Mrs. Thorpe.

"Nurse?"

"I'm sorry to disturb you." At that point, she realized that he would be coming to see Mrs. Thorpe and she had no way of escaping. "I believe the consultant is coming to see you. Let's make you comfortable." Sophie fluffed the pillows. Even in her groggy state, Mrs. Thorpe gave Sophie an odd look.

Firm footsteps of a long stride approached the screen. Sister Kay was explaining the patient's condition. Sophie swallowed hard and held her breath as Sister pulled the screens back. "Ah, good. Nurse Romano, Mr. Wainwright, our new head of orthopaedics, is here to see Mrs. Thorpe."

Carlos froze to the spot and stared before clearing his throat. "Nurse Romano, a pleasure. Nurse Romano and I have worked together before, several times. It is good to see you again."

Stunned, Sophie could not answer. Sister Kay frowned, forcing Sophie to say something. "Hello Mr. Wainwright." Her heart beat so hard, she put her hand on her chest, quite certain everyone could see it pounding.

# The Return

Why hadn't she realized Carlos was the new head of orthopaedics? Andrew had told her the overseas hospitals were closing. Did Andrew know Carlos was coming back? Even Paola mentioned Harry was being moved and she hadn't seen Carlos. Sister told her they were expecting an experienced ex-serviceman. She should have asked who it was. Why did it matter? Hadn't she pushed Carlos out of her mind? It was the shock. She would have liked some warning. That was all. She certainly had to get used to the idea of Carlos being around, particularly as she now had the reputation of being skilled at treating traumatic limb injuries.

By the time her shift was over, Sophie was exhausted. Her chest felt so tight, she thought she would burst. The thought of the new comfortable rooms and Hillary's companionship put a spring in her tired legs as she walked home.

Hillary had lit a fire and made tea when Sophie arrived.

"Dare I ask what kind day you had?" Hillary asked, as Sophie literally threw herself on the sofa.

"Carlos is back at the Bartley as Head of Orthopaedics."

"What!?"

"We had three patients admitted today as a result of motorcar accidents and one patient has a badly mangled foot. Guess who was the consulting orthopaedic surgeon?" Sophie went on to tell Hillary the whole story.

Hillary listened carefully. "When you think about it, it's not surprising. Do you think Andrew knew he was coming back?"

"Maybe. If he did, why didn't he warn me?"

"What if he did?

"How? He said nothing to me. Except that nonsense about my heart belonging..." Sophie did not finish the sentence. "Do you think he was referring to Carlos?"

Her eyes wide, Hillary nodded "I think it is quite possible. For an intelligent woman, there are times you surprise me, Sophie."

"Ah, there's the dinner bell," Sophie said with some relief. The conversation was stretching into places she did not want to go. Andrew's reasoning for departure was beginning to make sense and she wondered if Carlos had known Andrew was leaving.

Fortunately, Hillary had studying to do after dinner and Sophie hid her head behind her Agatha Christie book, thinking but not reading. She just had to remember to turn the page occasionally until she eventually left Hillary to her studies and went to bed, falling asleep almost immediately.


After a good night's sleep, a long chat with Hillary and a rationalizing lecture to herself, Sophie felt confident she could handle Carlos, the surgeon, and she would work on the personal side, if necessary.

Carlos had been in to see Mrs. Thorpe early before the

day shift had started and when Sophie arrived on the ward, Mrs. Thorpe had already been taken to the operating theatre. The operation would take several hours. She wondered if Mr. Thorpe had been informed. Usually, with trauma patients, relatives hung around, waiting for news and she didn't recall seeing anyone near Mrs. Thorpe. Then she remembered seeing a man sitting on the bench outside the ward when she'd arrived.

"Mr. Thorpe!" Sophie said, stepping out of the ward.

A pale, tired gentleman in a pinstripe suit looked up at her. "Yes."

"I'm Nurse Romano. I took care of your wife yesterday. I understand she's in surgery this morning."

"Mr. Wainwright talked to me this morning and explained her injury. He said he'd be able to repair her ankle but the foot was going to be complicated. He warned me she could lose the foot." He rubbed his forehead, his eyes full of tears. "I told her not to go out. I know how she drives and it was slippery. But she insisted. I should have stopped her."

"It's not your fault. She spoke to me yesterday. It wasn't her fault either. The motorcar slid into a wall on a patch of ice. I can tell you she has the best surgeon in the world. I served with him in Passchendaele and I've seen him save limbs and feet blown up by explosives. If anyone can save her foot, Mr. Wainwright can. It's going to be several hours. Why don't you go home and get some rest?"

"I can't. I have to be here."

"In that case, go down to the canteen and get some breakfast. I'll come and get you if there's any news."

"Alright. I could do with a coffee. You'll let me know if you hear anything?"

"Yes. Now go and take a break."

Sophie sat at the nurses' desk hoping she hadn't given Mr. Thorpe false hope. He was young and probably hadn't served in the war. Perhaps they'd only been married a short time.

"You are good at talking to people," Nurse Harrington said.

"Thank you. You learn that it is important to listen to relatives, as well as patients. That poor man is worried sick about his wife, but he needs to eat to keep his strength up for his wife. He also needs to know that the doctors and nurses will do their best. You'll make a good nurse, so remember that. How are things with you and Nurse Fox? Still squabbling?"

"No, we learned our lesson. I'm taking Dotty home for Christmas. I asked Sister if we could have the weekend off together."

"That's nice of you. She must be excited," Sophie said.

"She's nervous because she thinks we are too posh. My father won't be there. He never is. And Mama is busy with her charity stuff, except for Christmas Day and we'll be together for a few hours. Edwin is home so he's coming to pick us up. I want Dotty to meet my brother. I wanted you to meet him too. I've told him so much about you."

"I'm sure you and Dotty will be more than enough for the poor man. Now back to work."

It was late in the afternoon and after visiting hours before Mrs. Thorpe was brought to the ward. Her husband, who had sat a vigil on a hard bench outside the ward all day, desperately wanted to see her. When Sister went for her break, Sophie beckoned him in and pulled the screen around the bed so he would be there when she woke up.

To her surprise, Carlos came into the ward and went straight for Mrs. Thorpe's bed. She followed and when he walked in Sophie said, "I can explain, Doctor. Mr. Thorpe has been waiting all day…"

Carlos cut her off. "It's all right, Nurse. Mr. Thorpe is exactly where he should be, with his wife, and I need to talk to them both about the surgery. Then I'll explain to you what needs to be done for the recovery." His eyes lingered on Sophie a few seconds too long, which started her heart racing.

Catching her breath, she squeaked out, "Thank you, Doctor." Closing the screen, she walked down the ward to Sister Kay.

"Mr. Wainwright is with Mrs. Thorpe, and her husband is there too. He wanted to speak with both of them. He also mentioned there would be some special instructions for Mrs. Thorpe's care,"

Sister glanced at her time piece. "I'll wait for Mr. Wainwright. You go ahead. It's getting late. I will pass on his instructions tomorrow morning."

Sophie didn't need to be asked twice. She wanted to get as far away as she could.


Mrs. Humphries was serving dinner when Sophie arrived, full of apologies for her tardiness.

"No need, Miss Romano. I understand people get held up. Sit yourself down. There's a letter for you from Scotland." Mrs. H grinned. "I had one too."

After they ate, Sophie picked up the envelope from the hall table and felt strangely comforted by Andrew's handwriting.

*Dear Sophie,*

*How pleased I was to receive your letter and delighted that you and Hillary have moved to Mrs. Humphries' attic flat. She will be so pleased and I know you will keep an eye on her. She was so kind to me through some very dark days.*

*I have settled at Dalkeith Castle. It is a rambling, old stone house with decorative turrets, but not a real castle. Unbeknownst to me, my appointment included a flat right here on the premises. It is quite large, with a sitting room and bedroom that have a magnificent view of the hills. They were purple with heather when I arrived and now have a dusting of snow. I have my own kitchen and I have become quite adapt at cooking, although I do confess to eating some meals in the staff dining room.*

*My work is exactly as I expected. The staff are nice, supportive and passionate about the patients. Even Matron is amenable and the nurses are dedicated. The patients have many different mental ailments. I treat them all with varying degrees of success and have several research programs planned.*

*I have a confession, and you may have already guessed. By now, Carlos will be back at the Bartley, and yes, I did know he was returning, although how I found out was purely accidental. I literally bumped into him at the Italian restaurant. When they closed the overseas military hospitals, he decided to return to civilian life and was offered the position at the Bartley.*

*We had a serious discussion regarding opportunities, both personal and professional. I told Carlos that I had broken our engagement. He was surprised and very angry with me for hurting you, to the point I thought he might hit me. I had always known he cared for you but until that moment I had not realized his affection for you was so very deep. Carlos is a good man. I think you know that. I will say no more, except to ask you to consider what is in your true heart.*

*Please don't be angry with me for not warning you that Carlos was returning. I made a judgement that it was not up to me to interfere in your business. However, here I am, interfering as a friend.*

*I miss you. You would love it here, although it is rather cold, Mrs. Humphries place is much warmer than a drafty old castle and although the food is good, the meals do not come close to Mrs. H's cooking.*

*Your affectionate friend,*
  *Andrew*

"What does Andrew have to say," Hillary said, looking up from the bureau.

"Interestingly he's settled in and likes his new position. He confessed to knowing Carlos was back at the Bartley, with an apology for not telling me." Sophie pouted. "But I'm still angry. He also made some disturbing comments about Carlos."

"What do you mean, disturbing comments?"

Sophie passed the letter to Hillary. "Here. Read it."

Hillary raised an eyebrow after reading the letter. "Is it disturbing because it's true? When are you going to stop punishing Carlos for something that happened years ago? From my understanding, it was his mother's lies that prevented him from contacting you."

"Hillary, I'm surprised at you. I don't wish to discuss it further." Sophie left the room. Resisting slamming the door, she was angry, mostly with herself. She didn't know how she felt and she was afraid of the truth in her heart. "Why can't life be simple?!" Embarrassed by her tantrum, Sophie went to bed.

She pulled the covers over her head and curled up in a ball, wanting to be invisible in both body and mind, but her mind would not shut off. She went back to the day she was in a Base Hospital in France after Carlos had saved her leg and both Carlos and Andrew sat at her bedside, unsure if she would live or die. She had heard them talk, but not dared to think about it since that day. Carlos had broken her heart when she heard him say 'Goodbye, my dear Sophie.' She'd felt his tears on her cheek, telling her how much he loved her. Then he'd kissed her forehead and told Andrew to take good care of her.

She had wanted to call after him, but she was too ill and it was too late. And from then on, every time Carlos appeared in her life, she pushed him away, wanting to believe he would marry Rosamond. It made it easier to think he was not available. But, seeing his ringless finger in Italy, she could no longer pretend Rosamond was keeping them apart. She'd selfishly hidden behind Andrew and that was a terrible mistake because, in doing so, she'd broke Andrew's heart. Now her heart ached for Carlos and she wept tears of love lost until she fell asleep.

# Love Declared

The rain, wind and depressing grey skies of late November were brushed away by festive Christmas preparations. Streamers were strung across the wards and the scent of pine from decorated Christmas trees lifted the spirits of both staff and patients.

Sophie had managed to avoid Carlos all through the autumn, except in a professional capacity, especially with Mrs. Thorpe, who had made a remarkable recovery. Carlos had promised she could go home for Christmas if she could walk with a cane. Today was the day Mr. Wainwright would agree to discharge her. Sophie gave her an encouraging smile when he arrived on the ward.

"Good morning! Mrs. Thorpe, you are looking well. I'd like you to stand up from the chair and walk to the end of ward and back. If at any point you feel you have to stop, just raise your hand and Nurse Romano will come to your rescue."

Sophie stood next to Carlos, the smell of his cologne stirring some disturbing feelings inside her. Every time he came close or spoke to her, she had the desire to touch him, a desire she denied, squashing it like a bug under her shoe. It was becoming increasingly difficult to maintain her aloofness. She held her breath, and not for Mrs. Thorpe as she picked up her cane, but to block Carlos from her senses.

Mrs. Thorpe stood up from the chair and walked at a brisk pace to the end of the ward and back.

Carlos clapped. "Bravo! Well done. You may go home and have a wonderful Christmas." He turned to Sophie and more quietly said, "Bravo to you too, Sophie. Mrs. Thorpe's recovery is because of your nursing. Thank you." Carlos stared at her. Still holding her breath, she thought she might faint. His whispered breath tingled down her spine. Could he be feeling the same way? He cleared his throat, his attention now on the patient. "If you encounter any difficulty, call the hospital and they will contact me. Remember, light walking is good, including a short walk every day, but no running and elevate the leg when resting."

"Nurse, would you escort Mr. Thorpe to the ward. He is waiting in the lobby."

"Of course." Sophie began walking down the corridor and realized Carlos was at her side. Having given herself a good shake from her fantasy, she said, "Did you send me to the lobby so you could walk with me?"

"I've been trying to get your attention for weeks. You have been avoiding me ever since I returned to the Bartley. If it wasn't for the patient, I would never see you." He stopped and took her arm. "Please, Sophie, can we talk?"

Sophie looked around thankful the corridor was clear of people. "Not here. After my shift." Trying to cool the flush that covered her face, she hurried on to the lobby, not daring to look back. After her revelation the night before and feelings that morning, she felt panic. Was it possible that Carlos was aware of her thoughts and feelings? She shook herself again. *I'm being ridiculous. Of course not. It is just a coincidence.*

"Mr. Thorpe, I have good news. You can take your wife home today. Follow me. She's all ready to go. You'll be together for Christmas."

Sophie always felt good when patients walked out of the hospital fully recovered. Mrs. Thorpe was special. It had been touch and go as to whether the foot could be saved, and not only was it saved, but, with exercise Carlos predicted she would be walking normally without a cane in just a few months.

A cold wind whipped around the corner as Sophie waited for Carlos, part excited, part panicked and partly wondering what the heck she was doing. But she had decided that she needed to talk to him and ask questions, particularly about Rosamond. She resolved not to get involved. She just wanted answers and then she could tell Hillary and Andrew that any romance between Sophie and Carlos was long dead. They had both made irreparable mistakes and what once might have been, was long gone. "Calmly clear the air and then we can both get on with our lives," she stated to herself.

Sophie jumped six inches off the ground at the sound of his voice "I hope you haven't been waiting long." *So much for being calm*, she thought. *did he hear me?* "It's cold. I suggest we go to the café across the street."

Carlos guided her to a quiet table for two and ordered tea. She felt awkward, waiting for the tea, and tried to fill the time with idle chatter.

"How are you settling in? It must be different after being in the army for so long."

"It is, but in some ways it is as though I've never been away.

I am discovering that running a whole department is rather challenging, especially as we are understaffed. My so-called right hand man, Dr. McDonald, is young and inexperienced and not even a fully qualified surgeon, but he has high praise for you."

"Poor fellow tries hard, but he did not know what he was doing. I had to show him the signs of infection on a poorly splinted leg. He started off, full of himself and a bit arrogant, but he was humble enough to take my advice about the leg injury. Not many young doctors would have done that. I think he has promise and, with a good mentor, he'll do well."

The waiter placed the cups and teapot on the table with a large plate of assorted cakes, scones and porkpie.

Sophie giggled. "Hungry, are you?"

"Starving! My landlady is not the best of cooks and if you're late, which I frequently am, she doesn't save dinner."

"Mrs. Humphries is the opposite. It doesn't worry her if you're late. She keeps your dinner warm, but the plate hardly resembles food once it has dried up in the oven," Sophie said, laughing.

"I'm not sure which would be worse, nothing at all, or having to eat something inedible," Carlos added, joining in the humour.

Laughing eased the tension and Sophie poured the tea and helped herself to a scone. Her insides were fluttering like a hundred butterflies and she wanted to giggle.

Carlos looked at her seriously. "Sophie, I've been a complete idiot and I'm sorry."

"Sorry for what?"

"I don't know where to start. I feel as though I've made a mess of things between us and whatever I do, I make it worse or don't do anything and that makes it even more terrible." Carlos slipped his fingers under his collar and loosened it.

"You are not making sense, but I think I understand what you are saying. May I suggest you start at the beginning? Maybe after your mother deceived us both by not giving you my letter and telling you of my father's death and the terrible situation I was in."

"Had I known, things would have been very different. I wish I had tried to find you. I would have married you, Sophie. I loved you then as I love you now. I never forgave my mother, but then she never forgave me for breaking off my engagement to Rosamond. She died last year, a victim of Spanish flu."

"Oh, I'm so sorry. I didn't know. And your father?"

"He's doing well, still runs the import/export business. The war took its toll, but he survived."

"I thought you had married Rosamond. Hillary scoured the newspapers and she kept telling me she had seen no announcement. I should have inquired but I was in Belgium and, as far as I knew, you had gone on leave to marry and then you disappeared."

"Every time our paths crossed, something intervened and parted us. When I agreed to marry Rosamond, I honestly believed I would never see you again. Imagine my surprise when you turn up at the Bartley as a nurse and then again in Passchendaele. I remember wondering how it could happen and then it was too late. I tried, but you kept pushing me away."

"Yes, because you were engaged to be married. I was not going to be accused of coming between you and your fiancée. You seemed quite happy."

"I was until I saw you again and I finally told Rosamond the week before our nuptials. She called the wedding off. My mother's fury went beyond anything I'd seen before. I didn't come back because my orders were to go to the front. When I returned, you and Andrew were dating."

"That was a mistake on my part. It should not have happened. But, after the bomb explosion in Passchendaele, Andrew saved my life." Sophie sighed. "I was so ill and then you saved my life and my leg. I wanted to thank you and I overheard you tell Andrew to take care of me, I thought it was over."

"I have never regretted anything more than that day in France when I walked away. I thought I was doing the right thing. I did not deserve your love and Andrew did."

"He did, Andrew stayed with me and he loved me but I confused my feelings of friendship with love. The war ended and I never thought I would see you again."

"After the war I was sent to a hospital in Lucca. That brought back memories. When Harry told me he had met you at the Jazz Club, I thought I must be hallucinating. When we came by the villa, I had told Harry I was going to tell you I loved you. Being at the villa was just perfect, taking us back to the silkworm days. But when you said you were leaving the next day, I couldn't. There you were, slipping through my fingers again."

Sophie gave him a big smile. "You know, it might have worked. That was the day I saw your naked finger and realized you were not married. But then you disappeared yet again. I was already betrothed to Andrew. He proposed to me after I recovered from the bomb injuries and I had happily accepted. But, as time went by, I had niggling doubts and was reluctant to set the wedding date. When Andrew picked me up in Dover. I decided you had flipped in and out of my life one time too many and Andrew was stable and reliable. During the drive back to London, it felt like the right time to name the wedding date."

Carlos ate a piece of pork pie and Sophie buttered another scone as they fell silent.

"Andrew knew all along that your heart belonged to me. It is because of Andrew that I'm talking to you now. He loves you as much as I do. He was afraid you would regret marrying him. He told me in no uncertain terms to make you happy. Sophie, I can promise you I will not disappear ever again." He leaned across the table and took her hands in his. "I love you and always have. Please give me another chance?"

Sophie swallowed hard and sipped at her tea, tears filling her eyes. Carlos, moved his chair next to hers, lifted her chin and whispered, "Please say yes." He kissed her she returned it, wanting him so badly she thought she might burst. But she was afraid, afraid he would disappear again.

"It is too soon, Carlos. I love you with all my heart, but you will not break it again."

Carlos stared at her, his expression that of a guilty little boy. "I am sorry for the past and I promise I will never break your heart. Can I start by asking you to have dinner with me?"

Sophie placed her hands on his cheeks and kissed him. "Yes, that would be a good place to start. Now you can take me home for a dried up, inedible dinner."


Preparing for the impending Christmas holidays kept them both busy and the closest they got to dinner was the canteen or across the street at the café. Carlos' new duties kept him at the hospital and Sophie had agreed to work over Christmas to allow Nurses Harrington and Fox to spend Christmas together. Only a skeleton of staff was needed at holiday times as most patients were discharged to be with their families.

Christmas on the wards was festive. Each ward had a Christmas tree and garlands were strung form the ceiling. A corner of the ward was screened off to hide a table of snacks and a bottle of sherry. Sister Kay invited the doctors and nurses for a glass before the arrival of the bird. A small capon was delivered to each ward at lunchtime and one of the doctors was invited, usually with his family, to carve the turkey. Dr. Wilcox was not available, much to everyone's delight, and Mr. Wainwright was asked to do the honours.

Sophie watched Carlos carve. Not having any family to celebrate with, it felt good to be together. If it wasn't for being on duty, Sophie would have been with strangers. Hillary had gone to her sister's to be with her father and family. Mrs. Humphries had planned a dinner for those boarders who had no other home to go to. Sophie had chosen to be at the hospital, working a double shift, and was glad.

Carlos picked her up when the night staff took over and drove her home. They had drifted into a comfortable courtship, mostly on hospital grounds. Carlos had made no attempt to push her beyond where she wanted to go. Sophie surmised that having two medical careers, a good portion of their lives would be spent at the hospital and this would perhaps be normal and she liked it. Neither of them had expressed any interest in a family and Sophie was okay with that, but a house would be nice. She had found herself thinking about buying a little house again and she had no reservations about sharing it with Carlos. She wondered why sharing property, either a house in London or the villa, had seemed to be such a problem with Andrew. The reason probably related to the Villa di Seta, because Carlos, not Andrew, belonged there. Perhaps it was the same for a London house.

Carlos parked his motorcar. "Is everything all right? You are very thoughtful."

"Miles away, thinking about the villa."

"Italy! I'd like to go back with you, just the two of us. A trip down memory lane."

"I'd like that. Do you think we could get time off at the same time?" Sophie said thoughtfully.

"Maybe in the spring, but not before."

Sophie kissed him and waved goodnight, feeling excited at the prospect of returning to Italy.

# Poor Dotty

Christmas Day and Boxing Day had been fun. She'd enjoyed spending it with Sister Kay and the patients and, of course, Carlos. Because she'd worked both days, she had an extra day off. Taking advantage, she slept late. It seemed odd not to wake up to Hillary sleeping or studying. The whole house sounded quiet, making Sophie feel anxious. She always liked lots of people around her.

She decided to visit River House. There were always people there and she wanted to visit Cook and give her a Christmas present; a set of wooden spatulas she'd bought from Selfridges.

Cook was delighted to see Sophie and anyone would have thought the spatulas were studded with diamonds, she was so pleased with them. It appeared that bamboo spatulas were the best one could buy.

"You couldn't have called on a better day," Cook whispered. "I have a problem and I don't know what to do."

"Cook, whatever is wrong?"

"It's Nurse Fox. She was supposed to spend Christmas with Nurse Harrington. The chauffeur picked them up Christmas Eve and they was so excited. Nurse Fox's eyes were as big as saucers when the chauffeur opened the motorcar door for her. It was a treat to watch. And Nurse Harrington was so proud."

"So what happened?"

"Nurse Fox was driven back 'ere late Christmas afternoon. Edwin, Nurse Harrington's brother, brought her back. She were crying some'at awful. He was very kind, trying to console her, but she ran up to her room and locked herself in. Mr. Edwin said he was sorry, but something had happened and she'd been sent home. He said it was none of her doing and asked me to take care of her. I asked him when his sister was coming back and he said he didn't know."

"Has she been downstairs since?" Sophie's forehead creased with worry.

"No. I knocked on the door last night, thinking she might like a cup of tea, but she said she was all right and needed to sleep. I went back this morning and she told me to leave her alone. I'm worried about her."

"And with good reason, Cook. Something terrible must have happened at Beech Hall. Lords and Ladies can be quite cruel and I suspect Dotty didn't fit in. Would you like me to talk to her?"

"Oh, would you? She likes you. In fact, both of them miss you since you moved out. They looked up to you. I missed ya too."

"You are too kind. I'll go up now and see if she'll talk to me."

Sophie knocked on Dotty's door. "Dotty, it's Sophie Romano. Cook tells me you are upset and she's worried about you. Can I come in and talk to you?"

A rustling sound and then a throat clearing and a nose blowing. "Nurse Romano, I want to be left alone."

"Dotty, what happened? Perhaps I can help. It's a bit rude

talking through a door. Can you open it for me?" Relieved to hear the key turn in the lock, Sophie had her foot ready to push her way in if necessary. But it wasn't, as Dotty opened the door wide and fell into Sophie's arms.

She cradled her and they sat on the bed. "Shush, sweet Dotty. Tell me what happened."

Sophie took a clean handkerchief from her pocket and wiped Dotty's face, which brought a smile to her lips. "Mi mam used to do that." She took a deep, uneven breath. "I wish she were here. She'd know what to do."

"I'm sorry you miss your mum. I'm a good listener."

Dotty sniffed and wiped her face dry. "Are you sure? It's a long story."

"I am sure." Sophie slipped her arm around Dotty and let her rest her head against her shoulder.

"It was so special. The chauffeur picked us and drove us to Beech Hall. I've never been in a motorcar driven by a chauffeur. Clarice was quite the lady knowing exactly what to do and say. Edwin met us at the door and we had a posh tea. He is very nice and handsome in his uniform. Did you know he's a military doctor?"

"I think Clarice mentioned it."

"Clarice showed me around the house. It is enormous. I stuck with Clarice, afraid I'd get lost. She loaned me one of her dresses for dinner and a maid came and did our hair. It was just the three of us for dinner as Clarice's parents were out. In fact, I didn't meet them until lunch on Christmas Day. Clarice had told me that they had their Christmas dinner at lunchtime. And, then there was some kind of ceremony around the tree before opening their presents." Dotty began to cry again. "I never got to see that."

"Take your time. What happened next?"

"We had this big dinner, not turkey. They 'ad roast beef. It were the size of a donkey. There were other things and Clarice helped me with the courses and cutlery. Lord Harrington were cold and angry, shouting at the servants. It weren't very pleasant. Anyway, we had the beef and then it were time for pudding. They turned the lights out and the butler walked into the dining room, carrying a plum pudding on fire. Blue flames were all around the pudding and I was so shocked I shouted 'core blimey!' Lord Harrington banged on the table and glared at me. I knew I shouldn't have said that and Clarice jabbed me in the ribs. Lady Harrington tried to smile and told the butler to put the pudding on the table. Everyone clapped and cheered." Her tears were flowing now and Sophie squeezed and rocked her a little.

"Something else happened?"

Dotty nodded her head and sniffed. "He told me to stand by his chair, so he could get a good look at me. He stared into my face again and asked me my name. I said Dorothy Eva Fox. I thought it better to use my full name. My mam's name were Eva. I never use it. He went crazy and told me to get out. He said I was a gold digger and to get out of his house. Lady Harrington, shouted 'Thomas, calm down. You're frightening the girl.' Edwin tried to defend me and that made him even more angry. Clarice stood up and he ordered her to stay where she was and yelled, 'Get out!' Edwin got up from the table, ignoring his father's demand to sit down, and he came with me to collect my things. He said his father was injured during the war and was known to have unreasonable outbursts that could last for many days. Under the circumstances, he thought it better if he drove me home."

Sophie had a strange feeling that she had found what she sensed was missing, but she needed more information.

"I'm so very sorry, Dotty. You must have been terrified. I had a feeling from Clarice that her father was a cruel man, but this is unfathomable."

"What did I do wrong? I don't understand and now I've lost the best friend I ever had."

"Hey, look at me. You did absolutely *nothing* wrong. It is Lord Harrington who is wrong. Clarice will be back. You haven't lost a friend either. Now let's dry those eyes and go downstairs and have Cook make us something to eat. I promise you, we will work this out."

Cook already had the kettle on and a bowl of hot soup ready for Dotty when they arrived in the kitchen.

"Dotty had a bad experience with Lord Harrington. He lost his temper, nothing to do with Dotty, but he saw fit to take it out on her. Rather than be abused, she decided to come home. Clarice will be back after the holiday, I presume." Sophie made it a statement, not wanting Cook to pry. Dotty could tell her more when she was ready.

"You poor lass. Them posh people have no manners. Here, have some soup and I'm heating up some mince pies. Don't you take no notice of the likes of them. You's worth ten of them, Nurse Dotty."

Sophie drifted off into thought. Lord Harrington's behaviour bothered her. Something must have set him off. She was familiar with shell-shock, but there was something about this that was different. His outburst was excessive towards Dotty. She needed to know more, but it was unlikely she'd find out more about the Harringtons. Maybe she could learn more about Dotty.

"Dotty, what do you remember about your father?"

"Nothing. He left us when I was little. Mam said he just upped and left. It's been just me, mi mam and mi brother, till he were killed."

"Did your mother help you get into the nursing program before she died?"

"No, but she said to go to this solicitor office after she died and he would help me. It was a big fancy office, Grenville, Grenville and Sons, and he said I had a benefactor who would provide for me to go to nursing if that was what I wanted. I asked who it was and he said he couldn't tell me. It were confidential."

Sophie smiled at Dotty's attempt to improve her grammar. Was and were seemed particularly difficult for her. Clarice and been working with her, but it was going to take a long time.

"Cook, may I use your telephone, and do you have a directory?" Sophie asked.

"Go ahead. Directory is under the telephone."

Grenville, Solicitors was listed on Regent Street in London. Sophie dialled the number, not sure if the offices would be open. She was in luck when a receptionist answered. Sophie asked to speak with Miss Dorothy Eva Fox's solicitor. She was put on hold and was expecting the receptionist would ask questions, but she didn't. She said Mr. Arthur Grenville was on holiday and asked if madam wanted to leave a message. There was no message. She would call again. *Well, at least the solicitor exists so the rest of the story must be true,* Sophie thought.

Picking up the telephone receiver again, she telephoned Carlos at the hospital. "Carlos, I can't explain now but I may need your help. Do you know the solicitor, Arthur Grenville?" Carlos did not know him but Grenville senior had been his father's London solicitor for years. Sophie thanked him. *Perfect,* she thought. *I'll take Carlos with me to see if I can get any answers as to the identity of Dotty's benefactor.*

Cook removed steaming hot mince pies from the oven and poured more tea. Dotty, although red-eyed and puffy from two days of crying, was looking more like herself.

Sophie was wondering if Dotty's long lost father was her benefactor. She needed to see documents. "Dotty, do you have any of your mother's papers, things like birth or marriage certificates? Those kind of papers?"

"No. We didn't have much and the landlord threw me out. I had just a few clothes. The solicitor gave me money for boots and the uniform. Oh, I have a box Mam said to keep safe. I never looked inside."

"Can I see it?"

"Yea. It's in my room."

It was a small, polished wooden box and it did indeed contain documents. Dotty's birth certificate, her brother's, plus his death certificate as well as her mother's birth certificate, and a marriage certificate between Eva Grimes and Albert Fox, dated four months before Dotty's birth. Eva had already been pregnant when they married. There were some letters and the document from Grenville, Grenville and Sons.

"Dotty, would you mind if I took this for a day or two? I'd like to read through the legal documents."

Dotty shrugged her shoulders. "Okay by me. Are they important?"

"They could be. If there is information about your benefactor in here, it might be useful for your studies."

Dotty shrugged again.

"Will you be all right?" Sophie directed her question to Dotty and Cook. "I have some errands to run and then I'm meeting Carlos."

"I'll take care of her," Cook said, patting Dotty's shoulder.

Sophie called Carlos again. She had an idea and, if she was right, she thought she knew the identity of Dotty's benefactor. She asked Carlos to meet her at her digs after dinner. It was a bit risky and Mrs. Humphries might object as Hillary was away, but she wanted Carlos to look at the documents and, if truth be told, Sophie was getting tired of the assumption they would misbehave if not chaperoned.

# More than Friendship

Mrs. Humphries had a visitor for dinner that night. Her sister from Croydon had come for a Christmas visit. Once dinner was over, she entertained her sister in the kitchen. Sophie stood at the lounge window waiting for Carlos, planning to be at the door before he rang the bell.

She had tidied up and made the sitting room look cosy with a fire and, when he arrived, she quickly whisked him upstairs.

"This is lovely. You and Hillary must be comfortable here." Carlos stood in front of the fire, cold from the drive over.

"Thank you. We really like it. Hillary studies over there and I like to read in front of the fire."

She sat on the sofa and Carlos settled next to her. It felt good sitting together alone, not worrying about other people in a restaurant or co-workers in the canteen or corridor at the hospital. Carlos casually stretched his arm across the back of the sofa and Sophie wanted to smile at his not too subtle move. She wondered if this was such a good idea. She wanted to kiss him and every time she saw him, her desire for him increased. She really wanted to trust him, but doubt kept creeping into her thoughts. Would he leave her again? Did she want to spend the rest of her life with him? She knew the answer to the latter. It was the former that frightened her.

He gently pulled her towards his side but made no attempt to kiss her. They just relaxed, feeling warm and good.

"This is nice," Carlos said. "How did you get it past Mrs. Humphries?"

"I didn't tell her. She was busy entertaining so I decided I'm an adult and see no reason why I can't entertain gentleman callers in my sitting room."

"A gentleman caller, indeed." His fingers ran through a strand of Sophie's hair. "You are a very modern woman and I like it. I do think we have gone beyond Edwardian drawing room etiquette. We fought a war, it's 1920 and that has changed things."

"I hope I am as brave when Mrs. Humphries scolds me." Sophie took Dotty's wooden box from the table. "There was a reason I asked you here tonight, beyond your charms, of course." She giggled.

"Ah, the mystery of Dotty the nurse," he said, teasing.

"This is serious. Ever since I met Dotty and Clarice, I've sensed there was something different but, for the life of me, I cannot explain what." Sophie went on to describe their different backgrounds, strong friendship and of Dotty's experience at the Harringtons, finishing with the connection to the solicitors.

"I'm not sure how I can help. My father was and probably still is a client of Mr. Grenville, senior, I believe he has two sons in the business now. I do find it odd that his son Arthur is Dotty's solicitor. Lords, earls and knights are mostly the firms clientele."

"If I make an appointment, would you come with me? I want to find out who Dotty's benefactor is. You or your father know the Grenvilles and they might tell you."

"Information like this is confidential and no matter who I am, they will not tell me." He frowned. "Why do you want to know?"

Sophie took a deep breath. "I think Lord Harrington is Dotty's father and benefactor."

"What! Sophie darling, where in the world did you get that idea?"

"Dotty's mother worked as a maid in a big house and was forced to leave. I bet she was pregnant. Dotty thinks her father ran out on them when she was a little, probably after he realized Dotty wasn't his." Sophie opened the box and pulled out the marriage certificate. "See the date and now see the date on Dotty's birth certificate, only four months after they were married."

"That doesn't make Lord Harrington her father. Albert Fox is listed as her father. It sounds more like Albert did the right thing and then regretted it."

Sophie sighed. "What about the similarities, their unusual green eyes and the strong friendship? And this?" She waved the Grenville document in the air.

Carlos took it. "The similarities are coincidental. Lots of people have green eyes and the girls are good friends. You are seeing things that are not there. Now, this document is a different story. I grant the benefactor is a mystery and this might tell us something." Carlos settled in to read the legal language.

Sophie tucked her feet under her and gazed around her sitting room, enjoying the domestic scene and realizing how natural it felt with Carlos. She appreciated his willingness to help.

She opened the wooden box and removed some scraps of paper with brief messages, mostly meeting places. There were no signatures, but there was a letter.

*Eva,*

*Under the circumstances, I cannot see you again.*
*I enclose £50 to do what you have to do.*
*T*

Was the T for Thomas Harrington? Sophie assumed the money was for an abortion. Then she smiled. It was written on Harrington letterhead.

"I was right all along!" She handed the paper to Carlos.

"I agree that is pretty damming, but vague enough not to be proof, although the letterhead is a giveaway. I've read this document from Grenville's and I do think you are right." He leaned over, giving her a kiss and a smile. "Yes, I am admitting I might have misjudged the situation. However, the clauses regarding confidentiality are tight and Dotty would lose if his identity was revealed."

"I think that has already happened."

"How?" Carlos asked, puzzled.

"When Lord Harrington challenged Dotty, she gave her full name, Dorothy Eva Fox. That was when he told her to get out. I think he realized who she was."

"So, exactly what do you want me to do? Are you planning to tell Dotty? And what about Clarice and the family?"

"I don't know, except you could approach the Grenville's. I hadn't thought about the family, but I think Dotty should know who her father is and that Clarice is her half-sister."

"You do realize that this could end badly." Carlos gave her a stern look. "Leave it alone, Sophie. Dotty is happy being a nurse and having a friend in Clarice. If you promise me you will leave things as they are, I will speak with Grenville, but only to make sure Dotty is protected."

"All right," Sophie agreed with reluctance, acknowledging she had not thought of the consequences.

Carlos got up to poke the fire and Sophie poured them a sherry each. "Sorry, it's all I have. You would probably prefer brandy."

"With you, it will taste like nectar. Have you thought anymore about us? I know I was supposed to take you to dinner and I haven't done that yet." He hesitated. "Sitting with you here is better than dinner out. I imagine one day this will be us every day. Please tell me you would like this too?"

Should she tell him she had had those exact thoughts?

Sophie glanced at Carlos. "Someone is coming up the stairs." Sophie went to the door. "Mrs. Humphries, what a surprise. Come in."

"I thought you had company," she said with pursed lips.

"Mrs. Humphries, allow me to introduce my very good friend, Mr. Carlos Wainwright."

"Pleased to meet you. This is highly irregular."

"I don't think it is irregular for me to entertain my friends in my sitting room. Mr. Wainwright and I have known each other for a very long time and if my father had no objection to us keeping company, I don't think you should either, Mrs. Humphries. Now, won't you join us for a glass of sherry?"

Lips tightly pursed and a with a little waggle of her head,

Mrs. Humphries said, "I don't mind if I do."

By her second glass of sherry, Mrs. Humphries had loosened her lips and was chatting away about her sister's visit and a little bit about Mr. Humphries, who was lost in the war. When Carlos expressed his desire to leave, she insisted on escorting him down the two flights of stairs, chattering all the way.

Two days later, Sophie received two surprises. Carlos had contacted Grenville, Grenville & Sons. Mr. Grenville, senior, confirmed in a roundabout way that Sophie's suspicions were correct. The benefactor had withdrawn his support for Dotty but another had stepped forward and Dotty was required to attend his office. Hearing the news, Sophie insisted on being there and Carlos drove them to Regent Street.

Edwin and Clarice Harrington were already in the office when they arrived. Clarice jumped up and gave Dotty an enormous hug. "I can't believe we are sisters."

"Sisters? I don't understand." Confusion written all over Dotty's face, she looked to Sophie for an answer.

"If you would all take a seat, I will explain," Mr. Grenville said from behind his oak desk and gestured towards the vacant chairs.

"Miss Fox, your father is Lord Harrington, who was also your benefactor. Your mother made sure you would be provided for in the event of her death. A strict condition of confidentiality was part of the agreement, which he believed to have been compromised and rescinded that agreement.

"Upon discovering he had another sister, Captain Harrington has taken on that responsibility and will provide for you

314

and his sister Clarice. Captain Harrington will explain the rest. I wish you all well. Good day!" He turned his attention to Carlos. "How is your father?"

"He is well, a little lonely since mother died, but still running the business. I will tell him I saw you."

Sophie took Dotty's arm. "Everything will be all right Dotty. I'm sure it was a shock."

"It was, but I knew there was something different about Clarice. I can't believe I have a sister and a brother and a father. Poor man, he must have been so shocked when he saw me at Christmas. I honestly did not know."

"You are very kind, Dotty, but I doubt he will be a father. I'm glad you found a sister and a brother. Edwin will take care of you."

Sophie had the distinct feeling that Lord Harrington had disowned the girls. Edwin was his heir so he would not disown him and Edwin knew that and was protecting his sisters.


Sophie and Carlos returned to the Bartley. Carlos had a new surgeon to introduce and train, Dr. McDonald had moved on, deciding surgery was not for him. Carlos was looking forward to Mr. Kent, a well-trained surgeon who had served in the war. Sophie rushed to the nurses' lounge. She had to change into her uniform before going to the ward. She expected to be in trouble as she was extremely late for her shift. She had notified Sister Kay she'd had an emergency, but her reasons were not exactly an emergency, and would be difficult to explain.

Nurse Swindon and a new probationer looked frazzled

when she arrived and Sister Kay was nowhere to be seen. She sent the probationer for a break. Nurse Swindon informed her that Sister Kay was in a meeting with Matron and the governors. She checked the charts before sending Nurse Swindon off for a break when the probationer returned.

Sophie was aware there were major changes coming to the hospital. The war and the aftermath had changed things and the hospital needed to change with the times. The shortage of doctors had eased as military doctors were demobilized. Many women, having worked during the war, were looking for opportunities and nursing was one, so there was a steady stream of probationary nurses, which pleased Sophie as she loved training the young girls.

# Celebrations

Sophie stared down the ward at empty beds. She couldn't remember a time when the ward had been that empty. There was a case of pneumonia, a car accident, a heart condition and two patients under observation, which usually meant the doctors didn't know what was wrong. Nurses Harrington and Fox had returned from their holiday and momentous discovery.

Sister Kay ordered the probationers to clean cupboards and chores that were often neglected when they were busy. Nurse Swindon attended to the patients and Sophie was surprised to be summoned to Matron's office.

Beth, Matron's secretary, was all smiles. "Nurse Romano, Matron will be with you soon." She lowered her voice to a whisper. "Reprimand. Caught with boyfriends on hospital property. Sister MacPherson's ward."

"Beth, you hear it all. Anything new?"

Getting up from her desk, Beth whispered, "Changes coming. After the big board meeting, I heard Matron and Sister Kay talking, but I didn't have all the information and didn't understand, other than lots of changes."

Matron's door opened and two somber nurses stepped out and rushed past Sophie and Beth.

"Beth, can you come in here, please."

Beth disappeared into the office and returned with files in her hand. "You can go in now. Good luck."

Sophie hesitated, wondering if she needed it.

"Good morning, Matron."

Sophie didn't like the scowl Matron had. She was usually cheerful. "Good morning, Nurse Romano. Although, so far, it has not been the best."

"I'm sorry to hear that, Matron."

Matron looked up. "Forgive me. I find reprimanding mostly good nurses taxing."

Assuming she was not expected to answer, Sophie sat quietly and waited for Matron to finish writing notes in a file. She looked up and smiled, relieving Sophie's anxiety. "As you may be aware, the hospital is making some radical changes to departments and services, as well as staff. Sister Kay will be working with me on some special projects. Nurse Romano, I have great pleasure in offering you the position of Sister for the Women's Ward."

Sophie held her breath, speechless. *Say something. Open your mouth. If you don't breathe, you'll faint.* "Um, I don't know what to say." Sophie bit her bottom lip and a broad smile stretched across her face. She slapped her hand on her heart, which was pounding. "I could hug you, Matron. Oh, I'm sorry, that was very inappropriate."

"Not at all. You deserve this more than anyone else I know. You will make a wonderful nursing sister."

"I can't believe it's the Women's Ward too, literally a dream come true. I have big shoes to fill. Sister Kay is one of the best teachers and Sisters."

"Have faith. You will fill those shoes more than adequately."

Matron opened a drawer and handed Sophie a Sister's cap. "The rest of your uniform will follow. You'll be starting your new duties in two weeks' time. Sister Kay will work with you for the next week or so. Now, my dear, go and celebrate."

"Thank you, Matron."

Beth, who heard everything in Matron's office, rushed to her with hugs of congratulations. "I am so excited. You are one of the best. I am so happy for you."

"Thank you, Beth. What did I do to deserve such praise?" Sophie tried to wipe the grin from her face, but she just could not. She couldn't wait to tell Carlos and Hillary.

Sister Kay and the nurses were waiting for her when she returned and in unison said, Congratulations, Sister Romano. Even the patients clapped. Sophie thought she might burst with pride. Suddenly everyone scuttled off to their work. Dr. Wilcox, with only two juniors, walked on to the ward.

"I hear congratulations are in order. Well done, old girl. Couldn't happen to a better nurse. The only one who has ever put me in my place." He gave a gaff-aff, which Sophie assumed was meant to be a laugh. "So why don't you start by joining us for rounds this morning?"

Sophie glanced at Sister who nodded. "Thank you. Dr Wilcox, gentleman, this way."

It seemed that everyone in the hospital knew of Sophie's promotion, except Carlos, who had been in surgery most of the day. She left a message for him to call that evening.

Mrs. Humphries was delighted about the news and Sophie phoned Hillary as soon as she arrived home. She would have liked to celebrate with her friend but a telephone call would have to do for now. She wanted to call Andrew but hesitated, waiting to tell Carlos first. She didn't have to wait long. Carlos did not call but drove over, already having heard the news through the hospital grapevine. Mrs. Humphries insisted he stay for dinner.

New Year's Eve looked to be a non-event for Sophie. Even though she had New Year's Eve and New Year's Day off, there was nowhere to go or at least nobody to go with. Hillary was still away and Trixie and Chris were at a masquerade party at Beech Hall. They had invited her, but Sophie had declined. Carlos was working. All the boarders were out for the evening and Mrs. Humphries had gone to her friend's house.

Sitting by the fire, feeling a little sorry for herself, she heard the telephone ring and debated whether to run down two flights of stairs or let it ring. Curiosity set her feet running. It could be Hillary or Trixie.

Carlos' deep voice filled her ears. "I have a surprise for you. Put on the very best dress you own and I will pick you up in an hour."

"Where are we going?" Sophie asked, feeling excited.

"It is a surprise. I'll give you a hint. It is your very favourite place, plus a surprise." Carlos hung up.

Sophie ran upstairs, inspected her wardrobe and took out her Romano silk dress, the very best dress in her wardrobe. She only hesitated a second. Was this a wedding dress? She shook her head. It had never been a wedding dress. It had always brought back memories of Italy, Romano silk, her father and Carlos. This was the perfect dress for tonight. She had a quick bath, and did her hair, finger waves in the front with diamanté clips she had bought at Selfridges and let the rest of her hair fall loosely on her shoulders. She slipped the dress on, allowing the silk to slide sensually over her body. The butter blond colour contrasting her dark hair and olive skin, she felt radiant.

She stood behind the door. Hearing his footsteps on the steps, she waited for the bell to ring and opened the door. The hall light shone on the most handsome man in the world wearing a white dinner jacket, black bowtie and a smile that lit up his whole face.

He held out his arms and stepped inside. "Sophie, you look beautiful." His hands brushed along her long tresses and she felt him shudder. "You know how to bring a fellow to his knees." He frowned as he felt the dress. "Romano silk?"

"The closest I've ever seen since Derby." She pulled him to her and kissed him, his response mirroring her love and desire.

Carlos gently pulled away. Breathing heavily, he said, "We had better get going."

Catching her breath, Sophie slipped her arm in his. "Where are we going?"

"Dinner and dancing at your favourite place. The Kingfisher Club, a special dinner and music followed by dancing.

Fairy lights twinkled all around the club, candles glowed on each table and Christmas trees stood floor to ceiling on the stage. Hundreds of lights flashed on and off, reflecting on the trumpets and trombones. The band wore red sequinned jackets and the stage was an explosion of light. Sophie blinked as the hostess lead them to a secluded table.

The dinner was magical. It was rare that Sophie ate in the club and she could hardly remember what she ate, but she would never forget how she felt as she peeled off every bit of resistance. So full of love, every time Carlos touched her, she tingled like nothing she had felt before. His eyes told her he felt it too.

Kissing her gently on the cheek and squeezing her hand, he said, "We have more than the New Year to celebrate tonight. First, I am the luckiest man in the room, or maybe the whole of London, because I am here with the most beautiful woman in the world."

"And don't forget the most handsome man. Such compliments are enough to make me blush." Sophie slipped her head to one side, teasing him.

"We have more to celebrate, Sister Romano. I am so proud of you. I don't doubt you will be matron one day. Between us, we could run the hospital." Carlos made her laugh, and yet, it was possible, she thought.

Reaching into his jacket pocket, he nodded to the waiter, who pulled his chair to one side. Carlos bent on one knee. "My darling Sophie, will you marry me?"

Without any hesitation, Sophie said, "Yes." At last, she knew everything would be all right. Carlos slipped a diamond ring on her finger, a bottle of champagne popped and their glasses bubbled. It seemed the whole club had heard and a roar of cheers and clapping vibrated around the room.

"To us!" Carlos raised his glass.

"To us!" Sophie repeated, beaming with happiness.

The band began playing a slow waltz. Carlos held his hand out and led her to the dance floor. Holding her tight, they danced so close she could feel his every move and moved with him as one. Resting her head on his shoulder, she closed her eyes. His cheek rested lightly on her head and she felt his warm breath flutter in her hair. Blissfully unaware of their surroundings, they swayed gently with the music until they realized it had stopped. The mood broken, Sophie lifted her head and leaned back on Carlos to face the band, clapping to the loud chants and feeling the anticipation and excitement of a brand new year. Carlos wrapped his arms around her and they both yelled in unison with the crowd as the countdown began.

10 9 8 7 6 5 4 3 2 1 and a roar of Happy New Year!

Carlos held her close, kissed her and whispered, "I love you, Sophie. Absolutely nothing will ever part us again."

She believed his every word and trusted him. She felt safe, secure and unconditionally loved. The warm, loving sensations inside filled her with desire for this wonderful, handsome man. She wanted to stay in his arms forever. Finally, she knew for certain she had always loved Carlos, her one and only true love and he would never leave her again. "I love you, Carlos. My heart has always belonged to you."

# Epilogue

Sophie and Carlos were married in Lucca, at the villa in March 1921. Sophie did not sell the villa, but kept it as their getaway place. She and Paola remained friends. Sophie did buy a small house in London together with Carlos, where they settled into a long, loving and happy married life. They chose to be career orientated and not have a family, but enjoyed their friends' children.

Carlos excelled in his position as Head of Orthopedics and eventually became Chief Physician at the Bartley. Sophie worked hard at changing the probationer's program and the Bartley had a reputation of training exceptional nurses. Eventually, when Matron retired, Sophie was appointed the new Matron at the Bartley.

Andrew stayed at the Dalkeith Clinic in Scotland and did amazing work with shell shocked soldiers and troubled civilians. He became world renowned with his advances in psychiatry, treating trauma and shock. He never married, but one could say he was married to his work. He remained Sophie's best friend.

Trixie and Chris settled at Beech Hall a little sooner than expected as Chris's father became ill. Trixie delivered a little boy, Clive, named after Chris' brother. Sophie and Andrew did their duty as Godparents and Andrew became a great friend of both families. Clive was the first of three boys.

Hillary passed her exams and finished her training as a Houseman under Dr. Wilcox at the Bartley, qualifying as MD along with her three female friends. She and Reggie married and set up their own general practice in London.

Clarice Harrington and Dotty Fox became excellent nurses on their own career paths. Lord Harrington never admitted to being Dotty's father and, because of Clarice's friendship with her, he disowned her. Edwin, always treated Dotty as his sister and took care of them both. The earldom was entailed, so as much as his father would have liked to disown him, he could not. Lord Harrington died the year after the disastrous Christmas. As the new Lord Harrington, Edwin welcomed his siters to his home on the estate. Even his mother welcomed Dotty, although she was now to be called Dorothy. Clarice was happy to be reunited with her mother.

*In the Wake of Sophie's War* is the third and final book in the Sophie's War Novels and it has brought Sophie's story full circle, almost finishing where it started, with many references to the prequel, *Ruins in Silk.* I highly recommend you download this free offering from my website https://susanajennings.com or buy the prequel from the retailer of your choice.

If you missed the Prequel (Free download from my website) or purchase from Amazon along with Book 1 Prelude to Sophie's War - https://geni.us/MWT3 and Book 2 Heart of Sophie's War – https://geni.us/SophiesWar2

# Acknowledgments

I think perhaps this is the fastest I have ever written a book and I would not have been able to do this without the help and encouragement of my colleagues, friends and family.

Having spent six months in England taking care of my 101-year-old mother and then dealing with her estate, my mind was anywhere but writing. I had planned two books for 2022, but that was not to be. With help and encouragement from the Literary Ladies Writing Group (previously the Historical Writing Ladies Group) I managed to focus on Sophie's last book. My thanks and gratitude to Meghan, Susan TM and Margaret.

Thank you to Bob Barclay, a fellow writer and antique car enthusiast, who was able to explain cars, roads and travel during 1919 and 1920.

Many, many thanks to my editor Meghan Negrijn, http://ag oodideapublications.com who has now edited six of my books and re-edited at least four others. She understands my writing, even my thoughts. She never judges, although at times I'm sure she must be frustrated, but at the end of the day our goals are the same, an excellent book.

Proof readers, Kathleen Bigras, Rita Burke, Mary Rothschild and Rosemary Bann. I am always astounded at the typos that sneak through after multiple reads by myself and the editor and I am grateful for the diligence of proof readers.

There are some family members and friends that also helped this book along from the business side of writing. My daughter Rosemary, who has recently become my virtual assistant, allowing me to do more writing. I would like to give a shout-out to a group of women who have supported and encouraged me and given me so much confidence during the writing of this novel through our Wednesday morning Zoom meeting; Tanya R, Tanya PW, Abby, Coleen, Robin and Nancy. A special thank you to Nancy, who was not adverse to challenging my self-doubt, giving me a swift kick to keep going. Thank you, Nancy.

# Resources

- *Britain in the 1920s by Fiona McDonald*

This is an amazingly comprehensive book about all aspects of life immediately after the Great War. This book was tremendous help to me and for anyone interested in that time period. I can highly recommend it.

- *The Great Silence by Juliet Nicolson* - 1918 – 1920 Living in the shadow of the war

Another amazing book about this time period and one that is very readable. I highly recommend this one too.

- Various films and Google searches

# Disclaimers

**Historical Accuracy:**

I love history, particularly the early 1900s, the Great War and the 1920s. I am not a historian, nor am I a military person or nurse. I read copious books (many are listed in the resources section) and used the internet to search museums, historical and military sites to get an understanding of what life would be like between 1918 – 1920. I asked a million questions and I do my best to stick to historical facts. However, this is a book of fiction and, for the purpose of story, I have taken license in interpreting events and the social environment. If I have blundered badly, please send me a note and it will be reviewed and corrected in later editions.

**Italian words** – I have used some Italian words, which to the best of my knowledge are correct, but I am not Italian so if I made mistake, I ask your forgiveness and to please let me know.

**British medical titles:** Please note that in Britain a junior doctor or Intern doctor is called a Houseman. It is also worthy of note that in the UK when an MD becomes a surgeon he is referred to as Mr.

**A further note** regarding history and current opinions and understanding, particularly towards the LBGTQ community. The views, language and attitude towards homosexuality was intolerant, at best, in England 1920. These historical views are for the purpose of story and historical accuracy and do not reflect my views or anyone's associated with this novel.

## Canadian English:

It is important to note that English is perhaps one of the most dominant languages worldwide. However, there are many different ways of interpreting the English language. These interpretations are not incorrect, just different. You will find familiar words with different spellings in the U.K., Canada, Australia, America and most English speaking countries. I was born in Britain, but live and write in Canada. I choose to write in the Canadian style. So please, if you spot grey but think it should be gray, or colour that should be color or are tempted to replace an S instead of Z in realize, to mention but a few, these are not spelling mistakes, just the correct Canadian spelling.

I do hasten to add that as careful and thorough as my editors and proofreaders are, there are times when a pesky typo sneaks through and, for those infractions, I apologize and appreciate a note so that in future editions, the mistakes can be corrected.

# About the Author

Susan A. Jennings was born in Britain of a Canadian mother and British father. Both her Canadian and British heritages are often featured in her stories. She lives and writes in Ottawa, Canada and is the author of The Sackville Hotel Trilogy, a combination of historical fiction, a family saga and an intriguing love story. The Sophie Series, also historical, is a collection of novels situated during The Great War. You may recognize the main character, Sophie, from the Sackville Hotel trilogy. Taking a break from the historical genre, her latest series is women's fiction. The Lavender Cottage books feature the unusual backdrop of an English narrowboat marina with a later in life romance. Susan writes a weekly blog, which has been taken over by her doggy assistant Miss Penny, a Shih Tzu, filled with stories about living with an author.

Susan teaches the occasional workshop on writing and publishing. She is also available to speak at book clubs or other events. She is an avid reader of mysteries and historical fiction, especially of the Victorian and Edwardian era.

**You can connect with me on:**

- https://susanajennings.com
- https://twitter.com/sajauthor
- https://facebook.com/authorsusanajennings
- https://geni.us/SusanAmazon
- https://geni.us/SusanonYouTube

**Subscribe to my newsletter:**

- https://geni.us/NewsfromSusan

# Also by Susan A Jennings

## The Sackville Hotel Trilogy
Book 1 - The Blue Pendant
Book 2 - Anna's Legacy
Book 3 - Sarah's Choice
Box Set - All three books
Prequel – Ruins in Silk*

## Sophie's War Series
Book 1 - Prelude to Sophie's War
Book 2 - Heart of Sophie's War
Book 3 - In the Wake of Sophie's War (2022)
Prequel - Ruins in Silk *
*Leads into The Blue Pendant and Sophie's War

## The Lavender Cottage Books
Book 1 - When Love Ends Romance Begins
Book 2 - Christmas at Lavender Cottage
Book 3 - Believing Her Lies
Book 4 - Coming late 2021

## Nonfiction

Save Some for me - A Memoir
A Book Tracking Journal for ladies who love to read.

## Short Stories:
Mr. Booker's Book Shop
The Tiny Man

A Grave Secret
Gillian's Ghostly Dilemma
The Angel Card
Little Dog Lost Reiki Found

## Story Collections
The Blue Heron Mysteries
Contributing author to:
The Black Lake Chronicles
Ottawa Independent Writers' Anthologies